Infinity Point

Adam Hoss

BLACK ROSE writing™

First printing

ISBN: 978-1-61296-824-7
PUBLISHED BY BLACK ROSE WRITING
www.blackrosewriting.com

Printed in the United States of America
Suggested retail price $20.95

Infinity Point is printed in Gentium Book Basic

Infinity Point

In my solitude
I have seen very clearly
things that are not true.

– Antonio Machado, from *Moral Proverbs and Folksongs*

She felt her way along the cave wall, reading the world like Braille. The others didn't seem to have a plan. They huddled together and waited for death. She knew none of them by name. Soon they'd be ash and bones, a blur of human remains and extinguished secrets. Nobody spoke. A hush hung over them like the silence when somebody is about to cry.

A distant explosion shook the cave. She knew they were coming, the men and their machines, and she knew they'd be too late.

Here she stood, five hundred feet below ground, in possession of an object that broke the laws of physics, surrounded by those who, like her, had transcended the limitations of the human body, alone in the dark with their knowledge and their knives.

They faced more than death. A line of succession stretching back millennia would be broken within the hour. She had an heir in mind but no link to the outside world. She'd received instructions and did as she'd been told, hoping it might make sense to someone.

The Turk had burned first. She'd watched him die screamlessly, eyes closed, spine erect like a protesting monk. The stench of his suffering clogged the cave.

She unfolded the envelope in her back pocket. A name but no address. "To my daughter, Nikole Elizabeth Fink." The penmanship had faded over the years but the seal still held. She tucked the note in a crevice in hopes it would be safe from the heat.

A steel canister scraped against stone. Their executioner had returned, dragging along a fresh fuel tank.

Another boom, this time closer.

She couldn't leave this life taking everything with her. She had to pass on the knowledge. She had to pass on the blood. She couldn't let the secret die. She rubbed a hand over the flesh of her stomach and thumbed the sharpness of her blade.

The next part of her plan was going to hurt.

1

Nikole closed her eyes and tried not to think about what she was doing. Two stalls over, a toilet flushed. I could go to the ATM, she thought. I could spend all my money and then kill myself. Not a bad idea. I could hitchhike my way to Vegas, get eloped, shoot heroin, fly to the Moon. Then I'll swan dive from a skyscraper and, whatever they say about me, at least I'll know I'd been living a life.

In a public bathroom in the bowels of Penn Station, Nikole Fink fished through her own vomit in search of undigested pills, aware that she was not doing well. She hugged the toilet bowl, legs half lotus, trying not to puke a second time.

I can't believe Wally talked me into this bullshit, she thought. Said we'd change the world together, inshallah. Five years I wait, then they shove me in a coffin and cut the lights. Some dumbass juicer fried the fuse box and Natasha wants us to improvise. What does she think I can do? Miracles are not in my contract. I make faces into spotlights, deal with litigation from Dad's second family in China – long story – and panhandle video village for bathroom breaks. But I've got industry relations to consider, so I'd better rattle my way through another firing squad of chest pains and keep digging for pills, just one, please God, my kingdom for a milligram.

Her fingers touched something hard. She ventured a glance into the swamp and there it was, caught in the net of her fingers, a single half-digested shard of Xanax. She thanked a dozen deities and felt the world's noose loosen around her throat.

She shambled to the sink and rinsed her hands. She ran water over the rescued Xanax, a remnant of her morning binge, then slipped it into her mouth and swallowed.

Okay, she thought. Alright. I'll stick around this planet a while longer.

That's when she noticed the woman, a pale, slope-shouldered twentysomething whose eyes looked ten years younger than her face, doe brown and starstruck, her hair the color and shape of a torch. She had her face pierced in a place Nikole had never thought fit for jewelry. Clothed in denim and rainbow bracelets, she smelled of Clove cigarettes and wore the expression of a desert wanderer eyeing a mirage.

Don't speak, Nikole thought. Please God. Don't let her speak.

"Are you...?" the woman began. She trailed off and stifled a giggle. A familiar hush settled between them. Nikole knew what was coming next and hoped it would be swift and merciful, but understood it would not.

"Sorry. Are you Nikole Fink?"

Magic words. Alakazam.

"As in *the* Nikole Fink?" the woman asked.

Nikole bit her lip and said nothing.

"No way. You're her. Nikole Fink. Wow! *Kid Wizard* was, like, my *favorite* show growing up. I could tell you every episode. I watched them all. You were such a positive role model."

"Thanks," Nikole said, hissing the *s* through clenched teeth.

For a moment neither of them spoke. The woman giggled, reddened, palmed her mouth, looking embarrassed.

"I was just telling my friend Brittany the other day, like, wow, you know, what do you think happened to her? What ever happened to the Kid Wizard? You know?"

"Do I know? Is that what you're asking me?"

"Well, I mean... Sorry. I've never met a famous person. I don't know what to say. But I'm a huge fan. I love you. I mean... You know what I mean."

Nikole waited for her fan to leave but she didn't. They stared each other down through the mirror, huntress and prey. Nikole had the feeling that she wanted something but wasn't sure what to ask for or how.

"So, uh, you're still doing movies, right?"

Nikole nodded. "I'm in the middle of filming a new project," she said. "We're shooting a scene tonight."

Don't ask. Don't ask. Don't ask.

"Oh. That's good. I mean, it's good you're still working. Good to hear. I'm an aspiring actress myself, you know. Not a star. Not yet. Not like you." She paused and slid a hand into her pocket as though reaching for a weapon, unable to break eye contact with her messiah. "So what's your next movie?"

Christ. These people. The chasm between my existence and the world's perception grows by the nanosecond.

"Uh, it's a sneakers commercial," Nikole muttered. "A Japanese brand."

There was a pause as the planet's collected disapproval boiled down to a single syllable.

"Oh."

"I'm working with Natasha Kennedy."

"Who?"

"She was famous in the 1980s."

Nikole placed both hands on the counter. Breath clouded her face in the mirror like a blurred video of someone in witness protection.

Her huge fan drew her weapon, a sticker-plastered smartphone, and turned to where Nikole stood heaving in a sweat-stained mess over the sink. She aimed, steadied and snapped half a dozen photos.

I could live in a cave, Nikole thought. I could survive on roast bat and groundwater. In my solitude I'll find God. Loneliness will be my cross. But at least they won't take my picture. Natasha won't shove me into a room until I asphyxiate. My autopsied larynx won't become a tabloid sensation (but only if we hire a publicist, Wally would say). Carlos couldn't barge back into my life. I mean, what the fuck is Carlos doing on set anyways? Who called up Carlos? Why is Carlos there?

Some fucking week.

Something inside Nikole snapped. She'd gone numb to the woes of the world, sheathed by alprazolam, a web of scar tissue in her soul.

"Did I give you permission," she said, voice trembling, "to take my picture?"

Her fan grew sheepish. "Oh," she said. "I, uh, thought I could, um..."

"You thought what?"

"I don't know what I thought. I'm sorry. Can I, um, take your picture? Please?"

Nikole marched the length of the counter, her reflection keeping pace in the mirror like a stunt double. She wrenched the phone from her fan's fingers and spiked it to the floor. She stomped the screen and heard the glass crack.

"Get away from me before I do the same to your face," Nikole said.

The torch-haired woman reeled in shock. "I, uh... Sorry." She rescued the shards of her phone and scurried back into Penn Station.

The universe came into focus. Nikole lurched, her stomach somewhere unexpected, cliff-edge vertigo dulling six senses.

She spat at the mirror, disgusted at her beady eyes and potato-shaped skull. Sweat, spit and puke painted her flesh a shade of rigor mortis. She ran a hand through her blonde bob, trembling with self-loathing.

"You are beautiful," she whispered. "You're a star."

She watched her reflection like staring through glass at the zoo, fameless, fanless, heart jumped a boxcar and blood turned cement. Gotta face the world alone, Nikole. She pictured Wally the boxing coach, in the blue corner, taping up her wrists. This is why we need a publicist, kid. What am I doing here? Why aren't things different? What happened to the Kid Wizard?

She wiped strings of soul from her chin, swallowed, and turned to face the world and its cameras once again, still not sure which Nikole Fink she'd be today.

2

They appeared like ghosts, first an idea, then a cough, a groan, a splash of boots and sewage. They were sounds before shadows and shadows before men. They lugged hardhats, lunch pails, plastic explosives and skin turned transparent from lack of sun. They drilled holes through stone and blasted their way by inch and limb through prehistoric bedrock. They were cogs of urban machinery. Five hundred feet overhead, the city built on their backs teetered on a tightrope, one sandhog strike away from apocalyptic decay.

Rico plopped onto a heap of rubble and watched the sandhogs finish loading dynamite into the tunnel wall.

"You know what's good?" he asked. "Fucking pomegranate juice. Fucking amazing. Heaven washing over my tongue. I mean, even without vodka. Name something better than pomegranate juice. I dare you. You can't do it. Go ahead. Try."

Mickey could say more with a grunt than most world leaders could articulate in an address to the United Nations. He shuffled with an odd gait, top-heavy, as though his potbelly were weighing him down. His skin had paled as ghostly as the color of his beard. He gave a grunt equal parts gravel and grit.

"Yeah?" Rico said. "Well, all I'm saying is it's pretty good."

It's always raining underground. A trickle of moisture pinged against every surface. Half a dozen sandhogs – a wall of yellow raincoats and hard hats – stood under the glare of bare bulbs. They crammed dynamite into blasting holes with rods as though they were loading muskets. The drilled rock looked like a beast with a hundred eyes. A hum of ventilation echoed in the tunnel.

They were men of the underground, connoisseurs of fire, sons of immigrants. Their family trees were rooted in urban mines. They built Brooklyn Bridge and brought the city clean water. They worked in shifts, leaving memories of sunlight at the elevator door.

"Yo, boss," Rico said. "You ever find fossils down here? Mastodon bones? That kinda shit? I mean, if it's true when they say the rock's as old as the dinosaurs."

Mickey grunted in a way that said it was older than that, son.

"Yeah? Well, that'd be tight. All I'm saying."

Spray paint and blasting wires strung together holes in the rock. Clean edges, Mickey thought. That'll be Coop's handiwork, that kid from the midnight shift. Drill maestro. Hard drinker. Half these guys' age but a face two decades older.

"We good?" Mickey called.

Paul gave two thumbs up.

"Okay, okay. Pull back. Let's go."

Tony jumped down off his ladder the way he likes to do. The wall was a waterfall of multicolored wires and blast caps.

His sandhogs, their faces muck-splattered and weary, wore pyromania as masks. Crazy motherfuckers, all of them. Risking skull and fingers to play with fire a thousand miles from the sun requires a certain philosophy of life.

Mickey grabbed the spool and started unraveling the fuse. Down here it's never warm and it's never boring. The tunnels smelled like wet earth and gunpowder. Mickey walked backwards, keeping the fuse taut, using a sixth sense to keep up.

Rico yawned. "Hey," he said to the crew. "You guys wanna hear an idea I had this one time?"

Nobody spoke. They didn't have to. Their silence said no, but it carried also an understanding that they had little choice.

The symmetry of concrete loomed before them. They approached the quasi-finished groundwork, where they'd load in the mole in the coming weeks. Everywhere Mickey looked he saw not grime and bedrock but human ingenuity, a sprawling city below the city, a maze mined by groundhogs in search of treasure and electric wire.

"You guys think I'm just down here because my dad's the union boss," Rico said. "Right? Well it's not true. I got skills. I'm good at life. You know?" He paused, awaiting affirmation. "So I'm thinking, right, about doing my own TV series. I got an idea for a show. It'll be huge. It's about a bunch of dudes digging water tunnels under New York City. But, like, they find a *ghost* in the tunnels just, like, chillin' down here. But now it's *mad.* And they've gotta kill it. And they've got bombs. But it's all like, 'Boo, motherfuckers.'" He paused, awaiting compliments. None came. "Anyways, that's my idea. Been thinking about it a while now."

Water sloshed as they marched through the tunnel.

"That is the dumbest idea I've ever heard," said Rocky, a fourth-generation sandhog and walking wall of blubber.

"Ah, screw you guys," Rico said. "I'll go it alone. Just don't come crying when my name's all over buildings and I'm running for President. I could be President, I think. You guys think? No?"

They got a few football fields back and J.R. crimped the fuse. Mickey called for the horn to warn the cave's bats and rodents that there'd be a big boom. His men needed no reminders. He hooked up the fuse and the men plugged their ears with the coordination of synchronized swimmers.

"Three, two, one. Fire in the hole."

Mickey smashed the detonator with his fist. Red and orange strobe lights flashed from the depths, their light radiating around a bend. It sounded like firecrackers. The world was quiet a moment. Then the dynamite blew.

The whole planet seemed to shake. Mickey felt the shockwave hit his face like a splash of cold water.

Billows of dust ballooned through the tunnel. Mickey unplugged his ears and listened as the rubble crumbled on itself like a rainstorm of gravel.

It worked every time. Two decades playing with fire and he'd never lost his childlike enchantment with things that go boom.

But this time felt different. He studied the air with his ears as the ringing died and shuddered, feeling the presence of something new, something that didn't belong. He thought about *The Lord of the Rings*, the Mines of Moria, about what happened to the dwarves when they dug too deep.

The men trudged back towards the site of the blast, vanishing like spirits in the clearing smoke.

He heard commotion from his crew. They'd found something. A cave. Just when he thought he'd seen all the tunnels could throw at him. A crag the shape of Florida formed a dark spot in the wall where the light couldn't reach.

"Whoa," Rico breathed.

He dashed ahead. A giddy smile crossed his face wider than Mickey thought anatomically possible. Grabbing exposed rock like gymnastics equipment, Rico swung out his feet and ducked into their discovery.

Something stopped Mickey in his tracks. He had an odd feeling of being watched. He stood among rubble, still as a statue, staring at a point beyond the physical plane. He felt as though he'd lived his life to that point in a two-dimensional world and only now thought to look up.

The hole loomed before him, a cut in the earth. Something lurked inside. Something terrible. Something with fangs. Something of the darkness that belongs in the darkness. Something caged and ready to bite.

Rico popped out of the hole. He wasn't smiling anymore.

3

"You know what I hate about you? I hate how you've closed yourself off to the world. I hate how you don't speak unless spoken to. I hate when you interrupt me. At first I accepted your flaws. I liked the mystery. Now I realize you were doing it on purpose. I know nothing about your childhood, your family. And the plants! That's another thing. All you need is to water them. It's not natural, you know, the way you kill everything you touch. I swear to God, I buy you a plant and the next time I come over it's all wilted in the trash. And always with your sweatpants. Would it kill you to dress nice for once? I'm not talking miniskirts or nurse uniform, but just something a little sexy, just for me, just once."

"You could have asked me."

"There you go. Twisting my words. Turning it around like it's my fault. This is why we broke up."

Nikole sulked on a seat of shrapnel amidst bleary-eyed extras and searchlights, caterers barking pizza orders, the smell of stale coffee and cameras on robot arms. The pew had been built damaged, painted burned. A decorator scraped paint kegs across the floor. The lead grip – a linebacker-sized man named Tony – rehearsed his approach with an inactive Steadicam. Assistants shambled half-undead, mechanized drones programmed to please no matter the cost, parading in routine patterns with cappuccinos and Diet Coke, starry-eyed and clean-shaven, a crowd of pattering feet and softly-spoken apologies.

"You never think about things from my perspective," Carlos continued. "Like that time we went to Rick's for New Year's and I had to drink alone and feel like an alcoholic."

"I was on my meds," Nikole said.

"An excuse up every sleeve. This is why we broke up."

He'd shown up costumed as a Hot Topic vampire, complete with black nail polish, tacky rings and denim the color of midnight.

They're in my head, Nikole thought. It's all strategy. Psychological torture. Why else would Natasha cast Carlos? A random Mexican guy in a platoon of Russian soldiers? Diversity? Dada? A gift-wrapped aneurysm for her lead actress?

All for a thirty second sneakers ad and one month's rent, no residuals.

Carlos adjusted his glasses, jaws still mashing. Nikole had never seen a man go through so much chewing gum. Every snort and laugh he routed around a sticky gob. Sometimes, when they argued, he'd pluck it out of his mouth to deliver the zingers he'd practiced in advance.

"I'd say you handled it like a champ."

"Handled what?" Nikole asked.

"The panic attack."

"It was that obvious I was having one?"

"Ooh. Sore subject. Sorry. See, this is why we broke up. You can't feel happy for me. When Natasha Kennedy rang me up I thought it was a hidden camera show. I swear to God, Nikole, I was seeing spots. The woman is a legend. Well, *was* a legend. Back in the day. She asked if I wanted to be in her new short film. Hell yeah. So it's a shoe commercial. So what? Did you hear what she told me? I stole the scene! Here I was, thinking it was your big moment. I'm just saying. It's not a contest, Nikole."

When I die, Nikole thought, all my muscles will relax. Wally and his words. Said he'd make me a star. I *was* a star. I carried that dumb *Kid Wizard* show for six seasons. Twelve million viewers. Eight years old and unafraid. Now all I want is to hide. Now Carlos has wormed his way back into my life. Now I'm out of Klonopin and can't see Dr. Pills until Monday.

It's almost impossible, being alive.

"This is what Natasha does," Nikole said. "She plays mind games with her actors. Think about it, Carlos. She casts you out of the blue, and the fact we just broke up has nothing to do with it?"

Carlos studied the floor. "Well," he said, "we didn't *just* break up. It's been long enough that we're seeing other people." He paused. "*Are* we seeing other people?"

Nikole scoured the film crew for Natasha, desperate for a diversion. A mustachioed producer flicked to life a cigar and fumigated the stage.

I hate how I can taste it, Nikole thought. The chalk, the pills I took twelve hours back, the first stages of withdrawal. Noise from outside trickled through cracked concrete. A siren turned her heart to lead.

One of Natasha's assistants, a pasty starfucker named Jenna, bolted out of a back room in a frenzy of Starbucks and frazzled hair, glasses askew, panting. She spoke in a whirl of whispers, the effects of which rippled through the set: wide eyes, hushed tones. The film crew stopped what they were doing in segments as the news spread. Someone had found something and this changes everything.

"Where is she?" Jenna barked. "Where's Nikole?"

Nikole closed her eyes. All she wanted was to be alone with her darkness and her pills, burrowed in blankets until cancer takes her or an asteroid hits the Earth, whichever comes first. She'd never felt more alone than she did living in the city.

"Nikole," Jenna said. Her voice trembled. "You should see this."

"See what?"

She took a cautious step forward. "Well, they found a cave."

"Who is *they*?"

"Well, I don't know. Construction workers. The MTA. People digging a subway line, or whatever. They found a whole cave under the city."

"So?"

She left a pause that infused Nikole with anxiety. Something went unsaid that made Nikole involved. Underground engineers found a cave and somehow it's about Nikole Fink. All she wanted was the warm embrace of a grave.

"You'd better come see this."

Nikole and Carlos followed the horde over to video village where gaffers and grips elbowed production staff for position, all crowded around a single screen playing CNN.

"And I was like, holy fucking shit," a hard-hatted Puerto Rican was explaining to a newscaster.

"I have to remind you, Rico, that you're on live television."

The bottom of the screen screamed in reserved-for-serious-shit-sized font "BREAKING: MASS GRAVE DISCOVERED UNDERGROUND."

"I have to warn our viewers," the newscaster spoke, "that you may find the following video disturbing."

Nikole gazed in wonder at ashen forms who once were human, their limbs warped like exposed springs of a destroyed mattress. Clothing and skin had become a single sheaf of ash. Teeth, eye sockets and bare bone of exposed fingers were among the few clues identifying the species of the deceased. In the corner of the screen were the words "Video courtesy of Rico Ramirez."

"Tell us what we're seeing here, Rico," the newscaster said.

"Right. So it's just another day on the job. You know? Then, boom, we got ghosts. Real live *ghosts*. Well, I mean, not alive. But you know. I'm thinking NBC, maybe TBS. I'm looking to set up some meetings with producers, showrunners, hot shots, big daddies. You know what I mean. TV guys. The movers. The shakers. I'm calling my reality show *Cave Ghosts*. Working title. Anyways, guys, call me."

They'd moved from corpses to artifacts now. A forearm-sized bird statue looked lifted from a history museum. In cave art aesthetic, someone had painted a distinctive symbol on the wall:

The video became more baffling as it progressed. A corpse clutched a handful of diamonds. Another held an empty glass vial. The charred remains of a leather-bound book sat smoldering on the pile. Nearby, half an envelope splattered in blood spilled contents dissolved to ash.

"Whoa," Carlos said. "This is insane. I swear to God, Nikole."

A close-up of the envelope stilled Nikole's heart. Off camera they were interviewing a forensic expert, asking about the condition of the bodies and how long they'd been decomposing, but Nikole wasn't listening. There was text on the burned envelope that could still be read, small, in the corner, penned in faded blue ink.

"To my daughter, Nikole Elizabeth Fink."

4

Nikole stopped in the hallway outside her apartment. Number 404's door was ajar. Footsteps creaked opposite the wall. A Nikole-hunter had besieged her stronghold with the catapult of lock picks and sat waiting, claws sharpened, for its quarry to return.

For as long as Nikole could remember, the squat graffiti canvas she called home had been a neighborhood hotspot for jumpers. Last Tuesday there was another, his chalk outline all that remained by the time she'd come home. Neighborly gossip filled in fragments of a life: divorced architect, father of two, nothing out of the ordinary, quiet. And now he's dead. We never know a person's last thoughts.

Filming had run late. Midnight had come and gone before Natasha dismissed her crew. Nikole had scurried home over subway and sidewalk, scanning her surroundings every few feet.

A shadow had tailed her since Canal Street. Maybe. Low light and a fluttering heart clouded visibility and reason. In fine print her medication warned of hallucinations, stomach inflammation, heavy machinery. Footsteps sloshed in her wake. A van crawled curbside, keeping twenty paces back. The rain had stopped. Its remnants leaked from rooftop to gutter, plopping the nighttime full of percussion. Rats picked at a pink sneaker near their nest of plastic inside an overturned shopping cart. Nobody much comes here after dark.

A to B, she kept telling herself. Right foot, left foot. Just a few steps.

She'd checked for fresh suicides as she rounded Vandervoort and crossed Thames. Streetlights were devil eyes in the dark.

Polyurethane tickled Nikole's nose as she climbed the steps. She unfurled one knuckle at a time. She knew she should feel validation at her discovery, for uncovering proof of the perils of the sidewalks, but her bones ached and her brainwaves buzzed and all she wanted was to crawl under her table and chemically induce a coma.

She creaked open the door and took stock of her surroundings.

A teenage girl sat on Nikole's kitchen counter, her legs pendulums. She stood out against a sea of oak cabinets in jeans and an oddly colored hoodie that made Nikole think of radiation. Her face looked like it had been sketched in crayon by a child: eyes too big for their sockets, a snubbed nose too near her upper lip and bushy eyebrows that appeared better suited for a gruff lumberjack. She exuded mischief and perfume.

"Jesus, where were you?" the girl asked. "Reenacting the Ice Age glacier retreat in real time?"

She slid off the counter and slinked across the room. Floor lamps turned her brown hair blonde in patches. As she neared, a clash of citrus fumigated the air.

"Samantha?" Nikole guessed.

Sam palmed Nikole's face and groped. For an awkward half-minute they stood hand to face like a paralytic and preacher in the throes of divine healing.

"Welp," Sam said, speaking to an audience only she could see, "she ain't one of them Tupac holograms." She paused, looking Nikole head to toe. "It's really you."

The sisters made first eye contact in over a decade.

Nikole was unsure what to say. She chuckled. "When I left home you were *this* big."

"Yup."

Nikole tiptoed through the door. As she crossed the threshold, she felt like a prisoner in hood and noose, last rites read, whose pardon had just come through. The plagues of the world became dim noise washed out by fortress walls. She heaved relief and clicked shut the deadbolt behind her.

"I did knock," Sam said. "No answer, so I just sorta shimmied the lock."

"You did what?"

Sam shrugged. "It was that or scale up four stories." Her eyes wandered the studio's walls and floorboards, laundry-draped furniture, rodent droppings, weeks of unopened mail, loft bed above an aging television. "I see two... wait... five ways I could break into your apartment. Child's play."

Sam moved a stack of magazines and settled in the center of the couch, where the cushions sagged the most.

Nikole's eyelids blinked machine gun fire, her brain still processing the strangeness.

"So, uh, how's Dad?"

Sam shook her head. "That's one of them *loaded questions,* if you catch my drift."

"Not really."

She sighed. "I'm a street kid."

"What?"

"Dad started drinking again. Not that you know he sobered up in the first place. But he relapsed a couple years after you ran away. In an alcoholic's moment of clarity, he realized the cure to his mid-life crisis was to mail order a Cambodian bride and run off to Bangkok. He pulled the old Nikole Fink on me. He never even said goodbye."

"You're... homeless?"

"Mom disappears, you run away, Dad heads off to Asia. I'm all that's left of our family. What do you think happens to kids like me?"

"Jesus, Sammy. I didn't know."

"Of course you didn't. You never called. You never wrote."

"You're still in Rochester?"

"Nope," Sam said. "I hopped a cruise liner to the Virgin Islands, where I lounge in robes of mink fur. A male model named Felipe fans me with a giant leaf whilst I feast upon grapes and gummy worms." She paused. "Yes, I'm still in Rochester, dumbass. What do you think? I had to pick a dozen pockets this morning for the bus ticket down here."

"I'm sorry."

"Sure you are. But what can I say? 'Tis my divine punishment for mistaking Bilbo the calico for a speed bump a couple summers back. He was, what, *a thousand* in cat years? It's not like he's an endangered species. Say, you wouldn't happen to have any Vaseline and/or ice cream sandwiches, would you?"

Nikole hesitated. "Um, I don't think so."

"What are you, some kind of barbarian?"

Nikole eyed the creature on her couch and didn't know how to feel. She remembered Bilbo the cat, a ball of wet fur teetering between lives nine and eight, and imagined an underage driver at the wheel. I do not have nine lives, Nikole thought. I have one. Just like my parents. Just like everybody.

Right?

"So you heard the news about Mom?" Sam asked. "I saw it on the tube this afternoon and thought I'd pay you a visit."

"How did you find me?"

"I have my ways."

Nikole swept junk mail from a chair unused for the better part of a decade and eased herself onto a seat of dust.

"Yeah, I heard about Mom," she said. "One of the cave bodies."

She imagined her mother's corpse, world-damaged and scar-strewn like Darth Vader minus the mask. Nikole I am your mother. Was. Everything past tense now. A life in ruins, water-warped photographs, unsettled lawsuits – fossils of an unplanned life, things they found in the autopsy.

Sam leaped to her feet. "Well," she said, "what are we waiting for? I'd grab a set of waterproof boots if you got 'em."

"Where are we going?"

Her sister stared through her as though the answer should be obvious. "What do you mean *where*? The big hole in the ground. The dig site. I went snooping around a bit earlier today."

Nikole's eyes nearly burst from their sockets. "You *what*? You went down there? You saw the bodies?"

"Well I didn't make it all the way to the cave. But yeah."

"Isn't the construction site swarming with police?"

Sam laughed. "Swarming? A couple rent-a-cops and a chain-link fence. Child's play."

"But..." Nikole stammered. Is she fucking with me? Are we even related? Is this entrapment, retribution for my running away? "How...?"

"The elevator, stupid."

"Isn't it locked?"

Sam sighed, tired of the questioning. "Yeah," she said, holding a glistening shard to the light, "but I stole the key."

Making plans in life is impossible, Nikole thought. Because what happens. A bolt of lightning. A malignant lump. A meteorite. Today's five thousandth visitor. Now you're a footnote, a Buzzfeed fail, one of those things that's more likely to happen than a plane crash.

"Come on, sis," Sam said. "Our mom goes poof and thirteen years later they find her body in an Escher cave five hundred feet sub-subway, clutching a letter addressed to you, and you aren't even curious?"

Of course I'm curious, she wanted to say. But I don't do outdoors. I don't do danger. I do shoe commercials and liquor stores. I come home and pop pills and watch the walls and wait to die. I don't do trespassing.

"I get the feeling you're not exactly a risk-taker," Sam said.

"There's no way I'm breaking into a crime scene. Shouldn't we talk to the police?"

"Hell no, man. I don't talk to fuzz. I ain't no snitch. That, and I got a couple warrants out. Trespassing. Nothing major. But still. Let's avoid the..."

Someone pounded on the door.

Color drained from Samantha's face. Her eyes, already oversized, made to leap from her skull.

"Cops," she shout-whispered, finishing her sentence.

Nikole checked her watch. Half past one in the morning seemed odd visiting hours.

She held in a giggle. The Xanax in her veins and the walls shielding her from the world had surpassed the point of necessity and had plunged her into bliss. With the confidence of a movie star on the red carpet she marched to the door and peeked through the periscope of her peephole.

The hallway looked like one of the *Saw* movies. A flickering light cast shadows on plaster. The muffled sounds of a couple arguing radiated from 403, along with a humming noise that could have been a buzz saw or a misfiring radiator. A heating vent pushed warmth and the stench of sewage into the hallway.

Two men, clean-shaven and nearly identical, stood outside her door. They were dressed in sharp black suits, slicked black hair and black sunglasses.

Nikole put the chain on the door for effect and cracked it open.

"Nikole Elizabeth Fink?" asked one of the men.

"Yes?"

He dangled open a wallet like in the movies, flashing a cryptic identification card. "I'm Agent Johansson and this is Agent Johansson. It's important that we speak to you immediately."

"You're *both* named Agent Johansson?"

"We'll ask the questions, Ms. Fink."

5

They were serious men, humorless, the kind you see standing behind the president speaking into sleeves. One was balder than the other. Their suit jackets masked musty cologne. The men entered Nikole's apartment, arms crossed, glaring like boxing refs inspecting a fighter for signs of mischief.

A low pressure system spread across Nikole's chest. One of the Agents Johansson plopped into Nikole's well-worn swivel chair. The other plucked a banana from its bunch on Nikole's counter, helping himself to the fruit.

"Howdy, fellas," Sam said.

Divine punishment, her sister had called it. You can't go outside without a sphincter loosening of the gods. Evil spirits. Run away from home and what happens? A cosmic bowel movement. A switchblade to the soul. The universe is like that.

"Travel often, Ms. Fink?" asked Agent Johansson.

She teetered awkwardly near the doorway. "Not really. No."

"Do you leave the country often?"

"Well, I just told you I don't travel much at all..."

"So you don't often travel internationally, then."

"No."

"So you *do* travel internationally."

"Wait. What?"

"Interesting." The second agent, the one in the kitchen, scribbled notes on a yellow pad while holding the banana between his teeth like a pen.

"Are you guys cops," Sam asked, pulling her legs half lotus on the couch, "or just a couple of friendly dudes with candy and a van?"

The agents ignored her. "When and where was the last time you traveled abroad?"

"Well," Nikole began, "fifteen years ago, maybe more. Canada. With my family. Before, uh..." She looked away from her sister. "Before I left home."

"While in Canada did you knowingly have contact with any member of the Canadian intelligence community?"

"What? Of course not."

"And what is your favorite verse from the Quran?"

"I beg your pardon?"

"Your favorite Quranic verse, Ms. Fink," said the banana muncher, speaking for the first time.

"Well, I guess I don't have one."

"Oh, that's interesting."

"Very interesting," echoed the other.

Agent Johansson adjusted his belt. Both men still wore shades. "You see, Ms. Fink," he said, "we are not the police. We're from a federal bureau investigating claims of paranormal activity. Few know of our existence. No doubt you have heard about yesterday morning's discovery of bodies in a cave."

"How could we not?" Sam asked. "It's on every TV channel. You'd think they'd found King Tut's tomb."

Agent Johansson signaled silence with his hand. "As of a few hours ago," he said, "the federal government has taken over the investigation."

They sat in silence for a moment. The second agent started a new banana, again without asking.

"We'd like to ask you about your mother."

Nikole felt a sensation like jumping into a pool and realizing too late you're in the deep end. She struggled to stay afloat. Her eyes darted window to door. One exit blocked, the other fatal. She pictured herself as a chalk outline, neighbors clustered like refugees, a wailing ambulance far away.

She spent a moment composing herself. "It's a painful memory," she said.

"Take your time."

The agents flipped to fresh pages in their notebooks in unison.

"I was thirteen when it happened," she said. "Sam was three."

"When *what* happened?"

"When she disappeared."

Nikole looked at her sister, who had gone silent. Sam chewed her lip, keeping eye contact with a floorboard knot near her feet.

"Mom burst into my room one night," Nikole continued. "Her eyes were all puffy. She looked afraid. She took me by the shoulders and said remember. Over and over. Remember me, remember, remember."

"Then what happened?"

Nikole took a breath. "I woke up the next morning confused. Dizzy. Like I'd been in a coma. I had to check what month it was. I couldn't shake the feeling that something had changed about the world. I found Dad at his usual spot at the kitchen table, his eyes focused on something I'll never understand. That's when I knew. She was gone."

The agents sat quietly. Their faces were masks of patience.

"I mean *really* gone," Nikole said. "The insurance company had no record she'd had a policy. The state of New York had no record she'd been issued a license. The police they thought we were filing a false report. There was no evidence that Melanie Fink ever existed. Then things got weird. Relatives had memory problems. Medical records vanished. I'll never forget her. Her presence is imprinted in my soul. But," she said, tears swelling, "when I picture her face, it's just a blur."

Agent Johansson leaned forward and patted her knee in what Nikole guessed was an attempt at consolation. His touch made her deeply uncomfortable.

"It's okay."

"How is it okay?" Sam snapped. "It destroyed our family."

"Dad lost his mind," Nikole said. "Got mean. Wasted half my *Kid*

Wizard money. He took me to court. His own daughter. We couldn't leave his sight. That meant no casting calls, no season six, no acting career. You gotta understand," she said, half addressing her sister, "I *had* to run away."

She looked at one agent, then the other. They grimaced, pursing their lips like doctors preparing bad news. The sisters waited. The agents said nothing.

"So, Mr. Bond," Sam said, "what was our mom doing in that cave? Was she murdered, or what?"

They didn't answer. Nikole had a sense that the mood had changed.

"The Black Lotus," said the second Johansson. "What do you know about them?"

"The what?"

"They're dangerous, Ms. Fink."

"Extremely dangerous," echoed the other.

"It's a delicate situation."

"Extremely delicate."

A breeze rattled the windows with fresh rain and the stink of sewage. Dueling car alarms faced off in the night.

"This might be difficult to accept, but we believe your mother was involved in some manner of cult activity. She and her fellow worshippers landed on the Black Lotus hit list."

"The Black Lotus?"

"They are editors, Ms. Fink. They edit history."

The agents watched the sisters closely, measuring their reaction to the words.

"The Black Lotus specialize in erasing persons and events from historical records," the other agent explained. "They've been around since the Middle Ages, at least, likely off and on. We have, for the first time in centuries, physical evidence of a Black Lotus operation. We're pulling a thread at the edge of something remarkable. They didn't count on those bodies being found."

Nikole wondered if it would be impolite to fix herself a pill salad as they talked.

"So Mom was in a cult that was being erased from history," Sam said.

"Something like that."

Sam nodded. "Right. So, uh, what are you guys gonna do about it?"

"The Black Lotus will return to clean up their dirty work. They leave no loose ends. For now, we wait. We have reason to believe they are searching for something, a family heirloom, something missing from the crime scene. Can you think of any object - a piece of jewelry, perhaps - that might hold sentimental value to your mother?"

Sam rolled her eyes. "Ask Nikole," she said. "I'm just the asshole people keep running away from."

Nikole shook her head. "Not that I can think of."

This time the shift in mood was palpable. Menace had crept into the agents' eyes. They stared daggers through their captive witness. Nikole felt their glares go icy.

"Want to try again?" Agent Johansson asked.

Nikole ransacked her brain, searching for anything, a sepia-stained photograph, a necklace, a pocket watch made from precious metals, but the house was too distant, her life in-between a battlefield of pills and booze and track marks eating holes in her brain.

She didn't have to look at Sam to know. The telepathic bond between sisters radiated a frequency undetectable by foreign minds. The sisters were already in agreement.

"We have nothing else to tell you," Nikole said.

"What did your mother leave behind when she left?"

"Nothing," Nikole insisted.

The sat a moment more in silence. Nikole averted her eyes.

Agent Johansson smiled.

"Keep it somewhere safe," he said. "We'll be in touch."

6

Angel fell. The elevator took him down through layers of Earth striped like tree rings. Time moves slower at sea level. He'd read it in a book. Take an atomic clock up Everest and in a few Ice Ages it'll be off a hair. Spend a century without climbing a ladder and you'll grow your lifespan a couple thousandths of a second. Not much, but in his line of work, a thousandth can make all the difference.

They stood in a cage wide enough from twenty men. Light streaked at an angle, illuminating his face nose to scalp. The machinery required to plunge an elevator into so deep a chasm announced itself in a torrent of electric hum that scarred his eardrums with shellshock. He felt through his boots a tilt towards the corner where Genghis stood, holding his birdcage. He resolved to read more books on structural engineering.

"Right," Rico said. "So I've changed my mind. For the title, I mean. How about *Ghosts of New York*? Nah, scratch that. *The Ghost Files*? *Ghost and Order*?"

Angel and Genghis said nothing.

"You guys *are* from NBC, right? Sorry. It's just, you know, you don't look like studio execs. Not how I picture them, anyways. Uh, no offense."

They made no reply. Genghis set down his birdcage. He pulled a Beretta from his trench coat and clutched the weapon over his chest as though he'd been buried with it.

Sweat blurred the Local 147 tattoo on Rico's forearm. He looked at Angel, then at Genghis.

"Whoa," he said. "Easy there, guy."

If this job gets any weirder, Angel thought, I'm splitting. I'll go off the meds. Disappear. Stay at sea level. Would Genghis go rogue? Are we friends? He'd check, but the oaf would just grunt. Too late in the day to buy a syllable.

Angel hoisted his red toolbox to chest level.

"This is my toolbox," he told Rico. "You don't want me to open it."

Other things he had read in a book:

The speed of light in a vacuum is 300,000 kilometers per second.

There are over three million shipwrecks on the ocean floors.

Acta Diurna was the first newspaper published in Rome.

The word algebra is a Latin variant of the Arabic word *al-jabr*.

When your heart stops, you remain conscious for about eight seconds.

He'd read these books with the hope of understanding nature. Instead, he grew angry. It all seemed so important. People should know these things. Why had he never been told?

A chill rose from the depths like the tendrils of a giant squid. Blackness consumed them. The sulfuric stink of blasted rock ravaged his nostrils and he tried to breathe through his mouth. I've endured worse, he thought. The Lisbon sanitarium. The sewers of Bangladesh. He flicked his switchblade open and closed and waited, surrounded by skeletal remains of geology, a mass grave of bedrock and soil.

"Tell us again," Angel said. "From the beginning."

Rico's body language grew erratic, nervous. He swallowed hard and tried to keep his composure. "We use a mole – a boring machine – to dig out the tunnel, a four-hundred-ton metal snake. Big badass motherfucker. But first, see, we gotta lay the groundwork. We dynamite big chunks of rock – boom! – then we set down concrete so it's got a level surface, see, then we put down the tracks. It ain't fast. But, see, once we get the mole down there, it'll scrape out the next couple miles. Old times, they had to use blast mining the whole gig."

"Go on."

He looked at Angel, then at Genghis on the couch. "Who are you assholes? Detectives? CIA? The hell is this?"

"We are your friends."

Chaz chirped in his cage. His rainbow coat rippled. Angel choked down the urge to strangle the damn parakeet. "It's a sun conure," Genghis would correct him, even as he squeezed down on its fragile neck. He guessed from his menacing stare that the big man sensed his thoughts.

"So you took it upon yourself to explore this cave you found," Angel said. "And you took it upon yourself to shoot a video on your phone and release it to the media."

Rico nodded.

"When you entered the cave, did you see any additional entrances?"

Rico crossed his arms, growing more assured. "Nope. That's what J.R. was saying. How the hell did these people get there in the first place? But it gets even weirder. Mick – he's the site supervisor – checked geological records. They'd surveyed the ground before we started digging. Two years ago, they checked the ground from above and their tests revealed no cave. It's like both the cave itself and the people inside all came through a time portal."

"A time portal," Angel said.

He shrugged. "Well, what's your theory, guy?"

Angel glanced at his toolbox. "I'll need to open it eventually," he said. "They need air. I don't want them to suffocate."

"There's something... *alive* in there?" Rico asked.

He heard rock bottom before he felt it. A banshee scream of metal slowed their descent. Someone had scrawled "500 feet" with white spray paint.

"What did you find in the cave?"

He sighed. "Watch the news, guy."

"I'd rather hear it from you."

He stood still a moment, exasperated, unsure what to say. "Bodies," he said eventually.

They stepped out of the elevator into the manmade cavern.

"I really gotta insist that you guys wear hardhats down here," Rico said. "It's an active dig site."

Genghis set down his birdcage. If that bird gives us away, Angel thought, at least I'll have the upper hand in logic, if not strength, when I pierce its tiny heart.

"We are your friends," Angel repeated. "You have made quite a discovery, little man. Unexplained phenomena. Burned bodies. A secret cave. That sort of thing raises eyebrows. Our boss hates eyebrows. I am going to ask you a series of questions now. Try your best to be truthful."

Rico looked afraid. They stood in the light from the elevator shaft in a world consumed with darkness.

"What is the artifact?" Angel asked.

"The what?"

"Describe the artifact's appearance."

Rico squinted. His breathing increased. "I got no clue what you're talking about, guy."

"Who is Melanie Fink?"

"No idea. One of the corpses?"

"Correct," Angel said. "But Melanie Fink was an alias. What was her real name, and what was she doing in that cave?"

"How do you assholes expect me to know that?"

Angel and Genghis exchanged glances. Genghis gave a curt nod.

"Lead the way," Angel said.

Rico turned in the direction of the cave. Genghis raised his pistol and fired. Rico's brain exploded out through the cavity in his face and his body hit the ground with a thud.

An ambush predator relies on deception to trap prey. AKA sit-and-wait predators. Some float on the surface, others prowl the ocean floor. The devil scorpionfish – a quintessential bottom dweller. They come out at night, cloaked, far from the sun. And when they do, they are hungry. He had read these things in a book.

Angel stepped into the shadows, red toolbox in hand.

7

They crept through a world of taxis and fireflies, passing in and out of shadows, her hands at ten and two, sweating. Nikole eased her hatchback into a spot on 65th between a hearse and scaffolding.

"This is insane," she said. "This is illegal."

Sam yawned. "Would you just chill out?"

"We'll get caught."

"We won't. This is kinda my thing, sis. This is what I do. How do you think I get by on the streets of Rochester?"

"You've never done anything like this."

"True. So this is, like, the final boss."

Nikole nibbled half a Xanax bar as discretely as possible and gurgled it with lukewarm Poland Springs.

"Okay," Sam said. "I dunno how to put this delicately, or whatever. But what's wrong with you? There's something wrong with you, right?"

Nikole kept her eyes on the hearse.

"I'm fine."

The air outside was cool. Nikole focused on breathing like a normal person. A trove of tourists stumbled opposite the sidewalk like a drunk caravan of nomads seeking a fresh watering hole. Taxis stacked up at the intersection, their headlights a hundred eyes in the dark. Somebody was smoking marijuana upwind. Around them echoed ambiance of a city refusing to slumber: barking car horns, steam hissing from sidewalk grates, a distant siren, the machinery of a metropolis rumbling underfoot.

Central Park was a black hole. A chain link fence, reinforced with plywood, shielded view of the dig site. Sam scurried across the street without waiting for the light to change. Nikole looked both ways and followed.

Sam scanned the fence with her hand, searching for outlines of a hidden doorway.

"Stay close," she said. "If someone sees you, run back the way we came."

Nikole nodded.

Sam's fingers found their mark, a section of cuts in the fence strategically placed to give the illusion they didn't exist. She pressed inwards and revealed a slit barely wide enough for a body.

"This afternoon there were a couple cops out here," Sam said. "Must've caught 'em on their KFC break."

Sam waited for a pause in taxi lights and ducked inside, disappearing through the rabbit hole.

Nikole eyed the opening like it was the emergency exit to her life. Everything on this side, in her world as a struggling actress, felt like an illusion.

Maybe this is cheating, she thought. Maybe we aren't meant to find an exit.

On the other hand, she thought, staring out at the city, her old nemesis, alight in artificial suns and murky alleyways. Outside felt overwhelming, even as the pills went to work in her tummy.

She waited for the taxis to turn their backs and followed her sister.

Entering the forbidden zone infused her soul with stillness. She scraped her shoulder on exposed wire, unraveling her sweater and drawing blood.

Sam crouched near the treads of an earth mover and reconnoitered. The construction site was raw dirt and gravel, trailers plopped at angles, bulldozers, cranes and a crag in the earth that could fit five houses.

Nikole sunk in mud as she tended her wound.

"Something ain't right," Sam reported.

She didn't need to explain. The site was empty. As her eyes adjusted, Nikole saw wires and hoses crisscrossing gravel, wooden pallets in stacks, a parked van. The fence had deadened, but not muted, the sounds of the city. A single ingredient was missing: people.

"No cops," Nikole said, taking a knee by her sister. "Maybe they went home for the night. Maybe they figured nobody would be stupid and break in."

Sam shrugged. "There weren't cops earlier. A few guys in suits and what looked like private security - dudes in camo fatigues with machine guns who looked like they had a fever and pulling triggers was their only prescription."

"I thought you said a couple of rent-a-cops."

"Okay, so I was exaggerating."

Nikole squinted into darkness. She followed a bundle of wire to the point where it disappeared into the darkness of the pit.

"Did you actually go down? Or were you exaggerating about that too?"

Sam was quiet a moment. "I saw a couple dudes go down. Got a sense of how the elevator works."

"And the key?"

"Really, Nikole? It was the key to your apartment. I lifted it out of your purse in plain sight. You gotta be more perceptive."

Lights blinked on and off in apartments towering over the park. In their randomness Nikole saw smoke signals, secret code, signs of normal people living normal lives who weren't on file with the CIA.

Before Nikole could protest, Sam was off, moving nearly on all fours, scurrying through the night.

Nikole followed, keeping low to the ground, trying to remember what she'd learned auditioning for roles in war movies. They slinked around scaffolding glowing with moonlight. An odor of spent gunpowder and sewage wafted from the ground. Nikole pictured construction workers huffing the soil like wine tasters, arguing over notes.

They came upon a mass of beams and gate in grated blue. Sam went to work on a locked box mounted at waist level. A click announced success. Craning her neck, Sam pressed a few buttons and pulled the door open.

"We Finks are a crafty lot," Sam said.

The elevator made a sound like the space shuttle escaping the mouth of Mount St. Helens. If anyone didn't know the sisters had trespassed, they knew now.

We're doing it, Nikole thought. We're going down. It's happening.

"Got your flashlight?" Sam asked.

"Yeah."

"Now would be an excellent time to use it."

They entered the elevator. Sam did the honors of pressing the big red button.

As the elevator rumbled into bedrock, Nikole learned a new meaning of darkness. Her flashlight blinked to life and breathed a tight circle on prehistoric stone. She thought about open heart surgery, scalpels and X-ray machines, the sinewy guts of the city, a land before time. The sisters did not speak.

Nikole felt anxiety spread like cancer, first in her heart, then in her brain. As they inched further from the waking world, Nikole couldn't shake the feeling that she was entering her own tomb.

8

Juicy!

SO GOOD!!!!!!

Get it girl!

#caitlynsofierce

#SCANDALALERT

Antonio Noon aimed and shot. Click, click, click. Hands like a surgeon. Low light? No light? Honey badger don't care! His mind raced with headlines, all caps, seventy-two point font.

ACTRESS KILLS MOTHER???

Which pill-popping Z-list nobody from the '90s has resorted to arson to make herself relevant? Breaking and entering. A *Kid Wizard* reboot? Set in space? With Bob Saget? Oh the nostalgia. Oh the feels.

He hid behind a bulldozer and reviewed the photos on his camera. There's Nikole and an unnamed accomplice sneaking into the construction site. There she is entering the elevator. The Kid Wizard herself. All grown up!!! And who is this mystery girl? A coke dealer on a late night run? An accomplice to murder? That sweatshirt! What do you even call that look? Chernobyl chic? She's like a comic book superhero in that awkward phase between radiation and the power of flight.

So the rumors are true, he thought. Natasha Kennedy's staging her comeback, one shoe commercial at a time, both feet in the grave.

IT'S (still) ALIVE!!!!

Her hilariously over-produced commercials for Sensei Footwear read like a Wikipedia entry on desperation. Aliens, KGB assassins, topless mermaids and imitation CGI, all in the name of shilling sneakers. Pathetic, how we revert to childhood in our diaper years. And here's her star, living it up like she's a real celeb. Making a midnight rendezvous with a corpse.

WHAT WAS HER FAMILY HIDING???

Because of course it's a cover up. You don't come up in this world a child star without serious cadavers in the cupboard. Oh, how convenient. Back on TV and sweeping scandals under the casket. On the Upper East Side. I mean, really.

Still, working with Natasha Kennedy's a big deal. If the year is 1989. *Did you see her at last year's Oscars*? That dress! Black and white stripes?? Are we at the Academy Awards or Alcatraz?

He leered across treads, masked by shrubs. If this Fink girl's about to explode, I want in.

And then there's the mystery men who went down the hole an hour ago. He flicked back two dozen shots. A black guy, head shaved but for a ponytail, straight off the runway at Rikers fashion week. His pal had the weeping willow goatee you'd expect to find on a soothsayer wandering the Chinese highlands, or wherever. What was he holding? A birdcage? Was that a fucking birdcage? And that coat! What look is he even going for? The Trench Coat Mafia in Tibet?

He switched his SLR to full auto and scanned the graveyard of heavy machinery for signs of life.

And to think, he thought, I almost ignored that tip. But something's off. It seems staged. The strange tip, the van tailing me - oh, I noticed - no security, just like my source promised. I mean, really. The hell is this?

And it was the good source that tipped me off, he thought. The secret source.

And here we are, with a Z-lister nobody cared about until Natasha plucked her from the trash heap of obscurity as a desperation ploy. And what do you know? Drama already. I like this girl.

He sunk into the brush, sheathing his camera, and scanned the trailers. No one in sight. Or... No, that's nothing. Just the feels from a phantom gaze. I'm camouflaged, a clandestine agent clothed in shadows and fabulous fashion. Nikole Fink should thank me for throwing her to the piranhas of the blogosphere. Live by the lens, die by the lens.

Ooh, bigger question – who'll the old lady be wearing in her casket?

9

Nikole and her sister stepped into the city's ancient burial ground. Water dripped against rock, pipes and machinery, filling in the gaps in her vision like sonar pings. She batted her hands in the darkness and loose rock crunched underfoot.

"Kind of eerie," Sam said.

The sisters probed the chasm with flashlights. Pipes and wires lined rock walls. Nikole's beam vanished before hitting land. Every surface stunk of raw earth and ammonia. Nikole toggled between mouth and nostrils, experimenting.

"Um," Sam said, her voice brimming with reverb. "This way, I think."

Nikole's flashlight found what could have been a forklift and a string of lights. She sensed a beating heart; the city's underbelly was more a wounded animal than a grave.

She took another step and tripped over the rough draft of rail tracks, bruising her knee on a rock.

"Isn't there a light switch?" she asked.

"Probably. But fuck if I know what these buttons do. One of 'em's gotta by the dynamite. Don'tcha think?"

They felt their way into a labyrinth. Progress was slow. They scanned each step with flashlights, the world visible in bite-sized lengths before them, wondering about battery life. Water trickled through bedrock overhead. The air felt cold but not frigid. The tunnel walls were layers of sediment, multi-shaded bands of rock upon which a city had sprung. Five feet out was total blackness.

They came to a concrete tunnel. A stream of rain and sludge massed at its base like a river cutting through a canyon.

Nikole scanned her surroundings. She felt her sense of dread double, denting the Xanax armor of her midnight snack.

"This is crazy, Sam."

A distant rumble, barely perceptible, breathed from somewhere beyond the tunnel.

"Let's go back," Nikole said.

Sam marched forward and sloshed ankle-deep into the river as though she hadn't heard her sister's complaint.

Nikole's brain burned with anxiety. What if we suffocate? It happens to miners all the time. What about the Black Lung? Do they have ventilation? What if we get lost?

"Sam," she called out.

Nikole felt tendrils of darkness envelop her. Sam's flashlight dimmed like a satellite plunging out of orbit.

God, Nikole thought. What are we doing?

She bounded into the tunnel. Moisture soaked through her sneakers and socks. The earth's saliva froze her toes. She couldn't tell if it stunk less in the tunnel or if she was just getting used to it.

"Keep up," Sam called.

The tunnel seemed to stretch forever. Nikole tried walking on its curved edge to avoid the water but gave up when her shins began burning with tension on the angled surface.

They trudged through the dark for an hour, maybe more. The tunnel curved, ascended, descended. Nikole wondered about the mechanics and man-hours required to lay all the concrete. She pictured men in overalls and boots toiling in the clay, faces full of soot, hardhats carved with tributes to fallen workers, the looming threat of rogue machinery and collapsed caves.

She distracted herself by imagining an ant farm of workers burrowing underground and a city overhead ignorant of what happens every day below their feet.

After what felt like a forced march, they emerged again onto raw earth.

The air felt different here. Particles of virgin rock hung like dust motes. The looming silhouette of machinery sat idle near a wall marked with white spray paint. They had reached a dead end.

Nikole heard something move. She gasped, spun full circle, probing the dark with her flashlight. She found only shadows.

"Uh, sis?" Sam said.

All manner of horrors scrolled through Nikole's brain: waterboarding, a thousand years in solitary, a sadistic prison guard, her last rites and meal. You can't do this. You can't just walk into a cave full of bodies. You're not the police.

The rain resumed. Nikole's sweatshirt, already moist, absorbed groundwater working its way through the rock.

She searched for her sister in the abyss and found only the end of her beam.

"Check it out."

Rough edges formed a hole in the rock. Nikole took a step forward and detected a new scent. Something here had been on fire.

Sam didn't hesitate. She ducked through the gap and disappeared into the cave.

Nikole stood a moment alone at the bottom of the world. Maybe a monster breathed on her neck, or maybe she just imagined it.

She eased her way into the cave, and there they were. The bodies.

Sam stared at the pile of limbs. The air was thick with stagnation and seared flesh. Nikole pictured a gas chamber's aftermath, crackling bones, the kind of leftover heat that makes you wonder how hot it must have been up close.

The cave looked about the length of three buses. She saw an image painted on the wall in shades of ash:

Nikole felt overwhelmed, confused, gripped by a sudden urge to run and keep running, the feeling you can only get from looking at a dead parent.

Mom?

The corpses were beyond recognition. They looked like exhumed mummies. One had nothing left of its face. Another had both arms reduced to rubble. They were arranged in something of a pile, the remnants of cult ritual or firing squad.

"God," Nikole breathed.

Riches gleamed amongst the human wreckage: a fistful of diamonds, an ornate jeweled egg, a figurine of a pregnant woman that looked lifted from a Neanderthal museum. Near one body which must have been her mother, she found an envelope and ruined book.

Nikole knelt and examined the envelope. She pondered its destruction. Tear it up, she thought. Steal it. Erase all evidence that I'm involved.

The contents of the envelope had been destroyed by fire. Nikole thumbed through ashes, wondering what her mother might have been trying to tell her.

She found a warped photograph, blackened but for a corner. She saw the symbol again, this time on a storefront of what looked like a bookstore on a city street. Too much of the photo had been destroyed, she figured, to determine its location. She pocketed the picture.

"Check it out," Sam said.

She panned her flashlight across the wall. Words had been carved into stone. Nikole approached cautiously, testing the ground with her toes before she stepped.

In numbers the size of dinner plates someone had etched "205."

Nikole squinted at the number, trying to guess the meaning.

Sam panned the light lower. Another message, this one carved deeper. Its letters bore an intensity that conveyed the health of its sculptor.

She read the message three times, then four. Her brain coped in strange ways, rerouting the chemical embrace of her latest snack. Each second unfolded individually. Her eyes tried to escape their sockets.

The message said "Nicole F. burned me."

She read the words backwards, sure she was missing something.

"Huh?"

Sam shrugged.

"Mom blamed *me*? And she couldn't even spell my name right?" She turned and spat on the spot where she died. "I've seen enough. Let's go."

They climbed over their tracks through the ruins. Nicole burned me. Had to take one last pot shot, huh, Mom? Light at the end of the tunnel. But before she gets there, a quick graffiti job. Just to keep things interesting for the next tourist in the afterlife.

"Wait," Nikole said, stopping at the concrete tunnel's edge.

"Sup?"

"Two oh five."

Sam choked on smog and made a face.

"As in season two, episode five," Nikole said. "*Kid Wizard*."

"Got nothin' kid," Sam said. "I'll be honest. I never watched the show. I hated you so much after you ran away."

"Nicole Fox was a character on the show," she continued. "Nicole burned me. That was my line. But it wasn't a fire. She scammed me. I found a magic orb that'd make me stay a kid forever. It was supposed to be a lesson about the inevitability of growing up. But Nicole couldn't destroy the orb, so she hid it somewhere nobody would look." She paused. "It got kinda dark for a kids' show."

Sam illuminated her face from the bottom with her flashlight like she was telling a ghost story, asking with her eyes for Nikole to continue.

"The orb was the size of a pill," Nikole said. "Nicole Fox swallowed it, and then she committed suicide with the orb in her stomach."

The cavern creaked. The sisters as one turned their heads towards the cave. Nikole recalculated her loathing.

In the cave she fell to her knees, soiling her jeans with soot, prodding the torso of each corpse. The burned skin felt like flaking plaster.

She screwed up her face, held her breath, and tried to imagine she was on a film set. None of this is real, Nikole. They're just props. It's just the movies.

She punched a hole through a corpse with her finger. The flesh gave way easily. She pulled out nothing but ash and gagged, doubled over on the hard rock.

Sam shook her head and paced. "Nope," she said as Nikole hunted landmines. "I'm sticking clear of the splash zone. Not sure that Crest Vivid White is good at washing out dead mother. Maybe I'll call the mythical 'questions and comments' line."

"Does Mom's death not bother you at all?" Nikole snapped.

Sam shrugged. "You don't seem too upset yourself."

"It's different with me."

"Right. That's what everyone says. What do you think happened after you left me in the fit-for-child-rearing hands of our old drunkard of a dad? I've never had anyone, Nikole. I don't know what it's like, having a family."

"Poor you," Nikole said mockingly.

"You never wrote. You never called."

"What, you wanted me to lug you along in a suitcase? Look at me, Sam. You think you'd have fared better rationing ramen in a roach motel while I went in and out of psych wards and casting calls looking for work?"

"Well then. Brilliant life choice. You really made something of yourself."

"I'm a star," Nikole snapped.

"I bet."

"I'm in a Natasha Kennedy film. Well, a short film."

"Who?"

"She was famous in the 1980s."

Her hand hit something hard. Conversation stopped. Nikole moved her fingers slowly, as though sifting through sand. She reached into a dry chest cavity. The internal organs had a cooked, rubbery feel. The ribcage collapsed at the touch. Something unnatural sat in place of a heart. Nikole's fingers grasped a glass surface and she pulled.

It was an hourglass.

Sam squinted through low light. "There's no way someone could have swallowed that," she said.

A boot crunched rubble. The sisters locked eyes. Another footstep landed nearby. Someone else was in the cave.

Nikole's flashlight danced wildly from wall to wall. She caught movement, then it disappeared.

"Cops?"

I wonder if Wally has experience busting clients out of jail, she thought. Christ, I need another Xanax. Her eyes darted between corners, plotting escape routes. Bad idea, fleeing the scene. Did Sam bait me? Nikole Fink, criminal trespasser, born in a burn ward, not a star.

A flare hissed to life, flooding the cave with orange light.

Curious is the word we'll use. We didn't know it wasn't allowed.

Color drained from her sister's face. Was that a bird?

"Nikole," Sam said. "They're standing right behind you."

10

He had teeth that were hard to describe. Too wide for his skull, they'd grown at angles to compensate. His gums had fared poorly. Stained and filed like fangs, they looked like something from an oral surgeon's convention, or in a pamphlet they give you at the orthodontist's with the caption "Before." Here is a man who could make a handsome living, Nikole thought, modeling the oddities of the mouth.

"Um," she asked, "can I help you?"

He bared his fangs. The flare's glow turned his teeth orange. His wingman, built like a tank, kept focused on his birdcage.

Nikole's eyes had adjusted to the light. The man held a red metal toolbox in one hand.

"Hey, aren't you the *I'm the captain now* guy from that Tom Hanks movie?" Sam asked. She moved her neck through the full range of motion as she scanned his accomplice. "Um," she said, "what's the deal with your friend here?"

"Genghis speaks only when necessary."

"Does he have a little buddy in there?" she asked, gesturing with her chin at the cage.

The black man sighed, irritated. "It's a sun conure," he said. "His name is Charlie but he goes by Chaz."

Genghis smiled.

"Ah," Sam said, pressing into her cheek with her tongue. "Well I'm not a doctor or anything, but you might wanna think about upping the big guy's meds."

Nikole held the hourglass behind her back with both hands. She stared down the intruders, straining to look unafraid.

"Okay," she said. "I got his name. Genghis. And you are?"

The black man smirked. "Sit. Both of you."

"They call him Angel from Mogadishu," Genghis grunted, speaking for the first time. "Angel for short."

Angel rubbed his temples and grimaced. "Sit."

Sam took a step forward and there it was, a blink of flare light, the blade of a knife.

"Okay," Sam said. "Real things are happening now."

The sisters eased themselves onto the rock. Nikole tried to look bigger, to flare out the way animals do when threatened. Xanax had assumed control. Good timing, she thought, making a note to pop pills more often.

"Who are you and what are you doing here?" Angel asked.

"Who are *you* and what are *you* doing here?" Sam parroted, mimicking the rhythm of the man's African accent.

"We were curious," Nikole said.

Angel nodded, eyebrows arched. "Curious little kittens," he said.

Genghis yanked a cod from his coat pocket and crammed the fish into his mouth whole, scales, eyes and all, chewing noisily, his mouth open and stomach growling. He mashed tooth and bone as though he'd gone hungry for days. Then, with the polish of a circus sword swallower, he plucked the skeleton from his mouth intact, one rib at a time.

"The people I work with," Angel said, tucking his knife away, "each have their own ways of learning the truth. Electrocution, needles, serums. My tastes are more exotic. Are you familiar, little kitten, with the Loa Loa?"

"Loa Loa?"

Angel set down his toolbox and unclasped its latches.

"African eye worm," he said.

Sam leaped to her feet. "Nope," she said. "Nope, nope, nope, nope, nope." She marched towards the cavern entrance. As she reached the flare light's edge, Genghis stopped her and, with little more than a finger, flung her back to the ground.

Angel opened his toolbox. Its innards crawled with all manner of insects - spiders, roaches, wasps and ticks balled into a nightmarish gob of moving parts. Without so much as wearing gloves, he jammed his hand into the recesses of his zoo and plucked a wasp the length of his hand. Nikole wondered if he'd grown immune to bites and stings, or if he just ignored them.

"This is a tarantula wasp," Angel explained, dangling the palm-sized beast by a wing. "Its sting hurts worse than a chemical burn."

Sam curled up like a fetus, mumbling variations of prayer. Nikole surprised herself by staying calm. The scene was too strange to register as reality. Xanax sheathed her heart but she felt its armor wearing thin.

"I am going to ask you a series of questions now," Angel said.

"It was inside of her!" Sam shouted.

Angel and Genghis exchanged glances. Orange shadows danced across their faces.

"*What* was inside of her?"

"The... thing," Sam said. "I don't know. It's this glass thing. An hourglass, I think. We found it, then you assholes showed up."

"You're telling me the artifact is real," Angel said, his voice spiked with suspicion.

"You can have it. I don't care. Just, dear Jesus, throw your box of nightmares in a fire where it belongs."

"Who is Melanie Fink?" Angel asked.

Sam stopped squirming. She sat up, taken aback. "My mom?"

Once again, the intruders exchanged glances.

"You're telling me that Melanie Fink was your mother," Angel said. "I swear, if this job gets any weirder..."

Nikole saw it happen in slow motion. Sam reached into a shadow and came back with a rock. She wound up her shoulder. Nikole's lips could form no sounds. Sam hurled the rock sideways like skipping a stone. It smacked the toolbox with a pang. A mushroom cloud of exotic insects exploded across their assailant's body. Angel stood in shock for a moment, bugs crawling across his face and arms, then collapsed to the ground, wailing like a castrated banshee, rolling around as though engulfed in flames.

Sam lunged like a sprinter and disappeared through the cave's mouth.

Nikole's survival instincts took hold. She snatched her mother's last meal and bounded across her fallen foe in her sister's tracks.

11

Nikole fumbled with her flashlight. She moved without consciousness. Her body recited emergency protocol and genetic code. Her sister's footsteps echoed in a way that came from all directions at once.

"Sam?"

The cavern felt cool, moist, fragrant with death. Its darkness left her disoriented.

"Sam."

She panned her light across one rock wall and then another, trying to figure out which way was up. As she turned, she caught Genghis the giant in the beam squeezing his way from the cave. It looked as though the rock were giving him birth. In his hand, Nikole saw the unmistakable silver gleam of a handgun.

She tore away down the concrete tunnel.

The elevator, she thought. Safety. A to B. Right foot, left foot. Focus on the mechanics.

She sloshed through water as she ran, splashing as high as her face.

"Sam!" she screamed, not knowing what else to do.

Cold air flowed over the back of her neck. She lurched and staggered under the weight of what was happening.

The scrape of boots sounded at her back. Her pursuer limped through the tunnel with a certain inevitability, conserving energy, moving slowly with the knowledge that his prey would soon hit a dead end.

Just don't trip, Nikole, she told herself. Right foot, left foot. Don't fall. Then it's over. I've been in movies. I know how it ends.

Nikole ran through the tunnel. Water amplified the thud of her sneakers. She could almost feel the gun trained on her back the way you know you're being watched. A chalky taste formed at the back of her mouth like the memory of the smell of corpses.

A small part of her still-working brain recalled what the feds said about the Black Lotus, how they leave no loose ends. But the rest of the ruins inside her skull, drug-addled and melted, told her only to run and keep running, so she ran.

After a few minutes at top speed she slowed, then stopped. Her body trembled. She aimed her flashlight into the darknesses before and behind her.

There's only one way, she thought. I can't get lost. Why would I even think that?

The subterranean air did not treat her lungs kindly as she huffed. Adrenaline masked the pain in her knees but it couldn't keep up its act. She hadn't run a mile since high school.

Something splashed behind her.

"Sam?" she asked. Her vocabulary had shrunk to a single word.

Genghis came lumbering through the tunnel like a giant squid emerging from ocean depths: first a disturbance in the air, then ripples giving an idea of its mass, then a silhouette, and then there he stood, gun in hand. He heaved labored breath. He stopped, hands on his knees, then straightened his body, aimed his gun and fired.

The noise ricocheted. Nikole shrunk in the confined space, deafened.

She fell hard on her ass and lost the flashlight. Instinct took control. She lunged back into full sprint, groping at the hourglass as though looking for a power switch. It took hardly ten paces before she was overwhelmed with blackness.

She held one hand against the pipe and moved as quickly as the abyss allowed. She strained to see and hear, but all senses had been put on mute but for the copper on her tongue, a sometimes precursor to a panic attack.

The ground shifted timbre beneath her feet. She had emerged from the concrete tunnel. The pipe vanished. She stumbled into a new darkness, totally blind, arms flailing.

"Hey," she said. "Sam. Where are you?"

Nikole felt a strange pang of justice. She'd abandoned her sister and now her sister had abandoned her. Run away from home and what do you get? She pictured Sam watching her sister's funeral from a distance the way they do in cop TV shows, arms crossed, shielded by trees.

She stumbled. A panic attack punched a hole through her medicated shield. Machine guns of terror riddled her every organ. Heart attack. Collapsed lung. Kidney failure. Whatever it was. And what about the eye worms? Can you even see them? Her skin turned melting wax and tumors. Her mind turned mush. She spat and attempted to cry for help, only to emit a pathetic meow. "I need help," she whispered into the wet rock.

Footsteps crescendoed.

It's over, she thought. Aren't you supposed to feel calm? Isn't there supposed to be a light? She hated herself for believing their lies, then hated herself for dying.

A second set of footsteps approached. As Nikole's hearing returned, she heard something being dragged. She knew by instinct that it was a body.

Then everything went quiet. Nikole kept her eyes closed, bracing for the wasp sting, the bullet or the aneurysm, whichever came first.

Five minutes of silence settled over the cavern and Nikole realized she was alone.

"Sam," she whispered.

She sat up and pulled her phone from her back pocket. After running through a black hole, its screen blinded her. She quickly turned down the brightness.

Low battery. No signal. Of course.

She examined the hourglass with phone light. It ran backwards. Sand danced in a gravity-defying vortex. She flipped the object and observed the same illogic: grey sand settled, paused, then began trickling up.

A heavy sound brought back panic. She sheathed her phone and curled into a corner. Wait, she thought. I've heard that noise before.

The elevator.

She moved with purpose, right foot and then the left, in the direction of roaring machinery, wary for tripwire or booby traps.

She groped her way to the grated shaft. She counted to one hundred, then she did it again, just to be safe. She pressed the call button and the machinery roared back to life.

As she ascended from the depths, she again examined her find.

Sam was right. Nobody could have swallowed this. The hourglass was the length of her palm.

What is happening? Thirteen years later Mom gets unearthed, an hourglass in her tummy, a cryptic note carved in the wall that only I would understand. She wanted me to find it. Now scary people are involved. Federal agents. A sumo wrestler with a gun. A guy who carries around a box full of bugs. They all want what I have. Why? What do I have?

As the elevator neared the surface, hints of dawn rained through rusted cracks. God, she thought. How long were we down there?

The autumn morning smacked Nikole as though she'd dunked her head in ice. She shivered and pulled her soaked hoodie tight. The sun kissed the skyline, painting the sky pale fire.

Her eyes adjusted and there they were, bug man and Genghis and a body bag between them.

"Good morning," Angel called from across the construction site. "And what have you got there, my curious kitten?"

Nikole sprinted through the dig site, hopping cables and backhoe treads like hurdles. She squirmed through the hole in the fence and emerged in an unchanged world.

Sunlight and the smell of kebabs met her on the sidewalk. Dueling billboards oozed bird shit and towering breasts, buzzwords and movie stars. The morning's foot traffic was already swelling along Fifth Avenue. Nikole joined a clump of pedestrians and tried to blend in, head down, sweat pooling in the usual places.

Okay, she thought. The car. A to B. You can do this.

Taxis blew by all horn and tires, an urban chariot race. Soot-stained vagrants shambled like the living dead. A Vietnamese man yanked a steel curtain over his hardware shop. Sad faces stared out of buses above glossy perfume ads, movie stars hawking vodka, half-naked Rihannas and dates the circus will be in town. Nikole sidestepped a grate. A stampede swelled, children screaming you're it. Someone tried to sell her a gym membership.

She was outside without her pills and she knew what was that meant. The Xanax in her veins withered like a spent fuse. Agoraphobia nibbled her brainstem, whetting its appetite.

Nikole spotted a Cuban woman walking three poodles with one hand, done up in fluffy white coat and sunglasses, holding a pink phone in the other. Here is a woman who knows what she's doing, Nikole thought. She slinked through sound and began tailing the poodle walker the way you might follow a snowplow through a blizzard.

How do people do it? How do they walk out the door? So many things could happen. What if a dog gets loose? What if it has rabies? I could walk under a skyscraper at the exact moment of a window washer's worst nightmare. What if I see his body hit the ground? What if I hear the sound it makes? Could I ever sleep again? Or falling debris. That's another thing. It happens all the time. Someone got killed last year. Yes, she thought, I must keep vigilant for falling debris.

Eight blocks. Right foot, left foot. I am not a crazy person.

The poodle walker charted a crosswalk course. Nikole followed. Two cops spoke to a man bundled in bags. On instinct, Nikole hid her hourglass from their line of sight. Trees grew right out of the sidewalk. She never understood how they can grow like that. A fat Mexican, his hands more tattoo than skin, stood under an awning smoking two cigarettes at once.

Her hands shook. Air entered her lungs in starts and stutters.

She glanced across the street and saw him. Angel. The bug man.

Keep moving, she thought. Yes. An object in motion prefers. Everything's in motion here. All that stands still stands out.

A blind man jaywalked, tapping a cane, parting traffic biblically. An old man popped out of an ice cream shop who, for reasons lost in the mythologies of Brooklyn, had dyed his beard a bright shade of puke. He stunk of pot. "As the birds flocked to St. Francis of Assisi, so do the rats to me," the man proclaimed.

The city was conspiring. Everyone watching. See girl run. Hey is that, you know. That one girl. From the kid's show. Her. She killed dragons on

TV.

A cab slowed at the intersection. Fear clouded her senses. Her eardrums had been reduced to blown speakers. Her mouth went dry and vomit-tinged. She lost all attempts at dignity, moving like a crippled animal, nearly on all fours, scaring children and keeping baffled crowds at bay.

She broke into a sprint, shoving an elderly couple aside and claiming the cab, slamming the door.

"Drive!" she shouted, just like in the movies.

Two eyes danced in the mirror. They shrugged and the cab lurched into traffic. Nikole slumped into leather, drained and sore and unsure if she were alive. She realized she'd been crying.

"You alright, lady?" the driver asked.

Nikole mopped a cold sheen from her forehead. "I have a disability," she explained. Yes. That's right. I have protections. Rights.

"Sure. Where to?"

It didn't matter. None of it mattered. Not now that she had the world in her throat. There was no getting around it.

The hourglass was gone.

12

BLIND ITEM – WHICH Z LIST CHILD STAR WAS SPOTTED TRANSFORMING INTO A SHE-WOLF ON FIFTH AVENUE?

By Antonio Noon

Traffic slowed in Manhattan this morning as bicyclists and cabbies alike had to navigate a ten-car pileup of DRAMA involving an actress off her meds, some serious bling and a cheetah-print jacket fit for tribunal at The Hague.

Hammering away at his MacBook, Antonio Noon pulled his legs under him and fine-tuned the angle of his boner within the confines of his D&G chinos. Loving God I thank you for delivering unto me, etc. However that old Catholic school relic goes. Who woulda thought some fossilized loser from the '90s would be so damn interesting? *She* should be thanking *me*, he reasoned. I'm doing more to resurrect her career than anyone. Ungrateful bitch.

His stamp-sized studio was awash in tabloids, carpets like tattered flags, incense, garden gnomes, things stuffed from childhood, Barneys bags, books about Andy Warhol, two dozen flavors of lotion, a dead roach being cannibalized by its young, half-chewed hotdogs and wires. A radiator rattled near the window. Something scuttled opposite the wall.

Ugh. City of rodents. And I don't mean the Baldwin brothers. Zing!

Better bust out the glue traps. Had to fill the tub and Natalie Wood a whole family of whisker-having critters this time last year, he recalled. But there are things in this world worse than mice. Could be SATAN scratching at my wall. Could be house centipedes. Ew. No. I hate those things.

The hourglass crowned a coffee table cluttered with Mariah Carey cutouts. He studied it without shame. She dropped it right on the sidewalk. Common property at that point. Right? The New York five second rule. Some pleb would've snatched it up without knowing the first thing about blackmailing celebs. Perhaps I will one day open a museum of artifacts. COME ONE COME ALL!! Life is full of surprises! Behold the VERY PILLS pulled from Heath Ledger's stomach!

Ugh. Again. His upstairs neighbor was doing that... thing. Whatever the hell he does that sounds like a bowling ball through dominoes. A bass guitar, badly out of tune, shook the floor below.

He turned the hourglass over. The sand inside flowed backwards. He watched as the object defied physics, then turned it over and watched again.

Some kind of party trick, he decided. Magnets or something.

He plucked his iPhone and snapped a photo of his treasure. Time for some good old fashioned blackmail. A single taste of internet shame and Nikole Fink will come begging on her knees.

13

Nature documentaries permeated Nikole's dreams. Creatures from the deep. Amorphous, fangtoothed, bioluminescent effluvia building empires and armies half a planet underfoot. The comb jellyfish lives at the bottom of the sea. Shimmering it sinks through the ether, the last light at the end of the world. Jellyfish have no brains. Some live forever.

She shook off grogginess and checked the clock. She'd slept through the afternoon slouched over her desk. Xanax with the knockout. Sore spots littered her face, a fast-fading graveyard of pens and paperclips.

Nikole sorted medications in her kitchen. Dexedrine and Ritalin, Valium and Oxys, uppers, downers, painkillers, muscle relaxants, and something called Finnegan that's supposed to fight nausea. A snack for every hour. Cough syrup lined up like shot glasses. And you, my precious, she thought, rattling a vial of Xanax. There is only one lord of the pills.

Nikole ate four Coricidin tablets from the stash and a bottle of Formula 44, consumed in measured doses at ten minute intervals to stave off stomach demons.

The TV played a special about a female boxer from China. Cut her teeth fighting bareknuckle in underground fight clubs. Shaved her head, went in disguise as a man. Developed early Parkinson's. In her village they call her a hero.

She fixed cereal and crawled into a comfort, bringing with her chicken salad and pills, bottled water and boxed wine. Just in case.

She flipped channels and watched herself move a matchbox with her mind. Another rerun. Uncle Steven can't start the grill. Fire from her fingers. The family taken aback. Uncle Steven, played by Lance Fielding. What happened to that guy? IMDB search. As an exercise in masochism, Nikole searched herself. Nikole Fink. Played "Amy" on hit family show *Kid Wizard*. 62 episodes. An additional 12 film and television credits. All bit parts. Played the role of "Woman at Temple" in the Chinese knockoff *A Thousand Suns*. "Where is she now?" asked a commenter in the wasteland of her message boards. "I hear she's doing shoe commercials," replied another. "Sad."

She examined the burned photograph she'd pulled from her mother's claws. She saw books, a glass storefront, half a bicycle and the symbol. There was no way the picture had enough detail to identify the location. Maybe if I post it on Reddit, she thought. Is this evidence? Is this stolen? Could I go to jail?

Something vibrated against the floorboards. Phone! Christ, what time is it?

"Hey, Wally."

"You will do the John Stevens Show on Tuesday," said her agent, bypassing any semblance of pleasantry. She heard wrappers crinkle and could almost smell the fries. Wally spoke between gulps and fizz. "There's a signing Wednesday for the 15th Anniversary *Kid Wizard* box set in Chelsea. Dr. Harris will move your appointment to three thirty, inshallah."

She groaned. "I dunno, Wally. I don't think I can do this job anymore." She popped a Xanax and washed it down with warm pinot noir. "I hear Nikole Fink is doing shoe commercials these days. Sad. Where is she now?"

"You shall call in to the Steven Johnson Hour at seven o'clock sharp."

"I could live forever on the *Kid Wizard* money. They pay me a fortune for every rerun. ABC's ordering it into syndication starting in January. I could have a butler, even. Always wanted one of those."

"I have sent you material for the *Catman* audition."

"The what?"

Wally was silent a moment. "Catman. You know. Has a tail? Fights crime? Arch nemesis of The Giraffe? His mother was a seamstress and his father was an African lion? He's a superhero, but he's misunderstood. Huge franchise potential. Already they have cast James Franco as Catman. You shall audition for the role of love interest."

Nikole huffed. Woman in Background again, then.

"How is your weight loss going?"

"Weight loss?" Nikole asked.

Wally's silence signaled something that was supposed to be obvious. Nikole pinched a lob of blubber around her middle.

"You must lose ten pounds for the audition. I will arrange for you to see a dietary physician, one who will prescribe pills, inshallah. We must hire a publicist at once."

"Why all this, all of a sudden?"

Wally exhaled. "Mashallah, Nikole! You are my star, my angel! The 15th anniversary of *Kid Wizard* is upon us. Publicity! Interviews! Surely you will receive a big time role soon. Inshallah, of course," he added, restrained.

"I had a panic attack during the commercial shoot."

He gasped. "No good, Nikole. No good. You must tell me what happened."

"I acted my way through it."

"This is *precisely* why we need a publicist. You are doing the Steven Stevenson Show two weeks from today. On Thursday, there's a charity event in Greenwich Village that..."

"No."

He paused. "No to the charity gig? My God, Nikole, it's for kids with no legs. Michael Keaton will be there."

"No to everything, Wael," she said, using his real name for emphasis. "I'm tired of talk radio. I'm tired of playing woman in background. I want to be a star again."

"You see, this is what I do not understand. Finally you have positive publicity and it's like you don't want it. I knew this would happen."

"Wally?"

"You see, I am a man who understands the workings of, what's the word, the cerebellum. Yes.

"Hey, Wally."

"And while the cerebellum is a delicate mechanism, and I am far from a scholar, I implore you, Nikole, you mustn't..."

"I'll call you back, Wally," she interrupted. "Someone just broke into my apartment."

14

Lu Chen. That was the boxer's name. Nikole heard the crowd roar in her mind. Champion of the world. Belts made of gold. Raining confetti. Pound for pound, whatever that means.

Whoever had barged into her kitchen walked like a drunkard with ninja training, equal parts stealth and stumbling. Somebody's out there, in the red corner, getting ringside pointers from the coach. I am not a crazy person, Nikole thought. It's real. It's here. Nikole Fink versus the world.

She pictured herself bound, captive, ropes rubbing her raw, strapped to a folding chair and beaten by the mob, Angel opening his toolbox and explaining the venom of Brazilian worms.

The trespasser stepped strategically, experienced, evading the creakiest of floorboards. A throat exhaled. Lips smacked. She could smell the citrus from here.

"Nikole? Your door was unlocked, so..."

She attempted osmosis with furniture. Shallow breaths, shallow heart. If you try hard enough, can you stop your heart? Didn't a Buddhist monk do it? Suicide through meditation. With proper willpower, you can flip off life like a switch. She decided not to try, just in case.

The intruder came to a halt in the living room, hands on hips.

"Nikole," he began, "are you under the table again?"

Fear gave way to shame. If I could have one superpower, she thought, I'd like to disappear, and I don't mean turn invisible.

"Nikole? Will you come out from under the table?"

"In a minute," she squeaked.

The door was open. Shame shifted into frustration, passing through the cycle, everything in its proper place. An unlocked knob isn't an invitation. Because of course it's someone else's fault.

"Can I come under there with you?"

She exhaled. "Okay."

Carlos moved the tablecloth and half-kneeled awkwardly, hunched like an athlete going through a doorway. He stunk of egg rolls and Burt's Bees. Nikole shuffled into a corner. Her laptop was her lair's source of light. Carlos offered her a stick of gum. When Nikole refused, he shrugged, arched his eyebrows, and devoured double his share. He adjusted his legs, getting comfortable. "So this is weird. Just hanging out under the table?"

Nikole averted her eyes. "Don't look at me," she said. "I'm hideous."

She couldn't blame the world for long. Self-loathing came on hard. Here she was most dangerous. Unstable, was the word her doctor used. She fantasized about kitchen knives, shards of glass, bruises showing through mascara. And pills. Always more pills. I could destroy myself whenever I want, she thought. I have that right.

"What do you want, Carlos?" she asked, head down.

Here it comes, she thought. Wait for it.

Slowly, with deliberation, Carlos plucked the chewing gum from his mouth.

"I wanted to say sorry," he began. "I wasn't myself the other night."

"Okay."

"I was just thinking, you know, that you and I should..."

Then it scurried across the floor. Eight-legged and multi-eyed, the beast darted from crevice to crevice, moving with a speed Nikole thought unpossessed in the insect kingdom.

"Oh God," Carlos screamed. "Is it a spider? Kill it, Nikole! Kill it! Is it dead? Oh, Jesus. I can't even. Is it on me? I can't even, Nikole. Kill it!"

When I die, Nikole thought, my body will digest itself. Microbes will burst my membrane walls. I'll turn into earth and air. Molecules swept up in cosmic whirlwinds. Recycled bones. Born inside stars, bubbling around in my body, soon to be released into the wild. Am I living the best kind of life?

She crushed the insect.

"It's dead."

Carlos spent a moment adjusting to this new, arachnid-free world.

Nikole thought about offering him a Xanax in jest, but he'd be *concerned* all over again and she couldn't handle that right now.

"Anyways," Carlos said, unraveling a note from his pocket. "Here are the top five reasons we should get back together. One, you're under a lot of stress right now and I could give you massages and bring you chocolates. Two, I could get you groceries so you don't have to go outside because of your agoraphobia. Three, I could..."

"It's over, Carlos."

Entropy, it's called. We're part of the Earth. We're recycled. In the next life I might be a tree. No coffins or chemicals for me, trapped in formaldehyde prison, unable to birth dandelions and kings. Let me be free.

"I want to help you."

"Oh," Nikole said. "Um, no thanks."

"Why do you have to be so damn unreasonable about everything?" he sneered, banging his head against the table. "Do you just want to live in a cave all your life?"

Nikole shrugged. "Don't you have an acting class to get to?"

"So that's what it's about. I'm not good enough. Well, guess what? You can hide from it, but there's still a world out there. And nobody gives a shit about you. Not the way I do."

"Look, Carlos, I want you to be successful. Really, I do. But I don't want us to be together anymore."

"Why not?"

"Because," Nikole said. She paused, pondering the light from her screen. When I die, nobody will find me for months. "Because I want to be alone."

Carlos shook his head. Unbelievable, he said with his eyebrows. He stuffed his cheeks with gum, crawled from under the table and left.

As if on cue, Nikole's phone buzzed. New email. Sender unknown. She squinted at the screen as her ex-boyfriend's footsteps grew dim in the hall.

Nikole Fink,

What would you do with nine lives? I'd spend the first three reading Heraclitus and watching films from the silent era. Because you have to start there. Everything that can be said about life is in Chaplin's The Kid. *Then, once I'd figured out how to spend the next six, I'd move on to French New Wave and the utilitarians. Eventually I'd get around to first kiss, student loans, cubicle, etc. If I had to do it again I'd become a professional typographer. Life seven would be spent amassing appropriate prestige in my field. That way, life eight could be more wholly dedicated to my crusade against Helvetica. I hate Helvetica.*

Your mother died in possession of a fragment of the world's dangerous and forbidden knowledge. You know that by now. Here's something you don't know: there was one who escaped the fire. An old pal of mine named Snorri has shown up on the Lotus net. Odd timing. Snorri deals in curios, oddities. We're best buds. Sorta. Once I spent five months trying to kill him. Went undercover as a Viking named Auður. Some good old cloak and dagger. Methinks Snorri survived the flames. Do not waste this life, Nikole Fink. And be careful. The Black Lotus are hunting you.

Your friend,
Mouse

15

"Where did it come from?"

"No idea."

"I mean, when did it start?"

"Five years ago. Thereabouts."

"And how... I mean, like, you good right now?"

"It doesn't work like that. Agoraphobia isn't a force-field. When I think about how stupid it sounds, that just makes me feel even crazier. But when I'm on my meds, I can handle it. Most of the time."

Sam propped herself onto her elbows. The sisters lay side by side on the grass in Central Park, an oak dressed for autumn swaying overhead. Children's voices and the smell of soft pretzels wafted from the sidewalk.

"There was a stretch, though," Nikole said, "where I didn't leave home."

"How'd you eat?"

"My boyfriend brought me groceries. Then, once he was gone, my agent."

"Damn, sis. That's messed up."

She nodded. "It's from childhood, I think. They hovered. Everyone. Family, doctors, PR people, cast and crew. They knew the dark side. They knew what can happen to child stars. So they suffocated me. I led a life of privilege. I never learned to fight on my own. When I grew up, I didn't know how."

Sam yawned and adjusted her Tiny Tina book bag as a pillow. "Okay," she said, "don't take this the wrong way. But boo fucking hoo. You're telling me your head's screwed up because your childhood was *too good*? Notice how I haven't regaled you with any heartwarming coming-of-age tales from the life and times of Samantha Fink? Did you know I started drinking at age fourteen, just to deal with the pain of being alive?"

"What do you want me to do about it? We don't have a time machine, Sam. We can't go back."

Sam stretched out on her back. "Sure can't," she said.

Nikole swatted falling leaves from her face.

"Do you..." Nikole began. "I mean, aren't there shelters? Programs? Foster homes?"

"Fuck that," Sam said. "I'm a street kid. It's my choice."

"Yeah, but..."

"We look out for each other. It's the closest thing I have to a family. And don't worry, mother, I'm still in school. They don't know."

The sisters were quiet a moment, watching park-goers prowl sidewalks in twos and fours, normal families doing normal family things, pushing strollers, handing out balloons, walking in the park.

"What kind of a name is Snorri?" Nikole asked.

Sam flicked her phone screen. "Icelandic," she said. "So sayeth Google."

Nikole checked her own phone. New message. Somehow she'd missed the buzz.

Nikole Fink,

Your life is in danger. Nah. Kidding! Always wanted to start a message like that. Explosion of activity on the Lotus net last night. They've sent operatives to an address in Manhattan as we... well, we're not exactly "speaking" per se. And email isn't a continuous action so "as we" is a little weird. Anyways, you might wanna get clear of the blast zone. They found out about your hourglass, btw. They want it. Bad. They've marked it a Category Four artifact. The highest classification. Okay, I made that up. They don't do categories. But a firestorm's coming your way. Bang up job you're doing with the whole staying alive thing. If you wanna keep on keepin' on until we figure this thing out - as a certain Donald is wont to say - you should get out of town. Your mother knew a secret that could undermine our very understanding of human existence. She left a trail of breadcrumbs. For you, Nikole. You are the only one who can unlock it. Do not waste this life. I'll be in touch.

Your friend,
Mouse

She looked at the address and it wasn't hers. An apartment in Greenwich Village. Her heart skipped two beats. The hourglass. Let it go, Nikole. Let the Black Lotus claim their trophy. Why get involved?

Sam lay on her back using two fingers to swipe her phone screen. Halfway through a yawn she froze.

"Uh, sis?"

Birds twittered, children yelped. From this angle the world seemed pristine and windswept, an oasis of life tucked in a corner of outer space. Nikole had the feeling of a glass pane before a sledgehammer. Because obviously. You don't just stumble across an affront to physics and move on.

"There's, uh, something trending online," Sam said. Her voice had gone shaky.

She had the feeling of hitting "send" and being done with it. In someone else's court. The quasi-relief of making a big decision. Well, at least the decision is settled, if nothing else. Now all that's left is to go through the motions, the mechanics of the thing.

"You posted the hourglass to Instagram?" Sam asked.

She tilted her phone. Sure enough, there it was. The gravity-defying hourglass, etched into internet stone. Erase that, she thought. Go ahead. Try.

The dumbass waited one day. That's Thieving 101. Rob a bank, post it to Facebook. But you gotta wait to do these things.

"Who's Antonio Noon?"

Nikole sat up. "Say his name again."

"Antonio Noon," Sam repeated, enunciating like she was teaching a first grader to read. "You know him?"

Nikole rubbed her face. "By reputation. He's a celebrity stalker. Insufferable. Has he been following me?

"Fraid so."

"Jesus, Sam. He's got the hourglass?"

"Fraid so." She paused. "What the hell, sis? We stumble across Mom's lost treasure and, what, you stick it on a night stand near the window?" She squinted at the screen. "Which Z-lister got caught on a midnight drug run," she read. "This is blackmail, Nikole. Call the cops."

No time, she thought. And what would she even say? Lost relic. Not stolen, I promise! Oh, and the Black Lotus are inbound. They erase people from history.

"Or," Nikole said, eyeing the address Mouse had sent her, "we could pay him a visit ourselves."

16

Five black cats dotted the concrete steps, necks craned as one, fur draped like laundry spread to dry. The street was all fire escapes and sandwich shops, bicycles chained to sagging buildings, street sweepers and fallen leaves. Brick canvas above a sex shop bore erasures of yesterday's graffiti. Dogs yelped. Buses honked. A semicircle of immigrants bickered in fantastic accents near a cafe radiating espresso.

It occurred to Nikole that she hadn't the faintest idea what Antonio Noon looked like. The name chilled the spine of every Manhattan socialite. But the man himself stayed firmly behind his lens.

"They're calling it a hoax online," Sam said, sidestepping the felines. "Everything. The bodies, the cave, the hourglass."

"We'll get it back."

Sam stopped on the steps and nearly dropped her phone. "Really," she said. "That's your reaction. Mom was living a double life, a cultist in a magic cave with a magic hourglass, killed in sacrificial fire, and you're all, yawn, whatevs."

"When Mom left home, she left nothing behind. Her life was erased.

She escaped their white-out. She took the hourglass with her."

Sam's eyes bulged from their sockets, pupils dilating in sync, then returned to a skeptical zero point. "You're suggesting that our mother left of her own free will? You're suggesting she abandoned us?"

"I don't know, Sam."

"She got kidnapped," Sam said. "These cultists took her to their cave."

"That's what you think happened?"

Sam shrugged. "Well I dunno. Thinking about it makes my brain hurt. I didn't pay enough attention in whatever math is supposed to help you with word problems. If only she'd been traveling west at thirty kilometers per hour..."

"Look I don't understand it either. But that hourglass is part of the puzzle. She wanted us to find it."

Sam nodded. "Right. Okay. We'll get it back."

She tried the handle. Locked. Before Nikole could stop her, Sam mashed her hands across buzzers near the doorway. Eventually, the door clicked. As Sam pulled it open, the glass caught in reflection a well-dressed black man on the sidewalk in bowtie and pinstripes, Tom Ford glasses and a cap two shades darker than his skin. Even at this distance Nikole nearly choked on his toxic clash of colognes. He caught a glimpse of her face, dropped his Duane Reade bag and tore off running down the sidewalk.

The sisters swapped eye contact, then took off in pursuit.

Antonio Noon shouldered his way through a rap battle taking place under a neon sign. He leaped over a sidewalk menu like hurdles and jaywalked, drawing horns. Music thudded through the wall of a club. They jogged streetlamp to streetlamp, where garbage bags formed pyramids, the stink coming and going as they ran.

Sam darted across the street. The sisters ran parallel on sidewalks like sprinters in their lanes. Nikole's sneakers rattled a sidewalk grate. Antonio kept peeking over his shoulders, gaining ground then losing it, impeded by bicycles, panhandlers and tourists arranged in firing lines wielding city-sized maps.

A tree-chained dog nipped at her ankles. Air conditioners rattled and dripped. A Pakistani shop owner wore a coat made of cell phones and sale signs. No better deal, he kept saying. Sony, Samsung. Unlocked, upgraded.

No better deal.

Nikole sidestepped a fire hydrant and took stock of her psyche. Vital signs normal. Having her sister here helped. So too did actual danger. The world's scariest when there's nothing to fear.

Contractors climbed from a hollowed-out storefront like miners drenched in soot, surgical masks across their faces, radiating drywall. They plumbed fast food wrappers and wrenches in the back of their van. For a moment Ray's Contracting and Electric hid her view of the chase. Antonio Noon slid across a Honda's hood clumsily, setting off the alarm. He ran the double yellow like a tight rope until horns deterred him. He ducked down an alley and the sisters followed, Nikole now taking the lead.

An ATM outside a strip club was plastered with stickers beyond recognition. In black sharpie a flier announced auditions for a death metal band called Satan's Snowflake. Each bounding step shot adrenaline through her knees. She ate air in gulps.

They emerged onto a quieter thoroughfare of apartments and parked cars. Trees poked at odd angles from the cement, shedding leaves in the wind. Two Mets fans in full regalia crossed paths staring at smartphones, each not noticing the other.

Antonio Noon bounded down steps to a basement doorway and pounded.

"Open the door!" he shouted. "Mom! Open the god damn door!"

The sisters cornered him and he turned, arms raised in surrender.

"I don't have it," he blurted. He set his hands on his knees, gasping, looking near collapse. His crocodile loafers bore scuff marks. He examined them and sighed. "Look," he said, catching his breath, "I don't know what kind of Illuminati witchcraft you're into, but I'm going Hulk Hogan on your ass. When I posted the backwards-flowing hourglass on Instagram last night, I was doing so in character as Antonio Noon. The private citizen Antonio Noon is a delicate flower, and if you hurt my feelings I'll destroy you. My feelings are worth more than a medium-sized business."

"Where's the hourglass?" Sam asked.

"Jesus. Ask those goons you sent after me. Studio fixers. Bodyguards. That asshole with his birdcage."

The sisters traded glances.

"I sold it," Antonio said. "Okay? It's out of my hands. He had a gold tooth, Versace shades, Asian skin, a fedora with diamonds. Fabulous wardrobe from the neck up. His suit? Not so much. Men's Wearhouse meets garden shears. Awful tailoring. At first I'm thinking, okay, he's going for a sort of mid-century Parisian color palette, but with *those* shoes?" He looked at Sam with thinly-veiled disgust. "Who's this, your sister? What is she? A cartoon character come to life? Jesus, her eyes are the size of pool balls. Oh, and torn jeans. How edgy. What, you think showing a sliver of underage thigh will land you a TV spot? Get in line, honey."

Sam took a step forward and he flinched.

"I made those statements in character as Antonio Noon," he said. "My hurt feelings could bring down the space station."

"Goldtooth," Sam said. "Who is he?"

He shook his head. "No idea. Look, I've explained it already. Ask your friends."

"They're not here," Sam said. She crossed her arms and tried to look as tough as possible.

When I die, Nikole thought, bury me in a mass grave. But in life leave me alone. Movie stars and their mansions. Not me. Once I make my fortune I'll blow it all digging a hole. But this isn't always. I'll have a family. I'll go normal. Eventually. This is just until whatever blows over. I'll be more sociable in the grave. I'm not my sister. When Sam dies, she'll probably tell the whole world.

She heard voices, terrorists or schizophrenia, smudging crime scene fingerprints in her brain. Shades parted in a window. Antonio's mother, come to the rescue.

"Polygraph me," pleaded Antonio Noon. A lisp had crept into his voice, as though speaking through pain. "Look into my eyes. Are these the eyes of a liar?"

"Tell us what happened and we won't send our friends for a second chat," Sam offered.

"Goldtooth contacted me an hour after I posted the video," he began. "Told me it was hot. I thought he meant stolen. Offered me fifty grand. We met at Penn Station. He looked... I dunno. Chinese? Thai? He said he was taking it to some kind of magical library. That's all I know. He handed me a McDonald's bag. Fake money. Yup, I got screwed. Hope you're happy. Then your Somali pirate buddy and his sumo wrestler pal come rough me up. I have six million Instagram followers. Do you know what I'm capable of?"

The door opened. A woman with the torso of a mountain range stood under a junkyard chandelier. Antonio brushed past her, huffing with indignation. Safely inside he turned to face the sisters once more.

"You'll hear from my lawyers," he said. "Only a jury in Florida can understand how I've suffered."

The door slammed.

Sam's eyes went through that strange dilation again, growing right out of her skull. She mimicked the man from the other night, puffing out her chest and shoulders and holding an imaginary birdcage. Nikole nodded.

"Those assholes!" she shouted, kicking the air. "Well now what? We're back at zero."

Something clicked in Nikole's head. A magical library. He deals in curios. A bookstore on a city street. A symbol on a cave wall. You should get out of town. Do you travel internationally, Ms. Fink?

"Sam," she said. "How much cash do you have on you?"

"I dunno. Thirty bucks."

Her bones ached the way that people with bad knees can predict storms. She unfurled one knuckle at a time. What if I'm not back by the 13th? What will I tell Natasha Kennedy? Sorry. Trying to unravel an international conspiracy. Save me a role selling shoes.

"Let's go to the ATM and take out as much as we can," Nikole said.

"What for?"

Her intestines went butterflies but her brain relaxed. She'd made a big decision.

"We're going to the airport," Nikole said.

"The airport?"

"I know where they took the hourglass."

17

BLIND ITEM – WHICH Z LIST CHILD STAR IS IN TERRORIST BOOT CAMP?

By Antonio Noon

How the mighty have fallen! You might remember silver screen icon Natasha Kennedy as the catty, uterus-of-the-walk of yesteryear who hasn't done anything edgy since, I don't know, forever?? Rumor says she's run out of star power. Duh!! Not the '80s anymore, sweetheart. All she's got going these days is her shoe commercials and her DUIs. But things have gone from M.A.D.D. to worse as the one-time Hollywood powerhouse has had to resort to obscurity to find an actress desperate enough for her next ad. Things take a turn for the weird as this pill-popping former child star broke into a crime scene shortly after her mom took what Michael Jackson's doctor might call a "nap," apparently at the bidding of an ultra-scary terrorist group called the Black Lotus. Has she been radicalized? I must remain hush on my involvement in this sordid affair, my darlings. The only government database in which I want my name is the *too* fly list. Who is this actress? Post your guess in the comments. Reveal coming soon.

Wael "Wally" Algayar stared into the screen until his eyes went sandpaper. This is not my, what's the word, forte, he thought. I am a delicate man, a quiet man. I can perform the moonwalk. I have excellent taste in Latin jazz. Yes, perhaps I could have minded my mother more and, no, Allah might not approve of the magazines I look upon while on the toilet, but I am not a madman, nor do I have a family history of madmen, save for Uncle Cyrus.

He shuffled fast food wrappers and stained contracts, palms oozing sweat, mustard in his mustache. Nervously, he looked up from his meal.

"Are you sure?"

Antonio Noon held himself in the office doorway like an exotic dancer. "I'm *always* sure, honey," he said with glee.

"My God," Wally breathed. "Why would she do such a thing? You have photographic evidence?"

He nodded. "Got her going down the elevator and coming back up with buried treasure in her hands. I heard gunshots. But, what's more, somebody stole a corpse. I can only assume Nikole and her sister were in cahoots with the dudes with the body bag. That's how it looks, anyways."

Wally gasped. "A body bag!"

Gunther was working late again. Sounds of medieval battle radiated from the neighboring office. It sounded like a, what's the word, inquisition, wizardry.

"I have been humiliated," Antonio said, "and I have been wronged. I thought it was just a dumb party trick. The magic hourglass, I mean. Now I've got federal agents after me. There's something screwy going on, and that hourglass is the key. To the right buyer, it could be worth millions."

Or Franz. Whatever his name was. The German next door. Wally's memory had started to go. High cholesterol or amnesia. He knew fast food had doomed his soul. But surely Allah would allow the occasional Big Mac. Right? It's not murder. It's not deviance.

Wally used his eyebrows to suggest Antonio continue.

"The gossip press has more power than you can imagine. I could end Nikole Fink's career with the press of a button. She's done most of that work herself these past few years. But I've got connections, Wally. I could make or break her. I'm doing something for her either way – good press or bad press, depending on you. I've got her breaking into a crime scene, stealing a precious hourglass and colluding with body snatchers. And don't think I don't know about your little pill scam."

Truth is, he'd been only pseudo-observant for years. It's quite a thing, he mused, maintaining one's faith in a dollar menu-filled world. And now this. My God. Two decades without a break and what happens? I am a man who is cut out to deal with neither hooligans nor shenanigans.

Wally nodded, understanding. "This is a shakedown, no? You are blackmailing me."

The blogger swayed in the doorframe. He wore a pink bowtie and shaved scalp, movie star teeth and jeans matching the color of his skin so precisely at first glance it appeared the man was pantsless.

"Come now, Wally. Let's not use such harsh language."

"What do you want?"

"You're getting that hourglass back for me. That's step one. Then, I want fifteen percent of your cut on all Nikole Fink's future contracts. Look at it this way: now I have an incentive to help her out. That's a win-win-win. A threesome, Wally."

I am an expert in the art of delicate negotiation, Wally thought, but I have little in the way of high-G training. We are now in orbit. This blogger is staring me down, measuring my mustache.

"If you have indeed been wronged," Wally suggested, "why not contact the police? Surely they can help you recover lost property more effectively than Wally Algayar."

He reached for the phone, but Antonio stayed his hand. "You're an amateur, honey. I can tell. You don't want police involved. You want a private eye."

Antonio yanked a business card from his jeans, its rectangle of white striking against the black denim, and slid it across the table. "Like I said, I have a vested interest in Nikole Fink's well-being." He tapped the card's surface three times. Wally squinted. The card advertised a private detective with a name Wally couldn't begin to guess how to pronounce. "This man," Antonio continued, "is the best in the business at shoveling scandals into shallow graves. Google him. You'll see. Read up on what he did for Bradley Cooper."

"Why don't you contact this man yourself?"

He giggled. "Why get my hands dirty when I've got you? Look, I don't want my fingerprints anywhere near this thing. I've had enough run-ins with goons for a dozen lifetimes. Nobody outside of this room is to know about my involvement. I've got a blog to run. I've got celebs to stalk. You, on the other hand, have nothing to lose."

They stared at one another a moment, Antonio smirking, Wally stricken through with palpitations. He wiped sweat from his forehead.

"And this Black Lotus of which you speak," Wally said. "What if they target *me*? What if they target Nikole?"

He only winked. "I'm sure you'll figure something out."

18

Nikole watched a rainstorm mask the Atlantic like a burial shroud. Most of the passengers were sleeping. Sam snored loudly, her volume outsizing her physique. Ocean, cloud and sky were a single shade of night. At this altitude, the sky was an alien place. Moonbeams drew curlicues across the cloudscape. The scream of engines served as the only clue they weren't orbiting Neptune.

Nikole rested her forehead on the glass and wondered what she was doing.

In her head the puzzle pieces butted edges. A trail of breadcrumbs. A burned photograph. A symbol painted on a cave wall. Paranormal investigators. My mother. Edited out of history. But why?

Mom wouldn't have left me her breadcrumbs if she knew I'd turn into such a fuckup, Nikole thought. She plumbed her purse for the reassuring rattle of her Xanax. Fifteen tablets. We'll be back before I run out, she told herself. Right? But if I do run out... No, better not to think like that.

Nikole found herself overcome by a feeling that she wasn't alone. Her body became a soothsayer broadcasting precursors to chaos. A gallon of acid boiled in her stomach. Slime stuck to her neck. Trembling, she scanned the slumped passengers for anomalies, balaclavas and shoe bombs, a birdcage, fires on the wing. Nothing appeared out of the ordinary.

Satellites flickered among the stars and Nikole imagined the voices bouncing from earth to space and back, beamed to crackling television sets and radios in rented cars, to mobile phones and mobile clinics, to submarine bases in the Red Sea and sportscasters in Santiago. Their sounds transcended history. Secrets stored in code. The breath of magic incantations, some alive and some dead, hidden messages discovered by archeology or trash collectors or UFOs.

Nikole watched her sister sleep. She wanted to roust her, to feel her embrace, to sense her heartbeat through skin and fabric, to apologize for existing. She'd failed her family so many times. And now Sam is homeless, she thought. Sammy. My baby sister. She plumbed the chemically eroded black hole of her brain for childhood memories but came up blank. They were strangers.

Nikole realized her teeth were chattering and felt shame at her weakness in the presence of... what, exactly? She wondered about religious conversions, revelations, shell-shattered truck stops on the road to Damascus. The sisters hovered in the safety of the stratosphere. She may have hallucinated some deviation in the engines' hum. After a tense period of seconds or days, her senses settled and her body returned to its physical concerns.

We're going to find out about Mom, she decided. Who she was. What happened in that cave. And the secret. She took forbidden knowledge to her grave. But it's out there, waiting for those who know where to look.

I know where to look.

Her sister's snoring stopped, softened, started again. She squirmed in her sleep.

Nikole turned and watched clouds erase stars out the window, thinking how easy it would be, out in the cold and desolate patches of the world, to disappear forever.

19

The man made a face. Not contemplation. Not confusion. He didn't look annoyed or in shock. Just a face.

"Well," Nikole asked, "does the name mean anything to you?"

They stood in an office of manatees and dust. Photos of the ocean creatures crowded the walls. On the man's desk sat several specimens, this one cast iron, this one plastic, this one molded like a whiskered Buddha with fins. He looked up from his books. The man wore an orange Yosemite Sam mustache and drooping cheeks to match, wiry round glasses, an ankh in one ear.

"You're mispronouncing it," he said. "Auður." He said it like it rhymed with *other*.

Nikole's heart quickened. "So you know the name."

"Yes."

She looked at her sister. Sam nodded. Nikole wound up her breath.

"I've spoken to Mouse," she said. "We're here for the hourglass."

Snorri the bookseller blinked. For a moment, he said nothing. Then he curled his eyebrows. "Yes, I know Auður," he said. "Auður Jonsdottir,

Auður Helgasdottir, Auður who works at the lagoon, Auður who sells Skyr, both Auður the poet and Auður the professor of poetry, Auður the lab who leads Blind Magnus Ingvarsson to the liquor store and back, Auður from the theater, and Auður the whaling vessel, upon which my great-uncle had his right lung pierced by a walrus named Roy. Auður is a common Icelandic name."

Nikole deflated. Sam clicked her tongue.

The smell of books had baked itself into these walls to the point that, should they bring the bookstore down with flamethrowers, the whole city of Reykjavik would stink of paper. Snorri had a tag around his neck reading MANAGER in three languages. Whether an involuntary muscle twitch or as some sort of signal to leave, he began stroking a stuffed manatee on his desk with a balled fist.

"How about Auður the Viking?" Nikole asked.

He nodded. "Her too. Auður djúpúðga Ketilsdóttir. National hero."

"Is that Klingon?" asked Sam.

"Well," Nikole began, "Auður the Viking wants to talk."

His strokes grew erratic. Another face. Different this time. He held his head still between massive manatee eyes in the photograph behind the desk. Then he burst out laughing. "Who put you up to this?" he managed to squeak between guffaws. "Auður Ketilsdóttir has been dead a thousand years!"

Back outside, Nikole tightened her jacket and turned to avoid the brunt of wind. A man dinged past on a bicycle two sizes too small, laden with milk crates and scrap metal, a caged ferret and flags from two dozen nations.

"Run it by me again," Sam said. "Who told you about Auður the Viking? A talking rodent?"

Nikole struggled to keep a street map open against a gust. "Mouse is, like, some kind of code name," she said.

The cyclist dinged again and sped past a row of storefronts, narrowly avoiding an assembly of street musicians gurgling strange syllables, then disappeared behind the façade of Islenski Barinn Reykjavik.

Sam nodded. "And psycho secret agent lab rat – who sounds like quite the reliable narrator – says there's a dude named Snorri who knows escaped the cave, and you just sorta pieced it together... how, exactly?"

"The burned photograph."

Colored cottages and distant glaciers loomed in alleyways. Street signs bore fantastical names: Fríkirkjuvegur, Stjórnarráðið, Kirkjutorg. Nikole tried to guess how you might say them.

"Snorri is an Icelandic name," Nikole continued. "Mouse tells me he deals in curious and oddities. Her words. She says the Black Lotus are coming for him."

They wandered a sidewalk sandwiched by street art and stores selling microbrews. A spare billboard said something in Icelandic. Everyone looked fit, fur-wrapped, impervious to cold.

"So you figure he works at this mystery bookstore, which you've decided must be in Iceland. Really. It had to be Iceland. Why not Mar-a-Lago?"

"It's this or nothing, Sam. It's the only lead we've got."

"You couldn't get better directions?"

She shrugged. "The messages Mouse sent me – I had no way to reply."

Iceland. She'd never dreamed of being in such a place. She eyed the world like a museum, wondering if they have penguins here, if their sun goes down for half the year and if they see the Northern Lights.

"I mean, how many Snorris at bookstores can there be in Reykjavik?"

An art gallery's glass buckled in the wind. Someone had chained a dog to a sign saying no dogs. It lapped at a puddle as the sisters strolled past.

Sam made no reply. Nikole heard her fingers tapping. She turned to find her sister thumbing away at her smartphone screen, a look on her face that said I'm checking.

Nikole wrenched the phone from her hands.

"What did I say, Sam? They can track us."

Sam put both hands on her head and rolled her eyes. "How? From their evil Death Star phone tracker in orbit? And how do you know it's even in Reykj... however you say it?"

Nikole stared her down.

"Alright," Sam said. "Jesus. Give it back."

Nikole kept her eyes on the phone until it was completely powered down.

"Guess we're back to the Oregon Trail days. Take away our phones and it's just a few weeks before dysentery sets in."

They marched through breezy Reykjavik under clouds layered fire and ash.

The red corner restaurant ahead would have stood out had it not been flanked by equally eye-popping shades. Skullcapped men hoisted crates of crabs from the back of a Mercedes van and Nikole wondered if they were whalers. An amalgam of scarves that might have been a woman hurried after them with a clipboard.

Sam nudged her elbow. Across the street. Number 319. A bicycle leaning against glass. Orange light, volumes bound in leather, a man stroking his beard.

Nikole plucked the photo from her purse. The storefront's corner was the same shape but different materials. Gone were the bricks. Gone was the bird symbol. Could've been renovated, Nikole thought.

"This the place?"

"Let's give it a try," said Nikole.

Inside, the bookstore smelled of cedar and cappuccino. Books had been arranged by color. Yellow bled into orange bled into red with such seamless transition across shelves that customers were wary to touch. Here are books on world history, but just in pale green. Here's a blend of photography guides and bibles in black. Most eclectic was a sheaf of pink labeled "Wrestler Autobiographies, Lesbian Westerns, and Architecture of Post-Imperial Japan."

An employee restocked returns with the aid of paint swatches. She wore a bun of hair metal blonde, tights and a tank top full of skulls.

"Excuse me," Nikole said. "Does Snorri work today?"

The book stocker plucked out her earbuds. "Which one?" she asked.

"What do you have here," Nikole demanded, "a list of, like, a hundred things you're allowed to name your kid?"

"More than a hundred," the woman said. "But there's a list, yeah."

Nikole rubbed her forehead. "Listen," she said. "We need your help. We've come all the way from New York City. I don't know his last name. I don't know what he looks like. All I know is Auður wants to talk to Snorri and it's an emergency."

She nodded. "We have two Snorris: Snorri the cashier and Snorri in acquisitions."

Nikole drew breath. She looked for her sister and found her toying with a display of artfully arranged books on lost languages and films set during the Prohibition era.

"The second Snorri," Nikole somehow knew. "Him."

The woman nodded. "He's not in today."

Of course. Why would it be easy? Next she'll say he's taken the month off.

"Actually, he's taken the month off. Called us out of the blue. Sounded scared to death. Said he wouldn't be in for a while. Dunno what it's about."

Nikole palmed her face.

"But," she continued, "if it's important, I can call him."

The front desk was built from books. These ones weren't color coded. They were sorted by girth.

The sisters stood side by side as the purple panted bookseller dug through binders. Nikole stuffed fingers in her pockets to mask the tremors.

She spoke to Snorri in Icelandic, then handed Nikole the phone.

At first she only listened. His breathing sounded nasal, harsh, too fast. One of those things measured by a polygraph.

"Snorri?"

"Yes?"

His voice matched the raw energy of his breathing.

"Auður the Viking wants to talk."

The breathing stopped. For a moment Nikole wondered if he'd hung up.

"How do I know you are who you say you are?"

Nikole's heart lurched. She'd done it. Detective work. Two plus two. A to B. Photograph to phone call. Mom would be proud.

"Well," Nikole offered, "the Black Lotus wouldn't call ahead."

He chuckled. "They also aren't stupid enough to say The Black Lotus over the phone. You should know better, too." He paused. Nikole got the feeling he was waiting for a response but she didn't know what to say. "Something's fishy. Your timing's odd. Don't you think? I trust you've heard the news."

"The bodies," Nikole said. "The cave."

He drew a long breath and Nikole could sense in his inhalation a great hunger. "Do you have it?"

"Yes," she said, trying to sound like she knew what he was talking about.

"I'll only meet somewhere public. Somewhere well lit."

"Okay."

She heard sniffling, shuffling, something that could have been bullets slid into chambers.

"The Börn Náttúrunnarat café. Seven o'clock. Come alone. What will you be wearing?"

Nikole looked down at herself. "Uh, black jacket. Jeans."

"No good. Wear something colorful. Not that it matters. You'll recognize me on sight, of course." He paused. "You know, I've been looking forward to this."

"Me too."

Another pause. Something moved in the silence. Something large. She got the feeling Snorri was not alone on his end. "See you at seven."

The line went dead.

20

He wore the skyline as a belt, towering, Godzilla in a dress shirt, blotting the city at his back. Scrappy blonde and pale eyes, he beamed with pride and appointed himself, for the moment, Iceland's ambassador to table twenty-seven.

"First time in Reykjavik?" he asked. "You must ascend the Hallgrímskirkja! Hike the famous Eyjafjallajökull! Visit the Fjölskyldugarðurinn!"

Nikole's head swirled with syllables. Either the waiter was having fun with her, or she'd landed in Middle Earth.

An acting troupe was putting on a reenactment of a Viking saga in a square outside the café, complete with war hammers, plate armor and ice giants on stilts. A crowd had gathered. The players slinked through twilight, entering and leaving the world, shifting colors as they stepped between cones of red and green light.

"You may recognize me," the waiter continued. "I was on TV. I am world famous for my glacier lift. I lifted a whole glacier! Moved it sixteen point seven millimeters! They say I affected El Niño *and* the Olympic fortunes of our national handball team! That is the raisin at the end of the hot dog, as we say in Iceland. May I interest you in Reykjavik's finest ram's testicles?"

"I'm waiting for someone," she said.

Xanax dulled her everything. Throat swollen, she checked her surroundings for signs of gravity. The café sat nestled among storefronts, stone churches and skateboarders. Lights blinked on in clusters across the river. Sky and street formed a funhouse mirror on the water, evening bleeding into dusk.

She unzipped an inch of the yellow coat she'd bought for the rendezvous and wondered if it was an anorak. This'll be over before I run out of pills. Right? Of course I won't run out. But if I do... Better not to think about it. I won't. But if I do... But I shouldn't think like that.

"*Him*?" the waiter gasped, gesturing at a newcomer.

All her fantasies involved hiding. In a cave, under the sea, an igloo somewhere the sun sets for half the year.

"Yes, I know that man. Snorri. Lots of mystery surrounding him. They say he came out of the mountains, you know." He bent towards her and glanced both ways, softening to a whisper. "They say he's in league with the elves." He straightened himself. "Gott kvöld, Snorri!"

"Shut up," growled a voice.

She turned to see him and his face went white. She saw in his eyes a great spiritual hunger and a desperation to believe.

Snorri would stand out anywhere but at a Neil Young lookalike convention. His sideburns reached hook-shaped into pockmarked cheeks. For a moment he stood paralyzed among wait staff and impatient children, basking in the noise of clanging silverware and the smell of fish.

"Auður?" he said.

Nikole nodded.

His clay-colored skin turned to chalk. "Why now? After all these years?"

Nikole fought the urge to shoot her eyes five tables over, where Sam was sitting, lest Snorri think he'd walked into an ambush. She wondered if Snorri had his own people watching her.

"Um," she said. "Well, you know. They found those bodies in New York."

Slowly he slid into his seat. "I saw that," he said. "Bizarre. That symbol... I don't understand it."

What to say? Nikole hadn't brainstormed.

Snorri gestured at the city. "Reykjavik," he said. "It's still here. You'll forgive me for not speaking the old language. I... don't know if I remember how." Something seemed strange in Snorri's eyes, a shard of unreality amid a sea of blue. "When did you get into town? Never mind. Have you been there? Have you seen it?"

Nikole blinked. The things of her chest rattled like a misfired engine.

"Um," she said, swallowing glass. "No. I mean, not yet."

Snorri shuffled. "I don't know what I was expecting," he said. "It's just a plot of land. We spilled blood. Made grand speeches. Fell in love. And what's left? Hills and a handful of sheep. I do not wander in search of miracles, Auður. They're here already. I'm told there's a statue in Norway. History is strange. But what am I saying? This was after your time. Forgive an old man his rambling."

Nikole nodded.

He stared at the acting troupe and chuckled. "Erik the Red," he said. "Can you believe it? They're acting out the saga of Erik the Red."

The world turned up its decibels. Why did I think I could do this? Her stomach teetered with pre-panic attack vertigo.

"You appear to be under some duress," Snorri said.

Nikole cleared her throat. "I'm fine."

"Don't take this the wrong way," he continued, "but you look different than I've imagined you. There was a time I'd pepper you with questions about Vifilsdal and King Ingjald. Once I tried to edit you out of history myself. You have to understand. There were politics involved."

She flicked her pupils and watched Sam order what looked like half the menu. A team of servers paraded her with pastries.

The glacier-lifter returned. Snorri stared blankly and, after some awkward bantering, succeeded in ordering a shot of bourbon, raw fish and something called Skyr.

"History is the demise of the gods," Snorri mused, gazing at his countrymen like zoo exhibits. "Nobody can canonize anybody when we've got such good memories."

Snorri arched his eyebrows. He watched Nikole closely. Lips pursed, he shook his head, emitting from something between resigned chuckling and a bull after castration.

"You are a Black Lotus assassin, are you not?" Snorri said calmly.

Something might have moved in the shadows. Reykjavik after dark was a city of many caverns.

"I talked to Mouse," she blurted. "My mother was Melanie Fink." Nikole fumbled with her purse, searching for the seared photograph. "I mean," she said, slowing down, "I went down into the cave. My mother died holding a photo of your bookstore. I pieced it together." She paused. "So you weren't down there? You aren't the survivor?"

Snorri relaxed his stance and lit a cigarette.

"What a fool I was, believing Auður Ketilsdóttir had come to visit Reykjavik. As though the Black Lotus wouldn't find her." He paused, then looked into her eyes. "I have a gun aimed at you under the table."

A gun. Sound without meaning. She almost laughed.

"If what you say is true – that you innocently stumbled into this – you might as well be one of them. You have led them to me. You have confirmed my identity."

"She had an hourglass," Nikole said, struggling to get everything out. "Where is the hourglass? Do you have it?"

"And now we're here," Snorri continued, "and violence is inevitable. I am going to take you hostage. You have not been making your own decisions. The Black Lotus have been guiding you down a path. This was your first task."

Shapes danced in her peripheries. The combined momentum of her organs sent gears and vitals hissing. She wondered what a bullet might feel like. Her eyes leaped from tourists to locals, diners engulfed in laughter and beer. These people have no idea how I suffer, she thought. All inside. Crucifixion of esophagus and soul.

This will be my last memory.

Snorri leaned back, relaxed, and took a drag on his cigarette. "So you're telling me you don't know what this is all about?"

Nikole shook her head. "What was my mother doing in that cave? Who was she? What's special about the bird symbol?"

"Little girl, if we had until the end of time it would not be long enough to explain." He paused. "So it's true. The Black Lotus. They're hunting us down. Well then. I suppose I'm not much longer for this Earth. But still, why would they make their declaration of war so public? Something is off. They don't leave bodies behind."

"Who are the Black Lotus? I mean, I get that they erase people. But why?"

"Not just people. They exist to erase anything abnormal, anything that could be considered evidence."

"Evidence of what?"

Snorri lowered his face. "Evidence of the supernatural."

They let the words linger. Snorri positioned his arms under the table as though he were holding something. Then there it was. The click. Just like in the movies.

"Who are you?" Nikole asked.

"I am an adherent of humanity's oldest religion. Our order traces its founding back millennia before God told Abraham to sacrifice Isaac. We have been all but erased from history, swallowed up by bigger fish. There are only a few among us today who still know the old faith."

"And is my mother part of your..." She trailed off, searching for a better word than *cult*.

"Listen," he said. "Whatever happens to me, you have to get to Prague. You must find Mouse. She is the only person you can trust."

"Didn't she try to kill you?"

"Things have changed. No time to explain. What happens in the next five minutes will determine if I can trust you. I can take you somewhere safe. We can talk more about the... You said there was a survivor?"

Nikole nodded.

"Odd."

"Mouse says someone escaped the cave."

"Helena," Snorri said, nearly under his breath. "It must have been Helena."

"Who?"

"Listen, we're safe so long as we stay in the light. The Black Lotus prefer shadows. If we cause a scene, they'll flee. Get up and walk to the restroom. Try to appear calm. Count to one hundred and return. I will prepare our spectacle. Can you do that for me?"

Nikole nodded.

"Okay," she said, struggling to her feet.

She stumbled forward, reaching for the waiter as support. He didn't seem to mind. Her body ached. She gathered strength and pushed through patrons and crowded tables, inching towards her hiding place.

She expected the shot at any moment. You don't hear the bullet that kills you, or so they say on TV.

She staggered into the women's room and watched her face in the mirror. The world had aged her. Pressure bulged behind both eyes. What happens to the weak? What happens to the ones who can't take being alive?

A toilet flushed. A milk-colored woman in minks emerged. She had a lazy eye and two crosses around her neck.

"I need to use your phone," Nikole said, staring at her own eyes in the mirror.

The woman scrubbed faster, pretending not to hear.

"He has a gun," Nikole said. "Please help me."

She moved her hands into hyperspeed, shut off the faucet and scratched a handful of paper towels, breathing jaggedly. She pushed past Nikole and almost made it to the door.

Nikole grabbed the woman's head with both hands and bashed it into the mirror.

She crumpled. Her skull connected with the sink on the way down. Her bones made a sickening noise. The mirror bled a spider web of cracks.

Nikole stared in disbelief at what she'd done.

Someone started opening the door. She threw her weight against it and slid the deadbolt. Her chest caved. She felt a panic attack coming on. Moving on instinct, she dug through the woman's purse. Her victim moaned, showing signs of life.

Someone pounded on the door.

"Just a minute!" Nikole shouted, nearly hysterical.

Not here. Not now. At least let me dial... Well, what? Is there an Icelandic 911?

More rattling. Someone shouted in Icelandic. The woman at Nikole's feet had a gash on her forehead and her face was splattered cherry red, a good amount staining Nikole's sneakers.

Have I killed her?

She stood awash in noise gripping the phone. She'd done something. Who to call. What to do. Pounding in her head. Pounding at the door.

21

Wally felt as though he were stepping onto a spaceship. Every surface gleamed spotless ivory, glossy to the point of camouflage. Where were the corners? Disorienting geometry and clever lighting conspired to give the illusion of floating. A Japanese tree sprouted, twig-like, from a pit of pebbles. The desk was littered with gold trinkets and Apple products.

The detective himself lounged on a plush couch, its pink the only splotch of color in the otherworldly space.

"Dear sir," Wally began, "permit me to introduce myself. I am Wael Algayar, though you may call me Wally. My closest friends have bestowed upon me the nickname Walrus, on account of my mustache. I have contacted you on behalf of a confidential source for the purpose of recovering..."

"Sit," the detective interrupted.

Wally scanned the room and found no reasonable fixtures for the act of sitting. I am man ill-suited for high altitude environments, he thought. Space travel is not within my, what's the word, repertoire.

The precise age of private detective Akira Murakami proved difficult guesswork. He wore a stylish suit and thin red tie. His hair was slicked askew, a rouge strand curled below one eye. Here is a man of exquisite taste and uncanny ability, Wally thought. Here is a man I want on my side.

"I smelled you coming," Akira said.

"Your pardon," said Wally, checking his underarms for odor. "I beg it."

His office had a peculiar stench of whisky, cigars and something that might have been super glue.

"You have consumed garlic recently," Akira said. "My nostrils are unparalleled."

Wally shrugged. He had consumed nothing of the sort.

"As I was saying," he continued. "I am seeking assistance with the recovery of stolen property. An hourglass, to be precise. May I approach?"

Akira nodded.

Wally showed the detective the video on his phone, courtesy of Antonio Noon. The fifteen second clip showed an hourglass flowing in the wrong direction. Its sand spiraled upwards in disobedience of physics. Antonio Noon's hand reached into the frame and flipped the hourglass and, once again, its sand began flowing the wrong way.

Peculiar, Wally thought. Most peculiar.

"My – ahem – friend made what he believed to be an honorable transaction. He sold this item to an Asian man – he believes – with a gold tooth. The transaction occurred in Penn Station. He was told of a library of magical trinkets. The money was forged. This Chinese man – I do not know his name. My friend would like his hourglass back."

Two minutes of silence dissolved. He is measuring my mustache, Wally reasoned.

"Not interested," said the detective.

"Excuse me?"

"I am a busy man," he said. "I don't have time to go tracking down some gag gift. What does it use? Magnets? Just order another one, for God's sake. If you're that upset about it, bother the police. Or another detective."

"But..." Wally began. He did not anticipate the conversation would enter such a route. "If I pay you..."

"If what you say is true," the detective said, "I'd have no leads. A Chinese guy? You know how many of those are in New York? It is not a matter of money, Mr. Wally. It's an unsolvable case and, frankly, it bores me."

They stared one another down a moment longer.

Wally's phone buzzed in his hand. A strange number flashed on the screen. Is that an extra digit?

Wally groaned, irritated. "Excuse me," he said. "I must take this call."

He slid a meaty finger across his screen and pressed the phone against his ear, turning his back to the detective.

"Hello? Wally Algayar speaking. This is Wally. Hello?"

At first he heard only static. Then came sounds of weeping, a running faucet and heavy breath. Finally, there was a voice.

"Wally?"

Wally felt his vitals grind to a halt. He turned to stone, staring at a point on the office wall, unable to speak.

"You have to help me, Wally," the voice spoke. Yes, it was her. "I... I didn't mean to... Look, I did something bad and I need your help."

You know, he thought, perhaps I am simply not cut out for this industry. I am a delicate man, a sophisticated man. I enjoy tea from Thailand. I own a respectable collection of vinyl records. James Bond I am not.

"Yes," Wally said. "I know, Nikole. Do not worry. I am working on it."

"You...? Wait. What?"

"I have hired a detective. He and I are negotiating as we speak. This man is the best in the business. Surely he will help."

Nikole was quiet a moment.

"What are you talking about?"

"I know everything – the cave, the bodies, the hourglass, the Black Lotus, the body bag, the blogger's photographs. At first I was concerned, but now with the detective's help, we will settle matters. You needn't worry."

Wally tried to imagine the scene on the call's opposite end. He pictured Nikole drowning in pills and wine, her apartment a war zone of filth.

"How did you..." she began, trailing off.

Wally chuckled to himself. The lengths I go to for my clients!

"What is this odd telephone number?" he asked. "Whose phone are you using?"

"The, um, woman's. Listen, I can't explain. You have to help me, Wally."

"Everything is under control," he insisted.

A torrent of clatter rummaged through the speaker and the line went dead.

Wally sighed. "I should check on her," he said. "She has anxiety, strange phobias, panic attacks. She can be self-destructive. Then I suppose I will need to go searching for another detective. I am sorry to have wasted your time."

Wally turned to leave.

"Wait," Akira said, rising to his feet. "Mr. Wally, do you mean to tell me there is a connection between your lost hourglass and the cave full of bodies they found under Central Park?"

Wally faced the detective and nodded. "It was discovered in the tomb itself."

"I'll take the case," Akira said, speaking with a quickness that made Wally suspicious. "I'll do it for free."

"Did you not just inform me that the hourglass will be impossible to find?"

"Very difficult, yes. But I've got a hunch where to start. Do you happen to own a long black coat, a bowling hat and a cigar?"

Wally squinted, confused.

"Why do you ask?"

"Because, Mr. Wally, I need a partner. This case is bigger than a single man." He grew more animated as he spoke. His dark pupils danced with excitement. "My last partner is, well... We had a disagreement. He is currently on leave. I do not work alone. I must caution you, of course, that my profession is not for the faint of heart."

"You require my assistance?"

He nodded.

Wally shrugged, confused. "I will help however I can, detective."

Akira stroked his chin for a long time. His face morphed through shades of conflicted intrigue and intellectual arousal. Eventually, he smiled. "I have the feeling, Mr. Wally, that we stand on the cusp of a grand adventure."

22

The glacier lifter defeated the door with a single finger. Huddled beside him, two middle-aged diners brimmed with impatience and full bladders.

His face turned stone then jelly at the bloodied scene.

One of the women made a sound like a parakeet receiving shock therapy. The other fainted.

Nikole felt the world heating up. Her veins ached for Xanax.

Snorri flew into action and there it was, a flash of steel, his heart-piercer and negotiation tool.

"I..." Nikole began.

"Drop the phone," Snorri commanded, pistol at eye level.

Nikole complied.

"What have you done?"

Nikole watched it in slow motion. A figure moved at unnatural speed, pawing its way through shoulders of stunned customers, stalking.

Yes, it was him. The bug man. Angel from Mogadishu. And where was Genghis and his bird cage? Inside the restaurant, Sam's booth was empty.

Angel leapt like a clawed predator. Mid-air, he yanked a knife from his sleeve. He pounced on Snorri's back and stabbed him in the neck, knife piercing flesh to the hilt. A geyser of blood spray-painted the walls.

Snorri tried to gasp. His eyes flirted with the afterlife. A black bubble popped between his lips.

Snorri discharged his weapon as he collapsed. The bullet tore a hole in the ceiling and time, its echo deafening. Snorri convulsed. He clutched the air and then went still.

Angel and Nikole stared each other down, then scrambled for the gun.

Nikole touched its stock and had her knuckles slashed. She retreated. Angel came away with the firearm.

Splattered like a sloppy painter, he stood and aimed the barrel, a terrifying deadness in both eyes.

Nikole became aware. Each detail had a place in the order of things – the wide-eyed waiter quivering before the crowd, the mirror's flaking shards, a smudged sign of struggle on a stall door. A plate fell to the floor. She found it liberating, being at gunpoint. Here, on autopilot, nothing mattered. The gun made decisions for her. She couldn't be in trouble. I was at gunpoint, she'd say. They'd nod, understanding. You did what you had to, Nikole.

"The hourglass," Angel said.

What hourglass, she couldn't force herself to say.

Because that's it. Freedom. You wake up and jump out your window, bring a gun to school. You could be on TV in Tokyo. You could cut your wrists up and down and not across. Make the right choices and you'll be dead within a minute. Anxiety isn't a disease. It's an understanding. Anxiety is knowing, moment to moment, what we can do to ourselves, what we can do to each other.

But here's alright, at the end of a gun.

Angel turned to the shocked diners and aimed at an old man.

"Put down your phone or it'll be the last thing you do."

She felt it first. Tremors in the tiles. As Angel swiveled to his hostage, the waiter lunged. His momentum of muscles sent the assassin airborne. Nikole took a bounding dive over the bodies. She scanned the shock of aborted dinners and frozen faces. She knew to fear the shadows, the places she couldn't see.

Bloodied and stunned, Nikole limped through the suspended Viking Saga in the park square, passing between slack-jawed actors and spotlights.

"Murderer!" someone screamed from the café.

A faux Viking in full armor took a swing with his sword. She ducked.

A second shot rang out, turning shock to panic. Tourists dove for cover. Shrieks filled the air. An old man might have been having a heart attack. Nikole craned her neck. Angel was moving towards her.

She ran.

Psychosis or a coping mechanism projected hallucinations from brain to world. She saw or imagined an army of children standing mouths agape, faces from a Munch painting.

What will he do to me? He wants the hourglass, she thought. I do not have the hourglass. I'll be tortured, killed, dumped in the ocean.

She ran across a cobblestone plaza. A stone church rose like a spaceship. She tripped and rebounded without losing speed.

"Help!" she called out.

Balls of red fluff – more coat than child – screamed and scurried to keep pace with their pigeon-feeding parent. Japanese tourists snapped photos of the bloodshed, their faces the image of calm. Nobody moved to intervene.

The stars had disappeared. At an intersection Nikole chose a direction and kept running.

They leave no loose ends. I'll never learn the secret. I'll never find the next breadcrumb. And what about Sammy? My baby sister. I've failed her so many times.

Night found Reykjavik's sidewalks sparse. Two women shared a cigarette under the awning of a rehab clinic. They gazed at Nikole with disinterest.

She tried to call out for help but her voice stopped working. She had the feeling of waking from a nightmare with sleep paralysis, desperate but unable to move, certain something was in the room. Her feet kept moving.

Because that's what I am, she thought. A loose end. Where is she now? My fans need closure.

A cluster of hipsters appeared locked in competition, each trying to look more bored than the next. Police sirens sounded dimly. Their origins were masked by echo. Her brainwaves were blank but her legs knew what they were doing.

She stumbled outside the Icelandic Phallological Museum, where whale penises hung behind glass like baguettes. She failed to stop a passing Towncar.

"I'm having this total epiphany," a bearded drunkard said into his phone across Laugavegur. "The universe is flat and I can prove it."

Angel moved into the light, barely winded, gun gone but knife glistening.

Nikole cupped a palm full of curb water and flung it at his face. He retched and rubbed both eyes.

She used the curb as a springboard and tumbled through traffic. She felt an insect scuttle across her neck and down the back of her shirt. This one had many legs. She swatted wildly, trying to shake it out.

The bug bit hard. The pain was intense but brief. She felt dizzy, double-sighted, off-balance.

Parts of her brain began accepting defeat, reciting the what-ifs and at-least-there's-stills the way you do on election night when you realize your candidate is going to lose.

Dying's alright, she thought. Think of all I accomplished. I got to be on TV.

The world went black and white. Looking up she swore she saw a woman floating, anchored by her sneaker to a concrete wall.

But Sammy. What will they do to my sister?

She resolved herself to keep moving.

Angel popped out of an alleyway. Nikole stumbled across a grid of windows lit in tic-tac-toe stalemate.

Bass pumped from a nearby club. Nikole crawled up its steps. The bouncer, a meat husk with patriotic Russian tattoos, got a look at the bloody chase and dove for cover.

Yes, she thought. A public place. People around. The Black Lotus are allergic. It's what the man said.

Nikole entered and pulled the door shut behind her. For a half-second in the club's darkness she breathed and existed, nothing more. A Pixies cover band cranked out the opening riff of Monkey Gone to Heaven. An enormous Asian man stood watching, rolls of fat oozing from the back of his scalp like drapes.

Her knees did the talking. Forward march.

I have to get out of here, she thought. I have to reach the... What, exactly?

A line of career alcoholics slouched in shades of sadness, surrounded by shot glass graveyards. She felt the bass in her chest.

Keep moving, Nikole. A to B.

Fist-pumping partiers stood in near-fascist symmetry near the stage. A wiry-haired stage diver bared his belly before taking the plunge. They were a youthful crowd, exuding cannabis and sex, apart from an old man the shape of a skeleton smoking a cigarette under a NO SMOKING sign in at least eleven languages. The aberration wore more fabric than skin and stared as Nikole pawed body to body in search of an exit.

She made for a fire escape. A lesbian couple locked lips near the bathrooms, their glasses doing battle. Sensory overload was a hole punch to the skull. Through a veil of induced fog, Nikole fell and emerged amongst dumpsters in a urine-soaked alley.

She took two steps and staggered, her brain and body shutting down.

Something was burning. Unlike Mom's charred remains, this fire smelled of sulfur and brimstone. I'm dying, her body knew. She closed her eyes and fantasized about live burial. Years of wasted time swirled in her like reagents in a flask.

Angel seized her from behind and stabbed her in the neck. She felt a cold punch of steel, stumbled two steps and collapsed.

23

The land was full of ghosts. Bäckahäst, draugr, wills-o'-the-wisp. Steam carried fumes from the underworld. Up ahead, on a beach black as midnight, a mountain of onyx punctured morning mist.

Nikole crawled across dead steppe, trying to piece together how much time had passed. She saw light. Morning, then.

City lights glowed, distant, fading in the sunrise. Part of a cargo ship stuck out from fog. Rocks scraped her flesh, claiming blood.

Angel stepped on the small of her back.

"My curious little kitten," he said.

Heat poked tendrils through the chill. Cliffs rose like walls of Mordor and caves gaped black holes big enough for a family of trolls. Across a lava field, two dozen pygmy horses nibbled grass.

Nikole felt the gun's gaze like a laser on her skull.

She gripped a rock and felt sharpness ricochet through her bones. Angel relented with his foot. She heaved and kept moving.

"We meet again," Angel said. "I am glad. We have many subjects to discuss."

She inched forward through a cradle of geological oddities, fossils of an unformed planet. Puddles boiled with colors of the cosmos. Geothermal sculptures dotted this playground for elves, an echo of the Big Bang full of yellow brush and volcanic shards, perched on the cusp of the Milky Way.

Her neck felt stiff. She touched the spot where he'd stuck her with the syringe.

Hollywood stardom felt galaxies removed. Red carpets don't reach this far. Nobody's coming to save me, she thought. Not Wally. Not this mystery detective. And certainly not Natasha Kennedy. She'll just pluck another case study in desperation from the meat grinder of fame. I created this and only I can fix it.

How did Wally know I was kidnapped before it happened?

Angel paced like a vulture circling prey. With blood-stained sneakers, he stepped into Nikole's path like he was protesting in Tiananmen Square. Nikole grabbed his ankle. Angel kicked her away.

She felt it again, the laser beam.

"Who sent you to Iceland?" Angel asked. "Or did you simply know to come here?"

Nikole lay prostrate against the earth. She couldn't tell if she'd been shot. Starved for fuel, the machinery of life within her sputtered. "I, um, just kinda knew," she groaned. "I figured it out."

The laser beam focused its energy.

On the backs of her eyelids Nikole saw shades of white matter splattered on rocks, sinking into an ancient ecosystem, fertilizer in the circle of life.

"My mother was..."

"I know who she was, Nikole Fink." He sighed. "We did not count on you being involved. I'll admit, it was smart. It creates for us a giant problem. She knew it would. But still, we did not think a mother would do that to her daughter."

The beam dissipated. Nikole heard the gun entering a holster.

"Get up."

"Give me a minute."

They occupied a world silent save for the whispers of elves. Nikole breathed a mouthful of dirt. I could die here, she thought. The idea brought no comfort, but neither did it fill her with dread. She imagined meeting Snorri in the afterlife and rehearsed the things she might say, questions she'd ask. Who are you. What do you know about Melanie Fink.

With aching momentum, she sat up. Only now did she realize how her body had fared in the cold. Her fingers buzzed, numb. Her cheeks burned. She searched for her toes and counted, making sure nothing had come loose.

Angel stood admiring the landscape, his back to Nikole, guns on either hip.

The Earth vented warmth and Nikole rubbed her hands. The friction brought feeling. She checked her torso for wounds.

Angel pointed into the fog. "We are sneaking aboard that ship," he said. "We have a safe house on the mainland. There we will chat, safe from the ears of the world. There your fate will be decided. Genghis has already secured your sister in the hold."

"Sammy."

Angel nodded. "Do not worry, Nikole Fink. Your sister will not suffer greatly, so long as you cooperate. We have plans for you."

She felt something odd inside her skull. She pawed her head as though trying to swat away flies. She saw spots. The world grew blurry, then disappeared.

24

Wally felt the subway car braking and leaned into its momentum. The city's underbelly scrolled in the windows. Tourists bunched on the platform like refugees, eyes cast elsewhere, shopping bags bursting. The doors opened and an exchange of human bodies commenced.

Beside him, Detective Akira Murakami was fast asleep with both eyes open. The man slouched and snored amongst the ruckus of the subway, immune to noise. Peculiar, Wally decided. Most peculiar.

Akira had asked Wally to observe him and, should his eyes become bloodshot during his nap, to apply droplets from a medicinal bottle.

Wally examined his companion. Rose-colored tendrils had seeped into the man's eye sockets. He breathed evenly, back rigid as though meditating. Wally nudged the detective twice. Receiving no response, he concluded that the man's eyes required treatment.

My God, Wally thought, examining the medicine. Such a strange man!

He unscrewed the cap and extracted an eyedropper brimming with liquid. The bottle's label was of no guidance, encoded as it was in Japanese characters.

With great trepidation, Wally brought the dropper to the detective's eyes. His first attempt failed, spurting liquid down the man's cheek. A redheaded woman with enormous ears stared from across the aisle. Wally felt shame, both at his failure and at his coercion into this bizarre exercise. He made a second attempt, nearly touching Akira's pupil, placing the dropper at an angle he deemed best suited for the task.

I must not squeeze too forcefully, he reasoned, for such a burst shall surely disturb him. However, I must apply adequate pressure so not to leave another streak on the man's cheek. It is not becoming of a detective to appear as though he has been weeping, especially a detective of Akira Murakami's stature.

Various hypotheses considered, Wally made final adjustments to account for the mass of his thumb and forefinger and squirted the medicine into Akira's eye.

His whole body shook. The detective sprung from his slumber, turned to Wally and grabbed him the by the wrist.

"Do you smell that?"

Wally shook his head.

Akira sniffed the air. "Someone on this train is not who they say they are," he declared. Then, loud enough for surrounding passengers to hear, "Someone aboard has a bomb."

The large-eared woman lost a battle with gravity. Her jaw attempted a skydive.

Wally felt his heart rate increase. Commuters shuffled in their seats.

"Why have you attempted to blind me?" Akira asked, louder. "Is it because you know I am a detective? You know I am police?"

Wally stammered, unsure what to say.

Akira got to his feet in the moving train. "Whoever will detonate this device," he announced, "I will sniff you out."

For five tense minutes, the detective paced the car, sniffing. Every so often he stopped and cupped both ears, listening for deviations in the tracks. Murmurs rippled through nervous tourists. An MTA employee emerged to investigate and Akira shooed her away.

Wally couldn't help feeling that all eyes kept returning to him. He performed his own cursory scan. Just as I imagined, he thought. I am the only Muslim on this train.

Pressure grew. Wally felt the claws of panic entering his fellow straphangers. A balding father comforted his son. A dark-haired woman sunk in her seat, eyes fluttering. Two large men, athletes of some nature, Wally assumed, took turns standing and scanning the seats, attempting to look menacing.

After the commuters were riled to the brink of near-hysteria, Akira returned to his seat.

"I believe I have sufficiently frightened the hijacker," he said. He resumed a comfortable position. "I am glad you agreed to assist me, Mr. Wally. I had been worrying – ever so slightly – how I might pull off an assault of this nature without a partner."

Wally gulped. "An assault?"

"Yes, Mr. Wally. These cave murders have been unusual from the start, though I have several theories. My superhuman sense of smell permits me to accomplish tasks impossible to your typical detective, such as sifting fact from bullshit. Your secret VIP client Antonio Noon has deactivated his Instagram account. I was able, however, to quite easily hack his phone's cloud storage and examine additional photographic evidence."

Wally gasped, but Akira cut him off.

"I'm a detective, Mr. Wally. It is my business to know things. Antonio Noon has gotten in deep with dangerous people. This is not bullshit. I am a pacifist by nature, though my gut tells me violence may come to pass. Do you have firing range training with the Colt M4 Carbine?"

"Firing range training?" Wally asked, sweat spilling from his brow.

"Never mind. You can learn on the job. We are searching for a magical hourglass found in an impossible murder scene. I know of a place where these sorts of objects end up. A library, yes. I know of a man, a vindictive and ugly man, an authority on magic and magicians. His collection rivals most museums. It would not be above Bill Whitman to order a lackey to Penn Station with a bag full of fake money. At the very least, perhaps he knows of some connection between this hourglass and the crime."

"Yes," Wally said, "perhaps. Though I must stress, sir, that we are in search of stolen property with the intention of returning it to its rightful owner. I did not hire you to solve the cave murders."

Akira nodded. "Of course. I will sleep now. Should you see my eyes turning red, I'd ask you to apply moisture. My eyesight must be impeccable when I awake, as I may need to commandeer the train and steer it into station myself."

Within seconds he was snoring, eyes open, spine in perfect alignment.

My God, Wally thought.

Panic leaped seat to seat. Tourists and locals alike turned Wally a pincushion of scrutiny. Their eyes probed pressure points, scanning for unnatural lumps and vulnerabilities in his muscle structure. Yes. A, what's the word, cavity search.

But I am a clever man and I shall prevail. Should undue hardship present itself, I shall use my cleverness to elude it, he tried to convince himself as the train rumbled through the ever increasing darkness of the city's underbelly.

25

Fossils of induced sleep echoed in her brain. A to B was a mystery. Her body bore clues of captivity. Hands bound. Mild soreness. Socks and shoes intact. A stench of saltwater in the air.

"Welp," Sam said, "they got us."

Sam admired graffiti on the walls of their makeshift cell. A naked bulb lit her hoodie, a salmon-colored island in a sea of shadows. A fan on the floor rattled stale air. Mattresses, a metal pail and a jug of water poked edges in the dark.

"Poisoned darts and promised chocolate have lured me into this chamber," Sam continued. "Now I see, 'twas a sham. But the plight of a hostage can't be all bad. Think of the algebra tests I'll be missing. Plus, I get to chill with my big sis. This is one of them *bonding* thingamahoos."

"Do you understand the shit we're in?" Nikole asked. "We've been kidnapped, Sam. They're the people who killed Mom. They're killers. Do you understand that?"

Sam put her hands in the small of her back and let loose a ferocious yawn. "The bird keeper seems like a kind soul. Don'tcha think?"

They sat for hours in the steel shipping container, seasick, claustrophobia eating their sanity. The ship's horn growled distantly. Every so often Nikole imagined a starboard list. She imagined Wally panicking in his cramped office. What's the word, he'd say. Stowaways.

Genghis brought trays of spoiled veggies and something resembling potatoes. You could feel his approach in the floor. He stunk of seaweed. Lacking sun or clock, Nikole couldn't tell if this was the day's second meal or if night had passed and this was breakfast. He said nothing, left the food and slammed the metal door.

Sam paced the length of the cell, unfazed. "They can smuggle a leading lady but not Listerine?" she asked. "Savages."

"How are you able to keep calm after everything that's happened?" Nikole asked.

"I've seen things, kid. Things that can't be unseen. When you see what I've seen, it gives you perspective."

"Huh?" Nikole asked. "You're, what, fifteen?"

"Sixteen. I'm homeless. I'm a kid raised by wolves. What do you think happens to people like me?"

The stench. Soiled laundry and recycled sweat. Fear and loathing. A mural of toxic auras gleaming on every surface like a chemical sheen. Nikole coped by breathing through her mouth. Sam, accustomed to alleys and asphalt pillows, fared far better.

She felt the usual pre-panic attack symptoms: tight chest, tight throat, tingling in both feet.

"What will they do to us?" Nikole asked.

Sam shrugged.

Should have let it go, Nikole. Should have let the feds do their job. Who am I to solve a mystery? Follow the breadcrumbs and what do you get? Imprisonment at sea. In and out of consciousness. A man telling me I should cooperate.

Sam sat cross-legged and took inventory of her book bag: an empty perfume bottle, science lab goggles, a rancid sandwich.

"You know," she said, considering the sandwich, "this is the most time we've spent together in all our lives. I don't even know you. Who are you?"

"An actress," Nikole said.

"Helpful."

Nikole washed down Xanax with tepid water and examined her stock. They'd emptied her purse of cash and passport, but not her pills. Tiny victories. Twelve pills left. Gotta be careful, she thought. Time for famine rationing. I've been here before. I won't run out. But if I do... No, better not to think like that.

She forced herself to swallow sustenance. Can't jump overboard. The seas are swarming with sharks. Nikole pictured their fins slicing through the waves, jaws unhinged, their stomachs a landfill. She liked it here in her cage. If this is where they put me, she thought, it must be where I belong.

Sam's bag had been taken, sorted, cash and phone tossed overboard. But they'd let her keep an assortment of oddities, including a bizarre device: a baseball-shaped clump of twisted metal with mashed gears protruding like fangs.

"What's that?"

Sam grew solemn, zipped her bag, slid it behind her. "Don't wanna talk about it."

Nikole nodded, feeling like a good sister would know these sore spots in advance.

For a few minutes, the sisters said nothing. Sam looked wounded. She studied the space between her sneakers and hung her head.

"Dad changed after you left," she said eventually. "Lost his job. Got crazy ideas. For a couple years he was one of those assholes who combed beaches with a metal detector. Dude was obsessed he'd strike UFO bits, buried treasure, whatever. But every day he'd strike out. He'd come home empty-handed, stinking of filth, then hit the bottle and torture his mail order girlfriend while I locked myself in the attic and stuffed cotton in my ears."

Nikole chewed her tongue, unsure how to react.

"He took me with him once," Sam continued. "We hit up some forgotten beach along Lake Eerie. Empty as far as I could see. After a couple hours I found a hunk of scrap metal in the sand. Kept it for years. It's no secret hourglass. It's not made of gold. You won't find it in a museum or stashed in a secret safe. But it's all I have left, Nikole. It's all I've got to show that I used to have a family."

"You have me," Nikole offered.

Sam turned away.

That night, Genghis unbolted the cell door and escorted Nikole to deck. She'd grown so accustomed to the cell's stale atmosphere that coming into neutral air had a strange effect, like silence when an air conditioner shuts off. She tasted salt in every breath. The ship was puddle-laden and corroded, its endpoints lost in dusk. Tarp-draped cargo formed rainbow stacks. Lights on the bridge poked holes in night. Waves crashed below. The sky was aglow with waterfalls of light.

Angel stood starboard. Engines banged and hissed like a brooding dragon. The ship drank the ocean with a giant's thirst and spat, gargling, splashing in the night.

Angel faced the ocean. "I something to show you," he said.

Nikole approached. Angel turned his phone landscape style. On its screen, Nikole saw an image of a hostage bound to a metal chair in a brightly-lit room. She squinted.

"Is that...?"

A second man moved through the frame, wrapped in the anonymity of lab gear.

"I do not know this man's name," Angel said, pointing at the newcomer with his pinky. "But we know his as The Chemist. I am a nice fucking guy compared to him."

Nikole stopped in her tracks.

"Carlos," she breathed.

He ex-boyfriend struggled against the ropes, leafy hair askew. The Black Lotus had given him time to do makeup. He squirmed in his cell, decked out in freshly-painted black nails, eyeliner and a bullet on a chain strung around his neck.

"Carlos has nothing to do with anything," Nikole said.

"Hydrofluoric acid is a colorless solution that can cause permanent tissue death and organ failure," Angel explained. "It is particularly potent on the corneas, I'm told."

Nikole felt her skin erupt with sweat.

"Most people," Angel said, switching off his phone, "do not realize how much they have in this world to lose."

26

Sam screamed her voice box to tatters. "Help!" she yelled. "Sweet Jesus, somebody save us! He's got fucking roaches! Fuck!"

Angel straddled an aluminum chair. He eased himself onto the seat. His face was the image of patience. "Good," he said between outbursts. "Get it out of your system. Though I do recommend pacing yourself, little girl. We are only getting started."

The sisters squirmed in rope cocoons. Reverb suffocated Nikole's ear canal like a gong's leftovers in a small room. She pressed her cheek to the tile floor and saw the world sideways: cobwebs, boots, a red toolbox. The floor stunk of cleaning chemicals. Through its surface Nikole sensed heartbeats and something like the last gurgle of a drained pool as the embers of hope dimmed and died in her soul.

They'd arrived in Amsterdam as night bled into dawn. They slipped out of the docks unnoticed, Angel pledging upon Carlos all manner of chemical deformity should the sisters cause a scene.

As the city awoke, its canals swarmed with cyclists and cobblers, houseboats, coffee shops, churches and sidewalk cafés.

"This is turning into a pretty badass vacation," Sam said.

They'd walked along the canals. A line of trees made shapes on the water. Tourists patrolled in Segways. Sidewalks teemed with memory, seventeenth century sailors, scurvy, lost faces who plundered six or seven seas, battled Vikings and hid Jews in attics.

Nikole had stumbled along in a daze. She gazed into the faces of passersby and wallowed in their banality. None of these people will be tortured today.

"Keep moving," Angel barked. He nudged something that felt like a movie prop into the small of her back.

They came upon a row of houseboats roped along the canal. Some had rooftop gardens of potted plants. One had a hammock.

Torture. Her brain withered at the thought. It was too distant, too horrible. It happened to people on TV and in huts outside Baghdad. Not here, in touristy Amsterdam. Not to Nikole Fink.

Nikole knew the safe house from a block out. An off-gray houseboat with drawn blinds stood out from its neighbors in its disturbing plainness. The boat had no remarkable features, at least not from the outside.

Their captors had ushered the sisters through the door. Inside, every surface was sterile and soundproofed. Nikole felt like she'd entered a sound studio at Guantanamo Bay. They passed through locked doors. Genghis had tied the sisters into contortions of limbs while Angel held them at gunpoint. He produced his box of bugs and Sam lost it.

"I would like everyone to know I have a peanut allergy," Sam said. "No need to bust out your box of black widows. You could feed me a peanut and get the same result."

"Let's get out of the way what we already know," Angel said, addressing Nikole. "Just so we do not waste one another's time. Okay?"

Nikole couldn't nod. Nikole just swallowed.

"Before your mother vanished," Angel said, "she initiated you, Nikole Fink, into the Cult of the Bird Goddess. You learned their secrets and the names of their members. You know the places they would hide."

Fluorescent lights killed every edge's shadow. This room could have been purpose built for torture under industry guidelines.

Nikole tried to shield her brain from the thought police, just in case. She didn't have to try hard. Her brainwaves were a tangle of wires short-circuiting at the frays. She could hardly keep reality in focus, let alone form a coherent story.

"You have several options," Angel said.

Nikole closed her eyes. Her psyche played tricks on her. For a moment, she felt safe in her invented darkness.

"Option one, you will tell us the names of the members of the Cult of the Bird Goddess and then we will kill you. This is your best choice, Nikole."

Was it really a wasted life? I was famous. I had fans. Signed autographs, went on late night TV. It's just that there's so much of it left. That's the problem. Peaking too soon. Then you just sit around and wait to die.

"Option two," Angel continued, "you do *not* tell us the names and we will start on your sister and you will be forced to watch."

An odd chill radiated from Nikole's spine. Sweat broke out in the usual places – forehead, underarms, the small of her back. She could hear her heart racing. She had an intense feeling of self-realization. What sort of creature am I?

Angel was quiet a moment and Nikole got the sense that he was waiting for her to speak.

"I don't know anything," she said.

Angel stared, then moved his eyebrows. Okay, he said with his face.

He unclasped his toolbox with a dull clank. Sam went stiff on the floor.

"These are bullet ants," Angel said. He lifted a palmful of oversized black ants from a compartment in his toolbox. They scuttled overtop each other in the palm of his hand. "The most painful sting known to man."

He nodded to Genghis, who approached the sisters.

Nikole writhed in her rope prison, pierced by emotions difficult to define. Here was a man who dealt in human suffering. An engineer of pain. But in the bluish light, as he readied his bugs, the gaunt-faced man resembled more of a tired day laborer going about his routine. Here was a man who knew how to do his job and that was that, a cog in a machine, an actor in the drama of violence that Nikole's life had become.

"The Sateré-Mawé people of Brazil have the most excruciating initial ritual in the world," Angel continued. "Boys wishing to become warriors place their hands into gloves crawling with bullet ants."

Genghis stretched what looked like an oven mitt and Angel dumped his handful of ants into its open mouth.

"The goal," Angel said, "is to endure the unspeakable agony for a duration of ten minutes. This ritual is then repeated twenty times."

Genghis held the mitt at arm's length and approached Sam, who promptly began screaming once again.

"Helena," Nikole blurted.

Angel leaned forward. His eyebrows performed acrobatics.

"What?"

"Snorri," Nikole said. She struggled to keep coherent. "Helena."

A smile seeped across her captor's face. "Good, good. We are making progress."

Get me out of here, she thought, her brain unable to conjure much else. Get me out. Get me out.

"Of course you know the names," Angel said. "You know them all. Don't you?"

Yes, names, Nikole thought. Of course! Joe, Jim, Susie, Agent Johansson, Wally Algayar, Donald Trump. The cute one, the smart one, the one with a peanut allergy. The man wants names and I'll read him the phonebook. Anything, any names, please God, anything to get me out of here.

Angel squatted where Nikole lay suffering on the floor and dangled an old photograph before her.

"This man," he said. "What is his name – his *real* name?"

In grayscale, the image depicted a man cratered with pockmarks, eyes distant, hair like a soaked mop, holding the tatters of an American flag. He looked like a colonel who could have fought at Gettysburg.

"Uh," Nikole said. "Joe... Jonathon, I think. Yeah. Joe John. Last I heard he was hiding in an igloo in Saskatchewan."

She went red with shame like an actress bombing her audition. She stared at the toes of Angel's boots, bracing for a panic attack or broken nose. Angel only sighed.

"You must know *something*, Nikole Fink. You knew to seek out Snorri. You knew where he lived. Who were these people in the cave? Were they cultists? What was the secret they died protecting?"

Sam thrashed but her ropes held. Genghis rotated and shook his mitt full of ants, keeping the insects riled and in place.

"Is there a self-immolation ritual?" Angel asked. "Did they choose suicide over revealing their secrets? What was your mother doing in that cave and who killed her?"

Sam stopped struggling. The sisters looked at each other.

"Wait," Sam said, her voice ragged from protest. "We thought *you* assholes killed her."

Angel and Genghis exchanged puzzled glances of their own.

"Really," Nikole said. "We don't know anything."

Eventually, Genghis returned the bugs to their master.

"We must talk in private," Angel said.

He grabbed his toolbox and turned to the exit. Before he left, he swung open a switchblade, approached Nikole and cut the ropes binding her hands. They left the sisters alone in the room.

Sam heaved relief. Nikole untied her sister's wrists.

They sat in silence, each not knowing what to say. Nikole's mind felt free from thought. At a certain level, she knew they'd return. She knew there would be pain. But for what could have been five minutes or five hours, she simply sat existing in the world, a thing of blood and breath.

Then the door creaked open, and Angel and Genghis were gone.

27

Ember played with fire. Her fingertips sparked like flint. She palmed her fist, spoke incantations and, for an instant, held an orb of flames in the palm of her hand. She looked like a wizard winding up a lethal pitch.

"Anyways," she said, "I'm still learning."

Wally stood in a cave of books. Peculiar, he thought. Here we stand surrounded by parchment young and old, and yet this librarian uses fire as though she were washing her hands. Hands which, I believe, have not been properly insulated with OSHA-licensed flame-retardant material.

Ember was a jelly doughnut of a woman, a galactic parchment, a milk-colored canvas of outer space. She had the universe tattooed across her body. Strange worlds called her shoulders home. Wally spotted what could have been a constellation of healed track marks in the Venus of her forearm. An ancient mariner could chart his way home by studying her sleeves. She'd been sketched as concept art into a steampunk universe, the hacker chick with her head half shaved and something synthetic swimming in her blood, give or take three hundred pounds.

This sorceress and I have nothing in common, Wally thought. I can hardly do a card trick, and she can make the planets disappear.

"I've studied the classics, obviously," Ember said. "Thurston, Houdini, Blackstone, Dai Vernon. But the greatest illusionist of all time? The government, man. Fire magic's rad and all, but they control the fucking *weather*. It's insane."

Akira sniffed the air in a more subdued manner, as though he didn't want his fluctuating nostrils spotted.

"You're familiar with the HAARP weather station?" Ember asked. "Tsunami bombs? The earthquake machine? Here I am playing with flash paper while the NSA tosses funnel clouds and hurricanes across the globe like they're tumbling dice." She was quiet a moment, eyes downcast, shaking her head. "Anyways, guys, sorry. The School of Magical Arts isn't a public library. You need to have an appointment."

"Bill Whitman and I need to chat," Akira said. "We're old friends."

"Bill's at the station."

Akira squinted. "I beg your pardon? A station?"

"Yeah, a station. As in, you know, of the police variety."

Akira opened and closed his mouth, wordless. His brow writhed like an earthworm.

Ember's mood soured. Wally watched as the folds of her face drooped.

"They got to him, man. Fluoride, chemtrails, MK Ultra. Whatever toxic shunt they shoved in his brain, it worked. It's insane. I explained that to the cops. Think they listened?" She scoffed. "Fucking sheep."

"You – ahem – spoke to police?" Wally asked. "Regarding the, um... What, exactly?"

Ember looked confused. "This isn't about Tony? Well, shit, man, what do you guys want? Oh, God. You're *them*. Aren't you?"

Akira sniffed the air, sensing treachery afoot.

"We wish to inquire about an unnatural device," Wally said. "An hourglass. One that flows backwards. In your years studying magic tricks and illusions, have you come across such an object?"

Ember lumbered the length of the counter and tucked away her flame-producing materials. Her footsteps sent shockwaves through the floorboards. Wally watched her through several pairs of trick handcuffs behind the glass.

"Do I look like fucking Carrot Top?" she asked. "I don't do prop magic. That's why we hired Tony."

"And what happened to this Mr. Tony?" asked Akira.

"I told you already. Fuck! The *government*, man. The dude was studying theoretical physics. He had internships with NASA and shit. Prime of his life. No way a dude like that wakes up and thinks, huh, how about a gallon of drain cleaner and lye for breakfast? They got to him."

"He committed suicide?"

"This morning," Ember said, her eyes solemn. "His girlfriend found him. They rushed him to Mount Sinai, but it was too late."

Wally turned. Tucked behind bookshelves, a man in an overcoat stood watching their conversation with an open tome in his hands. He wore a Sikh turban and skin the color of oak. He averted his eyes and Wally swore he saw dust shake from the man's beard.

Wally nudged Akira with his elbow and gestured with his head. This made the Sikh nervous. He made to shelve the book and eyed the exit, only to find his escape route blocked. With the awkward indecision of grade school pupil caught cheating on his math test, the man buried himself in his book, willing away the world.

Akira walked over to the bookshelves on the opposite side of Ember's counter of curiosities. He clasped his hands over his belt buckle and stared at the Indian man, who was doing his best to pretend he was the last living creature on this planet. Akira leaned closer and, in a strange affront that seemed, to Wally, most offensive, with an enormous gust of wind in his nostrils, Akira sniffed the man's beard.

"Good afternoon," Akira said.

The Sikh did not look up. "I don't know anything about anything," he muttered. "I don't want to get involved."

Akira cocked his head and studied the spine of the man's book. "*The Gravity Thief*," he read. "Interesting title. What's it about?"

"I don't know."

Akira stretched his spine and towered over the man like an arc lamp. "You've reached, what, page 59? How about a synopsis? What's happened so far?"

Wally remained planted near the counter. Ember had lost interest and plopped herself on a barstool, her face illuminated by iPhone light.

"Who is that man?" Wally asked, half-covering his mouth as though he were attempting to confuse a lip reader.

"Raj?" Ember asked. "He's a regular. He's a conspiracy guy. He's woke."

Raj turned his shoulder to Akira's glare. For the better part of a painful minute, nobody spoke.

"Sera," Raj mumbled.

"Excuse me?"

"It is a biography of the Sera," he said.

"Intriguing! Do go on, sir."

Raj stood doubled over as though he'd taken a boxing glove to the abdomen.

"She was a Jewish mystic from Central Asia," he said eventually. "Lived during medieval times."

"Oh?"

Raj hesitated. "Yes. Claimed the power to reverse gravity. Claimed she could turn back time. Executed as a heretic. They took her out to Infinity Point and she was drowned. Not a rare text. No. Obscure, yes. Not valuable. I am doing my PhD. Personal interest. I know nothing about anything and I do not wish to get involved."

"Involved... with *what*?"

Raj slammed the book shut, sending skyward a mushroom-shaped puff of dust. "I know nothing about the bodies in the cave. I know nothing about Tony Shen. I am doing my PhD. Leave me alone."

Raj performed an about-face and buttoned his overcoat with a show of indignation. His face had turned orange, as though he were a chameleon matching shades with his turban. He glared at Akira with scorn. As he marched through Bill Whitman's collection of texts and oddities, he kept his gaze fixed on Akira, the source of his irritation, until he banged his knee on a metal bookshelf near the door. He nursed his injury and doubled the intensity of his eyes, as though casting blame on the detective for that as well.

"What an asshole!" Akira said once Raj had exited the library.

"Excuse me," Wally said, "but this gentleman named Tony, you said he once worked for Bill Whitman?"

"Yup," said Ember.

"And he has elected to end his life?"

"Yup."

"And what was his last name? Shen?"

"Yup."

"Shen," Wally said. "That is a Chinese surname, is it not?"

Ember shrugged. "Fuck if I know."

"This gentleman Tony Shen, the man who killed himself - is it possible that he had... a false tooth?"

Akira smiled, beaming with pride at his partner's neophyte detective work.

"No idea," Ember said. "I never met the guy. I'm a research assistant. Tony worked in acquisitions. I mean, I knew *of* him, but, like, in the way the NSA knows people."

Wally nodded. A Chinese man with a false tooth acquires a backwards-flowing hourglass, he thought. Two days later, a Chinese man who collects magical oddities commits suicide. This man worked for a private research center owned by a man described as ugly and vindictive. His collection includes a book entitled *The Gravity Thief*, which tells of a mystic who could turn back gravity and time. The man reading the book swears he knows nothing.

Do these pieces fit together? Is it, what's the phrase, a red herring?

"Excellent work, Mr. Wally," Akira said. "Remain vigilant. I think I know our next move. We must now enter a forbidden zone. A realm of the dead, Mr. Wally. A place off-limits to common people."

Ember scoffed, looking at something on her phone. "More like common *sheeple*," she said. "Am I right?"

28

The captives approached quietly, moving as one. Nikole remembered learning about how the Sioux stalk prey by stepping heel to toe and attempted to mimic the technique.

The door opened without effort.

Nobody home.

Nikole had the feeling of stepping off a film set. The houseboat had been reassembled. It looked like a vacation rental, untouched, ready for family occupation.

"Huh?" Sam said.

Angel and Genghis could have turned into butterflies. They could have swallowed a solution that turned them transparent. They were in a security bunker staring through a camera's eye, behind one-way glass, in Nikole's head, but they weren't here.

"Are they letting us go?"

It's a test, Nikole decided. A trap, a puzzle. Something sinister lurked behind the room's normalcy.

City sounds seeped through the houseboat's walls: voices, cell phones, the ding of passing bicycles, children yelping in the streets. The door had been left open. The midday sun lit its edges a shade of fire.

"They're letting us go," Sam said, her voice growing more confident with each step across the bamboo floor.

Nikole waited for the landmine, the tripwire, the punji sticks. Footstep to footstep, the boat creaked like a submarine under pressure. Her lungs burned from lack of breath.

The dormant parts of her brain began sputtering to life. They'll maim us, torture us, melt our flesh. But they're clueless. They have no idea about the bird cult or what happened in the cave.

Sam pushed open the door and winced from the sudden sunlight. Her hair turned the color of a meteorite aglow with leftover atmosphere.

They stepped onto the sidewalk. Once quaint Amsterdam had grown fangs. Bicycles were chained to every railing, sign and tree in sight, their beams a heap of metal glinting in the sun, arranged like limbs in a mass grave. Tourists prowled the tree-lined sidewalks in the shadow of brick buildings punctuated every so often with a glass storefront.

Nikole felt the aura of a pending panic attack, first in her ankles then in her knees. She trembled with each step.

"They're letting us go," Sam repeated, her voice free of disbelief.

A bicycle darted past and the sound of its bell echoed in the amplifier of Nikole's brain. She felt heat in her back, neck and ears. Someone shouted in German from a pedal boat drifting in the canal. Twig-like trees shed leaves in a breeze that stung against fresh sweat.

They picked a direction and started walking.

"Right," Sam said. "Let's find a police station."

It seemed like a good idea. It sounded like something one says in their situation.

Clouds crossed the sun. The sky had the texture and color of an iceberg's underside.

Angel had left Nikole with eleven pills. Ten now. That and the clothes on my back, she thought. It's all I own in this world. We are what we carry, and I carry my pills. There are many like them, but these ones are mine.

Sam stroked her chin as they walked along the canal. "Allow me to posit a hypotenuse, if you will," she said. "We got ourselves mixed up in somethin' that ain't right, sis. That picture the dude showed us! Who was that, a Civil War veteran? And now he wants to know where he's hiding? As in, today? Now? A century and a half later?"

"The man I met in Iceland," Nikole said. "The way he talked – it was like he was from another time."

"Are we talking time travel?" Sam asked. "Do they have a time machine? Oh, man. I got them heebie-jeebies. Gonna need me an ice cream sandwich or three."

A shudder passed through Nikole's body. Not here, she thought. Not now.

They kept walking. Prewar façades ran to the horizon on both sides of the canal, magnifying the echo of a distant police siren. Dutch voices radiated from a nearby bicycle shop, a structure built of three generations of brick, radiant new at the base and ancient grey at the roof.

Nikole stopped at a street corner. Bicycles swarmed around them.

"What would we even tell the police?" she asked. "My boyfriend's being held hostage by a secret cult of time travelers. They took my passport, phone and cash. All I have are these prescription pills that aren't in my name." Her voice grew agitated. "Oh, and if you could help find who killed my mother too. She worships the bird goddess. They have magical powers. Just ask the Federal Bureau of Secret Societies. They're both named Agent Johansson."

"Jesus, relax. We're free. It's over." She paused. "You okay?"

Nikole hyperventilated. The city conspired around her. Faces became grotesque masks. She felt needle-hot glares from each corner of the globe weigh her down like a death sentence by crushing.

"I am *not* okay, Sam."

Every noise startled her. The machinery in her chest performed acrobatics, a high wire act of internal combustion. Her vision blurred as she scanned each passerby, face to face, for assassination attempts or camera flashes or telekinesis.

What's the point of life when you're damaged like me? I have a car in New York and I can't drive it. I have to get loaded on meds just to walk down the street. Some days I can't even look out my apartment windows.

She realized she was crying. She squatted down, then sat on the sidewalk, her legs stretched in front of her. Sam was talking in tongues, telling her to get out of the way, but her voice was distant and washed out by noise.

Nikole stepped through a time machine of her own and witnessed her future self, death-bound and withered, full of everything she could have done with her life but didn't.

I wish they'd just do it, she thought. I wish they'd get me over with.

An Arabic man broke out of the pack of tourists and approached. He wore a white skullcap and matching robe that ended just above his ankles.

"What is the matter?"

Nikole attempted to wave off the well-wisher. He did not move. A second man, similarly dressed, stuck his head out of a nearby café, retreated, then returned with two others. They formed half a circle around Nikole on the sidewalk and spoke Arabic to one another in hushed, confused tones.

"Give her some space," Sam suggested.

A fifth man, much older, emerged from the café. A waterfall of white hair flowed past his shoulders, its ends dancing in the breeze. His chin sported a matching wispy beard. He shuffled slowly, hunched, assisted by two young Arabs who acted as human crutches. The elder squinted through circle glasses at the fallen actress. The others went quiet in his presence. He stared at Nikole, glanced skyward as though awaiting instructions from God, and then he said something in Arabic.

One of the younger men smiled. "She must come with us," he said.

Sam protested. Nikole, nearly fetal, felt hard pavement of the sidewalk in her bones.

"She is coming with us."

29

The waiting room swarmed with bodies in decline: self-medicated stab wounds, junkies nodding off in wheelchairs, children wheezing, coughing, sneezing blood, a woman in a leg cast screaming about elves and demons, a stretcher covered suspiciously in sheets, and one seriously pissed off detective.

"You can tell this Dr. Reiner that I will hunt him by combat drone if I'm denied access a moment longer," Akira shouted at a trembling receptionist. "I say nothing of what my sidekick will do to him. He's a sick bastard. Wait until you see why they call him The Walrus."

Wally hid his face. My God, he thought, unable to muster much else.

Lavender and pomegranate did little to mask the stench of sickness. Wally jumped as a boy in crutches brushed his arm. Masses slumped over armrests in symbiosis with hard turquoise and disease. Sunlight reigned in windows running ceiling to floor. Heating vents rattled and hummed. Wally wondered what they might prescribe to alleviate chronic shame.

"You can't just walk in there," the receptionist said. "Requests for autopsy results should go through the medical examiner's office. There's a procedure."

"I need to see the body," Akira said.

She looked befuddled. "Well it doesn't work that way, detective."

Not awaiting permission, Akira shouldered his way past the rabble into swinging doors labeled "Employees Only." The receptionist picked up a phone and began speaking rapidly under her breath.

Wally looked both ways, thought My God, winced, and followed.

The hospital hallways bore strange sights: vagrants in gowns, mangled limbs, chemo-receded hairlines, a blob of a woman sneezing profusely, Blackberries, checkbooks in shaky hands, nurses forcing smiles, medicinal incense in the air.

"This whole business reeks of abnormalities," Akira said. "Induced suicide? No, Mr. Wally. That is beyond the sleaze of a man like Bill Whitman. Tony Shen perished through unnatural means. But we need proof."

Wally struggled to keep up. "If you ask me, sir..."

"Smiling gatekeepers make their rounds," Akira interrupted, gesturing at stressed nurse in sprint. "But make no mistakes, Mr. Wally. It's nothing but a façade masking grotesque experiments. At least, this is my idea for a paranormal horror flick starring the two of us as buddy cops. *The Hospital from Hell.* Tagline: If it's immortality you seek, you'd best steer clear. Me, I'm going to live forever."

"I beg your pardon?"

"I'll never die, Mr. Wally, as soon as I figure out how. Lately I'm favoring cryonics. I'll bust my way from the ice in *The Hospital from Hell 2: Space Yetis.* Surely you will represent my screenplay and find us a director."

Rounding a corner, a security guard approached. With no hesitation, Akira punched the man in his face hard enough to send him crumpled to the floor. Horrified, Wally raced to help the man to his feet, only to feel the detective's iron grip on his shoulder.

"And so it begins," Akira explained, pulling Wally deeper into the hospital. "A genome rearrangement artist masquerading as 'doctor' silver-tongues you - as played by you - into entering his lair. Unspeakable mutilations are performed in the name of profit. You will do your own stunts."

Akira checked each room one at a time, slamming doors open and shut.

A panicked nurse ran towards them. Akira held out his hand. "Take one step closer and I will impale your first-born child."

"You madman!" Wally said. "Why are you behaving like this?"

"*The Hospital From Hell 3: Final Showdown*," he said. "We meet the boss: Doctor Scott Reiner, bowel mechanic, stitcher of scrotums. Gurney to gurney, his experiment grows. Strands mutate. Cardiovascular systems become self-aware. Bones and cartilage awaken. Then it's zombie time. Surely you will find me a director."

Finally, they happened upon the morgue. Akira charged in, headfirst. Wally took a breath and followed.

There he was, Tony Shen, dramatically lit, nude on the steel table. Cloth covered his face. Two white-coated technicians attended the corpse. He had a Y-shaped cut down the torso, exposing a stew of organs. Intestines spilled through the incision. Wally stood for a moment, captivated at the sight. He noticed several tiny holes on the man's thigh and lower leg, a red remnant of swelling around each puncture.

The morticians turned their heads to the intrusion.

"Where are you hiding it?" Akira demanded.

The techs exchanged quizzical looks.

Akira began pawing through scalpels, charts and vials on a nearby counter, sending tools clattering to the floor. He tore the cloth off the man's face and, sure enough, there was his gold tooth.

A cadre of baton-wielding security guards stormed into the morgue. Bringing up the rear, the guard Akira had punched stumbled in, clutching his bloody nose, and gestured at the unhinged detective.

"Halt!"

Security tackled Akira to the floor. He fought back. In the struggle, Akira slid something into Wally's pocket.

"Dear sirs," Wally shouted over the commotion. "Allow me to offer my sincerest apology for my colleague's unprofessional behavior. I made several attempts at restraint. However, the man refused to see reason. Therefore..."

"Listen, guy," a chubby officer said, his finger in Wally's face, "you've got exactly two point five seconds to get the fuck out of here or you're going to jail too."

Wally left the way he came in, alone this time.

He made it out onto the sidewalk, where cool breeze reminded him how badly he'd been sweating. He felt sick. Leaning over a patch of white lilies as though to dry heave, he felt the hard mass of the object Akira had lifted from the autopsy. He reconnoitered for SWAT vans before probing his pocket.

It was a vial of Tony Shen's blood.

30

He pumped his eyelids twice, three times, adjusting to the light. Flagpoles rattled in the plaza. Cops congregated around a cruiser, swapping jokes and KFC. An engine struggled to life. A herd of schoolchildren brayed and yelped as their teacher – all poncho and curls – pointed out landmarks.

Traffic hummed in and out of the courthouse parking lot. A sharp-dressed lawyer spoke to clients in baggy jeans. He slung a satchel over his shoulder so that he could use his hands more emphatically.

Wally sidestepped the man and passed through sliding doors.

He'd spent the night in a sauna of sweat. Writing on his mattress, Wally brainstormed the bamboo shunts and serums to which he'd surely be subjected as an accomplice to the insane detective's spree of rage. He'd begun doubting the existence of the mystery hourglass.

And what about Nikole? She'd shut off her cell phone. Not a good sign. Perhaps I will pay her a visit, he decided, once this business with the detective is finished.

Tasked with locating the hourglass, the man busies himself attempting to solve eight murders in a cave. That is like going to a toothpaste factory for a root canal, Wally thought. Yes. Though I am rattled and starved for sleep, I mustn't fail to take note of my metaphors. My ability to maintain cleverness under pressure results, I believe, from my excellent constitution.

He stepped to a counter and signed some forms, made out a check and, with great difficulty, succeeded in posting Akira Murakami's bail.

The detective sauntered through an alley-side door. By contrast, he looked well-rested and hungry for adventure. Wally sighed, shifted his ancient station wagon into park and leaned over to open the door.

"I am Shawshank," Akira said as he buckled up. "You did not need to bail me out, Mr. Wally. I had already begun digging the tunnel."

Wally ignored him and lurched into the post-commute traffic of Sixth Avenue.

"So what does your intuition tell you?" Wally asked. "Have you pieced together the location of Tony Shen's secret hourglass hiding place through a series of subtle observations, visual cues and hacked government files?"

Akira shot him a strange look. "No, Mr. Wally."

"So where do we go from here?"

Akira didn't respond. He stared into the glowing screen of his phone, a shocked expression sculpting his face. For the first time, Wally sensed genuine fear coursing through his detective friend.

"Impossible," Akira muttered.

Wally signaled a left turn. He began to wonder if the detective may be mentally unstable and, if so, what the implications were for his pending trial for assault and trespassing.

"I've been in touch with an old contact of mine," Akira explained, "a hacker from Bosnia. I don't know her real name, nor have I met her. On the dark web, she's known only as... Cathy."

"Really?" Wally asked. "All this cloak and dagger and she goes by Cathy?"

"Indeed, Mr. Wally. Cathy has been unable to locate additional information on our recently departed friend. There are no records that a man named Tony Shen was admitted to Mount Sinai Hospital yesterday. Of the four autopsies performed at the hospital's morgue yesterday, all have American names. All but one are female."

Wally struggled to keep his eyes on the road.

"But we saw his body!"

Akira nodded. "Indeed we did, Mr. Wally. Somebody has tampered with the records. Somebody with weight. This is KGB territory. I am beginning to wonder what we are up against."

"Did you see the markings on the body's leg yesterday?"

"Spider bites, it looked like," Akira said.

I have a vial of his blood, Wally thought. I have proof the man existed. Clearly labeled on the side in permanent marker was the name Anthony Shen, with double question marks in the field marked "Age."

A Chinese man with a mouth full of false teeth steals a gravity-defying hourglass. This Black Lotus organization – with powers of erasing medical records and inducing suicide – are desperate to reclaim it. It was stolen by Tony Shen. And now he is more than dead. Now he has been erased. It is as though he has never lived.

My God, Wally thought, what will they do to *me*?

"Stop!" Akira shouted.

Wally slammed the brakes and squealed to a halt, drawing a torrent of horns and middle fingers. Akira pointed. Wally followed his finger and gasped. Across a public square, affixed to a concrete building, a billboard advertisement for shampoo had been plastered over with a painted message.

In bold block letters, the defaced billboard said "HELLO, DETECTIVES."

Beneath the menacing message, a string of numbers read 4067974018.

Wally and Akira stared at the message while traffic bottlenecked around them.

"Do you still have the blood vial?" Akira asked.

"Yes."

"Okay, Mr. Wally. I have a plan."

31

Nikole looked Elvis Presley in the eye. His face stared through sepia and time. She considered him like a Shakespearean actress admiring a skull. Alas, poor Yorick. Elvis played the Memorial Auditorium in Buffalo, New York on April 1, 1957. Tickets were a dollar seventy-five. So says the poster, framed and protected by glass, a five cent print turned Picasso.

"It is living, yes?" a voice chirped somewhere unseen.

Nikole sat straight up, then regretted it. Her every inch ached. Her skull bore fossilized trauma. She unfurled her knuckles, battlefields of bruises.

She found herself lying on a beanbag chair in a room plastered with posters. The Stones, the Beatles, Jimi, Janice, Floyd and Dylan were heavily represented, along with a near wall-sized mural of the Grateful Dead. A slow-spinning fan pulled the stench of marijuana through the ceiling.

The Arabs crowded around her. A gaunt man with a red beard and skull-like face offered her coffee. She shooed away his gift.

Her brain was a black hole. She had a panic attack on the streets of

Amsterdam and now she was here, in the city's depths, her joints sore and throat parched. The intervening time had been rolled over with whiteout, erased as though it never happened.

"Where am I?"

The men spoke in Arabic, seemingly debating how to proceed. There were five of them and they all had beards, some thick forests and other wisps that danced under the breeze of the fan.

"We are the Hakim brothers," said the redhead. "I am Nasir. We are from Yemen. We own this coffee shop with our father, Mohammed. But down here, in the basement - here we have our laboratory."

Nikole rubbed her eyes. "Your lab?"

Again, the men argued in Arabic. One of the Hakim brothers, a stout man whose beard came off his chin in a line like an Egyptian pharaoh, grew agitated.

"We appear to be divided," Nasir said. "Fahad does not think it prudent to disclose the nature of our experiments."

Something seemed off. Nikole spotted a specter behind the Arabs' warm hospitality. Where is my sister? What about Angel and Genghis? Is Carlos alright? Somehow she knew to avoid asking directly.

"How long have I, uh... It's nice to, um... I'm Nikole."

The men bickered further in Arabic.

She stood and checked her bones. Nothing broken. Her eyelids felt like the Sahara. The brothers gestured to the door. Fahad crossed his arms and looked bitterly away.

"My brother has been overruled," Nasir reported. "You may enter the lab."

The basement was more a special operations headquarters than a science facility. Nikole and the brothers emerged into a living room filled with a Ping-Pong table, cameras on tripods, computer desks and leather couches. Arc lamps and overhead lights blasted the room with the blinding whiteness of a film set. Abstract art filled the walls. Nikole smelled something like burnt cheese and days-old coffee.

A clean-shaven man was bouncing a ping-pong ball back and forth with a one-armed woman.

"He is Ali Ali," Nasir said, gesturing at the man. "He will be the world's biggest Arab YouTube star."

"Yes!" shouted another brother. "The world's biggest!"

Ali Ali towered over the others, mixing basketball prodigy stature with movie star good looks. His skin was the color of cappuccino. A walking gob of hair gel and cologne, the YouTuber kept his caramel eyes glued to the ball, ignoring the intrusion, focused on the task at hand.

"He is playing ping-pong with a one-armed woman with Down syndrome," Nasir said. "He is letting her win. Is heartwarming, yes?"

"It gives me the feels!"

The brothers stroked their beards in agreement.

Green screens lined a corner of the basement room, green ceiling, beige carpet, cameras and a computer desk. A laptop running Minecraft sat on the desk.

"Ali," Nasir said, "let's hear some reactions."

Ali Ali set down his ping-pong paddle and walked to the desk. He made a show of straightening his button-down shirt and flicked his wrists like a concert pianist on a stage. With great pomp, he rested his fingers on the laptop and began chipping away blocks in his digital world.

"He will be the biggest Arab YouTube star," Nasir repeated.

Ali shrieked like an otter being electrocuted.

"Ali Ali is up to almost one million subscribers," Nasir said. "He will be an icon of new media. He will go on *Ellen*."

"Or the Maury Povich show," another brother suggested. "Is he the father?"

The brothers stroked their beads and spent half a minute debating whether or not Ali Ali was indeed the father.

Ali's character on the screen fell to his death. His jaw dropped and his eyes went wide. He was silent a moment, then made a noise like a horse disemboweled by a depth charge.

Nasir smiled. "Watch this."

He placed a small white box on the table. On its face, the box advertised a glittery new smartphone and Chinese lettering.

Ali Ali snatched it up and held it to the camera.

"The box has hard edges and runs approximately six inches in length," he said, turning it over in his hands. The brothers beamed with pride. "Really innovative packaging," Ali continued. "Highly disruptive branding solutions in real time. Synergy. SEO. TED talks. Okay, the next stage of the unboxing involves removing the tape. It's like scotch tape, but more disruptive. Oh man, you guys. I haven't even unboxed it yet and already this product is so disruptive."

"He is repped through Copperstone," Nasir said.

"Wait," said Nikole. "This guy has an agent?"

"Of course."

"But what does he *do*, exactly?"

The brothers fell silent. One by one, they all turned to look at Nikole. She felt their stares go icy. In a club chair by a stairwell, the woman with Down syndrome looked equally flustered.

"I am not sure what you mean," Nasir said. "He is Ali Ali. He is the world's biggest Arab YouTube star."

"Well, I mean, he's handsome," Nikole said. "He could do modeling or..."

"No!" Fahad shouted, speaking for the first time. His foul demeanor had only soured further as his brother divulged their secrets. "Modeling is *old media*. Ali Ali is a *new media* sensation. He will go on *Ellen*."

Nikole nodded. "Right," she said. "Okay. Just, you know, trying to help."

"Let's get a hashtag started," Nasir suggested, lightening the mood. "Ali, what is trending this morning?"

Ali minimized Minecraft and, with a few deft clicks, opened several Twitter accounts, each in different windows.

"There is a magician from the Czech Republic named Marco Lucks," Ali reported. "He claims he will make the Moon disappear."

"Start a hashtag."

"You got it."

"Next," Nasir said, "we will have him react to the newest Lady Gaga video."

"Uh, that's alright," Nikole said. "This is fascinating and all, but where's my sister?"

"We left her with a hookah in the café. She was demanding a gallon of orange juice, a box of ice cream sandwiches and a boy with an enormous leaf to fan her. She became quite unreasonable."

Nikole ascended creaky wooden steps into the coffee shop, where the stink of tobacco hit her full force. Tourists and locals mingled at round wooden tables. The walls were lined with Middle Eastern decor. American pop music blasted from a corner jukebox.

Sam sat sprawled on a purple couch like a mafia don, a copper hookah pipe on a table before her. Her lips were smudged with chocolate ice cream. The table was a graveyard of empty glasses, each with rings of orange juice at its base.

"His name was Lingling, I believe," she was explaining to Mohammed, the Hakim family patriarch. "Saigon. 1968. My first love. War is hell, kid."

Nikole gasped, then raced forward, arms outstretched. The sisters embraced.

"You're okay."

"Yup, yup," Sam said.

"We need to get to Prague," she said to Mohammed. The old man nodded and stared into space. He treated the statement like a profound mystery of the universe, pondering its every syllable. He said nothing. For a moment, Nikole wondered if the man spoke English. All around them, the café hummed with youthful gabbing and caffeine. Mohammed looked out of place in this century. Finally, he spoke.

"It can be arranged," he said.

The Hakim brothers huddled around Nasir's iPhone. "Check it out!" he exclaimed. "It is an article titled '12 Pastries that Look Like Gary Oldman,' and I *have* to click it right this instant. Ha! Look at number three!"

32

"And then there's the business with the tides. You can't knock the Moon out of orbit without kicking up some tsunamis. Everybody knows that. Well, most people know that. Point is, there's too many details. How far will they push this thing? They could use stock footage. They could hire actors. Will they start riots? Can they go full War of the Worlds? If Marco pulls this thing off, I'll eat my hat absolutely. I'll slow cook it for days. Lather it with buffalo sauce. Mark my words. You're listening to the Heinrich Show. We'll be back in a bit discussing Marco Lucks, a Czech illusionist who claims that, on October first, he'll make the Moon disappear over Prague. I'll marinate my hat in oil."

The driver switched off the radio.

"Thanks."

"What's that?" asked the driver.

"Thanks."

"Here's where the mortar went off," he said, pointing at his melted ear. "Ahmad thought they were fireworks. He was six. Forever six. Six until the sun swallows the Earth. The children used bomb craters as swimming pools. The things they turn into weapons – you wouldn't believe it. I used walk among the ruins of Aleppo thinking, they'll need me. I'm an architect, you see. A builder. Was. Now I have my truck. I have more than some."

Windshield wipers bobbed in rhythm with the cadence of his voice.

"Ahmed was barefoot," he continued, "stepping over rubble where a hospital once stood. Bones and bricks. Here's where the mortar went off, on this side of my head. Never did I think I'd be grateful for my deafness. You see, I never heard him scream."

"That's, um, quite a way of saying hello to somebody. I'm Nikole."

Nikole listened to the man's story and fingered the Xanax vial in her pocket. She wanted to binge. Eight pills left. Eight milligrams. No cash, no papers, no devices. Can't buy more. What will I do once... No, better not to think like that.

The sky brimmed and spat, laden with the load of something about to happen. She felt a big decision coming on.

"Mohammed Hakim speaks highly of you," the driver said. "You know the Hakim brothers, then. I am pleased to make your acquaintance. My name is Hassan. I come from Aleppo. Once I was an architect. Are you sure you are okay?"

"We're a little shaken up," she said, immediately regretting her words. Her. Nikole Fink. Shaken up. This man has braved minefields and the Mediterranean. He could win a staring contest with an AK-47 and I can barely handle a phone call.

"Let me know if you need the doctor."

A castle loomed atop German hills. Shrouded in rain, its spires pierced the mist, fingers gnarled heavenward like pillars of a crumbling faith.

Yes, Nikole thought. A big decision will come soon.

"So you are heading to Prague," Hassan said.

"Yes."

He nodded. "I can take you almost all the way."

They didn't die all at once. The thought came to her suddenly. The envelope wasn't burned. Its contents were turned to ash, but the envelope itself was intact. Someone planted the envelope in Mom's fingers after she had died.

The Cult of the Bird Goddess. Faces misplaced from history. A secret they died to protect.

Who were these people?

"What are you hauling?" Nikole asked.

"I am sorry. This is where the bomb went off. This is the side of Ahmed's passion. Perhaps Allah deafened me out of mercy. You will need to speak up."

"What are you hauling?"

"Rocks."

"Rocks?"

"Yes. They fill it up with rocks, I run them across the Czech border, then I come back to Dortmund and they fill it once more. Week after week. Year after year. Life after life."

The trucker looked emaciated, denim-clad. His features were blurred, joined in symbiosis with anonymous highway. Burn scars littered the right hemisphere of his head.

"How do you deal with it?"

"You need to talk louder."

"How do you deal with it?"

"Deal with what?"

"You know," Nikole said. "Being alive."

Hassan shrugged. He hesitated, opened his mouth as though he planned to deliver a grand monologue on the nature of faith and humanity. Then he rearranged the scars of his face and sagged sadly behind the wheel, saying nothing.

"Did you girls hear about Marco Lucks?" he asked, changing the subject. "He says he can make the Moon disappear."

Mile markers and guardrails passed in silence; the sky hid. The truck vented fire and lumbered across lanes, aimed at where the highway ends. Nikole ached, lost herself in suffering, endured anxiety-heart as a personal test and focused on the act of existing.

Then it was there and gone, the decision, already made. The hard part's over. Not today, she thought. Tomorrow. I'll do it tomorrow.

33

"In the future, movies won't have any talking at all," Pierre Laurent explained over a meal of smoked pork, potatoes, chopped onions, cabbage with an overpowering stench, a full wheel of cheese, fried garlic, mushrooms, a bowl of something off-yellow, a bowl of something steaming, red wine, crepes and a slice of chocolate cake. Pierre nibbled a bit at each offering then rotated the plates methodically, nibbling then rotating again like astronomical clocks. "I'm talking cinema pared to its core. None of this silly 'story' or 'dialogue.' The special effects have their own personalities. Soon mushroom clouds will be bringing home their own Oscars. Hell, let's replace the Oscars with more explosions. The punctuation of machine gun fire, a V-formation of Harleys, a post-apocalyptic wasteland – this is the future of film. A return to the silent era."

"And this is your latest project?"

He nodded. "It's a ten-hour experimental film. It's a zombie movie, but interactive. The audience becomes the undead. I'm talking vegetables. I'm talking feeding tubes. An orgy of explosions on the screen. What a time to be alive." He lowered his eyes. "Aren't you going to eat?"

Wally slunk in his seat, sweating rivers. "I am not hungry," he squeaked.

Pierre shrugged and took the world's tiniest sip of wine.

Beside him, action star Jackson "The Giant" Rivers made up for Pierre's humble consumption with a torrent of calorie inhalation, devouring shanks of beef with such speed that Wally thought he might slip up and swallow the plate as well.

Akira sat somewhat askew. "The studio has already cleared all necessary permits with the city government," he explained. "We have been cleared to film on location. We are insured, so you don't need to worry about doing damage to the site."

Jackson nodded, pausing between gargantuan heaves to explain for the fifteenth time that evening that he does his own stunts. Buzz-cut and steroid-riddled, the blue-eyed hulk burst at the seams, testing the fabric of his black turtleneck.

Beyond his meaty scalp, Manhattan shimmered in fading daylight. Silhouettes lugged shopping bags and prayer mats across a bike-strewn bridge. Flags and steeples cut black shapes against the sunset. In an alley near the restaurant a sausage seller pined for the evening's last customer. A couple kissed on a sidewalk bench, each looking past the other's head at their smartphones.

"Think I'll find the john," grunted Jackson Rivers.

A couple argued loudly at a nearby table. Waiters ferried ever more sizzling dishes in choreographed motions, their soles clacking on crunchy wood floors.

Wally waited until the hulk was out of earshot. "Excuse me," he said, lowering his voice. "But don't you think our plan is a bit, what's the word, unethical?"

"Relax," said Akira. "He thinks he's rehearsing for an action movie."

"Run it by me again."

"They were coordinates, Mr. Wally," Akira explained.

"On the billboard?"

"Yes. Latitude and longitude. They point to a warehouse. Red Hook, Brooklyn. We could be walking into an ambush. Better to let the big dumb actor go first, guns blazing. He thinks it's a movie."

"But what if he gets shot?"

"He is insured," Pierre explained, smiling. The acclaimed French filmmaker, pushing 80, took another tiny sip of wine. "He does his own stunts. What could possibly go wrong?"

Conversation hushed as Jackson returned. He shuffled into his seat, making a show of his muscles.

"Now," said Pierre, "I'd very much like to move the conversation back to explosions. My film doesn't even have a title. It's post-everything. Explosions are the future of art. I seek to deconstruct our notions of the atom bomb. I'm talking about a reboot of a reboot – a simulacrum – set in a post-apocalyptic, postmodern wasteland, a movie for grown adults with talking anteaters and the King of the Worm People and... Wally, are you listening? I could offer your clients work. I've already signed The Rock as Genocide Gerry. I'm looking to cast a love interest. Think about it." He stared out across the city, sipping his wine. "What a time to be alive, gentlemen. What a time to exist."

34

Nikole awoke in a burial ground. Cigarettes, rats and roaches formed pyres between the tracks. Empty wrappers rolled like tumbleweed. Two platforms over, a train hissed to a halt.

She shook her hair like wet dog and out rained a waterfall of filth. One of her roommates had risen early and lay flat on his stomach, bug-eyed and long-haired, watching her sleep.

Sam shuffled to life beside her. "Well, sis," she said, "you can check spending a night with the homeless off your bucket list."

First priority of the morning: pill count. She fingered her pocket and found her eight-pack of delight intact. Joints stiff, stomach scorched, she eyed a trash can. Not yet, she thought. I'm not that hungry yet.

New arrivals overtook the platform. Tourists clutched SLRs like rifles. Managers barked into Blackberries. From sliding train doors strolled day laboring migrants and apprentice sculptors, wandering vagrants and descendants of kings. They sidestepped the homeless without a stray glance. That's it, Nikole thought. I've learned how to be invisible. I've learned how to disappear.

Nestled among their encampment, a handful of oddities stood out. They wore suits and slick haircuts turned ragged by pillows of concrete. Chattering in German, they drank from paper bags and fished spent cigarettes from sidewalk cracks. A bow-tied man pushing sixty shook soot from his pinstripes and eyed Nikole. “Are you staying for the luncheon?” he called out.

Nikole stared.

“Oh,” said the man, embarrassed. “I thought you were part of the tour. You don’t look as – ahem – soiled as the natives.”

Sam scratched her ear. “The tour?”

“You don’t know? We’re executives from ConTech. This is our corporate retreat. We spend twenty-four hours among the homeless. It’s a team building exercise. That is our CEO,” he said, gesturing to a sandy-haired woman in a pantsuit clawing ravenously through garbage. “She’s a billionaire.”

“Ja,” agreed a fellow executive. “Ein billionaire!”

“I think it’s healthy for the homeless to see that billionaires are human, just like them. It creates empathy.” He faced a human form more bag than man. The executive smiled. “I must be so inspiring to you.”

“Ja,” his friend echoed. “Much inspiring!”

Nikole noticed a foreign texture in her pocket. She carried something other than pills. In her sleep, someone had slid folded paper into her jeans. She fished it out.

Nikole Fink,

Welcome to Prague! You know we have hotels, right? The White Dove on Lazarová Street has its sign set in Futura, hands down the best 20th century font. That or Ruit, typography’s white whale. I make decisions where to do business based on the typeface of a company’s logo. I will not fly American Airlines. It’s hard enough to vacation when there’s an international cabal of sociopath assassins tracking your every move. It’s time you and I had a face-to-face. Find the Queen of Thieves near the Kafka Museum, at the foot of the Charles Bridge. Meet her by moonlight and she will lead you to me. The password is Comic Sans. Okay, there's no password. But really there should be.

Your friend,
Mouse

The sisters stumbled into Prague and light of day, sore, starving and unclean. Nikole ran a hand over the prickliness of her unshaved shin and tried to avoid looking at herself in reflection. Thank Christ I'm not famous enough to attract paparazzi, she thought. I look hideous. How do the heroines stay so beautiful on TV?

She found a water fountain outside the station. This is it, she thought. I've made the decision already. The deciding is out of the way. Scratch the hard part. Pros and cons? Weighed. Consequences? Considered. All that's left is the mechanics of the thing. Big decisions are like that.

She washed down her Xanax two at a time until there were none left.

Empty stomach. Lightheaded already. Countdown to blastoff. Stratosphere, so long.

"Come on," Sam said, tugging her sleeve. "Let's see if we can find some food."

"We have no money, Sam."

Her sister smiled and fanned her fingers as though she were playing an invisible piano. "Not yet," she said. "Watch me work."

They floated through corridors of old world architecture. Gargoyles perched atop cathedrals and furniture stores, antiques markets and McDonald's.

Sam tailed a bald businessman or professor in a tweed suit. She matched his pace and crawled up behind him on the sidewalk. Nikole turned away. She didn't want to see her sister commit the crime.

Because we're innocent, she thought. Up until now, we've done nothing wrong.

I've done nothing wrong.

I have no reason to feel ashamed.

The pills were kicking in. She lost herself in the crowd and admired the city. Block by block you could see history like layers of sediment. Here are relics of monarchy, here of the Nazis, here the Soviets. A clock tower built during the plague inched through another hour the way it had for centuries, through occupation and revolution and reconstruction.

Sam caught up with her.

"Fucking cheapskate," she said. "Dude's wallet was empty. Got a couple drug store coupons, though." She looked at Nikole. "Uh, sis? You, um... You look kinda odd. You feeling alright?"

Nikole wiped away a string of drool and smiled.

"Right," Sam said. "Hold that thought. I'mma try again."

Nikole felt warmth in her stomach spread outward and her sharp bits of brain begin to dull.

Sam squirreled away through a pack of pedestrians.

A Mercedes snaked through tourist throngs, displacing autumn air and swirling exhaust around aromas of sausage and pigeon droppings. An elderly balloon seller scuttled across the cobblestone. On ancient bricks a masked youth spray-painted Cupid and an AK-47. The aerosol hiss drowned a shopkeeper's scolding.

Sam returned clutching a wad of crumpled bills with unfamiliar markings. "Are these Euros?" she asked, captivated by the thought.

"The envelope wasn't burned," Nikole said.

"Huh?"

"In the cave. And the hourglass – she couldn't have, you know. It's too big to... What's the word?"

"Swallow?"

Nikole smiled. Of course. Yes. Too big to swallow. Somebody had staged the crime scene. She wanted to share her revelation with Sam but the pills were in full force now and her vocabulary had entered a blender.

Fall colors draped the endpoints of an ancient bridge. Pedal boats meandered through its arches.

Something sizzled in a street vendor's cart and Nikole could taste sour flavors in the air. She salivated. Her stomach was beyond rumbling. She hungry to the point she'd stopped feeling hungry.

Not that it mattered. Angels of euphoria massaged her as she walked, spreading warmth and chemical bliss, induced medicinal romance, amnesia of the soul.

Sam tried to steal something from a hot dog cart but couldn't distract the vendor, a well-whiskered man from India with a face veiled by simmering grills. Isn't this her specialty? Survival on the streets? They passed buildings with red roofs, cinder embankments, watch sellers and spires, priests in skullcaps and businesswomen from China.

She held herself against a stone wall and dry heaved. Thank Christ I'm starving, she thought. Because I'd do it, right in front of my sister. I'd dig through my own puke for pills. Again. Absolutely.

"You look sick," Sam said. "You sure you're...?"

Nikole nodded.

The sidewalks were air. She drifted angelic through the city of spires. She knew it was all around her, the world. But, engulfed in chemicals, she'd shielded herself with a bubble of light.

In a cobblestone square, they discovered a Salvador Dali exhibition. Sam wanted food but Nikole wanted to melt her brain.

She spent the better part of an hour nodding off in caveman slouch, staring at *Swans Reflecting Elephants* while Sam went trash diving for table scraps.

It wasn't not like she didn't know. Sure, they'd wear off. Sure, she was out. Sure, she'd get crazy, writhe in withdrawal, scream at her sister, do desperate things, make more big decisions.

But none of it mattered. Not her mother's death by burning, not her career, her ugliness, not her family's secrets or kidnapped ex. Here, surrounded by tourist whispers and green-blazered security staff, her brain gone putty and limbs gone limp, she could drool her way through nuclear winter. This is what Buddhists train their whole lives to achieve. This is God's finger in the Sistine Chapel. For a single blissful moment in paradise, it felt okay to be alive.

35

They slinked through an alley of flaking pink and angels cast in iron. Accordions sang sadly; the wind wept. Rain had turned the world the smell of pennies. Sam clutched her stomach. Nikole felt it too. Oh, come on, she thought. Kids in Uganda and all that. John McCain and Elie Wiesel. You can go a day or two without food, Nikole.

"You know, I believed you," Sam said, "when you said you took those pills for your condition. I didn't know you were one of... Well, I didn't know you were like that."

She felt shame, sure. But panic played a bigger role. The problem was her empty pockets. Withdrawal would come on fast. The last time... Well, better not to think about what happened the last time.

They emerged onto a well-worn path along the Vltava River, a mirror of moonlight. River met shore along a retaining wall and pseudo-beach plastered with litter.

"This the place?" Sam asked.

They stepped over shrubs and a battlefield of plastic and plywood, half-depleted water bottles, empty beer cans, food wrappers, scraps of parchment and broken glass.

A pair of bald musicians sat on folding chairs near the water. Armed with a violin and accordion, they flooded the night with melodies of gloom. Framed between the musicians stood a woman with sloppy blonde haircut, homemade dye job and coat like a cape. She had her back to the newcomers and stood admiring the arches of the Charles Bridge cutting a well-lit line of day in the night.

Nikole approached. She stopped a safe distance from the bridge gazer and visually frisked her for weapons. The woman looked tense.

"Um," Nikole began, "I'm looking for Mouse."

Swiftly she held up a deformed hand. The music stopped. Her middle and ring fingers appeared fused. Between the first two knuckles they were a single digit. Her thumb looked stunted. A clunky steampunk ring adorned her pointer finger.

"Franz," she said, speaking silkily. "Is there a corpse standing behind me?"

The accordion player shook his head. "No, m'lady."

A strange thing happened as the Queen of Thieves turned to face her guests. Figures crept from crevices of the world. In the time it took her to pirouette, nearly a dozen henchmen had fallen in behind her.

The Queen's soldiers were a gallery of freaks and outcasts. A hobbled hunchback wore a bandanna covering one eye and necklace of dangling human teeth. A bodybuilder hoisted a gargantuan machine gun. A pigtailed girl no older than twelve twirled a switchblade that caught moonlight in strobes. Their faces stained with soot, they bore bullet wounds and battle scars. A woman in a shawl stared through a gleaming glass eye.

The Queen herself looked free from facial mutilation. Her bicep was tattooed with mechanical gears, silver muscles, wiring, circuit boards and mechanized tendons. Dark eyes exuded mystery. She wore a bullet on a silver chain, leather around her wrists and a three-finger ring that looked like brass knuckles.

"Holy crap," said Sam. "I'm not sure who would be more likely to come through here with a net – Jerry Springer or the curator of a nineteenth-century museum of medical maladies."

The thieves stood as one behind their queen.

"You've met Angel," said the Queen of Thieves, "and you're still alive.

I've never heard of such a thing."

"We need to see Mouse," Nikole said.

She nodded. "We all have needs."

She turned her back once again and the assembly parted, allowing her to gaze upon the full moon peaking above the bridge. The accordion player resumed his sad song. The violinist soon joined.

"Marco Lucks," she said, "claims he'll make the Moon disappear." She checked her watch. "Any minute now. Strange to think where we exist. A ball of rock falls into orbit. Gravity, plate tectonics, single-celled lifeforms. We don't live long enough to witness anything. Nothing cosmic, at least. We can't see God, so we have to settle for optical illusions. But you've found something that breaks the rules. That," she said, pointing to the Moon, "I can understand. That's physics, chance, Allah, whatever you call it. You've found something else."

"The hourglass," Nikole said. "What is it?"

She shook her head. For a moment it looked as if she was about to burst into song. Instead, she pined at the moon surrounded by hooligans, wrapped the warmth of music. A rowboat drifted under the Charles Bridge, blotting out lights one at a time.

She motioned for the music to stop.

"Were you followed?" she asked.

The sisters said "no" and "probably" overlapping, unclear who said what.

"You sure you don't wanna watch the Moon go poof?"

"Take us to Mouse," Nikole said.

She turned to take one last glance at the bridge. "Come now," she said to her band of misfits. "Let's go home."

The thieves fanned out behind her as she marched up the path towards Prague's baroque architecture. The musicians took up a peppy tune and joined the procession at its rear, prancing merrily as they followed their queen, now playing the pied piper, into dusky night. Nikole and her sister followed. A car alarm nearby broke the fairytale allure. Nikole turned her eyes towards an alleyway of ghosts and whispers. The parade marched along the riverbank through a galaxy poised on the brink of collapse.

36

Tucked into a basement of a basement, three purgatories removed from the underbelly of Prague, Mouse belonged to a lost industrial age. The city had piled over her in sprawls like layers of sediment in bedrock. Ducts heaved ghosts in the mist. Bricks bore water marks. A world full of gears and tubes, gyrating machinery and suspended dust gave the warehouse the feel of a peephole into a parallel world.

She had dark hair and lipstick to match, rodent-shaped ears and steampunk goggles that looked cut from a welding mask. She wore a leather jacket with seemingly endless pockets and a revolver welded from copper and LED in a shoulder holster. She looked hardly five feet tall.

"Are you Mouse?"

She flipped open her mask. Underneath was a face mired in freckles.

"Did you bring the hourglass?" Mouse asked.

"My boyfriend's been kidnapped by the Black Lotus," Nikole said. "Help us get him back."

"Yeah. Okay. Sure. The hourglass, Nikole."

Nikole shook her head. "I want answers first. Who are you? Why are the Black Lotus after my family? Who was my mother and what happened to her in that cave?"

Mouse shook her head. "No time to explain. Hand it over."

"I lost it."

The women dueled icy glares. Mouse appeared on the verge of psychotic break. Maybe her hand inched towards her firearm, or maybe Nikole imagined it.

Mouse gestured to the Queen of Thieves. Her minions leaped into action, seized Nikole by both arms and yanked her to the floor. Her hips connected hard with ancient concrete. A meaty pair of hands locked her skull in place. In her peripheries, she saw Sam likewise seized by ruffians, kicking and struggling.

Mouse approached, holding something the glinted in the torchlight. She removed her goggles and raised the object. It was a surgical scalpel.

Mouse grabbed Nikole by the chin and brought the scalpel to her eye.

"Don't move," she said.

Nikole winced. Her body went taut as a noose. She braced for torture. As the razor scraped across her pupil, she felt an odd grating sensation, not exactly painful, but itchy. It took the willpower of a self-immolating monk not to blink. She had the feeling of flossing out a scrap of food from between her teeth, one that had been there for so long she noticed it only by its absence.

Mouse retracted the scalpel. Dangling from its tip, nearly invisible, Nikole saw a writhing parasite hardly the width of a hair.

"African eye worm," Mouse said.

She blinked and shed blood, tears or both. Her eyeball felt violated, its lid coarse like sandpaper.

"Sweet Jesus," Sam said. "I don't got one of them creepy-crawlies in my eye jelly, do I?"

"I'll check," said Mouse.

At the worm's endpoint, barely perceptible, Nikole could make out the tiniest grain of metal.

"It's not mind control," Mouse said. "Even the Black Lotus don't have that one figured out. But they've been listening to your thoughts. They've been following you."

She moved to Sam, still restrained on the floor, and examined her eyes.

"No eye worm."

Sam shuddered.

Mouse dumped the parasite on the floor and ground its life out with her heel. Nikole's arm restraints relaxed.

She felt emboldened by safety. Here is a woman who knows what she's doing in life, Nikole thought. Someday, when this is all over, I'd like a lair of my own. I could plot and ponder, stroke my chin, study a globe. I could swim through life quiet and invisible. Because that's everything. Loneliness is my cross. But at least I can't be in trouble.

Mouse smiled.

"The Cult of the Bird Goddess, Nikole," she said. "The Black Lotus are hunting and killing cultists who claim to possess mystical powers. They are attempting to erase the bird cult from history."

"My boyfriend," Nikole said.

"Yes, yes. We'll save your boytoy. Well, *you'll* save him. Anyways, you've made it this far. Now that we've got introductions out of the way, how about you pull up a chair. I'll tell you everything I know."

37

"I joined the Black Lotus when I was thirteen," Mouse said. "My specialty was demolitions. My childhood was full of swing sets, playgrounds and homebrewing napalm in Uncle Jeb's toolshed. I like to blow shit up."

She unzipped her jacket and bared her arm. The metal one. In solidarity with her machinery, Mouse's prosthetic arm was a gold-plated gear collection of broken valves and moving parts.

"They called me Mouse," she said, pulling a sleeve back over her deformity, "because of these big ol' ears I got. Every trace of my former existence was scrubbed, even from my own brain. I don't remember what my parents named me. I don't remember my family. Angel's not his real name, either. We're forced to inject ourselves with memory suppressants. Certain details of our own operations are hidden from us. They monitor our thoughts through our eye worms."

"I would be totally okay with never hearing the words *eye worm* again for the rest of my life," Sam said.

Mouse's workshop thumped and hummed as though catching its breath. Nikole wondered if the racket was to confuse hidden microphones.

Nikole discovered a black lab curled between paint buckets under Mouse's desk. She nudged it with her toes a few times before realizing it was stuffed.

"A year ago I devised a workaround to fool their drug tests and stopped taking my shots," Mouse said. "I'd jab a needle in Mr. Spaghetti – that stuffed mutt you got your toes on – and infused his canine blood into my veins." She paused, then burst out laughing. "I lied! They don't do drug tests!"

Nikole couldn't find the humor.

"Anyways. My brainwaves cleared up and there they were – the cultists. They've found a way to transcend the physical limitations of the human body. Nietzsche's Übermensch. Their secrets, should they become publicly known, would fundamentally alter the understanding of human potential. Supernatural occurrences often can't be contained or destroyed. In those cases, our strategy is to eliminate everyone who knows about them. My curiosity was too much. I had to learn the truth. I went rogue."

"And what are their secrets?"

Mouse shrugged. "Nobody knows. Well, nobody except those dead bodies, and maybe a handful of upper-echelon Black Lotus bureaucrats."

"Who are the Black Lotus?" Nikole asked. "I mean, who are they really? They cover up supernatural occurrences. But why? What's their motive?"

"Oh, you know. The usual. Money, power. We erase parts of history that powerful people find unsettling. We help maintain a comforting narrative of a universe that plays by the rules and in exchange we get our members into the Vatican, the White House, secret societies, exclusive circles. It's in our mission statement." She exploded in another fit of psychotic laughter. "I just made that up! We don't have a mission statement! I lied!"

The sisters stared, stone-faced.

"And what about our mother?" Sam asked. "What about the people in the cave?"

"Beats me," Mouse said. "The Black Lotus wanted 'em dead. All I know is from the pictures I saw on TV. Which was weird. Ever since the Black Lotus started hunting them down, the cultists don't exactly advertise themselves. That symbol hasn't been used in decades."

"When they were questioning us," Nikole said, "Angel and Genghis said the Black Lotus didn't kill those people. They wanted *us* to tell *them* who did it."

Mouse froze. Her ecstatic body language and flailing fake arm sputtered and stopped like malfunctioning factory parts. Her eyes narrowed, then her forehead followed.

"You're kidding."

"We went down there," Nikole continued. "The whole thing seemed off. My mom died holding an envelope. The contents were burned but the envelope itself was intact. It all seemed staged."

Mouse's pupils swam circles in her skull. "It is highly abnormal that the Black Lotus would leave behind such a spectacular crime scene," she conceded. "Highly abnormal." She chewed half her lip, drawing the freckles on her chin into new constellations. "So you saw the bodies firsthand. What else do you know?"

Nikole told her everything, beginning with her mother's disappearance and subsequent family unraveling, her decent into addiction and obscurity, her painful regrets, her mother's unearthing, the *Kid Wizard* reference and the Agents Johansson, how she pieced together Snorri's hideout only to be kidnapped by the Black Lotus and inexplicably set free, meeting the world's biggest Arab YouTube star and waking up among the homeless in Prague. She reiterated the unexplained – the cave with no entrance, the symbol on the wall, the wrong way hourglass. By the end of it she found herself breathless, with a new set of priorities.

"Honestly," Nikole said, "I just want to go home. I want you to rescue Carlos and get us on the next flight to LaGuardia. I don't care about the bird people. I just want the Black Lotus to stop chasing us."

Mouse shook her head. "You can't stop them. You're in this thing now, Nikole."

"So you know nothing about the bird cult, you don't know who killed our mother, you can't tell me the significance of the hourglass and you can't protect us from the Black Lotus." She paused. "We risked our lives to find you."

"I was counting on getting to check out the hourglass up close. It's some kind of holy relic, I think." She stroked her chin with titanium fingers. "What was that name Snorri told you? Helen?"

"Helena."

"And who were these cops who showed up at your door in the dead of night?"

"Feds. FBI, I think."

"And why weren't they actually, you know, investigating the bodies?"

"They said they were waiting for the Black Lotus to come clean up their mess."

Mouse shook her head. "No, no. The FBI doesn't know about the Black Lotus. That's way over their pay grade. But we've got assets in the CIA. Maybe that goes both ways. Maybe the Agency's cleaning house."

Sam licked her lips. "Mmm'k," she said. "You got my brain canals all scrambled, lady. Lemme try and fathom some stuff. You're saying my mom got mixed up in some cult of magic-having superheroes, the Black Lemmings – renamed 'em, sorry – are guns for hire by the Illuminati, and now the *CIA* are involved? God dammit. A week ago I was trying to figure out long division and even that hurt my brain. And now you hurl *this* at me? Why?"

From hunger, revelation, or the Xanax-shaped hole in her head, Nikole began to feel faint. "I just want to get my boyfriend back," she repeated. "Who is this chemist person?"

"Ah, The Chemist. My old pal. Speaks of himself in the third person, thinks everyone's a spy, sharpens his teeth with a nail file."

"What does he want?"

"Dunno," said Mouse. "Hard to say what any of us are thinking. We're a ragtag clique of sociopaths and contract killers. At least three of our members are cannibals. We've got a guy named Worm Eater who earned his nickname the hard way. But we're pretty good at what we do." She tugged a book and revealed a hidden wall safe. Her mechanical arm interfaced with the lock, and in a few whirring motions it hissed open. She smiled. "There's nothing behind there. I just like doing that."

"Do you know where he is?"

"Yes. Your friend is nearby. I think they kinda figured you two were coming to see me. They want me dead real bad, see."

"Is that why they let us go?"

"Yep. They wanted to follow you a while, see where you'd end up. You led them right to me. Which means we gotta hurry. Let's split up. I know some useful idiots who can help. And when I say *idiots*... Well, you'll see.

They have an interest in a particular period of history. They are history buffs."

Mouse smiled devilishly and gave Nikole detailed instructions. Her plan sounded insane, homicidal and so far-fetched that Nikole wondered if she wasn't having fun with her.

"And my sister?"

"She comes with me," Mouse said. "One of my favorite hobbies – outside of typography and knitting – is to have a gander at the Black Lotus hit lists each week so I can keep tabs on who's getting acid baths, who becomes crocodile food, that sort of thing. They've got their eye on lots of folks. I'll check the database for persons of interest named Helena. If we want to know what happened in the cave, we'll need to find the survivor."

"I talked," Nikole said. "I told them the name Helena."

Mouse nodded. "I'm aware. We've got a tiny window to find her first. Let's meet up in Budapest on Monday. Here, memorize this address."

Nikole stared at a scrap of paper, rereading street and number a dozen times.

"You can't really miss it," Mouse said. "It's a... Well, you'll see. Good luck, new best friend! Should we get BFF trinkets and confess our celebrity crush? Or are we not at that point yet? No, you're right. Let's take it slow. We'll bond over swashbuckling buggy chases and mass shootings. Ours shall be a grand adventure."

She stood to leave.

"Wait," Nikole said, struggling to process the turn of events. "One more question. Why are you helping us?"

Mouse smirked at her in a way that suggestion the answer was obvious. "You really have to ask? Think it over on the way to Budapest. See you in a couple days. Don't die."

38

Mouse's rusty Volkswagen sputtered and purred and Nikole wondered what was older: her or the car. She meandered by moonlight, treading country roads, flanked by farmland and overgrowth, crunching up the gravel ascent to the Roman ruin Mouse had marked on the map.

The tower looked time-warped, medieval. Red lanterns burned in windows cut from stone. A village glowed orange in the valley below.

Nikole struggled to keep control of the car. Gin ate holes in her esophagus. In scar tissue and stomach lining she felt chemicals erode her soul. She pictured a bleary-eyed sit-down with Barbara Walters, studio lighting, a gentle hand on her knee, words in the teleprompter about hitting rock bottom, an addiction hotline scrolling at the bottom of the screen.

She rattled to a halt and flashed her headlights at the tower, not for any reason, but it's something she'd seen in movies. Nursing her chapped lips with booze, she struggled to find the handle and collapsed out the door into the night, still unsure what she was doing.

Mom wouldn't have gifted me her precious hourglass if she knew what I'd become. Drunk, druggie, waste of flesh, wasted talent. Step right up. See what's become of the Kid Wizard. If we could live forever, I'd just find ways to kill myself more slowly.

And yet here I am, coming to the rescue. They give people like me medals.

Nikole left the car running. She stumbled towards the tower and choked up her grasp on the fake metal hand.

"Hey!" she slurred. "It's me, Mouse! Don't you recognize me?"

She waved the metal hand.

"I've had an, um," she said, struggling to remember the script Mouse had taught her, "a conflict of couscous. No, wait. I mean conscience. A conflict of... Whatever. I'm turning myself in. Come arrest me. I am your prisoner."

She pictured barrel-chested city defenders swarming the tower centuries ago, brandishing sabers, protecting the princess.

I am no Lancelot. Inebriation is my armor. The problem is being conscious. Not yet, Nikole thought. I haven't made arrangements. Please, no flowers. Closed casket so they won't find my flaws. They're awful. Funerals. Spectators picking over your plastic corpse. Mom had the right idea. Sully your skin with enough scars and even the family won't look, let alone the world.

Nothing moved in the night.

"Up to you guys," Nikole said. "I could go down to that village, start knocking on doors, telling folks there's Black Lotus safe house up here under this historical, uh... thing."

Figures emerged at the tower's base. She felt eyes. More this time. Dozens of beady world-watchers stared from taut eyelids, an arachnid of trained pupils and silenced rifles.

Nikole felt still. The world stumbled around her. She waited for the bullet. But is it so bad? Dying? She couldn't decide, so she decided to keep drinking.

Masked soldiers marched through the shadows. They held assault rifles at eye level. She raised her arms in surrender, keeping awkward control of the metal hand's knob, careful not to show flesh out of the sleeve of her yellow anorak.

She knew The Chemist by his silhouette. A long-legged shadow filled the tower's doorway. He crossed the distance between them in what seemed like a single stride. He wore striking features Mephistopheles style, eyes like pale sky and a goatee which he seemed unable to quit stroking. His fingers looked warped. Even at this distance Nikole could smell the acids and reagents that had planted their flag in the man's heart like an old lover.

"What's going on here?"

"She claims to be Mouse," one of his soldiers reported.

Nikole felt naked. No pills, no treasure, no passport. Nothing but my yellow anorak. If that's what it's called. Well, at least I've got my bottle now.

"Mouse," said The Chemist. He spoke in an accent Nikole guessed was Russian. "The deserter." He peered at her in the starlight. "It does not look like Mouse."

Mephistopheles grabbed her fake hand and yanked, taking Nikole with it. She stumbled and hit the ground with her knee.

"This is some kind of bullshit," said The Chemist. "I do not understand it." He turned to his soldiers. "Throw it in the holding cell until we can figure out what it is."

He turned his back and the soldiers advanced. Understanding now that it was not Mouse in their midst, the grunts seemed to relax. Hands gripped her armpits and she lurched forward. Momentum and drunkenness warred in her stomach and she struggled not to vomit.

They took her down steps in total darkness. She felt as though she'd entered a refrigerator.

They reached a stone-walled room full of cobwebs. She heard the door slam before she realized the hands were no longer supporting her. Realizing too late, like Wile E. Coyote chasing the Roadrunner off a cliff, she staggered, tried to guess where her feet were, then fell flat on her face. She tasted blood.

A light hummed to life with electricity. Nikole craned her neck and spat a wad of dust.

Carlos coughed. The light rousted him from his corner. He pushed himself out of the sprawl of limbs in which he'd been sleeping. First priority: a stick of gum. He plundered his pockets by instinct but came up short. He scratched his ear. Halfway through a yawn, he recognized his new cellmate.

"Nikole?"

She pressed herself up on her elbows like a Sphinx.

"Hey," she said. "You alright?"

His eyes grew wider than Nikole thought possible. "Am I *alright*? Jesus, Nikole. Look at me. They threw me here in this, like, medieval dungeon and it has no windows, so I'm worried about the ventilation, like what if I suffocate, you know? There's cracks in the floor where there might be spiders. I swear to God, Nikole, this has been harrowing. Of course you're involved. It figures. Hey, do you have any gum?"

Nikole groped at his ankles and Carlos thought she was making advances. More bewildered than anything, he squirmed around her touch.

"Jesus, Nikole. You're a mess. I'm the one who got kidnapped. God, you're sweating like you're dying of fever. Gross. How drunk are you?"

"I'm out of Xanax," Nikole said. "You think I could rescue you sober?"

"A rescue. You're rescuing me. This is what you think a rescue looks like."

"They took my purse. I had to steal the booze."

She pushed herself into a seated position and touched her lip. Her hand came away looking like a red pen exploded.

"You're bleeding," Carlos said.

"Am I? Is that what this is?"

Her ex stared her down a moment, then forced an over-acted scoff. "Unbelievable. Why are you doing this to me? I had a career, Nikole. You had to get involved, didn't you? Now look what you've done. You had to go down into that cave. What do you think they'll do to us? I mean, now that they can't get their hourglass?"

Nikole steadied herself.

"How do you know about the hourglass?"

"I have ears, Nikole. I hear things. They say the hourglass is somewhere even the Black Lotus can't reach. They say the most dangerous people in the world have it. Now it's *us* they want. They're going to kill us." He paused. "We need a plan."

Nikole conjured images of secret agents and men with letters on their chests, famous generals and documentaries about bank heists.

"There are two of us now," Carlos said. "There's a single guard posted outside the door, and he looks like he's got the brain of an ostrich." Carlos paced around the cell. "Remember when I was in that Jackie Chan knockoff with Chris Plunk? They taught me karate. The basics. But still." He looked more assured as he paced. "I'll hit the guard with a Vulcan knockdown – a Jedi trick I learned straight from the death grip of Chris fucking Plunk." He spoke with his hands, growing more energetic. "Then I'll be all like..." He jabbed the air with uppercuts, mouthing crude sound effects. "Rachel, get his gun. He wears one on his hip."

Nikole blinked. "What did you call me?"

"Right," said Carlos. "Sorry. Go for his gun, *Nikole*." He rolled his eyes. "I swear, you'll never grow up. Once we get the gun he's done for. We'll blind him, knock him out, hold him at gunpoint and we'll be like, do what we say or else. Then I will carry you away, my princess, in my arms to a..."

Then it scurried across the wall.

His face turned pale. He staggered back half a step, eyes gaping, and let loose.

"A spider!" he shrieked. He went fetal on the stone. "Oh, God. Kill it, Nikole! Is it dead? Did you kill it? It's not on me, is it? Oh, God. It's on me. I can't even."

He tucked and rolled as though engulfed in flames.

Nikole wasn't listening. Rachel, she thought. Why did Carlos call me Rachel? A strange sensation rattled through her bones, not the feeling of being erased, but the feeling of being replaced with fiction. Nikole Fink is an actress, a child star, a Wikipedia entry with footnotes. She can't be forgotten. You can't just press delete. But they're doing it anyways, somehow.

Nikole killed the spider.

"I already have a plan," she said, "and you're not going to like it."

39

"I understand that you take this personally. I respect those who have, what's the word, gumption. This cannot be disputed. I have prepared several convincing arguments to demonstrate my admiration of gumption. However, it likewise cannot be disputed that you have ingested a questionable volume of alcohol. Highly questionable. My query for you, sir, is as follows: considering your intoxicated state, are you certain you should be brandishing a firearm of such caliber?"

Akira Murakami sipped from a silver flask. "This is not how I planned on spending my retirement," he growled in a fake Boston accent. "This is why my daughter will never understand. She can't know what it's like to get that call in the dead of night, to work on nothing but intuition and a clue scrawled in blood." He cleared his throat. "Was that okay? Or should I come off even more grizzled? You know, for my audition. For our buddy cop show."

Wally shook his head.

The warehouse was a crumbling brick block near the shipping port, sagging in places, with boarded up windows and faded lettering. The neighborhood stunk of sewage and seawater and Wally swore he heard a distant helicopter circling the scene.

"So that's it?" Wally asked. "You want to star in the movies and all this is for show? You want to be the world-famous detective who solved the cave murders so you can go on TV? Do I have it right, sir? Do I have you figured out?"

"Do you hear that?" Akira grunted, taking another swig. "The streets of Boston, Mr. Wally. They call me back home. This is why my daughter will never understand." He paused, then added "I am Ben Affleck."

Hollywood action star Jackson "The Giant" Rivers rapped one knuckle against the driver's side. Pierre Laurent, behind the wheel, cracked his window.

"So the bad guys are holed up in their seaport hideout," Jackson said. "I love it. Are they stunt doubles? Extras? Do they have weapons training? How many and what are their positions?"

The director and detective looked to one another across the center console.

"You see, Jackson," Pierre began, "we are trying to make this authentic. You're playing Agent Bruce Shields, remember. He doesn't play by the rules. A loose cannon, but he gets the job done. It is the role of a lifetime, Mr. Rivers."

Jackson grunted. "Hell yeah."

"Now remember, Jackson," Pierre continued, "we'd like you to treat this like the real thing. Once filming starts you'll need to improvise. So if anything goes wrong in there, just..."

"I do my own stunts," Jackson said proudly, beaming an ivory smile.

"Yes, you've told us that many times."

"So, bust in, kick ass, chew bubblegum and blow shit up?" From his back pocket, he flicked a set of sunglasses. "Another day at the office," he said, resting them on his face. Toting the shotgun over one shoulder he sauntered across the gravel lot humming a battle hymn.

"God, he's dumb," said Pierre.

Akira turned. "We'll wait until he's inside, and then sneak up behind him. We're his reinforcements. Pierre stays in the car. He's not insured. How badly do you want to retrieve your client's hourglass, Mr. Wally? Are you prepared for combat? Are you prepared to pull the trigger? Can I count on you?"

I am not the sort of man, Wally thought, who is cut out for midnight raids. I enjoy fresh apple cider. I have been told that my mustache is a work of art. I have opinions about Art Deco style. I desire nothing more than to own a mansion sizable enough to display my collection of vintage bottles. Violence is not my, what's the word, purview.

"I am eager to wrap up this business and return the hourglass to its rightful owner, Mr. Noon," Wally said. "Are you certain of its whereabouts?"

Akira's smile widened. "You are not a perceptive man, are you, Mr. Wally?"

Wally pondered his career and his fate. A string of failures ending in bizarre shootout in an ancient cave. Am I a man consumed by greed? Do I resort to such tactics thusly? Like any man of the world, I thirst for success. Long I have plowed through middle age on breadcrumbs and fading talent. But what will I tell Allah? Behold my mustache, most merciful God. See how its ends twist upward? All I've accomplished in life can be found on my upper lip. Nobody will remember Wael Algayar as anything other than "man in background" in Pierre Laurent's final and bloody piece of performance art.

Akira slipped back into his caricature Boston accent.

"Party time."

Then they were outside, marching towards a warehouse swarming with terrorists, desperate to do something, anything, worth remembering in this life.

40

"Huh. Well then. Looks like we got ourselves a regular whodunit."

The Queen of Thieves lay forehead to floor, bile-caked, body riddled with shrapnel and exposed bone. Her minions were sprawled in various stages of postmortem humiliation. Some had clean entry wounds, center-aligned between their eyes. Others had been mutilated at close range. The warehouse floor ran runny red and black ooze in patches, swamp-like. One soldier had been sculpted in an impossibly contorted death ball. Their weapons had vanished.

Mysteriously, the walls bore no marks of combat. Either the corpses had been relocated, or whoever had carried out the massacre possessed accuracy bordering on the supernatural. Every surface smelled of death.

"Black Lotus," Mouse said, stroking her chin.

Sam held her nose. Yup, she thought. Sure. Leave me with psycho bitch. I'll be fine. Here come the flashbacks of puppies and popsicles, never getting to see Daft Punk in concert and that one time I got extra credit on Mr. Braddock's trig test. That was tight. No with a thousand o's. Man falling from cliff. I wonder if they have ice cream sandwiches in

Heaven.

Mouse pulled a revolver from her leather pockets. It looked welded from scrap and copper coils.

Well, Sam thought, it kicks the crap out of dying from cancer. I mean, how many obituaries can actually use the phrase "in a hail of bullets?"

"We need to get to a public place," Mouse said.

They sidestepped severed limbs and bogs of fluid. Soaked floorboards squished underfoot. Sam breathed through her mouth and tasted gunpowder in the air. They crawled up stone steps towards lamplight seeping through. Mouse made a "shh" gesture with her metal fingers. Hey, you know, those might come in handy in life, Sam thought. Do they have multiple speeds? How easy are they to clean?

Delicately, she touched the doorknob.

A bird chirped. Out fluttered Chaz the son conure, bobble-headed and corpse-hungry, his feathers a ruffled rainbow. He perched atop a torso and cast black beads in their direction.

Sam moved to escape but Mouse just hung her head. "Too late," she said. "We're done. On the bright side, you'll go to the grave adequately educated about typography and what people look like on the inside."

Twin shadows formed a cross. From opposite corners Genghis and Angel stepped into sight. Lamps colored their skin a mix of coal and fire.

"Hello, Mouse," Angel said.

"Hey there, old pal. Hey, before you off us, do me a flavor. See to it that the text on my tombstone is set in Garamond. Adobe Garamond, of course. Not the one that comes with Microsoft Office."

Angel raised his weapon. Mouse raised her weapon. Chaz chirped and, for one final moment, the world was still.

41

"Shots fired!" Akira screamed. He darted through the warehouse door into a sea of blackness, flashlight in one hand, pistol in the other. Though the gate was indeed foreboding, it had been left unlatched and Jackson had swung it open single-fingeredly.

Wally followed to the cusp where reality caught up. He stopped short, heart teetering on implosion, tremors rippling him eye socket to toe. A hundred feet of warehouse separated him and the hourglass, him and battle, him and what's the word. He began reciting the names of Allah. I am not a man cut out for martyrdom.

He heard no further combat, just a single shotgun blast, but he'd lost trust of his senses. Voices traded harsh syllables. Feet shuffled and skipped. Much like a sports fan losing power during the last pitch of the World Series - a most excellent metaphor - Wally awaited horror or triumph. Who won?

He peered into the warehouse.

The interior stretched a football field's length of despair and disuse, stripped but for a single length of rope, a red support post emblazoned with the number 56, wood shavings, dust motes, the stench of rotting pallets and a sizeable rodent population. At the far end, an open door cut a patch of dim light from darkness.

Wally gulped a gallon of oxygen, tried to decipher the cocking mechanism on his firearm, and shouldered his way forward into war.

At least twenty light switches line the wall, but Wally didn't bother. His eyes adjusted and he peered into dark corners. Rusted I-beams ran the length of the ceiling, his dress shoes creaked loudly and cracked glass filtered streetlight into figures on the floor.

The temperature dropped noticeably upon entering. Wally swung his flashlight beam wildly. He kept his pistol raised, still unsure about the safety, and rushed to catch up with Akira's light in the dark.

They found Jackson Rivers standing before a canvas of broken machinery. At the actor's feet was the carcass of a pigeon shredded with shotgun flak.

"You didn't tell me her kidnappers shapeshifted into motherfucking birds," he said. "I love it. Take me to the king of the bird people."

Save for the machinery, the warehouse looked empty. Wally stopped in his tracks. Something didn't feel right.

Akira darted around shelving units. He led with his gun, moving precisely, action-starved and confused by calm. Water dripped somewhere nearby. The small space still rang with gun blast.

My God, Wally thought. Where was I? Name seven or eight?

"We must delve further," Akira said.

Wally shook his head. "Mr. Akira, we were mistaken. There is no hourglass here. There is no tripwire, no ambush."

Akira's face remained hopeful, though in his eyes Wally saw a creeping sense of defeat.

A false lead, Wally thought. We are at square zero once again.

Akira scanned the walls with his flashlight. His beam revealed nests of rodents and graffiti, but nothing nefarious.

And then there was a sound: footsteps.

Yes, Wally heard it clearly. They were not alone in the warehouse. At least four feet were on the move, cloaked in shadows.

Wally turned as one to a doorway sandwiched by baling machines. A fluorescent bulb flicked to life inside. Jackson Rivers moved to investigate. He strutted, head bobbing, shotgun raised.

Wally only now understood the impressive nature of the actor's bird mauling feat, considering factors ranging from low light to sunglasses. Here is a man able and competent with a firearm, if not intellect, Wally thought, feeling slightly more assured.

Jackson filled the doorframe with muscles and peered. He glanced backwards into Akira's flashlight beam, baffled. Akira positioned himself for reinforcement.

A detective I am not, Wally thought. However, my cleverness, in combination with Akira's nostrils and Jackson's muscles, make for a trio most impregnable.

At once Wally found himself weeping. He might as well have stumbled across his own severed head. Surely we will never find this hourglass, and surely Antonio Noon will bring about my ruin. He cursed himself for falling under the Hollywood spell. A career revival. A star in the making. Sure. A mansion large enough for his vintage bottles. All he needed was to keep quiet. Now he stood on the cusp of his own dismemberment, death without dignity. His metaphors were not enough.

Voices spoke nearby. Strangers. A new, what's the word, timbre.

He shuffled across the stone, attempting to mask his approach.

"Wait," he heard Akira speaking distantly from the lit room. "You guys are *both* named Agent Johansson?"

"We'll ask the questions, detective."

42

Genghis and Sam squared off, elephant and mosquito, strength versus speed. Mouse socked the big man's skull with her metal fist, making a sound like a crushed can. Sam lost her balance. She landed ass first and fell out the doorway. Genghis doubled over, clutching the point of impact. Angel scrambled to find his dropped blade.

"Go!"

Sam set her feet like a sprinter and ran.

The narrow street looked abandoned, yellow orbs lighting cobblestone, a stone wall plastered with fliers for indie bands and missing dogs, graffiti, overflowing ashtrays and shops shuttered until morning. An open apartment window flooded the streets with Czech folk tunes. A shirtless man stood smoking on a balcony.

Holy crap, Sam thought. Real things are happening.

She ran through green space in a square and hopped the hood of a parked car. She spotted a backpacking tourist fifty paces ahead dipping in and out of the light and moved faster, pure instinct, knowing not to look back.

Really now, she thought. I mean, seriously. Of *course* they have ice cream sandwiches in Heaven. What was I thinking? But still. Holy crap. Don't let me die until I catch up on my shows. Gotta make small talk over something in the afterlife. That, and I need to brainstorm what I'll say to Bob Marley.

Mouse caught up.

She pulled Sam down a slit between buildings. The tourist had disappeared. Sam heard lumbering footsteps. They emerged onto a porch overlooking a canal of black and stagnant water.

Dead end.

"Jump."

"Uh...."

Mouse cannonballed into the abyss. Sam hesitated a moment, then leaped.

She hit the water and sank like concrete, thrashing, weighed down by denim. The shock of cold sent air out her nostrils.

Mouse took long breaststrokes, already half a football field downstream.

Fuck, fuck, fuck, fuck, fuck, Sam thought. She squirmed out of her hoodie. She kicked off her shoes. Nothing but oxygen mattered in her life. She flailed limbs in desperation, wondering how Mouse made it look easy, forcing her muscles into action and thinking fuck, fuck, fuck.

Mouse dove and surfaced. In the moonlight her metal arm glistened.

Sam's brain went blank. Adrenaline flatlined. She slowed and sank, then thrashed her way from the depths. Fuck, she thought, unable to conjure much else.

Foul water splashed down her throat and up from her lungs.

Nikole left me for dead. Again. A sister is not a goldfish. You can't just flush me, toss me, feed me to piranhas. Sure, sis, let's go to Iceland. Bring a coat. The hell was I thinking? As if the bitch wouldn't dump me down a sewer. It's what she does. Why am I crying? Why does it still hurt so bad? Beat me, starve me, don't take me to see Daft Punk. But don't fucking leave me. I can't take more alone.

The thought was there half a second. Let go. Stop struggling. This time it's me leaving you. How does it feel?

On the other hand, think of all the mint chocolate chip ice cream left uneaten in this world.

She resolved herself against death and kept pushing.

Her vision bobbed black and blacker, half a head afloat. Somehow, she reached land.

Aching and lightheaded, Sam clawed her way up stone steps into a shopping district. Every movement was agony.

Stray locals roamed a square of stone, statues and cafés painted flamboyant colors. Silhouettes crossed paths on an ancient bridge. A soccer fan with the Czech flag painted on her face stopped and stared at the dripping runaways.

"This way."

Mouse kept moving. Sam wasn't so much running as dragging along. Soaked skin to marrow with freezing water, starved of sustenance, nauseated from the fog and stink of sewage, she felt her everything dwindle. Something odd happened in her bones.

Mouse gestured to stop. Scanning her surroundings, Sam saw nothing of note but heard heavy boots thumping and sensed something else in the air, cobras coiled and ready to strike.

Sweet Jesus, she thought. Not like this. I never got my license. I never beat Big B's record in Mario Kart. I never returned *A Clash of Kings*. I only got first place in laser tag once. At least give me one last ice cream sandwich, Lord, descended from the sky on a beam of light.

Mouse took off and Sam rushed to follow, lunging as hard as she could, legs like twigs.

She moved forwards in jolts, then started to feel dizzy. Synapses fired inside her calorie-starved brain, bouncing between survival instinct and curses for her sister.

She saw ahead a vast crowd assembled on the bridge.

Right. The magic dude. Moon go poof.

A figure waddled in an underpass. Sam recognized the bold outlines of Genghis the giant. She turned to find Angel shouldering his way through a clump of beer guzzlers.

"Come on," Mouse called out. "Keep up."

Mouse leaped ahead, making for a ramp leading to the bridge. Charging forward like electrocuted cattle, Sam punched the air, picturing her sister's face.

A stone arch advertised tourist information. Mouse and Sam huddled in a doorway.

"Did we..." Sam started. Speech felt impossible. Mouse shushed her.

Angel arrived first and started bustling about like a headless sun conure. His silver eyes shimmered in lamplight. Sam felt Genghis in bootsteps before she saw him, birdless. Echoing in the archway, the Black Lotus assassins paused and exchanged whispers. They nodded and pressed onto the bridge.

Sam felt her body giving way to hunger and chill. Cold cut through her torso but she felt the warmth of hope.

"We need to increase our visibility," said Mouse.

"Right," Sam said. "The last thing you'd wanna do when getting chased by terrorists is call 911."

Mouse gazed at the crowd on the bridge. They huddled close for warmth, tugging their coats.

"You're right," Mouse said. "We need cops. We need O.J. Bronco chase. TV cameras. Maximum exposure. Black Lotus is allergic to publicity. I just hope we don't air on one of those news channels that has scrolling text set in some pleb typeface like Tahoma."

Sam shuddered and rubbed her hands. Her fingers felt cold under the skin.

"The magician," Mouse said, scanning the crowd. "Marco Lucks. We're going to kidnap Marco Lucks."

43

At first the Moon just flickered. Tourists waited alongside heroes cast in granite on the Charles Bridge, brandishing biker jackets and binoculars, gearing up for a space odyssey. Hidden speakers breathed the unmistakable crescendos of *Also sprach Zarathustra*. Streetlights painted onlookers and statues a single shade of copper. Across the river, spirals and cathedrals decayed into darkness.

All eyes were on the boy with orange hair. Elevated on a simple stage at the bridge's midpoint, he toyed with fireflies and levitated a globe.

Mouse shouldered through the crowd, co-conspirator in tow. Food, Sam thought with a million o's, shambling like the undead. Right. Punch magic dude in the dick. Get arrested. Can I get ice cream sandwiches smuggled into jail? Will I have to shank a bitch?

Marco Lucks teased his audience with a flick of the wrist. He moved his hand before the floating orb and cast a shadow on the Moon far above. The onlookers gasped with delight.

A single security officer crossed arms near the stage, separated from spectators by a barricade.

Sam went numb from the neck down. Cold, wet and hungry, she felt the bridge or world shift balance beneath her feet. Her socks were soaked. Her jeans were soaked. She was happy about Leo finally winning his Oscar and all, but Hugh Glass never got any awards except, you know, not getting digested by a grizzly and the ability to breathe another few years. Dying of hunger in a city filled with pastry shops. Dying of cold in October. Really? Her head burned. I'm sorry, Jesus, for pondering ice cream sandwiches and Bob Marley tunes when I should be all, praise be, or whatever. Got some stuff I wanna do. See the Grand Canyon and punch my sister in the ovaries. Not ready to go just yet.

Mouse stopped. Water and clumps of sewage littered her hair.

Sam got a whiff of herself and choked. She scanned faces. Their pursuers had gone Waldo. Mild irritation and hardened feet impeded their path, but everyone was too focused on the sky to go Gandalf. Tourists peppered the night with accents and smartphone shutters. The Moon, they kept saying. The Moon, the Moon.

Another crescendo.

"Follow my lead," Mouse said.

Sam felt something internal about to snap. An overwhelming frustration – at her surroundings, her sister, her lack of options, her brain's inability to produce anything but filth and one-liners – boiled to the surface, edging her towards uncharted territory.

If I could do magic, she thought, things would be different.

Thirty yards back a disruption of bodies rippled across the bridge. Somebody else was elbowing for position. Mouse pulled her seaweed-stained gun and kept it low. Eyes skyward, nobody noticed.

A bulky man in flip-flops huffed indignation as the twosome shouldered towards the stage. Sam could see the magician better now. He had what looked like Christmas lights in his hair. He wore a silky black coat and a crucifix around his neck.

If I could do magic, Sam thought, I'd make my sister suffer the way I've suffered. Because there's no common ground. Nikole Fink is an actress in New York City. Had to learn that from Facebook. Runaways don't think about the sister-shaped hole they leave behind. Other girls dream of diamonds and pearls. All I've ever wanted was a sister. Now I have one and she pops pills and lets me die. Fuck her. Fuck the Black Lotus. Fuck this planet and everyone on it.

"Hang on," Mouse said, stumbling. "I feel kinda off."

Cameramen faced off on stage, jockeying for angles, swirling about the conduit of make-believe. Marco Lucks took a final breath. The music climaxed. He covered the floating globe with a black cloth.

Up above, the Moon blinked out.

The disappearing act defied physics. The sky's newfound blankness twinkled with stars and satellites. Nothing glowed. Sunbeams silenced. The Moon was gone. The crowd gaped, dumbfounded, but Sam had experience. Life's too short. Everybody knows that. But what they don't tell you is you'll spend most your time waiting around anyways. Then someone goes away and you realize something about our species. We need food. We need warm. But we need each other just like we need to breathe.

Marco Lucks gestured to his handiwork, half-bowed, awaiting applause, but the crowd was too stunned. As the music died, a faint hum of insect-like noise took over the night.

If I could do magic, Sam thought. If only.

Music resumed. Marco Lucks juggled planets. Only now did the onlookers understand applause was expected and hammered out a meek meeting of palms, still shaken by the impossible occurrence in the sky. Sam found herself crying. The full moon – or lack thereof – was transforming her. She fantasized about switching places with the Black Lotus, killing her past with memory suppressants and executing Nikole Fink. Her loathing swelled and pushed against some internal boundary she never knew existed.

"Distract the guard," Mouse began. "I'll..."

Sam reached out and grabbed Mouse's gun.

The tinkerer, unprepared for such a steal, put up no resistance. Sam gave her no time to react. I'm no illusionist, she thought. I can't draw shapes in the sky. But, now that I've got my own magic wand, I bet people will do what I say.

Marco Lucks added more celestial objects to his juggling routine. At several-second intervals he set a baseball-shaped planet on invisible wire. Slowly he built a model of the solar system floating in halo above his head.

The mustached rent-a-cop, himself succumb to spectacle, paid no notice to Sam's trespass.

She climbed the stage and held her handgun at eye level. Marco Lucks dropped his planets.

"Cut the music," she said.

Marco signaled offstage. The speakers died.

They stared a moment locked in silence. The magician went pallid against his coat. He said something in Czech. Sam moved on instinct. She pounced and grabbed his throat. Pistol to temple, she addressed the camera. "If you want to see the Moon again," she said, "you'll meet me at the docks in two hours with five million Euros in unmarked bills, one gallon of chocolate milk and, I dunno, five or six chicken nuggets. I love me some nuggets."

The sea of faces bobbed somewhere between amusement and curiosity. They think it's part of the show, she thought.

"This is not part of the show."

Neither security nor onlookers showed the slightest alarm.

The night had swallowed her companion. Sam felt dizzy. The river had sapped her adrenaline. She lost track of which way went up. What now?

She aimed at the Moon and fired.

Panic erupted. Onlookers gasped and ducked, clutching necks and air and children. A poncho-wrapped grandma near stage couldn't decide whether to clap or cry. The cop dropped prone. He appeared unarmed. On both sides the crowd swelled like a pre-tsunami sea. A human wave lulled, crested, and so began the Charles Bridge Stampede.

Bodies tumbled. Screams peppered the air. A thunderstorm of boots and sneakers sounded like hooves. A diver built like an Olympian leaped off the bridge. It took a small army of mothers to prevent a blonde adolescent from doing the same.

Sam reveled in her chaos. Through her hoodie she felt Marco's heart pounding harder than her own.

Mouse jumped onto stage. Amidst the scrambling limbs below marched two familiar Black Lotus assassins.

"Run!"

44

The trio scrambled for shadows. Hypothermia, hunger and a wail of police sirens barked at their heels. Sam strode quickly. The gun added weight to her soaked jeans.

Marco Lucks made no attempt at escape. He bounced along, in fact, thrilled at his own kidnapping, guiding his captors to the city's cubbies, speaking excitedly in Czech every few paces. Mouse battered her way through screeching moon gazers and sobbing children. The bridge had become a war zone brimming with shell shock and refugees.

Sam blubbered her lips. Are we doing the thing? She blinked rapid fire, unsure if they were indeed doing the thing.

They made it off the bridge. Midnight traffic hummed under a mix of centuries: trendy storefronts and remnants of castles, baroque walls and glass towers, sports cars, trolley wires, lines snaking out of nightclubs and bass pounding through walls.

"We lost them," Mouse reported, glancing over her shoulder. "I think."

The stampede melted into sidewalk traffic. Remnants wandered dazed and lost, craning necks skyward to check on the Moon. Had it been part of the show after all? Yes, they decided. Nothing out of the ordinary. Sure, we're down a celestial object and some spectators got crushed, but at least it's part of the show.

Marco Lucks marched head down and hood up, sheathing his orange hair.

A black miasma chased them along streets with unpronounceable names, broken in places by headlights and halos. Sam felt herself changing.

I'd want Ellen Page, she thought. No one else will do. I mean, okay, it wouldn't be *my* biopic, but, after all, I'd play a part. Emma Watson could play Nikole. Will they come live with us? You know, to study our quirks and personas and all? Scratch that. I'd want Bill Murray. Nontraditional casting, sure. But I woke up feeling gender fluid today and who are you to judge?

A police cruiser squealed around a parked bus.

"Shit," Mouse said. "Run!"

So they ran.

The alleyway spilled into an intersection. Horns blared and tires screeched around a stray kitten who couldn't decide on a sidewalk. A dark-skinned sailor held his ankles. Two of his shipmates arm-wrestled on the flat table of his back. All around loomed the allure of stone and plaster, sports chants wafting from noisy bars, the smell of sausage and steam rising from the streets.

Marco led the way. Mouse spoke into Sam's ringing ear, encouraging her to drop the gun. Police cruisers were impeded by foot traffic. A homeless man urinated on a cruiser's windshield.

They slinked through Prague casting no shadows, passing between glass and concrete, exploring the city's endless alleys and spires.

An obese officer in all white lumbered behind them. Gun drawn, he screamed in more languages than Sam knew existed.

"Stop!" he coughed. "Stůj! Arrêtez! Halt! Alto! Lõpõdaq! Taxawal! Ndalo! Shecherdit!"

Marco found an opening between bricks, seemingly by sense of smell, and ushered his captors down a dumpster-lined lane. Sam's feet sent pangs from shin to knee with every step. She shifted in and out of numbness and full body aches, wondering if she was already dead.

Nah, she decided.

Ellen Page would be better cast as Mouse, Sam thought. She's got that jawline. Murray's my go-to but I'd settle for Benedict Cumberbatch.

Underfoot the sidewalk felt taut, about to crack.

Marco, Mouse and Sam took cover near a contractor van and watched police dart past. The multilingual mountain of flab lagged thirty paces back.

"That was brilliant," Marco said, speaking English for the first time. "Did Lazlo put you up to it? I'd be pissed that he didn't clue me in but, no, it was perfect. The look on my face! The crowd really bought it!"

Sam felt strange as she stood. Her legs didn't want to unfold.

"Well," Marco said, cracking a smile, "how long will you keep me prisoner? The audience has reassembled at the bridge, awaiting return of their precious Moon. People need things like that. Anchors. Objects in the sky that never change, never go away. We need that to make sense of life." He gasped. "What if you hold me for a week? Panic! Disorder in the streets! And then, on the seventh day..."

The cops doubled back as the trio crossed the street.

"It's them!" one shouted.

They sprinted up another cobblestone crevice. The blackness seemed absolute.

Ahead, trees peeked from behind a plaster wall. A blue dumpster made an effective stepladder. Marco eyed it first.

You know, Sam thought, if they're gonna make me into a movie, I gotta up my game. I'm not badass enough to fool a dude, even at gunpoint. Gotta get me some skull tattoos.

Marco scaled the dumpster and hopped over the wall. Mouse and Sam struggled to follow.

They found themselves in a city of the dead. Jutting in mist, a thousand ancient gravestones battled for space in confines so tight that the dead must be buried ten deep. Headstones flaking with age ran right up against the wall. They formed piles and barricades, in patches torn asunder like victims of an earthquake.

Movement was a chore. Sam banged her shin into a grave older than America and felt no pain.

Her sneakers crunched leaves and gravel. Commotion echoed from the land of the living. Here ghosts lay in repose, silent but somehow alive, an army of bodies six feet and as many centuries removed.

Mouse wrenched back her gun.

"We make quite the team," she said. "If you have even a passing interest in graphic design, I'd love to collaborate." She aimed the gun at Marco. "You," she said. "Chill with your ancestors here a while. Then leave. Tell the cops what you want. Make up a story."

He looked disappointed.

Five feet from the cemetery gate, Sam stopped.

"Wait," she said. Something lurched inside her.

Mouse trembled, looking impatient.

"I can't move," Sam said.

Reminders of the canal bath rattled her spine. Another breeze and she nearly choked. The passage of air in and out of her lungs became slower.

"Please," she said. "I gotta eat something. I gotta dry off."

"No time," said Mouse.

Sam willed her feet into motion. An off-white Volvo approached outside the gates.

Mouse stopped the car with gun drawn. Sirens sounded in the distance.

Sam fell to one knee, heart exhausted.

Mouse hoisted her to her feet. She was speaking something but her words were blurry shapes. She felt herself entering a stolen car.

Sam wanted to sleep. Her muscles had begun a pre-death ritual, shutting down one at a time, prolonging the fuel of her body's core. The world felt far away. A shadow crept from another plane. Nothing mattered. Not as much as this thing that's like sleep but isn't quite sleep. She hung her head. The world went blank behind her eyes and vanished as completely as the Moon.

45

The angel came up Church Street. He drew figure eights outside the butcher's shop, iris-eyed, stubble-headed, sheathed by dawn. Stray dogs chased his bicycle. In city steam the boy found wings and halos. Wally rested his forehead on the hotel window. Tribeca was awake already, abuzz with taxis and beggars and bald men barking into phones. One World Trade Center loomed over urban sprawl like a distant mountain peak.

Wally imagined a virus leaping body to body and wondered how quickly plague could take Manhattan. What did they call it? The Black Death. Yes, blackness creeping in clouds, insecticide for humans, washing us clean. Because every so often a planet needs a new beginning. He didn't have the heart to record the metaphor.

Agent Johansson joined Wally near the window and rested his hand on Wally's shoulder.

"We understand you are upset, Mr. Algayar," he said, "but understand that we intervened for your own protection. You don't seem to understand the situation. You're playing a perilous game."

The other Johansson walked through the hotel room and placed his palm on his other shoulder, an unwelcome advance.

"Extremely perilous," he said.

"Who are you guys?" Akira asked, sitting legs akimbo at the corner of the bed. "Are you CIA?"

Johansson smiled. "We are your friends," he said.

"You see," Wally began, "I am not a political man. I am more, shall we say, a scholar. I can count to ten in five languages. I have investigated several unsolved mathematical theorems. But I am not well-versed in the art of espionage. I must insist you cease and, what's the word..." He trailed off, frustrated beyond vocabulary.

The agents stood stoic, arms crossed.

Will you please expand upon this 'Black Lotus' menace?" Wally asked. "Will you tell me what is going on?"

"That's classified."

"Though it's interesting you're pursuing such a line of questioning," the other added. "Do you travel internationally often?"

He shrugged.

"Interesting response."

Both men scribbled notes on legal pads, using their thighs as tables.

"We cannot have you poking about town," Johansson said. "Your meddling threatens to undo our progress. Do not worry. We will keep Nikole Fink safe, Mr. Algayar."

Wally squinted. "Nikole Fink? She is in danger?"

The Johanssons craned their necks in unison and stared as though Wally had uttered an incomprehensible riddle.

"Officially we have no comment, though I will say that we warned her against getting involved. Everything was constructed precisely, down to a science."

"An extreme science," the other echoed.

"But the hourglass we did not anticipate. Rachel seems to have conjured it out of ether."

"Rachel?" Wally asked. "Who is Rachel?"

"Nikole," Agent Johansson said. "Sorry."

Wally and Akira shared a glance.

"The hourglass is the great unknown," Agent Johansson continued. "Someone must have planted it after we'd left the scene,"

"The scene? You mean you two were in the cave?"

The agents said "no comment" with their eyes.

The agent nearest Wally smiled. "It is all for the greater good, though the details are classified. Rest assured no harm will come to her."

"Though there is one final detail," the other Johansson said. He hesitated a moment. Wally noticed that both men were hovering their hands near their hip-mounted firearms. "You are in possession of stolen property, are you not?"

Wally felt his heart rate increase.

"A vial of blood," Agent Johansson specified.

The two men stood shoulder-to-shoulder and began boxing Wally into a corner. They moved laterally and shielded Akira from view.

"This blood is useless to you, Mr. Algayar. It must be destroyed. You cannot fathom the magnitude of the object you carry."

"Extreme magnitude."

Wally swallowed. "I, ahem, must defer to..." he began.

Johansson drew a stun gun from inside his jacket pocket, keeping his other hand near his pistol.

"Proceeding to subdue target."

Daggers pierced his ribcage and Wally found himself paralyzed. Confused as to why his muscles disobeyed orders, he stood for a moment a grotesque sculpture framed in the morning light, gasping for air before collapsing to the floor.

"Target is subdued."

Johansson crouched over him and began probing his pockets. His fingers touched something hard. The vial. Wally, you imbecile, he thought. Why not squirrel it away in a floor safe or cubbyhole? Yes, he decided. I must demarcate several cubbyholes in my home at the soonest opportunity, though I fear the idea has reached me too late.

Akira leaped from the bedside. He wrapped an elastic cord around the standing Johansson's neck and pulled. A gurgling noise came from his throat.

The crouched agent turned. Akira swiveled his kicking captive into the man's path and sent him sprawling. He reached for his gun.

"The taser, Mr. Wally!" Akira shouted.

Wally struggled to move. His arms felt run through with metal rods. Every movement was a marathon.

He tapped the stun gun with his foot and succeeded at kicking it to within arm's length. As Johansson drew his firearm, Wally aimed the nefarious device and fired into his back.

"The gun, Mr. Wally!" Akira shouted, straining to keep control over his victim.

Wally felt his motor control slowly returning. He flopped onto his belly and swiveled, then crawled forward the way he'd seen soldiers in war movies advance on enemy positions.

What madness! Does he expect me to slay the man?

Wally retrieved the stunned agent's firearm and took aim.

Akira let go.

Agent Johansson raised his hands in surrender. Akira yanked the gun off his hip.

"There are so many things we can do to you," Johansson managed to cackle, swallowing hard, "that you will find worse than death."

My God, Wally thought. What are we doing?

Akira retrieved the blood vial. He helped Wally to his feet. The fallen agent eyed Wally through broken sunglasses. In his pupils, Wally saw a newfound respect.

Akira motioned for the standing Johansson to sit on the bed. He complied.

"Your keys."

Johansson reached into his jacket and Wally thought, my God, this is it. Surely we will be killed. But the agent dutifully retrieved his car keys and nothing more.

Then they were sprinting down the hotel hallway, hearts pounding, out of breath, checking every so often over their shoulders.

Perhaps a gymnasium devotee could descend seven flights faster than Wally Algayar, but not without bruising a few bones. His ankles took the concrete hardest. Adrenaline roared to life, clouding his senses and dulling pain.

Wally shoved his stolen gun into his pocket and pulled his sweatshirt over the butt.

They emerged into the hotel lobby. A pair of brunette women in red vests juggled phones behind the reception desk. They paid the would-be assassins little mind.

They raced across the parking lot towards the agents' white

contractor van. Just like the movies, Wally thought.

Akira used the man's keys and shifted into reverse. Wally scanned the mirrors for pursuers, and the hotel windows for snipers.

"You are insane!" Wally shouted. "We will be killed!"

Akira said nothing. He lurched the van into traffic.

Wally made to stash his gun in the glove box. As he clicked open the glove box, his jaw dropped.

There it was, a rip in the fabric of physics, engraved with zigzags and words of distant ancestors, the secrets of heaven and earth or a paperweight.

"We have found your hourglass, Mr. Wally," Akira said.

46

The Chemist took turns stabbing his teeth with a toothpick and examining his fingernails. His body bore the deflated skin of recovering obesity. Two partially eaten hamburgers – one waning, one waxing – served as paperweights on his desk. "Officially," he began, "this chemist has orders to set you free."

A trio of masked soldiers finished chaining Nikole to the wall in crucifix pose. She felt too sick to move, let alone speak. She knew they'd done it to Carlos too, the eyeworm, and secretly took pleasure in this fact. Her body ached from her most recent panic attack and already she felt another coming on.

Carlos outstretched his arms for the shackles as though he'd had practice.

"We were meant to observe you," The Chemist said, making no eye contact. "Now I must explain to my superiors why you are my prisoner. You show up in costume as Mouse with the aim of springing your friend from captivity." He paused. "Surely you are not such a fool to think your scheme would work."

A plumper, oranger man stood in the corner of the concrete room, his arms crossed, his gaze unsettling. His face, punctuated by floppy ears and a stubble of a John Holmes mustache, looked decidedly void of mercy. Nikole knew to fear him.

She'd been warned about Xanax withdrawal from every corner of the internet. Yes, it could kill. No, it shouldn't be done cold turkey, not alone, not without trained medical staff within puking distance. Seizures, respiratory failure, cardiac arrest. Rare, sure. But long term abuse rewrites your DNA.

Nikole squirmed inside her anorak, still wondering if that's what it's called, sweating, aching, her intestines a tangle of wires.

"This chemist has a theory that you are in league with the American spies."

Nikole's eyes made soup of the world. She slouched mired in soreness. The cuffs were already rubbing her wrists raw.

"The Johanssons?" she asked.

The Chemist scanned his captives, bound against the wall like a gallows waiting room from medieval times. His head swiveled with the sloth of a bulldozer in a neck brace. A thunderous bout of laughter escaped his lips with such unexpected force that its shockwave sent Nikole reeling.

"So it is true!" he said, catching his breath. "You have been working to bring down the Black Lotus all along. Everything has been an elaborate scheme, no?"

Carlos shot her a dirty look. "God dammit, Rachel."

The second officer, the orange man, had singled Nikole out for an unwavering stare-down. She knew instinctively that he was the real threat. A glimmer of sadomasochism enveloped him like a satanic halo.

There was a knock on the door: "Sir! We have situation!"

The Chemist held up his palm.

"Not now, Dmitri."

He lit a cigarette and shuffled paperwork. There was a tense silence. Nikole felt the orange man's gaze like radiation from a distant star.

"Vladimir," said the chemist, "what should we do with these spies?"

The orange man only drilled deeper with his stare, maintaining military silence.

"Vladimir is not in a speaking mood," The Chemist said. "This is a very bad sign for you. When Vladimir is not in a speaking mood, it means his thoughts have become very sick. Vladimir, have your thoughts become very sick?"

Again, the orange man was silent.

"Oh, this is not a good sign for you. Vladimir's head is a sick place."

"Please," Carlos said.

The Chemist grew giddy with delight and drummed his fingers against the desk. "Oh, my favorite!" he exclaimed. "When they beg - that is my favorite. Right, Vladimir?"

Vladimir did not respond.

"Oh, this is a very bad sign for you." As The Chemist stood, every fold of his excess skin shuddered separately like a ripple moving through jelly. "Excuse me," he said. "I must make a shit. I will leave you with Vladimir, but I must warn you that if he begins acting on his sick thoughts, I will be too far away to hear your screams."

The subordinate returned, to the door, blocking the chemist's path. He looked tremor-stricken, post-nightmare, gobs of sweat poking through his flesh.

"Sir!" he repeated in broken English. "We have situation!" He paused, then added, "We have school bus!"

The Chemist sighed, screwed up his face and buried it with a palm.

"You see, Vladimir," he said, "this is why we do not make safe house in historical site. This chemist told you there would be consequence. Now we must gas a busload of children on field trip." He turned to his lackey. "How many?"

The man hesitated. "Well," he said, "to begin, they are not children."

They've arrived, Nikole thought. She couldn't remember the next part of the plan. Her brain had become a stopwatch. Thirteen hours, twenty-seven minutes, fifteen seconds and counting. Sixteen, seventeen. Her head kept ticking, reminding her how long she'd been without her Xanax. She knew it was about to get worse, the hunger, and not the kind in her stomach. She felt a big decision coming on.

"They are... how shall I say?"

"Speak!" yelled The Chemist.

"They are dressed like Hitler, sir."

The room went quiet. Even stoic Vladimir jerked his head in reaction to the strangeness.

The Chemist stared at his underling. "Hitler?" he asked. "As in Adolf?"

The messenger nodded.

"You are telling me that a school bus full of Hitler impersonators has pulled to our doorstep?"

He nodded.

The Chemist looked at Nikole. "What are you scheming, spy?"

Nikole's eyelids slid like sandpaper. She blinked hard, drawing no moisture. Vaguely she recalled the next part of Mouse's plan, but behind her forehead she was plotting her own route, A to B, understating that the *to* part is where things might get rough.

"Are they armed?" The Chemist asked.

"Yes, sir. They speak of rescuing the princess and impaling the infidel."

"Rescuing the... Dammit. Our cover's blown. Already we have broken protocol." He turned to Nikole. "You win today, spy. But this chemist will remember his humiliation. This chemist will find you. You cannot hide. We will meet again."

The Chemist ushered out his soldiers and Vladimir, who cast Nikole one final glare of impalement, and slammed the door behind him.

Carlos groaned and tugged against his shackles.

"I don't even want to ask," he said. "What the hell have you gotten us into now, Rachel?"

"Why do you keep calling me that?"

Carlos rolled his eyes. "Because that's your name. I swear to God, Rachel, you'll never grow up."

Commotion radiated opposite the door, a petrified slab of cedar. Voices spoke excitedly in German, jumping between giddy elation to barking orders to mumbling something about "the infidel." Their voices grew as they neared.

"Okay," Nikole said, "this is the part you aren't going to like."

"Wonderful."

Nikole slouched against the wall and waited, feeling ancient coldness through her anorak.

Then she made a big decision.

47

A gaggle of Hitlers filed through the door.

Their hair was dyed and combed over, their mustaches ubiquitous. Some were short, others tall. A particularly unconvincing doppelganger came wearing glasses, a mustache that looked more like a waterfall of carpet, a green turtleneck and jeans. Some sported full regalia Nazi uniforms, but most opted for casual attire. They buzzed with excitement. Numbering a dozen or so, the men congregated around Carlos.

"The infidel!" gasped a Hitler in a tracksuit. "We have found the infidel!"

Elation rippled through the crowd. "The infidel! The infidel!"

"See how he has chained this innocent woman to the wall!"

"What?" Carlos asked, eyes bulging with surreality. "I'm chained up too, you fucking lunatics."

Nikole's existence played like a VHS tape rewound too many times. She couldn't account for three of the last six months. The pills had made Swiss cheese of her brain. Memories eroded and in their place came noise. Did I set fire to my mother? What's one thing I did in August? I've lost all my friends. Every one. I pop pills and watch reruns of my life on TV. Sometimes, when it goes dark behind my eyes, I weigh the pros and cons of destroying myself. I'm still in the deciding phase on that one.

Their cheer soured into a shouting match. The room became a circus of Nazi salutes and harsh German syllables.

Nikole wondered if she were hallucinating. She sagged or swam against her bonds, feverish, joints and sockets askew.

But she'd made the decision. She had a plan.

Step one: get out of here.

A newcomer stepped through the fray. His presence calmed the others. He came dressed not as Hitler, but like a Nazi propaganda poster come to life. A spiky pseudo-mountain of dyed blonde rested on his scalp. His uniform spared no expense. Emblazoned with epaulets and medals, its red fabric looked regal in fluorescent light. The stench of chewing tobacco hung heavy with his each exhalation.

One of the Hitlers bowed his head. "Commandant," he said.

The Commandant stopped in the middle of the room and removed his leather gloves one finger at a time.

"Gentlemen," he said in a painfully overacted accent. "As part of this year's Hitler lookalike contest, I am pleased to announce the commencement of the twenty-third annual infidel hunt." The Hitlers nodded, barely concealing their excitement. "I shall now unchain the infidel. He must run, and we must catch him."

"God dammit, Rachel," Carlos shouted. "It can never be easy with you. What the fuck is this shit? What have you dragged me into now?"

Nikole's throat thudded with panic. She tried to brainstorm talking points, negotiation tactics, but all that played in her brain was static.

The Commandant unclasped the iron shackles that held Carlos to the wall. He fell knee first to the floor, breaking the momentum with both hands. He cowered for a moment in a sea of combat boots, then looked up at Nikole, asking with his eyes what to do.

"Run, infidel," the Commandant commanded.

He hesitated.

"God dammit, Rachel."

Carlos darted through the doorway. The Hitlers waited with tobacco-stained smiles. A minute passed, then two. Then they tore away in pursuit, jockeying for position, shouting over one another in German, drowning the world in an artillery barrage of clambering boots and shrieks of joy.

The Commandant stayed behind. He unhooked Nikole and sent her likewise stumbling to the ground. She swallowed and spent a moment mired in dust, then painfully pushed herself to her feet.

He stood and performed a military-style pirouette, painfully over-acting a Nazi salute – a click of the boots, a pump of the chest and a hand extended forty-five degrees.

"Heil!"

Nikole stared a moment.

"Um," she began. "Hi. Thanks for, uh... Mouse had told me to, um..."

The man stood stoic, arm extended, silent.

"Could I, um..."

He repeated the salute and Nikole got the feeling he was awaiting reciprocal. Awkwardly, she returned a limp variation of the salute.

"Sorry," she said. "Where I'm from, we usually just shake hands."

He laughed shrilly.

"Call me Commandant Kovac, Hero of the People. Yes, I know your friend Mouse. I figured she'd call to cash in her favor one of these days. You meet some interesting people in her line of work. Don't you? You'll excuse my men. They're short on brain cells. I, on the other hand, am a man of great honor and skill. You see, we are not *Nazis*. We have particular historical interests. We are history buffs."

"Oh," Nikole said. She blinked, unsure what else to add.

"We seem to have scared off your friends," he continued. "They thought us to be armed. Ha!" He laughed shrilly, baring teeth the color of milky tea. "Like I'd trust those morons with a slingshot! I, on the other hand, am a man of great stature and, I should add, a born natural with the Luger."

He showed Nikole his antique pistol.

"Um... okay."

"The fate of all Europe – indeed the world – rests on my shoulders," the man continued. "Pride yourself, American, on having met the hero of the Battle of Jánosík. Yes, this humble hero single-handedly overthrew the communist rat Viktor Bartok and threw him into the Hall of Traitors where he will rot for his transgressions." He laughed more bizarre noise. "Those idiots running around in their costume mustaches know little of the world. I, on the other hand, am a man of great..."

Nikole waved her hands. "Look, Mr. Hitler Youth," she snapped, "I don't give a fuck about your historical interests. Yeah, dressing up like a Nazi. Great hobby you got there. Meanwhile, back in reality, I'm sick and I need medicine. And you aren't fooling anyone with that dye job. So can you help me, or would you rather fuck yourself?"

She didn't know where it came from. The anger. Is it inside me always, masked by pills? Is this what I'm like in my natural habitat? And, more importantly, is it a real gun? I'll need a gun for the next step.

The Nazi only smiled. "It appears we have arrived at a misunderstanding. An impasse, if you will. I am something of a doctor myself, having sewn up many combat wounds and created many more."

Nikole shook her head. "I need medicine."

"Well, in that case, perhaps we should go into town. There is but one pharmacy in Central Europe that passes my stringent tests of ideological purity. Fortunately, it is not a long drive."

"Can you take me?"

He smiled wider. "As I have already explained, m'lady, I am a man of honor."

"Will you bring the gun?" Nikole asked.

He narrowed his eyes. "Of course."

Onto step two.

48

Because all that's left is the A to B of it. The mechanics. Just following orders, sir. I've already done step one. Step three is eat the pills, so I'm a third done with the thing already. Too late to change course. Soon I'll have them. Then we can deal with lesser concerns, like water and food, Sam's survival and figuring out what Mom died to protect.

In the mirror, Commandant Kovac flashed fake blue contact lenses. "I assure you, American, this is the most ideologically pure pharmacy in all of Europe."

Nikole mumbled noise. She felt post-trauma, pre-tumor, doused in nauseous sweat, ready to strike.

One parent goes poof, the other up in smoke. You wonder how the world keeps going. Don't these people know that one day it'll happen to them? And yet they keep clocking in and out, climbing the career ladder, Folgers, mortgage, missionary, morgue, in the agreed-upon pattern. The rules. What you're supposed to do. Never mind the cancer behind the curtain. These things won't happen to you.

Nikole's seatbelt was a cage. Forest fires burned in her stomach. Every surface felt abrasive to the touch, as though the world had turned into sandpaper. The last time she'd gone cold turkey... Well, best not to talk about last time.

"We are close."

At its outskirts, the city of Lučenec, Slovakia, was filled with unkempt fields and decrepit concrete, cars older than Nikole, colorful houses and gated apartments, farmland in various stages of seasonal shutdown and powerlines, everywhere powerlines. A shirtless farmer in overalls stood on his porch, pitchfork in hand, his face from a famous painting.

Nikole kept her eye on the gun.

A dark-skinned man and his son walked curbside lugging toolkits.

"See that man?" asked her neo-Nazi chauffeur. "See how he's trying to make a better life for his family? He could be a secret terrorist, you know. Those are the worst. The kind who pay taxes and send their children to school and work in our factories and don't blow themselves up. They live their lives peacefully and die in old age and nobody ever knows they were terrorists. Best not to take chances."

I've never fired a gun before, Nikole thought. But it seems easy enough.

Downtown Lučenec looked Prague lite, a European fusion of baroque and glass, cobblestone and electric cars, old churches and a timeline of monuments to dictators and invasions.

Then there's the safety. Right? Some kind of switch. But I'm smart. I've been in movies. I can figure it out.

The pharmacy advertised itself as an apothecary. It occupied a stone building that looked more like a pint-sized mansion than a CVS. It sat behind a waist-high fence and garden. Its bushes and brick walls served as shelves for litter.

Nikole tried to view this world through the eyes of the Commandant with varying degrees of failure. She brainstormed lines from manifestos, closed her eyes and tried to fill herself with revolutionary zeal. All you do is aim and shoot.

"Well," said the driver, grinning widely, "we have arrived."

She didn't hesitate this time.

Nikole lurched forward and snatched the Nazi's gun from his waist, giving him no time to react. She tumbled into the avenue. Her heart felt flimsy, frozen, about to break.

She didn't look back. Left, right, left. Forward march. Soon they'll be mine. Soon I'll be better.

She burst through the pharmacy door, holding the gun the way she'd done in movies.

Pill bottles lined the walls. A man in a red windbreaker shuffled euros across the counter. A beaker of fluid sat atop a wooden counter. Minimalist paintings were mounted on the walls beside disclaimer forms and diagrams of internal organs.

A white-haired woman noticed the gun. She reeled, eyes wide, frantically tapping her husband's shoulder. Nikole raised the weapon and the woman, already pale by nature, turned transparent.

Nikole locked the door with its chain. She moved quickly. The cashier trembled and readied the register. Nikole shook her head.

"No," she said. "Xanax."

She felt her grip on false reality fading. Just like the movies, she told herself. It's just the script. These are just lines. I'm holing a prop, playing a part. None of this is real.

Nikole aimed at the ceiling and pulled the trigger, just to see how it felt.

No new chaos emerged. As the gun blast died, Nikole noticed the stillness. Customers went fetal as though hiding from a predator who sensed through movement.

A customer breathed Slavic curse words. Nikole shot a glance outside and saw a passerby speaking hurriedly into his cell phone.

"Faster!" Nikole shouted.

The man in red had gone chalky. Black veins stood out in patterns. Nikole had never seen color drain from a person like that.

Nikole snatched a paper bag from the pharmacist's hand.

Five paces towards the door, she stopped.

It didn't feel like a panic attack. No. This was something different, something new. Every cell in her body grew still. Sound became tinnitus became silence. She tasted blood and copper. A customer lunged and knocked her to the floor. Helpless, Nikole watched a bottle of Xanax roll out of her reach. She felt the gun torn from her hand. Someone spoke rapidly into a cell phone. "Políciu! Políciu!" When I die, Nikole thought, I won't know what happens tomorrow.

•••

Nikole blinked. Paramedics. Passed time. A forest of feet surrounded her. She knew what it was. She didn't have a panic attack. She had a seizure.

She tried to move her hands only to discover they'd been cuffed. Her neck grated as she scanned the room. Police took statements from a cashier. That's it, she thought. I'm done. Put me in the chair. Throw me in the hall of traitors. Hang me by neck until dead. I'll confess. I'll sign your forms. Anything to stop the pain.

A bearded cop studied her on the floor.

"You are under arrest."

49

Red and blue lights flashed in the mirrors. Mouse looked afraid. She pulled over to the curb.

"Okay," she said. "Let's think this through."

A mass of rain moved across fields like a locust swarm. To their left, highway traffic hummed under an overpass.

"Were you speeding?" Sam asked.

"I don't know. I don't fucking know. Okay?"

The vastness of the Hungarian countryside stretched before them. A hatchback zipped by blasting Beethoven's Fifth. Car-high shrubs lined the road in a line stretching to the horizon.

"Do you understand the situation? We're in a vehicle that we stole at gunpoint, we have no ID and we've got two illegal weapons in the car. If he's got a partner, he'll come stand by the passenger door. If it's just one guy, I'll take him down hand-to-hand. If he's got a partner, you'll need to open fire."

"What?" Sam gasped. "They're *cops*."

In the Volvo's mirrors, Sam watched a white door emblazed with the word "Rendőrség" swing slowly open.

"Shit. He's got a partner."

They'd spent the night in Bratislava, paying for the hotel with cash. In the morning, they hummed through the countryside rested and freshly showered, stomachs satisfied. Sorta. Two thousand calories of milkshakes and chicken sandwiches later, Sam still felt hungry. She examined the fabric of her new pullover and pined for her tattered hoodie. Curse you, Prague sewage. Where will I find that color again?

The problems started when they crossed into Hungary. They'd traveled hardly a mile past the border when police lights corralled their stolen Volvo to the curb.

Sam slouched in her seat. The partner made it as far as the rear passenger door and stopped, his lower half – firearm and all – visible in the mirror.

Mouse rolled down the window.

"Good morning," said the cop, speaking English. He had a faint mustache and potbelly and exuded an odor of spoiled bananas. He leaned into the driver's side window. "Where are you ladies heading?"

"Valuska," Mouse said, truthfully telling them the name of the small Hungarian village that was their destination.

"I'm afraid you're mistaken," the officer told her. "No such place exists."

Mouse kept her eyes trained forward.

"Go ahead," said the officer, smiling. "Look it up."

Mouse slowly pulled her smartphone from the cup holder, swiped and typed. Sure enough, the village of Valuska had been erased from Google Maps. As Mouse worked, Sam heard firearms leaving holsters.

Black Lotus.

Mouse didn't wait for what happened next. She floored the accelerator. Sam's body lurched against seatbelt and fabric as they skidded into traffic, leaving the officers scrambling for their cruiser.

"Hold on!" Mouse shouted.

They zipped between hills shaped like breasts, their forests ablaze in autumn. Shacks sagged on farmland of shrubs and muddy rivers, exotic flowers and outcroppings of sunbaked rocks.

A shot rang out, ricocheting off the passenger door.

"Fuck!" Sam shouted. She tried to flatten herself against the seat, compressing her spine. "Can't you call the cops? The real cops, I mean?"

"They *are* real cops," Mouse shouted over the engine. "They're being manipulated. Eye worms."

"So what do we do?"

"Dunno. Thinking."

Deeper into the Hungarian countryside they plunged, puppet cops in tow. A red Peugeot darted past, impervious to the hazards of the chase. An eighteen-wheeler played it safer, spraying their windshield with road waste. The mirrors filled with flashing colors and potholes.

"This is going badly," Mouse said.

She slammed the gas. Sam bounced window to console.

Their stolen car skidded across two lanes of trucks and then some. Mouse turned too hard and they slid across rumble strips onto the shoulder, trading paint with a guard rail. Sam clung to her seatbelt. Her skull connected with the window.

Sam looked at the sky. Sup, Jesus. So about last night. I kinda figured we had all my karma issues sorted out in the sewage. Could you not?

A second cruiser joined the pursuit.

What if you close your eyes and that's it? A feeling of gloom came over her. Death felt real this time, closer than it did in Prague. Sam curled into a ball. No stimuli, she thought. Total darkness. The thought gave her soul frostbite.

Trees stretched across a valley out the passenger side. A blot of fuzz moved like liquid crystals and Sam had to stare a moment before she realized they were sheep.

"Should I shoot back?" Sam asked.

Mouse had a look on her face that might have been laughter under different circumstances. "Don't get yourself killed, kid."

The engine roared. They slid across lanes. Mouse's own skull tasted window. The growling decibels of police sirens gained strength. Terrified motorists squealed tires on a stone bridge ahead.

"So what do we do? What the fuck do we do?"

Horns blared as she maneuvered around brake lights.

"The Black Lotus arrange historical forces against us," said Mouse, her voice the picture of calm. She sat with impeccable posture, hands at ten and two. "History is what we're up against. How familiar are you with the Roma people?"

"Um..."

"Gypsies."

"Um..."

"The most hated people in Europe. An easy target. Helena thinks she's clever by hiding among them. But she's wrong. An entire settlement could disappear and no one would care. Valuska is a Gypsy settlement. Looks like it's already gone."

"Sure," Sam said. "Whatever. It's just, you know, we won't be breathing in a few seconds, so..."

Another gunshot rang out and Sam's side view mirror splintered into highway debris.

"Shit!"

A third cruiser joined the chase, then a fourth.

Maybe it's real, she thought. The pearly gates, the angels, the clouds. Shouldn't there be a password? There's gotta be some safeguard. You can't run around picking pockets and stealing cars and then, two seconds before the curtains close, pledge to play nice. Right?

They zoomed around a lake held back by an ancient retaining wall. Evergreens poked through the brush. Signs in Hungarian advertised alien messages.

One of the cops gunned it and pulled up beside Sam. The bearded officer flashed a firearm. Another cop remained stoic and steely-eyed, hugging their bumper.

Sam cradled her head. A gallon of acid boiled in her stomach and she thought she might throw up.

"I might throw up," she said.

Mouse lifted her pistol from her coat. The cop's eyes bulged and he fell back. The cruisers settled into an arrowhead formation.

A symphony of noise flooded the highway. Mouse pushed the Volvo past redline. SUVs and hatchbacks pulled to the shoulders, traffic parting like the Red Sea. A truck couldn't decide on lanes and blocked both, stalling the police.

Mouse slid to the shoulder, but this time met no guardrail. One wheel touched dirt and she almost lost control. Two cruisers back, a cop wasn't as lucky.

"There!" Mouse shouted.

A lumbering eighteen-wheeler crawled near a barrier. The sign was in

Hungarian, but Sam understood the big flashing arrow perfectly well. The two-lane highway's right lane was closed ahead.

The car wobbled, lurched, roared with fury. Cops swarmed like wasps.

"Gotta time it right."

The truck gained speed and began to merge.

The cops entered death throes, turning their cruisers into battering rams. Sam's bones jolted as metal met metal. The rear passenger window cracked with gunfire. Shards of glass washed over Sam's neck.

"Now!"

The engine screamed in protest. She pushed three digits of speed. The truck and Volvo converged on the single open lane. More metal and sparks as they traded paint.

Mouse's rear bumper was smashed between cab and concrete, but it stumbled through. In the mirrors Sam watched the truck lumber at tortoise pace, blocking the pursuit.

Holy shit, Sam thought. It's working. Bob Marley, you and I will meet another day.

Empty highway stretched to the horizon ahead.

Trembling, Mouse didn't let off the gas. "Okay," she said. "That'll buy us some time."

50

Sam busied herself checking for pursuers. So far, the road was empty. She touched her chest and felt her heart decelerate. The road turned from asphalt to gravel to dirt, then back to gravel again. Their stolen Volvo handled the terrain admirably.

"So," Sam breathed, "that was, um, yeah. Wow. This Helena chick better be worth it. You sure she was in the cave?"

"No. But the Black Lotus want her dead. They don't want us to find her. They are taking extreme measures. I assume they have a reason."

They rode in silence for a moment, listening to the sounds of the road.

"Anyways," Sam said, still catching her breath, "have you put any more thought into it?"

"How about Whiskers?"

"Fucking *Whiskers*? Do I look like a seedy contractor who shaves his mustache in patches and walks out of sex shops with his face hidden in shame?"

"Well if you're gonna be my sidekick, you need a nickname

subservient to mine. I can't have you being the Saber-Toothed Tiger. How about The Flea?"

Sam nodded. "I could live with The Flea."

They rode in silence a moment longer. Sam's vitals flirted with normal.

"So," Sam said. "It's for real, then. Secret societies. Cultists. The CIA. Next you'll tell me we've got ancient aliens on our hands." She paused. "Whoa. No way. It's aliens, isn't it? Tell me it's aliens."

Mouse made a puffing sound that could have been stunted laughter.

"No aliens," she said.

"Yeah? Well, I dunno what to believe anymore. It's like I've come out of a coma in a parallel universe. If these bird cultists break physics and make gravity go backwards in an hourglass, what else? Can they bring back David Bowie? Can they make ice cream sandwiches part of the food pyramid?"

"You're an odd one, Whiskers," Mouse said.

Out the window, Sam watched strips of farmland, each with its own texture, filled gaps between forests dotted with smoke-pumping chimneys and traffic circles.

Mouse stroked her chin in contemplation. "Truth is, I don't know much about them. I don't know what makes them special. But I've got a hunch. Are you familiar with the Kurgan hypothesis?"

"No."

"Back before written history, if you believe the hypothesis, the first civilizations in Stone Age Europe were peaceful utopias ruled by women. Some archeologists argue that they worshipped a female deity, and that the oldest religions in Europe were matriarchal. But, surprise, it didn't last. In rolled the dude bros from the East. The Kurgan invaders had battering rams and war gods. 'Free Hugs' signs don't do much against that. So ended the era of peace and began an era of patriarchy and persecution. Western religion – beginning with the Greek gods – was a political perversion of far older themes."

"And what does that have to do with my mother?"

"That symbol on the cave wall," Mouse said, "was originally discovered in a 5,000-year-old cave painting in Spain. The triangles, the hourglass shape – symbols of rebirth, regeneration. There may be a connection with the ancient practice of goddess worship."

"So this all happened in the caveman days."

Mouse smiled. "Oh, no. They're still out there, Whiskers. The practice of goddess worship never went away. It continued in the shadows, edited out of the narrative of history, but never truly erased. There are still adherents of goddess worship hidden in plain sight among us today, and the Black Lotus have a vested interest."

"And, what, they have superpowers?"

"I don't know. But I think we're about to find out."

They rattled up gravel leading to a shantytown. Shacks rose around them like curtains, sagging into soil. The homes were built from a dozen materials, at least half of which were unsuitable for construction – bedsheets and cardboard, packet mud and oil drums, flaking plywood, tree bark and rags.

"Meet the Roma," Mouse said. "A thousand years of discrimination and hatred later, they're still here."

Children darted from doorways. Steam rose from a shack crisscrossed with clotheslines. Mouse shut off the vents in a futile attempt to stem the stink of trash. A girl stood on rubble, face all hair, drawing water from an ancient pump.

They rattled to a stop. This was the end of the line – by choice or not, as the ground became so strewn and twisted ahead that the Volvo lacked the horsepower to press on.

"Is this..." Sam asked. "Are we...?"

"Valuska," Mouse said. "They've wiped it from the map, but not the earth. Not yet."

"What can we do?" Sam asked.

"Nothing. The Black Lotus have committed to the destruction of this settlement."

Children squatted in the dirt, eyeing the newcomers with suspicion. Eyes peered from gaps in bent wood and broken shingles. More children – younger – swarmed the car with glee, shouting something Sam couldn't understand.

Mouse and Sam wandered through the village. A shirtless man sat in a plastic chair, feet planted in a pail, washing his underarms with a sponge. From inside a shack Sam heard the crackling sound of violins. She stopped to listen, but Mouse nudged her forward.

Mouse asked in Hungarian, then English, for directions. She had trouble expressing what she was seeking. A soot-faced child with flowers in her hair pointed to a shack.

"Keep up, Whiskers."

The shack was little more than a door. Sam noticed that all the doors looked different and realized that each had been salvaged from a separate scrap pile.

Mouse knocked with her mechanical hand. Receiving no answer, she pushed the door open. Inside, a woman looked up from her knitting.

"Helena Tarr?" Mouse asked.

The woman's eyes fluttered with anxiety.

"Relax," said Mouse. "I'm not Black Lotus. Not anymore."

Helena Tarr was a question mark of a woman, her spine like a sickle, wrapped in a cardigan and a sash the color of Mars. Her bun of brown hair sparkled with hints of silver. She kept her hand beneath blankets and waited for someone to move.

"Okay," Mouse said, "well technically I'm still on the Lotus payroll, but that's a loophole more than anything. Point is, I'm not going to hurt you." She paused. "Okay, well I *might* hurt you. But not a lot." She paused. "Maybe a lot."

"Were you in the cave?" Sam asked. "Did you know Melanie Fink?"

Helena's eyes narrowed with suspicion. Her pupils were so blue they looked alien. Hints of freckles poked through her tan.

"Nikole?" Helena asked.

Mouse and Sam looked at each other.

"That's my sister."

"Oh."

For a minute or longer, nobody spoke. Helena appeared rapt with confusion, indecision and something not unlike hope.

"How did you find me?"

Sam gestured at Mouse with her head. "My new best bud helped me with that."

"I see." She turned to address Mouse. "And who might you be?"

"I'm the only person on Earth who can save you from the Black Lotus," Mouse said. "They'll be here in ten, twenty minutes tops."

"So you knew her?" Sam asked. "You knew Melanie Fink?"

"I had a message for Nikole. Why should I trust you? How do I know you're speaking the truth?"

Sam shrugged. "Well I don't exactly have ID."

"Here," Mouse offered. "As a sign of good faith, I brought you a present. Well, okay, it's not with me, but look."

She showed Helena a photograph on her cell phone of the backwards hourglass.

"My God," Helena breathed. "You found the hourglass. Can it be true? You are Sera's daughter? The message worked?" She paused. "But how? It wasn't me you were meant to find."

"Who is Sera?" Sam asked.

Helena hesitated. She pulled her ankles under her and sat cross-legged. "And you," she said, addressing Mouse. "What's your role in this madness? What do you want from me?"

"Your story," said Mouse. "Who you are. Why the Black Lotus are after you. What happened in the cave."

"You want to hear a story."

"Yes."

Helena stared into space. Sam watched her larynx shift like an insect beneath her skin. Her mouth made a wheezing noise as she breathed. For a moment it looked like she'd resign herself to silence, preferring the bullet over divulging secret knowledge. Her face brimmed with sadness but no trace of tears.

"Alright," Helena said. "I'll tell you a story."

51

"The flowers. Those I noticed right away. White petals, pink edges. They were the same sword lilies that grew in his garden. I found them in shop windows and sidewalk cracks. Now and again nature sends us reminders that we haven't been around this planet very long. Whole civilizations can sink into the clay, disappear forever. I've seen it happen. But where I'm from, everything still stands.

"No one's sad about it anymore. But, even today, the city is divided into before and after. The land remembers trauma. The people see souvenir postcards.

"I sat at a café, the mountain in the distance. Trees blocked my view. Tourists chatted and sipped wine and snapped photographs. They asked one another to imagine. What was it like? Children shrieking, the sky all dark. Who were these people? Did they blame the gods? Did they understand science? But those lives were too remote. They couldn't imagine it. A fake sadness hung in their voices.

"There was a woman, her jacket made of stripes and stars, peering at my table. When she opened her mouth, you could see a gap between her teeth. She said howdy, asked me if I was part of the tour. I replied with a smile. Her husband craned his neck. He complained about the bus driver. He said I looked upset. They kept saying, you know, it was all once upon a time.

"I looked away and accidentally saw the mountain. I must have made a face because the wife chuckled. 'It's like you were there,' she said. 'But that isn't possible. We can't imagine it. Nobody can. Nobody can imagine what it was like, the day the fire came out of Mount Vesuvius.'

"I took a sip of water. They were right. Once upon a time. Only I remember. I'll never forget.

"Virgil and I were young. Pompeii was our first taste of city life. We moved into an insula – a sort of apartment building – east of the House of Venus. The view! We never imagined such excitement. Cattle carts hauling hay, pottery makers, sculptures of legionnaires, men in togas, stray dogs and donkeys, servants with water buckets, gladiators in chains, ivy, twittering birds. Pompeii. Virgil found work as an apprentice glassblower. We talked about starting a new chapter. This was before I met the scientist.

"I have seen many wars and I have met many veterans. The scientist rarely spoke about his past. He'd fought at the Battle of Medway. He had a Z-shaped scar on his chest. I always wondered about that scar. His face had hardened with age. He'd inherited a villa, but no slaves, from a wealthy uncle on the city's outskirts. Here is where he conducted his experiments. His name was Plinius but everyone called him Pluto, because of the rumors.

"We met in springtime. The Pompeii market was noisy that morning. I can still hear the sounds. Wheels clacking on cobblestone, mules braying, customers haggling. It's all there in my mind. Fat Balbus the melon seller's cart overflowed. A trio of legionnaires, steel from head to toe, stood laughing and groping apples. Their armor grated as they walked. I wandered past tents and peppers and pottery, loose livestock, children playing board games and women gossiping in shawls. Pluto was showing the soldiers a coin trick. When they weren't impressed, he quoted Diogenes the Cynic. 'It is not that I am mad,' Pluto told them, 'it is only that my head is different from yours.' This was the first unusual thing about him.

"Day to day, it feels like you'll live forever. But we can't understand forever. We aren't built to last. The affair I had with the scientist would've ended soon enough. He was pushing mid-sixties in an era of short lifespans. But that's not sorrow when you're living it. That's just what happens next.

"We developed a routine. I'd wait for Virgil to be gone an hour, just in case. Pluto's wife spent time in Rome, caring for elderly parents. They'd fallen out of love decades ago. I'd alter my route to disguise the pattern. Adultery was a serious crime. Sometimes I'd scale his back wall. His villa was overgrown from laziness and lack of slaves. He had a garden full of sword lilies. You can go to Naples and see them growing today.

"He was my father's age. At first I hated myself for what we were doing. I can't say what attracted me to him. I'd known him by reputation. He was a recluse who spoke in riddles. Rumors said he was trying to bring a corpse back to life. Imagine my disappointment when I entered his workshop. He had pipes and pulleys, detailed schematics, but no bodies. It's only in hindsight that I see he was on the verge of inventing the steam engine.

"I told him that I'd like us to be together. He laughed, but I hadn't meant it as a joke. Still, I saw the illogic of it, the impossibility. I wasn't beautiful enough. 'You are too beautiful,' he told me. 'I don't like beauty. I like decay.' This was the second unusual thing about him.

"One day there was commotion outside Pluto's villa. A neighbor had complained about sounds and odors. Another thought there'd been a fire. I hid in his workshop as he argued with the authorities. Adultery could get a woman killed. I cowered between machines. The workshop pumped and purred. I sat in the workshop like I was inside his heart.

"He tiptoed in the hall, as was his habit. Conceal all evidence, even when the wife's away. We were never so brazen. But still, he'd wipe down every surface. I kept telling myself that one day I'd be a real adult, with a family of my own. But I knew it couldn't be with Virgil. He was not the one I loved.

"Now the neighbors had been pacified and he'd removed half his toga. He lifted me by the underarms and we walked to his garden.

"'I live for you,' he whispered.

"I kissed his wrinkled skin. I realized he'd let the workshop run loud as cover for our lovemaking. He called me baby girl. Virgil never called me that.

"We walked laps around his garden, sometimes nude, always holding hands. 'Poor flowers,' I'd say. 'It's nice when they bloom, but then they wither and die.'

"'You are such a child,' he told me. 'Old flowers like me need to wilt. We're making room. For the common good, you see.'

"I nodded and pouted like a child. Warm breeze whipped the pillars of his home, carrying the stench of sulfur. I thought it was from his experiments.

"There had been earthquakes, yes. But earthquakes were not uncommon in Pompeii. Pluto and I watered flowers and right-side-upped his pottery after each tremor.

"He told me a story from his childhood. His great-grandfather had forded the Rubicon with Julius Caesar. He'd never met the man, so he'd fantasize. He pictured his ancestor felling enemies by the hundreds, taking arrows to protect his king. He played gladiator with his brother, who suffered from horrifying birth defects. He couldn't stand and went pale in the sunlight. When he was born, his head was a ball without holes. Physicians had to poke nostrils and cut a mouth. If only he were born two thousand years later. Maybe by now he'd be cured. Pluto remembered the day his brother died. 'His heart just stopped,' he told me. 'Out like a torch.' By then he'd already enlisted, and any fantasy of battlefield glory had been long dulled. Of his own combat experience, Pluto was tight-lipped. It had changed him, was all he'd say. You could divide his life before and after. When he'd come home, he got married straight away.

"'Children?' I asked. He shook his head. Something inside him didn't work. That was his theory. Some Romans had families. Pluto had his machines.

"Pluto did not go out like a torch. His heart didn't stop. But something happened to it.

"I returned from the wine cellar with another jug. The sky had darkened. Pluto was on his stomach, shivering. His limbs were arranged at strange angles. I dropped the wine.

"I offered to get help but he told me to run, to save my marriage. I begged. He wouldn't relent. 'Get out,' he told me. 'Please. Don't ruin your life. Happiness is not the same as living a long time.'

"Maybe those weren't his last words. It was long ago. In any case, I fled.

"Dogs barked in the insula across the street. Horses acted strange. They say animals know things in advance. A shingle fell from his roof.

"I've seen videos of atomic bombs. I've read about Hiroshima. But the explosion that Tuesday in August was like nothing from this earth. Night fell mid-afternoon. People milled about the streets, more stunned than afraid. They were all starting the same direction. I walked quickly. Maybe I was looking for Virgil. Maybe I was looking for home. My ears rang and my lungs neared collapse. Plumes of black rose from Vesuvius to hide the sun. Gaius the carpet merchant wiped blood from his ear. I reached to my own ears and came away bloodied myself, as though I'd stuck my fingers in red ink. Something went splat on a nearby roof. I thought it was bird. Then it happened again. Pumice the size of my fist rained from the sky.

"The clouds looked devil-horned, streaked with lightning and fire. Legionaries urged calm but nobody listened. Evacuation became a stampede. All of Pompeii ran in one direction. I walked the other. There was a constant roar and the ground shook. Ash fell faster than I could move through it, ankle deep then knee deep within the space of ten minutes. The air grew hot. Animals were going crazy. People trampled each other. I thought about Pluto, face down in his garden, one of those contorted plaster molds you see in museums today.

"Darkness swept over us like a flood. Midnight doesn't do it justice. We were blindfolded, groping. I heard screams of infants and wails of dogs. Some called out for the gods, others for parents and children. Some, feeling the heat intensify, prayed for a quick death. I was crushed by bodies and dust. A foot pinned my neck. Light returned, but not the sun.

"Surely, I thought, this is the end of the world.

"I choked. In the fire's light, I saw my body, then I saw my skin. I'd slipped right out like leaving a robe. The strange thing is, I don't remember pain. The sadness was too much. We'd failed as a species. Ash was still falling when the clouds parted. I remember seeing the city in rubble. Mount Vesuvius kept churning pillars into the sky. To the west, the sunset peeked through, painting the sky in bloom. Sound faded. The heat was suffocating. I don't remember my final breath.

"I awoke nude. A man with dark skin chanted over my body. I saw a great tree and a beam of light. I heard a choir. This is it, I thought. The underworld. Pluto's domain.

"I looked right and left, but found neither husband nor lover. There were others from Pompeii. I recognized Sabina the priestess. We kept in touch. She was running a car dealership in Alaska when she killed herself in 1971. While my neighbors reunited in Heaven, we were forced to keep living. Denied death, we were imprisoned in Hell.

"Centuries passed. Wars were fought. Disasters scourged the earth. People were born and they died. They loved each other. They conquered the New World and invented the light bulb. I remember everything.

"I met others. There was Aelia, who one day outside Jerusalem witnessed Jesus nailed to a cross. Enrique of Malacca, Magellan's slave. Maarav and Mack, the twin Mayan astronomers. My story is boring in comparison.

"I bounced around, life to life, never staying in one place long enough to draw suspicion. Yes, I had more lovers. Yes, I had children. But I had to leave them before they could see I wasn't aging. I had to take new names. It's what we all did. I was living in London when I learned they'd unearthed Pompeii. People thought that day was important to preserve. Finally, towards the end of last century, I mustered the courage to visit.

"Tourists swarmed, chatting, snapping photographs, children smiling and playing hide and seek in houses where laughter once rang, arguing, running, holding hands. But I didn't see them. All around me I heard sounds of Roman life. My mind spoke Latin. Hooves clacked, merchants haggled, soldiers bragged of battlefield valor, prostitutes offered discounts to traveling scholars, poets recited verse, philosophers debated the afterlife. I looked at Vesuvius now, inert, harmless. Its shape had changed.

"To these tourists wandering ancient streets, tomorrow is a guarantee. They'll live forever because forever is beyond their grasp.

"As I strolled through the decay, I saw everywhere the white petals of sword lilies. They sprouted through the ruins in an ancient cycle of time. Maybe the eruption changed something about the soil. But they're still there, season after season, the same flowers that bloomed the day I died.

"Why me? Why do I get to see them in bloom, year after year? Why not Virgil? Why not Pluto? I thought by going back I'd feel closure. Instead I just stood and listened, a ruin among ruins.

"I watched the flowers until the sun set. I wanted to make sure it could. Now I am here and I have told you a story. Please, do not call me Helena. Call me Olympias of Jericho. You are the first person who has known my name in a very long time. You asked why the Black Lotus is chasing me. You asked what makes me special."

"The Fountain of Youth," Mouse answered for her. She stood a moment half-smiling, staring at air, rapt in epiphany. "They're hunting and killing people who drank from the Fountain of Youth. And you're one of them. Do I have it right?"

"No fountain," Olympias said. "But yes. We bear the curse of eternal life." She looked at Sam, then at Mouse, then at the photograph of the hourglass. "Do you know what you've found there?"

52

Hurried voices were the first signs of conflict. Sam wiped tears from one cheek but not the other. The Black Lotus, editors of history, civilization's paint thinner. They're here. Sort of. Sam pictured spy planes and combat drones, satellite uplinks, blank faces in underground bunkers crowded around computer screens. The destruction of this settlement is a historical inevitability.

Mouse got to her feet, unmoved by the story.

"Where is the Fountain of Youth?"

She asked without charm. In her eyes Sam saw an emptiness sharpened by years of hunger.

Olympias shook her head. "It's not that simple."

Mouse drew sharp breath. "But it's real," she said. "Eternal life."

The Pompeii survivor hesitated. "You are young," she said. "Your body clock is screaming at you to live. That's what makes it scary. But the rules exist for a reason. Break them and you pay a price. I've watched the plague take Europe and I've read about Genghis Khan. In the evenings, I watch the news. And I think, so what? See the soil and see me. We are no different. We watch the world with nothing, nothing, nothing to do."

"If life is so painful," Sam asked, "why not commit suicide?"

"I've thought of it. I don't know. Maybe I've been waiting to tell someone my story."

Mouse nodded, impatient. "Okay," she said. "Alright. I'll keep that in mind. Where is the Fountain of Youth?"

Glass broke outside and the three women turned their heads as one. A new urgency rattled the air. People were shouting, throwing stones. Footsteps hurried past the door.

"It's not what you think," Olympias explained. "There is no fountain."

Mouse peeped outside the tent, then ducked back inside. "Shit," she said. "Black Lotus."

Sam turned to Olympias. "Fuck your secrets," she said. "I just wanna know what happened in that cave. Were you down there? Did you see the others get burned? Did you know Melanie Fink?"

"We were lured to the cave with the promise of safety. It was a trap. There was a single killer, wearing a mask. We were burned one at a time. It was strange. It was as though I was set free intentionally."

"But how did you get in and out?" Sam asked. "There was no entrance."

She made a strange face. "What are you talking about? Of course there was." She paused. "You mentioned the name Melanie Fink. I believe you mean Sera."

"Who?"

"A mystic from Tbilisi. Half my age. She built that hourglass. She gave it to me as a gift. The Black Lotus took to calling her The Gravity Thief."

The commotion outside magnified. A scream pierced the air. Engines rumbled. A police megaphone boomed in Hungarian, then in English. The settlers were being evicted.

"She gave you the hourglass?"

"She'd had a premonition. A dream. She thought I'd need it. Sera was going by an alias, like the rest of us." Olympias hesitated, unsure whether to divulge more. "Last I know, she was going by the name Melanie Fink. She gave me the hourglass years ago, along with detailed instructions on how to pass it on."

Sam blinked. An understanding began to dawn on her.

"You're saying that *you* took the hourglass into that cave?"

"Yes. Sera wasn't down there. She resisted temptation."

Time stopped. Sam reeled as though hit by the force of a runaway train. She sputtered, tried to speak, screwed up her face.

"She's alive?" Mouse asked for her. "Melanie Fink is still alive?"

"I will answer all of your questions if you can get me to safety. Just don't ask me about the way to eternal life. Don't ask about joining the bird cult. You could torture me to death and I'll never tell. You cannot understand, young as you are, that not knowing is for your own good."

Something exploded nearby.

"We need to get out of here," Mouse said. "Come with us to Budapest."

Olympias nodded. "Lead the way."

A Molotov cocktail ignited the tent. Sam jumped to her feet. "Did the Ohio State Buckeyes just win a championship?"

"Run!" Mouse shouted. "Go!"

The three women ducked through a collapsing doorframe into trampled mud.

Where she expected chaos, Sam found the world potent and still. A bulldozer sat among trash, a single splotch of yellow on a lifeless plain. On one flank police stood in firing line formation, head to toe riot gear, batons and bulges on their hips. On the other stood the engineers. Men and women in hardhats, they'd come with sledgehammers and axes, tools of unmaking.

"Black Lotus," Mouse breathed. "They're here for you. They'll bring down the whole settlement to hide your death."

They felt it before they heard it, heard it before they saw it: heat lighting up their bodies, the crackling of flames. The engulfed husk of a car pumped smoke into the sky. A woodpile exploded.

The Roma settlers darted in and out of shacks, scavenging heirlooms and children, speaking Romani.

Police spoke through a megaphone first in Hungarian, then in English. "For your own safety," they said.

Fake police – or real police, manipulated – advanced. Two cops tore children one by one from a camper engulfed in garbage.

The settlers looked accustomed to such treatment. They squatted and sat. Some packed suitcases. Nobody looked afraid. Another eviction. Go through the movements.

Bulldozers came over an embankment like tanks, leaving treads in the mud. The backhoe bit into a shack and children came pouring out like ants.

"Move," Mouse barked. "Go."

"We can't just leave," Sam said. "We have to do something."

"These people aren't worth your life."

Rioters, their faces more bandana than skin, began seeping through the police line. One threw a Molotov cocktail. The police didn't seem to notice or mind.

The stench of burning tires was nearly overwhelming. Faces smoked brown and black, children, dogs, men in rags and winter hats, boot prints left like fossilized suffering, smog sheathing the sun, darkening and darkening, sky snowing ashes, the end of the world. Engineers sheared the landscape with tools. Warsaw, Poland, 1943. A grainy photograph come to life.

Sam jogged towards to attackers in riot gear, unsure how to stop them but knowing it was her duty. Boots with red laces. A child holding his bloodied leg. A dog, all ribs and fur, tugging at its chain. The fire closing in.

Rioters moved in eerie lockstep. Metal clanged. Pottery shattered. Glass cracked. The boots kept marching, mechanical. A man with a length of pipe stared down a family of squatters with unfettered malice.

Sam followed her two targets into a shack and watched as they turned cabinets to splinters and bedding to feather puffs. Children swarmed their ankles.

Someone coughed behind a plastic curtain. That got their attention. Weapons readied, the rioters approached and tore it away.

Behind the curtain, a bony man pushing one hundred huddled naked in the shower, chest rising and falling, faded numbers tattooed to his wrist. He looked more defeated than afraid. You survive Auschwitz. Then what? History is remembering what happens. We have photographs and monuments, but that's not being there. You can kill everyone who knows a thing, or maybe you can't. It doesn't stop it from happening again.

The man bowed his head, overwhelmed with sadness. The rioters looked ashamed. They exchanged glances. Sam studied the man's breathing a moment longer. She felt something primal. Here stands a monument of the human condition, a skeleton out of time, suffering for our sins. Her body was racked with chills.

Back outside, Sam staggered shell-shocked through scenes of carnage. Comets of fire drew lines against clouds and Mouse gazed upon them in profile, wisps curled around her head. A shack made of cardboard ignited like a castle hit by trebuchets. A child stood like a statue. Twin flames from a burning house looked like angel wings at his back.

Planks crunched and cracked as they were uprooted by rioters and construction crew, working side by side to expedite the process. Helicopter rotors drowned sounds of sobbing. Sam saw a priest holding a crucifix to the sky, marching through violence calmly, like something out of the Bible. Smoke engulfed the crucified Christ. Temptations from another plane. The priest spoke prayers in a strange language as boiling wind kicked up his robes.

Mouse snatched Sam with her mechanical arm.

"We need to leave. Now."

They made for their Volvo, its siding soot-smudged but its windows intact.

"Where's Olympias?"

They turned and watched it happen. Olympias of Jericho held her hands in surrender before a line of police. A burning structure at her back looked like a cross. She extended her arms like Christ, then lunged at the cops, reaching as though for a weapon.

Sam gasped.

And so died Olympias of Jericho, taking with her two thousand years of memory, cut down in a hail of bullets.

"No!" Mouse shouted.

As Olympias slipped to the ground her face was still, but Sam swore she saw movement in her lips, a smile struggling to cross her face.

Mouse shoved Sam into the Volvo's backseat. She leaped in and they were off. The car bounced across uneven ground, its engine straining. As they escaped children gave chase, fanning out in crowds, arms outstretched like a U.N. convoy passing through an African village. Sam stared hard into the fire and in its depths she saw yellow eyes and a goatee, a grin of cinders, a pitchfork and horns and she couldn't help the feeling that all had been eternally, irretrievably lost.

53

"Remind me."

He had floppy ears and a head bulging at the temples, grime between his teeth, coal-colored eyes and a birthmark the shape of Italy. He stood between copper pipes and walls defaced with swastikas. Water tanks hissed and roiled a blanket of white noise. When she took a step forward he clamped his arm across the door.

"Are you a good girl or are you a bad girl?"

She saw her face in the reflection of his glasses. She knew she was about to get raped but didn't know what to do with the knowledge. Her heart couldn't decide whether to race or stop beating altogether.

Nikole bowed her head.

"I'm a good girl."

A machine whirred to life. Nikole rested her hand on a metal surface, only to recoil from the heat.

"Say it louder."

Nikole shook her head. "Let's just get this over with."

The prison guard's smile widened. His breath smelled like tobacco and blue cheese.

"I like to talk to them first," he explained.

Her mouth tasted like vomit. Earlier, when they'd left her in the holding cell, after puking blood and bologna, hugging the toilet with all her strength, she thought about destroying herself. Just do it. All the way this time. Panic attacks prodded her body like a torturer's awl, coming on like clockwork.

Her jailers shuffled her around, marching her down hallways with checkered tiles, past cells packed with migrants clamoring in Arabic with outstretched hands, men packed on top of men, a multi-headed wall of flesh. They had trouble verifying Nikole's identity. Through an interpreter she'd asked for pills and a phone call. They shuffled paperwork and peered into security monitors and said we'll see.

The guard loosened his belt. "We get Americans time to time," he said. "Drugs, mostly. But armed robbery? That's serious years. That's Leopoldov. Nasty folks at Leopoldov."

Nikole held a spot above her bellybutton where the knives were sharpest.

At the clinic, they'd given her square tablets. For pain, they'd said, unspecific. She waited for the words "treatment program," a call from the embassy, a diplomat en route. She pictured her name scrolling at the bottom of CNN.

Suicide. She hadn't made the decision yet. Nothing final. But at least it was on the table. At least she was getting a good look at what it would take.

The guard had his dick in hand, not fully erect but getting there.

"As long as you don't cry," he said. "I hate it when they cry."

He'd given her advance notice. This same guard had paraded her through jail like an emperor flaunting spoils of war. Female prisoners – detainees, they called them – lounged in a room of bunk beds, squatting, sitting cross-legged, playing with each other's hair. She was ushered past a room with children's finger paintings plastered on the blue walls where women with neck tattoos held babies. Then they'd reached the unmarked door. Sounds of machinery and rape radiated from the other side.

"The important thing is you don't fight back," the guard had told her. "Then it's resisting. Your lawyer will explain. Whatever you do, you don't resist."

Nikole mumbled.

After vomiting her second attempt at dinner, she'd tried to score pills off a detainee with fantastic orange dreadlocks named Markéta.

For my disorder, Nikole tried to express using grunts and sign language. Her throat had swollen shut. Everything seemed blurry and blacked out, like a transcript redacted by the CIA.

Something lost in translation led to violence. They swore in Slovak and kicked ribs. Tattooed women lunged from the steps where they'd been lounging. A fat woman belly flopped on the pile. Alarms blared. Nikole waited to be stabbed but only felt a flurry of fists on her thighs, then her stomach, then her face. The pain felt far away.

Guards rushed the bodies, screaming threats and swinging batons. Nikole watched a black woman take a taser to the back and waited for the same. The guards peeled off one sweaty body after the next like refs at a football game. They shoved her in a private cell and spoke grave warnings of added years and Leopoldov.

Then came dead of night and a baton knocking her cell door. She hadn't been sleeping. Twitching, she pulled herself to her feet. It was her floppy-eared friend with the teeth. "The judge will see you now," he said. Seemed an odd time.

The common area had emptied. Nikole stood alone in a spotlight. "Walk towards the light," said a voice.

The guard escorted her through empty corridors. Everything was white: walls, floor, ceiling. The duo's footsteps were the only sounds. Nikole felt a chill in her spine and knew what was coming.

They reached a boiler room and the guard shoved his baton into the small of her back.

A last-minute knock on the door saved her from being raped. The guard looked embarrassed. "Tomorrow's another day," he whispered, tucking his dick in his pants. "Then there's the day after that. We'll get to know each other well."

A night passed, a century. She was working out how to do it, how to tie the knot, when new men came for her. They were muscular, clean-shaven. "Are you the American?" one asked. "Come with us." Nikole marched down the checkered hallway flanked by muscles. They held her by the underarms whenever she started stumbling. Her crotch tightened as they approached the boiler room.

She struggled. Whatever happened, she wasn't going back behind that door. She squirmed and spat in the guard's face.

Next thing she knew they were on the floor in another pile of weight. She took a baton to the shin. She couldn't tell if she was having a panic attack, had surrendered to psychosis or had been hypnotized and hooked to wires in a mad scientist's lair. They hoisted her, bloody and shaken, to her feet.

"Stop resisting," a guard barked.

"Fuck you," she said.

"Don't you get it? You're being released."

They took her to an office and presented paperwork. A hunchback in a tan suit sat behind a computer. Upon gazing into her bruised eyes, he asked why she had been making trouble.

"Serious years," he said in a wiry voice. "Leopoldov Penitentiary."

She wondered about this Leopoldov prison. On her eyelids she saw a penal colony, forced labor, men wearing vertical stripes who had been caught resisting.

The hunchback mumbled something about friends in high places. She knew they'd send a diplomat. "These orders," he said in a strange accent, "came from *way* up the ladder. Who are you?"

"I told you people a thousand times," Nikole said. "Google me. Search IMDB. Nikole Fink. I'm an actress. You'll see my picture. I'm famous."

The man typed something on his computer.

"There is no IMDB page for a person named Nikole Fink," he said.

Nikole's heart twitched. The world, already distant, all but disappeared.

"Wikipedia?"

He typed.

"There is no Wikipedia article for a person named Nikole Fink," he said. "As far as I can tell, no such person exists. You're providing a false name. That's serious years."

"Search for *Kid Wizard*," Nikole said, feeling desperate. "It was a TV show."

He stared at her a moment, rolled his eyes and typed.

"Ah, here it is," he said. "*Kid Wizard*. I'll be damned. There's the name. Nikole Fink."

Her vitals veered towards normal. She sighed relief. See. I told you.

I'm real. I exist.

The man's eyes narrowed. "That's odd," he said.

"What?"

"'Nikole Fink was the stage name of American actress Rachel Lipinski,'" he read off the screen. "'She is best known for playing the role of Amy on the sitcom *Kid Wizard*.'"

He turned the monitor. There she was. Rachel Lipinski. A Wikipedia article complete with footnotes. The woman pictured looked like Nikole, but it wasn't her.

She struggled to process this new information.

He swiveled the screen back to his side of the desk. "According to this website," he said, "Rachel Lipinski is dead. How can that be, if she's sitting across from me?" His eyes narrowed further. "Well that's especially odd. It says here that Rachel Lipinski died *today*."

They wrung their hands and whispered rumors and escorted Nikole to the gates and pushed her into the light of day. Her knees wobbled and she wondered how far she'd make it before collapsing like roadkill. The Slovakian countryside stretched before her, foreign, directionless.

A silver car approached. Two silhouettes stared within the windshield. Both doors opened at once and they emerged – Genghis the Giant on one side, birdcage in hand, and Angel on the other holding his red toolbox.

"Hello, Rachel Lipinski," Angel said. "Let's go for a ride."

54

"As of now," Angel said, "you no longer exist."

Rock bottom. What bullshit. There are always stairs leading down.

This was supposed to be the part where she started noticing birdsong and blue skies, cool autumn air, the details of nature dulled by drugs. She pressed her face against the glass and tried to focus on the flowers. A motorcycle tore around them, engine blazing. Through manicured greens she spotted edges of grandiose architecture. A Hungarian rap song crackled from the radio. Ahead a bridge lay flanked by weeping willows and something that looked like the Taj Mahal. Life felt clouded, grey, remote. She looked at the bridge and wondered how far you need to fall, just to be sure.

"We did a job here once," Angel continued. "Or perhaps I am thinking of Bucharest, Romania. Damn memory suppressants. Genghis, do you remember the Gül Baba job?"

Genghis grunted.

They entered a circle full of statues. It looked like a cross-section of the Coliseum. Tourists roamed in packs, spilling onto the road. A bus honked long and low. Tents offered trinkets and sausages. Chaz fluttered about his cage. On the center console, Angel's red toolbox of insects shimmered in the light.

Angel adjusted the mirror. His eyes grew serious.

"If you needed medicine you should have asked," he said. "Your arrest complicated things. Lots of Lotus resources involved."

They drove past buildings lost in centuries. She saw a man slouched on a bench, a spider web tattoo filling his bald head, phone aglow between his knees, staring at nothing. She sensed this man's suffering and thought, we will never meet. If she had telepathy, it's what she'd tell him. We never know a person's last thoughts.

Genghis parked along a street full of pink-shaded buildings.

Nikole thought about the *Kid Wizard* finale, the episode in which she vanished to a dimension where kids stay kids forever. No parents! No homework! No rules! But it's not them. It's never the ones who disappear. The tragedy is that the rest of us keep living. When I die, I'll take the world with me.

Genghis held up his hand to indicate five minutes, then disappeared into the door of a clinic. As soon as he vanished from view Angel turned to face Nikole.

"Look," he said. "I am sick of it, you know? We want to split. That hourglass was our ticket out. I've been skipping my memory suppressants. I know how to escape. Listen, Nikole, I am sorry you got mixed up in this bullshit. Do you hear me? The Black Lotus have ruined everything. These things I can never have – a family, a house to live in, a swimming pool in the backyard and a fucking dog named Fido. You know?"

Nikole glued her face to the window. Is he buying pills? When can I have the pills? How long before I have pills? How many milligrams to a pill? Pills to a bottle? Doesn't he need a prescription? What if things go wrong and I end up back in jail? Do jails in this country give inmates the right pills? Where are the pills? I need my pills.

"Come with me," Angel continued. "We are blank slates. Nobody knows us. We could start over, here in Budapest. I know someone. A collector. What he's offering for your mother's hourglass – it's the kind of money you put in hedge funds."

Nikole squinted through the glass. A dog barked and Nikole jumped. He's probably in line now, she thought. He's paying for the pills.

"Are you listening?"

"What's taking him so long?" Nikole asked.

"For fuck's sake, man. I am telling you something important. I think I love you, Nikole."

After what could have been five minutes or five hours, Genghis filled the clinic's doorway with his hulking frame. He clutched a paper bag in one hand. Nikole could feel her veins salivating.

Pills, she thought. They're close. The pills are close. I need my pills.

He climbed in the driver's seat. Can't look too anxious, Nikole thought, failing terribly, her whole body shaking. Like a sorcerer unveiling an ancient relic, Genghis peeled back the paper tomb and revealed an orange cylinder filled with tablets. How did he get them? Can you walk into a shop here and just buy Xanax, no prescription? If that's the case then sure, I'll stick around this planet a while longer. Like those grand bridges of Europe torched during the World Wars, I can be rebuilt. I just need pills.

Genghis twirled the bottle between meaty fingers and showed Nikole the label. Alprazolam. With forehead wrinkles he asked if it was the right kind. She nodded, sweating, a starved dog with eyes on steak.

He set the bottle on the center console. Nikole grabbed it.

Angel's hand clamped her wrist.

"Wait," he said.

Nikole's heart was at a breaking point. Waterfalls of sweat poured down her spine. She realized Genghis was aiming a pistol at her from between the seats.

"First you must make a promise," Angel said. "I like you Nikole, so I will let you live. But your sister knows too much. She has just discovered the big secret. It's your fault. Samantha Fink's brain has become dangerous and forbidden knowledge and as such it must be destroyed. I tried to be friendly. But now we have a problem. Now the boss man is involved. Promise you'll help us kill your sister."

Nikole considered his eyes, then looked at Genghis. Both men were void of mercy. The bottle glowed in her hand like a beating heart.

She felt sacred knowledge. Obligations. She'd failed her sister so many times. What would she do in the name of pills?

"I promise," Nikole said with no hesitation.

They let go. Don't binge, don't binge, don't binge, she thought as she shoveled pill after pill after pill into her mouth.

55

Dr. Apolline Fournier, the self-described historian of ideas, turned the hourglass over in her gloved hands and observed its gravity acrobatics. She tapped the symbol etched on its base:

"Goddess worship," she said. "It's a fringe theory. Mainstream historians reject it outright."

"Yes," said Akira. "This symbol, I believe, is our only way forward in attempting to guess the object's significance."

She had a blonde bun and a bulging eye, enlarged, Wally guessed, from years hunched over a microscope. Vintage science posters filled the walls of her office, crammed, fighting for every inch like a chimney claimed by ivy. Diagrams of specimens from bacteria to elephants dotted the parchment. Wally busied himself studying a labeled jellyfish, then took Akira aside while the professor continued her examination.

"If I may, sir," he said quietly, "I did not hire you to solve the mystery of the cave murders. I hired you to reclaim Mr. Noon's property. Now that we have achieved our goal, I insist we return the hourglass to Mr. Noon and be done with the insanity. I must check on my client Nikole Fink. That man's words regarding Ms. Fink have rattled my constitution."

"Mr. Wally, we are on the cusp."

"The cusp of *what*?"

Akira turned his attention back to Dr. Fournier.

"I figured you'd know something about it," he told her.

"I'm better versed on the history of science," she conceded. She set the hourglass on her desk and watched its lead-colored sand trickle upward. She turned it over and watched the process in reverse. "Magnets, I'm assuming."

Akira nodded. "The symbol etched on its base, I'm convinced, is crucial."

Madness, Wally thought. Here we have accomplished what the detective deemed impossible, and yet he strives to make things harder. We have the hourglass. But this is not why he performed for free. He wants to be famous, Wally understood. He wants the world to know he's the detective who solved the infamous cave bodies conundrum. And he will use this fame not to further his career, but to launch his TV drama.

"There is no evidence that matriarchy ever existed, anywhere, at any time in history," Dr. Fournier was saying. "And the evidence for so-called goddess worship is shaky at best. The archaeologist Marija Gimbutas spent half her life trying to prove the existence of ancient utopias ruled by women. It's a nice story, but the evidence just isn't there."

"So," Akira said, "if someone wanted to prove the theory of this Mrs. Marija, would this hourglass be compelling evidence?"

Dr. Fournier shrugged. "Not really. We're talking the Stone Age, detective."

Wally could imagine academics sparring over Stone Age particulars.

Sure. But why would anybody care *so dearly* about the religious beliefs of cavemen that they'd resort to murder, abductions and the involvement of the CIA?

The archaeologist handled the artifact gently, rapt by its edges.

"Regeneration of the body," Dr. Fournier continued, "was a prevalent theme in the goddess religion."

Akira had a look about him like he was starting to piece something together. Puzzle pieces flashed, reconfigured, butted heads in his eyes.

"But this is a controversial theory," he said. "Correct?"

The archaeologist shrugged. "These people aren't alive anymore, detective. We can't ask them." She tapped her finger against the symbol once more. "Note the hourglass shape. Triangles, according to Gimbutas, represent the vulva, which represents rebirth."

In the corner of her office a small television played the news on mute. Wally did a quadruple take. For a moment, he thought he saw a photograph of Nikole Fink on the TV. On closer examination, it was someone who resembled her likeness, but certainly not Nikole.

"How about The Gravity Thief?" Akira asked. "Does the phrase mean anything to you?"

"I'm afraid not."

"We have been told," Akira continued, "of a female mystic from the Caucasus Mountain region named Sera, who..."

"Wait," she said. "Yes. Sera. A boring historical figure, to tell the truth. A charlatan in an era when charlatans weren't rare. Female charlatans perhaps more so, but there's nothing interesting about her. I wouldn't have even known the name if not for the hoax."

"Hoax?"

"Some joker, a couple years back, claimed to have met Sera, alive and well in Tbilisi, Georgia. That's Georgia the country, I mean."

"Ah," Akira said. "Georgia the country. I've heard of it. Remind me where that is."

"The Caucasus."

"Ah."

"There were pictures floating around the internet. Conspiracy theorists claimed it as proof of reincarnation. Amazing, what people can believe. We are a species with an inherent spiritual hunger. This takes work to overcome."

A strange thing happened as she lifted the hourglass and turned it sideways. The sand began moving in a figure-eight pattern, increasing in speed the longer she held it aloft. Soon the sand formed a continuous blur around the edges.

"Huh," she said.

Wally again became distracted by the television. A square-jawed man with greying hair was giving an interview. A familiar face. Lance somebody. One of Nikole's co-stars. The screen's news crawl scrolled in microscopic text, though Wally could make out a phrase: Kid Wizard.

"Can you turn up the volume?" he asked.

Dr. Fournier combed her cluttered desk for a remote, found it, pivoted in her chair and aimed.

"And I kept thinking," the actor was saying, "this kid's gonna go far. Rachel was a joy to work with. I'm still processing what happened."

Rachel, Wally thought. He plumbed his brain's crevices and came up empty-handed.

The camera cut back to a well-dressed woman in the studio who, after a vague segue, launched into a story about a dam removal project in New Jersey.

Wally felt his heart pound. Something peculiar was afoot.

He moved closer to inspect the news crawl. Words at the bottom of the screen announced that child star Rachel Lipinski, better known by her stage name Nikole Fink, died this morning from a drug overdose, just before the 15th anniversary of her show. It said she was an addict for years.

Wally felt mired in granite. The posters returned his gaze.

Photosynthesis of plants and the food chain, scientists unearthing ancient bones, comets barreling towards earth at speeds beyond grasp of the human brain - all motion slowed and slackened and, by turn, the universe stopped working altogether.

"Are you alright?" asked Dr. Fournier.

Rachel Lipinski, he thought. There is no such person. He remembered how Tony Shen's medical files vanished, as though he'd never lived, and a shudder crept up his spine.

In contrast to Wally's frozen gaze, Akira's face performed acrobatics. Wally watched his jaw loosen, eyes go wide, evidence of revelation. He looked like a math prodigy processing an unfathomable equation. He looked at the television, then at the sideways hourglass making its infinity pattern, then once more at the professor.

"Georgia the country, you say."

The professor nodded.

"I can't believe it."

"Is Nikole dead?" Wally asked.

"No, Mr. Wally. Nikole Fink is alive and well, and I believe I know where she's heading."

Wally waited for the smug smile, but none came. Akira simply stared, dumbstruck, at the nothingness before him, then he grabbed the hourglass.

"Check your luggage," he said. "Phone a friend. Ensure all pets are properly cared for. We're going on a trip. It looks like I am going to miss my court date."

"Why is that?"

His smile finally bloomed. "Because, my dear Wally, I believe I have just solved the mystery of the cave murders."

56

She watched the castle besieged by ghosts and thought about the art of dying. All she needed was to say a few words and walk A to B. All mechanics. Big decisions are like that. I was at gunpoint. They'll understand.

Pedestrians moved like liquid crystals on the sidewalks below. Statues of men on horseback endured bird shit and history. Cameras clicked and tourists gabbed. A man marched through selling hot dogs.

Nikole wandered the castle grounds in a Xanax-induced daze. She bought a hot dog. Tourists from Korea asked her help in snapping their photo.

From this vantage point above Budapest she saw all the buildings and wondered about the people inside them. Millions of people in cubicles and county jails, soaking in steam baths and curating museums. And they'll all be dead. Every single one. The one thing we can say for sure about life is that it ends. Take that away and there's nothing you can say for sure about life.

Someone tapped her shoulder.

She checked over her shoulder. Nobody. She rolled her eyes.

"God dammit, Sam."

Her sister lunged and embraced her from behind.

"I can't even, sis," Sam breathed. "I dunno what you've been through these past couple days, but I'mma take a gander and say our tale tops yours. Stealing cars, kidnapping magicians, then I saw a lady get shot in the head. But it's cool. Nothing like chicken sammiches and a road trip with your new BFF to take the edge off. Clean underwear helps too." She paused. "Guess what?"

"What?"

"Guess."

"Just tell me, Sam."

"Mom's alive."

Nikole blinked. "What? No, Sam. We saw her body."

"We saw a skeleton with her face burned off." She paused. "Well, his or her. Nah, pretty sure it was a her. Boobs and all."

"You're saying that Mom escaped?"

"Nope. She wasn't down there in the first place."

"Then who wrote my name on the envelope?"

"Dunno. Oh, and by the way, she drank from the Fountain of Youth. Minor detail."

"Don't fuck with me, Sam. Don't give me hope."

"Well," Sam began. She squinted at the sky. "Yeah. Not sure you'd believe me. *A long story* doesn't really do it justice. It's been a weird couple of days."

"So where is she?"

Sam sucked in air, making a hissing noise. "Yeah, about that. Our informant got kinda sorta martyred before she gave us an address."

Nikole pressed a finger across her lips. Then, slowly, she pointed at her eye.

Mouse came closer and examined.

"No eye worm," she said.

Nikole nodded. "They're planning an ambush," she warned. "They want me to lure you and Sam into the Calvinist Church along the Danube. I'm supposed to tell you it's a cultist shrine. We need to split town before they realize I've betrayed them."

Mouse shrugged, weighing her options. "Or," she suggested, "we could strike first. You know, go have a little chat with our buddy Angel."

"Are you insane?"

"We have no leads, Nikole. I have no idea where mommy's hiding. I don't know who killed the others in the cave, or why. And as for the Fountain of Youth, I doubt it exists, at least in the sense it's a fountain somewhere. But we met someone. Immortality is real. It's the secret they died to protect."

"And, what," Sam said, "we're just gonna go in there and ask about it nicely? They'll kill us."

"Not if I talk them out of it."

Nikole watched the hotdog seller juggle ten varieties of ketchup and thought, everything you do is irrelevant to me. Maybe you're having an affair. Maybe you'll get cancer of the bone. We'll never meet again but we have something in common, a self-destruct genome buried in our DNA. The best part of dying is you get to do it alone.

"Okay," she said. "Let's go."

57

They took a tram down the hill and walked along the Danube, where migrant workers tended flowerbeds. Three Hasidic Jews sat at a sidewalk café framed by pillars. They spoke intensely in Yiddish, their faces black in silhouette. Nikole fingered the reassuring weight of the Xanax in her jeans pocket.

"See, Western religion is, like, a variation on a theme," Sam was explaining. "These people – Mom, the dude you whacked in Iceland – they're part of a goddess cult." She paused. "Or something. Hey, you guys think they've got KFC here? Got them munchies. Got 'em bad."

Tourist-clogged boats drifted in the Danube. Everyone seemed to have their gaze fixed in one direction, necks craned, cameras cocked as though awaiting a parade.

The Calvinist Church cast shadows on the sidewalk, bricks and jagged edges and spires. The sign said Closed. Not a pedestrian in sight. Mouse approached Nikole and tugged the zipper of her jacket. She pushed open

Nikole's yellow anorak as though joined in symbiosis. Nikole saw two handguns in inner pockets. Mouse lifted one and transferred it covertly to Nikole.

"Stay behind me," she said.

"Whoa," Sam said. "Wait. We're just gonna walk in there?"

"Yup."

"Won't we get murderslayed?" She was quiet a moment. "Murder... *slew*?"

"Nope."

Sam moved her head rapidly, looking at Nikole, then Mouse, then Nikole again. "But..." she muttered. "How..."

"I told you already," Mouse said. "I'm going to talk them out of it."

Saying nothing more, Mouse creaked open the wooden doors and disappeared inside. Sam hesitated a minute longer, then followed. Nikole brought up the rear.

Every surface glowed yellow. Mouse clicked shut the doors and in rolled tidal waves of silence. Bibles were tucked in seatbacks. The pews looked cramped. A chandelier dangled over a wood-carved altar, painting yellow walls warmer. Not a soul in sight; they'd gone to rapture or home for the day.

Mouse raised her pistol and fired a hole in the ceiling.

"Gentlemen!" she shouted, her voice drowned by lingering decibels. "A word, please."

Men in balaclavas crept from under the pews. They blocked the exit. They held sleek black submachineguns and you could see in their eyes a steely detachment earned through years learning not to feel.

Mouse twitched. Her head darted crevice to altar.

Then there it was, the rainbow bird, fluttering across the nave. Angel stepped from the shadows, first his body then his face. The silencer of his weapon peaked from under his coat.

"This time," he said, "you can't run away."

Genghis lumbered behind him.

Mouse calcified in place, counting assailants. Four total. No. Five.

"I have a proposition for you," Mouse said.

"Not interested."

"You can't do this," said Mouse. "We swore an oath and sealed it with blood." She paused. "Well, I mean, okay, Black Lotus don't do blood oaths.

But we should. Anyways, could you not?"

Angel said nothing.

"Really, you guys? You'd rather see a job done than live forever? It's the Fountain of Youth you're trying to erase. I met one. A cultist. She talked. Yeah, I know, the whole 'comforting narrative' thing. But think about it. Immortality. All we need is to admit this job is bigger than us."

Angel said nothing.

Mouse turned to face her rear assailants. "Nobody?" she asked. "None of you are interested in cheating death?"

They only stared. Sam inched closer to Nikole, whose heart had entered overdrive.

Mouse turned to the altar. Every muscle in her face drooped.

Christ in plaster watched from his cross. Nikole couldn't tell if the ticking she heard was a bomb or Sam's watch. She stood at the edge of a cliff. Something was about to be lost. Faces from history, goddess cults, life without end and a fleeting chance to meet her mother – through fate or schemes plotted on dusty maps, a lone candle approached the event horizon of memory.

"Please," Mouse said to Angel. "Don't let them do that... *thing* to my body. I don't want to be recycled."

Angel nodded. He began to look conflicted.

Mouse turned and aimed her gun directly at Nikole's head, cocked and released the safety.

"No!" Angel shouted.

Mouse smiled. "Ah, the mighty Angel, laid low not by a hail of bullets, but by a weakness of the heart."

Then Nikole remembered. The memory came on quick as a bullet. A distant afternoon. Washington Square Park. New York had faded into an inter-season blur, emaciated trees, drifting snow. Freaks trickled from sidewalks, dancing, drumming, urinating, whispering prophecies doused in acid. Under the arch a doo wop group of black men sang "Winds of change blow 'round my door, is this the year I've waited for?" Mom waddled along, pregnant. Nikole pictured her face clearly for the first time since she'd vanished. A man wearing a beanie cap and a shirt that said MUSIC SAVED MY LIFE asked for an autograph. The hush of celebrity presence rippled through tourists. Heads turned. Is that the girl from the, you know? The show. The TV. Nikole saw her mother's every detail, thin eyebrows, milky skin. An ancient queen or high school dropout. Their breath formed clouds that faded into space, chasing warmth that disappeared. Mom turned and said, Nikole, promise you'll never forget me.

Nikole yanked her own gun from her jacket and fired. The shot missed badly.

Angel ducked, unprepared for the blast. In the confusion Mouse yanked her mechanical pinky and tossed it into the church. The gunmen watched it roll across the stone and exchanged glances, asking should we shoot with their eyes. Before they could decide, the detached pinky exploded in a flashbang of blinding light.

Nikole reeled, disoriented. Gunshots erupted. She saw Mouse go down, clutching her metal arm, flicking levers and pumping the church with billows of smoke.

The church turned black. More gunshots. Nikole turned and fired again, squeezing the trigger, and fell backwards, connecting hip to the floor. She struggled to breathe. All her senses were clouded. She tasted something that could have been blood. Between shadows she watched her sister's body racked with bullets. Sam crunched to the floor with a sickening thud. A knife entered Nikole's midsection. The world grew blacker, then disappeared.

•••

Nikole woke from a dream in motion and found herself limping through Budapest. To her right the Danube drifted, unchanging through the ages. The Parliament building rose like a castle on the opposite bank – a stretch of Gothic spires and waving flags, grand domes and stone embankments. Evening turned the sky royal blue. People stood on the opposite bank in bunches, awaiting something drastic to happen in the sky.

She felt the inside of her jacket and withdrew fingers dripping with blood.

Forward march. A to B. Keep moving and you'll get somewhere. Sidewalks are like that.

A backwards glance revealed the church harmless and inert. Her brain stopped short of understanding. Something happened and now I'm walking.

She staggered onto a patch of bricks across from Parliament. Orange lanterns lit the building's backside, evenly spaced, diabolical in evening light. They reflected in stripes of fire on the river's surface. Everything about the sight was perfectly symmetrical.

Then, a voice.

"Nikole."

Movement was a chore. With great effort, she craned her neck, then her shoulders, then turned to face her pursuer.

Angel stood stained with smoke, unarmed, his eyes a shade of flesh.

"Let me help you," he said.

She tasted copper and bile, smelled charred flesh. The ringing in her ears hadn't stopped.

"We'll live forever," Angel said, arm outstretched. "It is only us now. Do not be afraid. I will take you there, to the graveyard. Sighişoara. They will perform a ritual tonight and we will join them. I have made plans. I am leaving the Black Lotus." He paused. "With you."

Nikole felt sick in a spiritual way, without physical symptoms.

Three gunshots rang out, dull thumps in Nikole's ears.

Angel looked at his torso, stunned.

He took a jagged step. His three bullet wounds turned black, then red, then oozed down the front of his coat. He lunged and wrapped his arms around Nikole.

Mouse stood behind him, her gun raised. A wisp of smoke rose from its barrel.

Nikole held Angel a moment but her strength was fading. As he slipped down her body he left a trail of blood like wounded animal. His breathing slowed and then stopped.

Fireworks exploded over the Parliament building. Plumes of fire streaked the sky. Cheers tore through tourists watching from the bridge. Pop, bang, sizzle. Wind carried the smell of burning. Nikole felt tears run down both cheeks. She staggered through falling debris. Orbs of light descended around her. She held her arms to the sky and cried out, surrounded by spent fireworks and embers drifting through the sky like ashes from Mount Vesuvius.

58

He bounded down the stairs, taking them two steps at a time. The concrete shuddered under his weight. Solid construction, he thought. I would need many tons of Semtex. Take out the supports.

He noticed flaws, security holes, weaknesses in the design. One point for entry and exit. Blow the stairs, trap everyone below. When the apocalypse begins, we will be safe in our concrete bunker. But there's the issue of food. Two cases of MREs divided by eight staff plus two guards plus him plus me. Three point six three meals per head. Ration them in thirds, stretch it three, four days. Then what? I could kill them all and have a feast. But even then, how long? An advancing zombie horde buries us in rubble and I go on concentration camp rations and – assuming the stray rodent – I'd last nine hundred ten days, give or take a few hours, before the snake swallows its own tail.

He had it all figured out in his head, down to the last milligram. In the corridors, he examined the pipe. This one labeled hot, this one labeled cold. Interesting. Vents rattled overhead.

I'm too big to fit, he thought, but I'd need to make sure none of the weaklings crawled through the air ducts to freedom. I should remove their hands as a precaution. Then again, one cannot properly salute with flesh stubs alone. I believe that saluting one's superior is no empty gesture, and that hierarchy is vital to the continuity of any post-apocalyptic commune. So we'd have to deal with prosthetics as a temporary fix.

He reached the door. The guard gave him a curt nod.

"The American will see you now."

His office was a room. Desk, chair, walls and no windows. Nothing ornate. A room. You couldn't say anything else about it. He'd shaved his eyebrows again. Hard to say why anyone does anything. His head was perfectly hairless, a clay-colored dome. Deep-folded wrinkles looked like battle scars. He wore a black blazer, black shirt, no tie. His office smelled of port wine and aftershave.

"Report," The American said.

He mused a mocking salute but subdued his urges, satisfied with the knowledge that this man they call the American, but whose identity had been scrubbed since birth, may one day become his handless minion.

"Fucked."

The American drew his lips like leather. "I don't suppose anyone's accused you of being long-winded," he said. He took a long drag on a vapor cigarette. "Are we down a man?"

He nodded.

"Two red alerts in as many weeks," said the American. "Getting a Hollywood actress involved." He arched forehead stubs where once he had eyebrows. "Mind telling me what you were thinking?"

He shrugged.

"Did you know, Genghis, what I wanted to do this weekend?" the American asked. "I thought we could, just for once, have ourselves a nice little afternoon. Maybe see if we can get the furnace to stop making that sound. You know what sound I'm talking about?"

Genghis nodded.

The American spent half a minute mimicking mechanical disorders with his mouth. "It's making me nuts. You know what else makes me nuts? Failure. Do you know, Genghis, what the Japanese Samurai used to do to themselves when they failed?"

Genghis nodded.

"Stabbing a man in Reykjavik. Shooting up a church in Budapest. You realize you're a god damn psychopath, right?"

He nodded.

"As far as I know, never in history has the Black Lotus attempted to erase someone famous. We've got no precedent. We're going by feel. But it does occur to me that the first thing I'd do if I were trying to erase someone is, you know, *kill her*. Mind telling me what the hell you were thinking?"

He shrugged.

"You were like, yeah boss. We can handle it. Do you know what the Aztecs did when people back then had bad ideas?"

He nodded.

"Of course you do, because I told you about it. And now winter's coming and they'll put salt on the roads. My Lexus isn't made for salted roads. Do you understand, Genghis, what the salt does to my car?"

He nodded.

"But you were like, yeah boss. We'll nab the hourglass, off Mouse and finish the job in one swoop. Do you remember standing in this very office and using the word *swoop*?"

He nodded.

"And what about Angel? I mean, what the actual fuck? He was my star gunslinger. And now I get word he was thinking about going rogue too?"

He shrugged.

"Did you know that the Korowai people of New Guinea are the last known living tribe of cannibals? Until 1970 they were uncontacted, unaware anyone else occupied this earth. Wild, don't you think?"

He shrugged.

"How do you think, Genghis, the Korowai would handle failure?"

He shrugged.

The American paused, holding his vapor cigarette in contemplation, rolling his tongue around the insides of his cheeks.

"You did kill the sister, correct?"

Genghis nodded.

"Good. The way I see it is we gotta neutralize this thing for good. The propaganda division's done a bang-up job littering the media with stories of Rachel Lipinski's death. PsyOps is in the brainwashing phase. The only problem is the flesh-and-blood girl is still alive." He paused. "In a way I'm grateful. This fuckup has revealed a web of cultists far more sophisticated than we'd previously imagined. Have you been monitoring Wally Algayar's eye worm?"

He nodded.

"That hourglass! A brilliant piece of code. You know where we're heading, then?"

He nodded.

59

"We're close."

"To what?"

"What do you mean to what? To *it*."

"What's it?"

"The truth."

"What, it's a place? It's something you can look at? The truth?"

"You know what I mean."

"I don't. What's the truth?"

"Well I don't know everything."

"But the truth."

"It's an idea that can be distorted but not destroyed."

"You're sure of this."

"It's an idea bigger than us."

"How much further?"

"Top of the staircase."

"Then the truth."

"Would you stop talking and climb?"

She labored up ancient steps. The day's dying light streaked through slits between wooden beams. The covered staircase felt tomblike, ethereal, witness to centuries. Its endpoint was washed white in contrast. A gnarled tree stood center frame. Sediment cracked beneath their feet.

Nikole's stab wound had stopped itching. A dull ache burned her gut. She brainstormed anatomy, pictured those medical charts you see in waiting rooms. Her bodily functions continued unimpaired. Whatever had been pierced couldn't have been vital. Still, the pain seemed ominous. She endured it as a personal test. Already she spotted signs of infection near the bandages. Years of pill abuse had rendered her immune to corner store Tylenol.

Mouse kept walking uphill. Nikole followed. They emerged near an old church. Trees decked out in autumn colors shrouded the stone walkway. Cigarettes and fast food wrappings littered the ground. A breeze pushed around dead leaves like ripples on a lake.

"Before he died," Mouse said, "Angel talked about a cemetery here in Sighişoara, Romania. He said the bird cultists were performing a ritual."

"I was there," Nikole said. "I heard him."

"This must be the place. This is where they make people live forever." She paused. "Or something. We're going to find out, Nikole. We're going to learn the secret."

Nikole rested her hands on her knees. "Hang on," she said. "Let's wait."

"For what?"

"For my sister."

Sam came huffing up the covered staircase, arm in a sling, bits of bandages poking from under her sleeve, its dark stains hinting at the extent of her injuries. Her breathing sounded gargled as she exerted herself. She kept clutching her forearm.

"Well," Sam said, "at least I'm ready now to embark upon an exciting career as high school guidance counselor. You know that most of those chumps haven't even been shot? Severe trauma should be part of the licensing procedure for therapists. Just so they know what it's like. Sure, Mr. Weiss has his fancy degree, but he's never woken up on the operating table or anything."

They ascended towards the cemetery, accompanied by the sound of footsteps. Tourists had vanished for the evening.

A brick mausoleum, baked by centuries of sun, stood watch at the cemetery gates. Sweeping views of Romanian countryside sprawled beyond the church, full of hills and castles, forgotten battlefields and shallow graves, vineyards and brick streets bisecting villages.

Mouse gestured towards the mausoleum.

"We'll hide here until sundown."

The women slouched in the shadows. Nikole winced and rearranged her body, hoping to distribute the pain more evenly throughout her midsection. Sam eased herself down with the shaky consistency of an old man entering a hot tub.

"You okay?" Nikole asked.

Sam nodded.

"You sure?"

"Yup. Got shot in the arm. But you know. It's cool. I've got Advil."

Nikole turned to Mouse. "My sister needs a hospital."

"Soon," she promised. "We won't get another chance at this."

Nikole rested her head against the brick wall.

"Have you thought about what you'll say?" Sam asked.

"What?"

"To Mom. When we find her. What will you say?"

She shrugged. "Haven't had time to think about it."

"I'll forgive her," Sam said. "I'll tell her it's okay."

Nikole put her hand on Sam's. "I'm glad you're with me," she said.

Sam made to wipe her tears but stopped halfway through the motion, wincing, and retracted her arm. "The problems start with hallucinations," she explained.

Nikole narrowed her eyes.

"What?"

"You know," Sam continued, "because of the *extreme fucking trauma* you assholes caused me? Grey men from Mars take me aboard the Mothership for a thorough ass-prodding, and all I can think is *why are they wearing Richard Nixon masks*? Then I get it. Holy crap, these aren't masks at all. They're *actual clones* of our 37th president. Mr. Weiss pats me on the head and reassures me I'm just 'seeing things.' But he's never been shot so what does he know?"

Nikole couldn't laugh. Nikole just smiled.

"How did they meet, anyways? Do we know how they met?"

"Who, Mom and Dad?"

"No," Sam said. "Bonnie and Clydesdale, the bestiality phenom from Phoenix touring this summer at eighteen county fairs and Bone-a-roo. Yes, Mom and Dad, dumbass."

She shrugged. "Never got the story."

They sat and waited. Nikole's eyes fluttered. This repose from violence allowed her body to take stock of its exhaustion. Her head drooped. She closed her eyes and within half a minute fell asleep.

In her dream, Nikole climbs the spaceship bridge to watch KX-131 go supernova. Her family's waiting. Light years from the nearest neon sign, Earth visible via telescope, atmospheric interference is a nonissue. The command center is dark at this hour. The asteroid miners of the *Phaeacian*, exhausted from thirteen galactic hours of drilling, have fled the orange cabin glow, the computer screens and sweeping expanse of space for their daily allotment of pre-sleep vitamin therapy.

KX-131 pulsates against brown arms of the Milky Way.

"I thought it would be more exciting," Nikole says.

Sam tells her to chill. "It hasn't started yet."

Not that, she feels like saying. Escape. Leaving the world behind. It felt right at first, strapped in a cockpit at escape velocity, Earth at our backs. The forbidden rush, the freedom of an open road, gravity's vanishing act. Then you drift into the void and think, wait a minute. This is it? This is all we're made of? Stuff?

KX-131 becomes for a moment a gateway to the Kingdom of God: light that blinds the blind and warms fossilized remains on dead planets light years away. Dad shields his eyes but Mom stares transfixed.

"KX-131," Mom says. "Four billion years. Survived by nobody."

The star spills across the cosmos. Nikole extends her thumb, closes one eye, and blots out the exploding star.

"If humanity went extinct tomorrow and you could only save one person," Sam asks, "who would it be?

Nikole shrugs. "I don't know."

"Yes you do."

"I mean, I don't even know how I'd approach that decision."

"Think about it."

"One person?"

"One person."

"I guess I'd save myself."

A web of colors paints the spacescape with abstract oils. Soon the behemoth of radiation will collapse into a scar, the galaxy's PTSD, the only reminder that one time, somewhere, there was a KX-131, and one time, somewhere, it gave a world the chance to live.

Sam shook her awake. Nikole reeled for a moment in post-dream asphyxia, pondering whether it was some sort of holy vision or meaningless synapse splatter.

Night had fallen. The air had chilled. Mouse stood vigilant, head forward, body pointed like a figurehead mounted on a ship.

Five men toiled in the cemetery, pulling up chunks of soil. They worked at a distance, quiet but for the percussion of their shovels. It was like witnessing birth, watching a body come out of the ground. Mouse stifled a gasp as one of the workers pulled off his sweat-soaked shirt. Ghostly pale in the moonlight, Nikole saw on his chest the unmistakable plate-sized scar of ancient impalement.

"The fountain," Mouse said. "They're taking the body to the fountain."

60

The dwarf had pink hair. Part of her act, she'd explained. She sat on cushions and used pedal extenders to reach the clutch. She had her hair in an unnaturally colored bob, swept to the left, one side of her head shaven. Tattooed skulls and stripes formed sleeves on either arm. She smelled like peanut butter and jelly sandwiches and marijuana. A gold ring tugged her nostrils. She kept looking in the rearview mirror.

"She's fine," Mouse said.

Sam had gone feverish and clammy. Glistening with sweat, breath shallow, she sat clutching her stomach as though seasick. She made to speak but thought twice, choosing to conserve energy.

Ruined castles and prairie grass loomed on hills as the pickup truck neared the dusty sinkhole of Viscri, Romania. A bandaged river of pavement cut through farmland. The road was narrow enough that you weren't sure there'd be room if a car came the other way. Wind kicked up the stink of manure.

"Don't follow too close," Mouse cautioned, gesturing at a rusted SUV two football fields ahead.

"Why?"

"I'll pay you double what we agreed on," Mouse said, "if you stop asking questions."

Wildfire had erupted across Nikole's midsection. She ventured a peak at the knife wound under her shirt. The skin surrounding the slit had grown green and warped like leather. It gave off a smell that made her sick.

People milled about town, perusing melon stands, jaywalking and jay-jogging, tending livestock and speaking with their hands. Cowboy boots and jeans poked out from under a truck on jacks.

"Gotta say," said the driver, "thought I was getting robbed. Nobody's ever hired me as a driver. It's weird."

She had a peculiar accent. Nikole remembered getting in the car with a Laura Magnolia from Bucharest, but whether that was last night or in grade school was a mystery. Clad in scrappy jeans and an unwashed t-shirt, puffy lips and pasty skin, this dwarf-sized woman – if Nikole recalled correctly – likes magic mushrooms, the Doors and defrauding the elderly.

Mouse looked tense.

Their pickup ascended dirt towards an old fortified church. Its peaked roof jutted above brush and trees in a way that reminded Nikole of a Japanese palace. The church was concrete and flaking plaster, holy white, at once pristine and ancient. Slits for bows and arrows littered the parapets. A bush of roses grew taller than the man tending it.

The SUV pulled near the church entrance. Laura Magnolia from Bucharest pulled behind trees. The doors opened and out came the graverobbers, dressed now in suits. They made no attempt to hide the fact that they carried a corpse.

They slid the coffin like a cigarette out of a packet. They looked somber, bored even. They lugged the coffin into the church.

"What now?"

"We wait."

Sam was deteriorating by the minute. Tan had drained from her face.

"Hey, you guys," she said. "Still here. Just, you know, a reminder."

The driver stared into the mirrors.

"Okay," she said, "it's obvious the girl needs a doctor and it's obvious you're avoiding a hospital. She's a mule, right? You're smugglers?"

"Shut up," said Mouse.

The countryside looked like the end of a tunnel. Nikole felt rattled. A depression rippled across her chest. My sister is dying. She'll never meet her mother. Not in this life. Now I'll get gangrene. When I die, make sure the casket stays shut.

"There's a doctor I know who's very discreet," said Laura. "He travels with us. We've got illegals in the circus. People who can't go to a hospital." She paused. "Well, okay. So technically he's not a *doctor*," she said, making quotation marks with her fingers. "But still, very discreet."

"Circus?" asked Nikole.

She nodded. "I walk the tightrope. We tour villages and..."

Mouse pulled a gun. "Shut the fuck up," she snapped. "You so much as breathe too loud and I'll take you behind that church and bury you alive."

Laura stiffened. "Can I," she squeaked, "at least take my medicine?"

Mouse hesitated, then nodded, keeping the gun trained on her vocal chords.

Laura popped the glovebox and removed a vial and a syringe. She pierced the seal with pudgy fingers. Nikole watched with fascination. Laura pumped her fist. Nikole noticed track marks on the inside of her elbow. She found a vein. Nikole averted her eyes. Laura let out a sigh and slouched.

"What is that?" Nikole asked.

Laura shot a glance at Mouse for permission.

"I mean," Nikole said, "is it heroin?"

Mouse rolled her eyes and nodded.

"Xylazine," Laura said. "Horse tranquilizer. We use it as anesthesia on the donkeys."

Nikole cleared her throat. Her heart swelled.

"Um," she began, "can I try?"

As one the driver and passengers turned to look at Nikole. Even Sam paused her suffering to screw up her face.

"The fuck, sis?" she asked.

Nikole reached forward, grabbed Laura by the hand and pulled her hand to her exploding heart. "Feel that?" she asked. "I have a medical condition. I need sedatives."

Nobody moved. Nikole figured this meant nobody objected. She reached forward and dug around Laura's paraphernalia until a needle pricked her skin. She retrieved a used needle and an unused vial.

"Just a drop," Laura warned. "Your body's not used to it."

Nikole shook off her grasp. "I take anywhere from two to eight Xanax a day. My body's plenty used to it."

"Yeah, but it's a different..." Laura began, then trailed off in a way that indicated she knew firsthand the futility of junkie logic.

Because that's what I am. An addict. Isn't that step one?

But now's not the time. Once this is over I'll give sobriety another go. I just need to make it through the day, through the week. Just like every day. Just like every week.

She'd shot up before. She knew the drill. She'd done heroin. Once. A few years back, in a nightclub, with other actors. They'd wrapped filming a Nike ad. She played Girl in Background. Guaranteed pure, said a guy named Cannon. That's the kind of guy you trust, Nikole thought. When it comes to drugs, you trust a guy named Cannon.

As she readied her homemade memory suppressant, one of the graverobbers left the church, got in the truck and shifted into drive. The others – and the body – stayed behind.

Laura asked with her eyes if she should follow.

"Yes," said Mouse. "Wait. No. Let me think."

"Make up your mind quick. Dude's getting away."

"He's not the one we're after."

"Who, then? The body?"

Mouse nodded.

"Hey, you guys?" Sam asked from the back.

"Shut up," said Mouse. "This is it. We've found it. We've found the shrine of the goddess. One of them, at least."

"Hey, Mouse?" Sam asked.

"What is this supposed to mean? A sacrifice in reverse? Bringing a body to life? Or is this a safe house? An underground railroad? I wonder about the corpse, its story. That body is like going to the library, opening a book and reading the last page first. You know how it ends and maybe why it ended, but nothing of the characters, nothing of the plot."

"Okay," said Laura. "This is out of my league."

"These people know the forces that regulate humanity. They can close your wounds. Don't you think? You didn't deserve it. Getting shot, I mean. They'll understand."

"Hey, Mouse."

"Whether our place and time is right or wrong is irrelevant," Mouse continued. "We don't have an invitation, but we came to this stretch of road the same way they did."

"Mouse," said Sam.

"What?" she snapped.

"Nikole isn't breathing."

61

"What if it's real, Mr. Wally? Secret Agents. Medical files that disappear. An international cover-up. Extortion. Murder. Do you really believe this is about settling an academic dispute between archaeologists? What if this gravity thief has been reincarnated, and this hourglass is proof of her unnatural existence? What if they aren't magnets, Mr. Wally? Tony Shen was another. His blood, if tested, would reveal that he too was reincarnated. Perhaps he had the tooth of a thousands-year-old corpse. Now how about you go slurp from the fountain over there and give me a minute. I must speak with the pigeons."

The man, Wally thought, is insane. My God! He schemes without end. Never have I seen a man scheme such as he. Always it amounts to, what's the word, poppycock. His latest scheme is pure folly. Reincarnation! To believe in such a thing is to abandon reason.

They'd arrived in the small nation of Georgia that morning. Wally had succeeded in sleeping through the latter half of the flight. His sleep-starved body was no match for suspicious glances and turbulent skies. The runway rattled him awake. He looked at his watch. He looked at the sun. They didn't match. The day and night cycle had been rearranged so radically that the phrase "time zones" seemed insufficient.

To sleep, he thought, is to pass through a tunnel. But I have encountered a detour. I have, what's the word, wiped out, skidded and wrecked. They have affixed to me tow ropes and pulled me through a hidden passage. Yes. I shall record this metaphor in my yellow notepad so I may deploy it at an opportune time. For I am indeed a clever man, and if others are unaware of my cleverness I have only myself to blame.

Groggy, Wally had shouldered his way through throngs at Tbilisi Airport and, with great exertion, succeeded in reclaiming his suitcase. He utilized his potbelly as a battering ram to the consternation – and, quite frankly, suspicion – of his fellow travelers.

Customs pored over his passport for an uncomfortable duration. Wally had expected such treatment. He'd brainstormed several convincing arguments to demonstrate his American citizenship, for example his thorough knowledge of fast food dollar menus, but found such tactics unnecessary. Showered in glares and whispers, he was permitted to enter Georgia without special accommodation.

Akira crouched among a flock of birds in the square, surrounded by stone buildings and minarets. Under a tent, old men congregated around plates of hot bread. The smell of bread seemed to be everywhere in Tbilisi, Wally thought, along with statues, churches and reminders of war.

Akira found his bird. Around the creature's tiny ankle, a coded message had been affixed to a rubber band. Wally had to avert his eyes in shame as tourists watched the detective give chase to the bird around the square, speaking to it in an invented language. Finally, he caught the animal and, needlessly sniffing the air, retrieved the message.

"I have the address," he reported.

"That was highly unnecessary. We already had the address."

"Yes. But you forget, Mr. Wally, that I don't play by the rules."

They wandered a stone alleyway overflowing with metalwork. A shopkeeper smoked his pipe before an impressive display of copper drinkware. Another hammered a cylinder, much to a tourist's delight. Bullets and bullet-shaped coffee mugs overflowed a table up ahead.

All around were the sounds of capitalism, coins shuffled across counters, people bargaining in half a dozen languages, keys jingling and artifacts being pressed.

"What did you say happened to Nikole Fink's mother?"

"She vanished," Wally said, "some years ago. It is a sore subject, even today. There was never any closure, any explanation."

Akira smiled smugly. "I know."

"Then why do you ask?"

They came out of the alley onto a thoroughfare. Buildings jutted out of hillsides and forests. In this country, Wally thought, there is not a single flat piece of land.

He brainstormed geography and wondered where he might be on a globe. He resolved to research the Caucasus region in more adequate detail upon his return to New York. How embarrassing, he thought, not knowing where one is in the world.

"What if," Akira said, "this reincarnated gravity thief is Nikole Fink's mother? The secret agents said Nikole was being guided along a path. What if they are guiding her here, Mr. Wally, with the intention of drawing her mother out of hiding?"

Madness, Wally thought.

Ancient fortress walls and radio towers loomed on cliffs above town. The roofs were a rainbow and, staring in certain directions, the buildings seemed a jumbled mosaic, nearly built atop one another. Tbilisi is a place of spires and steeples, Persian rugs, street markets and houses consumed by ivy, opera houses and always the smell of bread. In every crevice, Wally beheld hidden treasures. Here a shop sold a hundred varieties of aged cheese. Here antique gramophones can be brought for service.

They wandered through a crossroads of empires, surrounded by relics of Soviet oppression and Arabian allure.

"You will recall the man in the magic shop, the PhD student. He said they took the gravity thief to Infinity Point, where she was drowned."

"Yes," Wally said. "But this was centuries ago."

Akira smiled. "You are aware, of course, Mr. Wally, that ghosts are most inclined to haunt the location of their greatest trauma."

"Ghosts! A new height to the madness!"

Akira hailed a cab. "The hourglass is not an hourglass," he explained as the yellow cab pulled curbside. "It's a map, Mr. Wally. It will lead the way."

"To *what*?"

"Something spectacular, Mr. Wally. Something unnatural."

"This is your theory. Ghosts. Unnatural occurrences. Reincarnation. An infinity map. Secret agents. All I wanted was to reclaim my client's hourglass."

"All in good time."

He entered the taxi. Wally studied a crack in the pavement, then looked at the sky as though awaiting divine guidance. He watched a flock of birds form a spear against clouds, thought My God, sighed, and, once again, followed the detective.

62

They stood in a semicircle under a hammer and sickle. Sun blazed through a dilapidated ceiling and drew slits across concrete. There was a smell like wet garbage. Graffiti ranged from crude gang signs in Cyrillic to elaborate frescoes of bearded communists and Soviet soldiers striking a propaganda pose. Everywhere the paint was flaking. From down a darkened staircase came footsteps and the sound of something being dragged.

Nikole propped herself on her elbows. Her lungs felt sore. Laura Magnolia from Bucharest looked at her in the way you might pop the hood to check a squeaky engine belt.

Three dwarf-sized men stroked their beards. A black man, shirtless with impeccable muscle structure, clasped his hands as though in prayer. Two female clowns exchanged stifled giggles. Above all towered a giant in dusty pinstripes, his hair flat like Frankenstein.

"My sister," Nikole groaned.

"Doc's patching her up," Laura said.

Nikole nodded and rested her head against the floor. From this angle the ruined Soviet monument looked like patchwork ready to collapse. Heroic typography embroidered in red, green and gold clung to glittering residue of glory.

"He sewed up two infected bullet wounds," Laura continued. "I don't know what the fuck you've gotten me into but I want out. I had to check the picture on the news to make sure it's you. Rachel Lipinski. You're supposed to be dead."

The word carried a certain weight to it.

"Where's Mouse?" Nikole asked.

"Gone."

"Gone?"

"She went into that church and I got the hell out. Your sister was doing CPR. She's the reason you're still breathing. I drove fast. For five hours you went in and out of consciousness. We kept a makeup mirror under your nose. Then, as soon as you got stable, your sister started fading. Jesus. Harrowing fucking drive."

"Where am I?"

"Bulgaria."

Nikole nodded. She laid back down and swatted her arms like she was making a snow angel, feeling for her Xanax.

"Somebody followed us," Laura said. "All the way through Romania, across the border. Somebody came out of the church and followed us. He's waiting for you upstairs. He wants to talk. Alone."

Nikole scanned the performers. They gazed with intrigue and fear.

She staggered to her feet. Laura gestured to a rusty ladder. Nikole climbed it to the roof, where concrete blocks and exposed beams were littered with bird shit and age.

Even in her rattled post-OD state, she had to stop and take it in, the landscape. Hills like sand dunes stretched to all horizons, dotted by wind turbines and patches of forest, dots of white cottages, valleys where sky shimmered purple in reflection on rivers, muted browns and greens of a land molded from clay, shrubs and monuments, villages shrouded in fog. The air carried a pleasant chill.

A Middle Eastern man stood with his back turned. He wore a green robe made less opulent from use and a matching turban. His beard was the color of snow

The man moved his head, but not far enough for eye contact.

"We had intel that Black Lotus would follow us to the church," he said. "Instead, you showed up. Who are you?"

"I'm not Black Lotus."

"Of course I know that. We have tabs on every member. What do you want?"

Nikole touched her face and felt dry blood or snot. She coughed more phlegm.

"I'm looking for my mother," she said. "Her name was Melanie Fink."

Birds quarreled overhead. They drew figure eights then scuttled away, drowned out by the hum of an airplane.

"I see," said the man.

She gargled phlegm and spat. I've been good, she thought. It was my first in a long time. Overdose, I mean. But this one wasn't a moral failing. This one was because of circumstance, she reasoned. No need to beat myself up. Still, she couldn't help steal a look at the edge and think about how far away the ground was from this high up.

He turned to face her. His face looked aged yet youthful, his eyes a shade of pale green dulled by the things he'd witnessed.

"Are you one of them?"

"A cultist?" he asked. "No. There is one path to eternal life, and that is through God. What you are seeking is foolish."

"I just want to know the truth. I want to know if my mother is still alive. I want to know who she was and what makes her special." She was struck by a sudden thought. "I want to know if I have it in me too."

His lips curled into a sad smile. "The cultists believe that the seed of immortality is inside us all. But it's not strong enough. You'd need a transfusion."

"A transfusion?"

"It's nonsense, of course. But I believe that faith is important to preserve, so I help them preserve theirs. The Black Lotus, on the other hand, seek to destroy faith."

"But..." Nikole began. "My mother's name was Sera. She was a mystic who lived during medieval times."

"You want so desperately to believe that."

"It's not true?"

"Her name was Melanie Fink. She'd been brainwashed into a cult. Nothing more. There is one path to eternal life and that is through God."

He paused. "If you'd like, child, I could tell you more about what they believe."

Nikole waited.

He turned his back and admired the landscape and, for a moment, the world was quiet and still.

"They worship an ancient fertility goddess. The Fountain of Youth, they say, is a person."

"A person?"

"She crossed the Red Sea out of Africa fifty thousand years ago. They call her Eve. According to the legend, Eve never aged past early adulthood. They worshipped her. A select few still do. They believe she's still alive, all these thousands of years later. Eve has been killed at least twice, the story goes, but both times rose from the grave. Her every cell regenerates. There's something nonhuman inside her."

"But it's not real?"

"Eve had many children," he continued. "Traces of her DNA can be found in almost all humans. The God Cell is already inside you. But it's not strong enough. Humans have never unlocked their full biological potential. We need a catalyst. There is truth in some of their creed. But no, they have no superpowers. That's the thing about the universe. It doesn't care about your feelings. It doesn't care about your hunger."

"So why is the Black Lotus chasing them, then?"

"I don't know and it doesn't matter. The Black Lotus have a variety of employers. It's politics. Somewhere, someone powerful doesn't want people to believe such things."

"What about the magic hourglass?" Nikole asked.

"An hourglass? I know nothing of a magic hourglass."

Nikole watched the clouds and felt shame. A cult like any other. Brainwashing. Politics. You wonder how people end up believing in Dianetics and UFOs. It's already inside us. We just need a transfusion of ideas.

"So none of it's real?"

He shrugged. "Who am I to say what's real? Maybe everyone else has it wrong. Maybe the bird goddess is the one true god. But I am not convinced."

"Who are you? Why are you telling me this?"

"I am a messenger with a warning. You wish to see your mother again. This is understandable. But maybe there's a reason she has not sought you out."

"Have you spoken to her?"

"Yes."

Nikole felt her pulse quicken. "So she's alive? She's out there?"

"Yes. That much I can promise is real."

"Where is she?"

"I don't know. This is by design. I help shield the cultists, but their final destination is kept secret. This way, should I be captured by the Black Lotus, they would have nothing to torture out of me. All I know is that she is somewhere across the Black Sea. Armenia, Georgia, Azerbaijan, maybe even Russia."

"The Caucasus Mountains," Nikole said.

"Correct. Unless..."

Nikole waited. "Unless what?"

His face remained still but she could sense gears moving in his brain. He looked at a point on the horizon. Everything about him seemed sad and lost.

"You said something about an hourglass."

"It belonged to my mother," Nikole said. "At least that's what I've been told. Somehow it ended up in that cave."

He nodded.

"The sand flows backwards," Nikole added.

"It is not an hourglass," the man said.

She waited. He said nothing. His face kept still as a mask. Nikole sensed he was weighing his options, deliberating what else to reveal.

"Use caution, child. You underestimate the forces you're toying with." He sighed and craned his neck, admiring the scenery. In his eyes, there was a constant sorrow.

He approached Nikole and whispered something in her ear.

Stepping away, he continued his oration. "I must return to my wandering," he said. "It is my curse. Be careful, Nikole. You are close to discovering your own."

The man disappeared into a corridor and he was gone, vanished like smoke.

Back inside, the monument was growing dark. Laura's pink hair looked irradiated. The circus performers were seated, playing cards. Sam sat with them. Color had returned to her face. She looked up from her game of Blackjack. "Hey, sis. Get your hourglass back?"

Nikole smiled. "Good to see you in high spirits."

"I'm a big roller now. Circus life's the life for me. I'll be famous. I'm days away from the part where I have to give a hand job to some shady talent agent named Bruce or Donny or Chad. Slicked hair, gold chain, tuft of chest hair, Hawaiian shirt, calls everyone kid, owns part of the Yankees. You know. *That* guy."

It feels good, Nikole thought. Being alive. She had the feeling a mountain climber must get when she's pulled back from the edge. Why not? Why can't this go on forever?

"The hourglass," Sam repeated. "Did that bearded dude give you back your precious hourglass?"

"He gave me something better," Nikole said. "He gave me directions."

63

"What are you doing?"

Sam held Nikole's Xanax at arm's length. The sea was black, invisible with night, but she heard its roar and she felt its bob. From that abyss, there would be no return.

Nikole trembled. She'd crossed the Sahara and here was her first sip of water, just out of reach. She feigned laughter at what must be a joke, pleaded, became angry, threatened to push Sam overboard with them, then settled on staring a space of deck between her feet.

"I get it," she said. "I have a problem."

The refugees clumped around them, watching the drama. They were black and brown, African, Syrian, men with faces full of scars, women with acid burns. Packed onto the fishing boat the way you see in pictures, they bickered about which direction faced Mecca using gestures as a universal language. A child, t-shirt and bones, kicked a clump of garbage while another said "goaaaaaaaal," repeating it, practicing his enunciation. Here a man sold passports. Here a man sold something called Crocodile that you inject like so. A dozen sex slaves sat stock still, their faces fossilized abuse. A Bulgarian man everyone called Hooks explained in broken English what to do if the Coast Guard showed up. Behind them, the coastal towns of Bulgaria smoldered with city lights. The boat smelled of rotting fish, fear and fatigue.

But now all was silent. Activity had stopped. Nikole and Sam – repeatedly mistaken for aid workers – stared one another down.

"You've gotta stop destroying yourself," Sam said.

Nikole went stiff head to toe. I'll jump, she thought. Like the pearl divers in *Tabu*, I'll explore the ocean floor. I'll fistfight sharks. I'll grab electric eels with both hands. Maybe I'll find Cthulhu. Maybe I'll end up in Hell. Maybe I'll die of drowning, but at least I'll die trying to reclaim my holy grail.

"You don't understand," Nikole said.

Sam's eyes bulged with tears. "I've lost so much already," she said. "I'm not losing you, too."

"I'll have seizures. The withdrawal could kill me."

Sam shook her head, disbelieving. Nikole looked to the migrants, hoping someone with experience could back her up. They stared through hollow sockets and yellowed eyes.

So this is it, Nikole thought. Tough love. A well-meaning death. She'll kill me with doing the right thing.

The standoff continued another tense moment. Finally, Sam relented.

"Okay," she said. "But I'll hang on to them. You get half a pill a day."

"Two pills."

"One," Sam said, falling into Nikole's negotiated trap. But even then, at the moment of compromise, Nikole was scheming ways to steal back the bottle. Or – who knows – bum something stronger off the smugglers.

I would have done it, she thought. I would have leaped off the edge. Nothing in this world would have stopped me.

The boat was a hunk of rust the length of a school bus, listing to one end, its mast a tangle of cables. A single orange life preserver hung near the cabin door. At least three dozen bodies were packed on the deck. The night was cold and most wore rags. Bits of battered flesh peeked through.

The black man from the circus, the juggler, had spoken highly of Captain Hooks. Laura had just shrugged. She wouldn't know. Nobody ever stops her when she crosses a border.

Nikole watched the migrants and their suffering seemed predestined.

She tried making small talk with an orphan who lost his whole family in Aleppo – aunts, uncles, grandparents, neighbors, even the family dog. "Bummer," is all she could think to say.

A woman with stubs for fingers and no teeth detailed her ordeal, captivity to captivity, as her family came apart one limb at a time on the trek from Somalia. A Muslim girl in a wheelchair wanted Nikole to describe New York City. She was insatiable. She wanted every detail. Tell me Chinatown. Tell me Wall Street. Tell me falafel stands and Central Park and do they hate Muslims. A father of four from Baghdad explained how the real problem is they don't let us work. "Not bad people," he said. "We want to work. We want to live." Even up close they looked far away.

Sam made a better attempt to show solidarity with the orphans. She taught them magic tricks. She wanted to know where the children were from and her eyes glazed over as they named places like Kobajjep, Qfeilun and Deir ez-Zur. Okay, back up. Let's start with the basics. Teach me how to say hi in your language. "Salaam," Sam said. "Like salami." The orphans stared, uncomprehending.

Nikole turned her attention to the darkness of the Black Sea. She felt exhausted beyond measure. The last few days were catching up with her. She noticed that many of the migrants were already fast asleep, sprawled in unnatural positions on the filthy deck of the ship in a way that showed they were used to such hardships, or that sleeping on an uncomfortable surface pales in comparison to what they'd been through.

She didn't finish the thought. The air felt cold. Waves crashed against the ship. Nikole slouched near her sister and let the sea rock her to sleep.

64

The hatchback left the monastery at dawn, rattling up a web of dirt carved like tributaries in grassy fields, a puff of dust in its wake. Mountains rose like great folds of earth.

Nikole rubbed her eyes, wondering how much sleep she'd gotten collectively in the past week. Sam stood hitchhiking in the center of the road. We made it, Nikole thought. We're here. Georgia. Mom's kingdom and I couldn't even find it on a map.

Engine grinding like a bag of hammers, the car came at Sam full speed. When it became clear she wouldn't budge, the driver maneuvered around her in the grass, hardly slowing. Sam flashed her middle finger and shouted a crude approximation of foreign curse words.

The sisters wandered a forgotten road surrounded by hugeness. Everything about the mountains was hard to judge. Ten miles away, or a hundred? A thousand feet high, or ten? It was only after Nikole spotted the white speck of a concrete structure at the mountain's base that she understood the proportions around her.

She brainstormed ways to ask Sam for a pill. She had to word it politically, like a favor-asking email to the boss.

"Nice scenery," Sam mused, a scratchy sleeplessness in her throat.

They reached a road overlooking a quilt of trees. Concrete blocks formed a guardrail. A brick shrine perched at the valley's edge. The air felt warm.

"It's a place inland," Nikole said. "You won't find it on a map."

"Infinity Point."

She nodded. "That's what it's called. Unofficially."

"And who told you this? A wandering messiah?"

"I trust him."

Sam resumed hitchhiking, less enthusiastic this time.

Nikole took stock of all she'd been through, from the café in Reykjavik to the shootout in Budapest. The gravity thief. A medieval mystic. A cult like any other. I need to hear it from her, she thought. I need to hear it from Mom. Then I'll believe.

And then what? We'll be a family again? Hounded by the Black Lotus, erased from history, my death already staged. We'll spend the next couple centuries in caves. Our fate has been decided. She knew she was angry about something but wasn't sure what.

A red minivan labored up the mountainside. Nikole made out a bearded blob at the wheel. He wore a fedora hat and leather jacket, and had what looked like crossbow bolts affixed to his forearm. Matted hair that hadn't been washed for days poked from under his hat. As the van ground to a halt Nikole noticed a pink My Little Pony doll dangling from the mirror.

The driver shifted his body to roll down the passenger window.

"Are you luffy hakiarnament?" he asked.

Sam stared. "What?"

"On YouTube," the driver clarified. "Your screen name. Are you luffy hakiarnament? You look like her picture."

"Um," Sam began. "No?"

"At 23:04 – military time – on September 24th, luffy hakiarnament made a very mean comment on a video titled 'Justin Bieber – I'll Show You.' I have reason to believe she used the 'n-word' and insinuated that Harry Stiles may be a closeted homosexual. Highly unnecessary."

"Cool story, bro," Sam said. "We're headed to a place called..." She turned and looked at Nikole.

"Tabatskuri," Nikole said, hoping she got the pronunciation right.

"Sure," Sam said. She turned back to the driver. "If you give us a lift, I'll buy you a lifetime supply of Faygo and Guy Fawkes masks."

"You mean the town Tabatskuri? Lake Tabatskuri? The nature reserve?"

"Um, the town, I guess," Nikole said. "There's a place called Infinity Point. There's a stone building that's been abandoned for years. That's all I know."

The driver made a face. "Hmm," he said. "The old church, perhaps?"

"Maybe."

He tipped his hat. "I will permit you to ride upon the Red Dragon, m'lady, under the condition you treat her with the respect she deserves."

The girls got in. Nikole climbed in the backseat and brushed aside weeks-old fast food wrappers covered in flowery Georgian script. Sam got in the passenger seat.

"Call me Jonah," the driver said as the van lurched into motion. "I am a troll hunter."

"A what?"

He smiled. "Internet trolls are the closest thing we have in the 21st century to Adolf Hitler." He spoke with a vaguely Russian accent. The car smelled of bacon and cheap cologne. "There is a man in Tbilisi, username BONERMACHINE9001, real name unknown. On August 17th of last year, he made an extremely mean comment on a message board for Naruto enthusiasts in which he compared OP – unfavorably – to the AIDS virus. Unnecessary. I have been hunting him more than one year."

"And what will you do when you find him?" Sam asked.

Jonah was silent, contemplating. "I will make him pay."

They drove through peaks of the Georgian countryside. Here live a people, Nikole thought, who have adapted to living in the crevices of the world. Here's a farm built at forty-five degrees, its crops jutting and its sheep moving as though affixed to the slope. Here's a town of ancient watchtowers carved from stone, untouched for a thousand years. A church sprung out of a mountain at an angle that looked like an artist making a statement about perspective. Satellite dishes clung to stone and mountain paths. Between towns, the valleys looked primordial. The land made her think of landscapes from documentaries, distant, unreal. The van was always ascending or descending a slope. Sun streaked through clouds like raining sparks. The rattle of the engine was all that reminded her she hadn't traveled through time.

Jonah peeled a banana and munched it in three gargantuan bites.

"By that mighty power," he said, mouth full, "made beings inspired from on high with souls celestial. To us he has given the world, infinite in variety we possess; from him is every monarch in his likeness. Oh one God, thou didst create the face of every form. Shield me, give me mastery to trample on Satan, give me the longing of lovers lasting even unto death."

Sam craned her body to the back and gave Nikole a wide-eyed stare.

"Shota Rustaveli," Jonah said. "The Knight in the Panther's Skin. If you're going to visit Georgia, you should know our greatest poet. And, also, our greatest anime artist... me."

He waited for a reply.

"Totally normal," said Sam. "Nothing's gonna happen. Nobody needs to get groped."

"I see myself as a modern-day Shota Rustaveli," Jonah continued. "I'm a romantic. They say chivalry is dead. Not in Georgia, m'lady. Not in the land of Jonah the Troll Hunter."

They approached a hamlet of old houses, battered barns, farmers' markets and general stores. The outcropping of structures adorned a riverside hill in a way that looked defeated by nature.

Jonah pulled the van to a stop outside a sagging blue building with the word "Guesthouse" in English and a pile of wood outside.

"Okay," Jonah said. "I need you to come with me. You're my henchmen. Stand in my flanks. Look tough."

Sam followed gleefully, Nikole grudgingly.

Inside, the guesthouse felt warm. Its innards looked rustic, full of wooden surfaces and ceiling fans carrying charm in their imperfections. Everything here was made by hand.

A middle-aged man with silver facial fuzz sat behind a counter carved from a single log. He looked up as the companions entered.

"Do you speak English?" Jonah asked.

The man nodded.

"Good. I'd prefer to conduct business in a common tongue for the benefit of my lady friends." He paused, adjusting his Victorian attire. "Are you Viagra_Overdose41?"

The man arched his unibrow.

"Excuse me?"

"I have reason to believe," Jonah continued, "that on June 21st of this year at 15:33 - military time - you made a very mean comment on a YouTube video titled 'Bucket of Sloths' in which you compared a fellow commenter to Mr. Joseph Stalin, when, for the record, the fellow commenter was not Mr. Stalin. For this transgression, I will make you pay."

The man was silent a moment. Sam stood with her arms crossed, trying to look as badass as possible. Nikole looked at the floor, embarrassed for them both.

"You're going to do what?" the man asked.

"Make you pay."

"Ah. Excuse me one moment."

The man walked into a back room and emerged with a sawed-off shotgun.

Jonah yelped and stumbled over his feet. Nikole and Sam, accustomed to violence, looked at each other and shrugged.

Back in the van, Jonah launched into a tirade of apologies.

"I would like you to know that I am far more assured than I appeared," he said. "I yelped and took flight for reasons of your safety. I am a gentleman, m'ladies. They say chivalry is dead."

They hit paved road and merged onto a highway. Shacks sagged on farmland of shrubs and muddy rivers, exotic flowers and outcroppings of sunbaked rocks. Signs in ornate script advertised alien messages. Jonah drank Pepsi from a two-liter bottle.

Halfway to Infinity Point, they realized they were being followed.

65

Jonah left them in Tabatskuri, a village of corrugated roofs and ugly satellite dishes clinging to overgrowth. Night had settled over Georgia. The sisters navigated a maze of dust, passing under crosses, wooden houses jutting over balconies, the sound of accordions. Trees rustled in cool breeze. Nikole rubbed her eyes, still rattled from her overdose.

"We could wait until tomorrow," she suggested. "We could catch up on sleep."

Sam marched with purpose. She kept her eyes focused. She said nothing but Nikole sensed her thoughts. They'd traveled half a globe and waited a decade and change. Nearby was an end to their trials. Behind one of these walls. She could be watching us right now.

"What do you think will happen, really?" Nikole asked. "Do you think she'll come home with us? You think everything will magically be okay? That we'll be a family again?"

Her heart thudded in a way like she was about to break the laws of physics, to poke her head through a curtain no one knows exists, to see things she's not supposed to see.

Tabatskuri resembled a ruin built during medieval times and left maintenance-free for centuries. Homes built from ancient stone had been reclaimed by nature, sheathed by grass and weeds like hobbit holes. It wasn't until Nikole spotted two men smoking near a crumbling brick wall that she understood this was a place occupied by humans.

The village spilled across an outcropping on the lake. A sign in Georgian script adorned what could have been a restaurant. Nikole heard voices on a balcony.

Her feet stopped at an alley's mouth. There it was: a stone building, vaguely church-shaped, perched on a lakeshore outcropping made precarious by erosion. The structure looked forgotten. A stub marked the endpoint of an amputated steeple. Dust and disuse settled on a wooden door, thirty yards out, emblazoned with a subtle but distinct symbol. The symbol was obscure and faded, hidden to anyone who wasn't looking for it:

Something tugged Nikole away. The sun was setting. They were some place new. A realization hit Nikole with the force of a speeding train.

Sam raised her hand to push open the door.

"Wait!" Nikole screamed.

Nikole pictured a physicist before a blackboard filled with equations, a web of photographs pinned to corkboard in a police station, the sinking sensation a ship's captain must feel upon realizing too late why they'd been listing to port.

"Do not go in there," Nikole said.

Sam screwed up her face. "Why?"

She breathed in and out, closed her eyes, felt the day's dying light on her face.

"Because," Nikole said, "I know what happened to the people in the cave."

•••

"The Navajo believe that when you die you're forced to walk across a tightrope. It doesn't matter about how good you've been about sitting still in church, or how many doors you've held for old ladies, or how many times you rode the sybian, or what you've snorted in the name of the gods. It's the prayers of the living that determine if you make it across. If you do, you're rewarded with an unlimited ability to slaughter animals. If you fall, you end up somewhere like this."

They'd taken turns keeping watch. Genghis sat upright in the driver's seat, eyes peeled. At the end of the alleyway, an old truck sat in shambles. Children in hoodies kicked a soccer ball, yelping in strange accents. A generator hummed inside a nearby building. Branches and leaves grew right out of the bricks.

Tabatskuri is a place at peace with nature, Genghis thought, and it makes me hungry. Everything looked overgrown, fusion, old and new, post-apocalypse chic.

"The Pacific Islanders," the American continued, puffing a vapor cigarette. "They're a riot. They think that when you die, your brain loses perception of time. You continue in a dreamlike state for what feels like eternity." He scoffed. "What if you have that dream where you're falling? And it goes on forever? That'd piss me off. You, Genghis?"

He nodded.

The American unholstered his firearm, an old-fashioned revolver. He toyed with the gun in his hand.

"A billion years from now we still won't have dying figured out," he said. "Who will teach our grandchildren? Once our species goes extinct and something takes our place, our guns will become fossils in museums with plaques. This is how human beings expressed themselves." He palmed a handful of bullets. "These are watercolors." He loaded six bullets into their chambers and put the gun to his temple. "This is a self-portrait." He held the gun still a moment. "Pow," he said, mimicking recoil. "When Picasso started drawing prostitutes, nobody thought it was art."

Genghis shrugged.

"Whatever, you fat moron. Keep your eyes peeled. Another hour until our shift's up."

•••

Ornate rugs lathered every surface. Tea whistled. From the kitchen came a clash of pans. Children's drawings had been taped to the plaster walls. The kitchen table overflowed with fresh fruit. A child no older than ten lugged firewood up the steps. The entire house smelled of citrus and fallen rain.

"I am not a man accustomed to such pleasantries, such servitude. I implore you promptly cease and desist with regards to your exquisite tea. You see, I am a man of delicate disposition. Already I am quite, what's the word, jittery. Additional stimulation – be it herbally derived or otherwise – is liable to rattle me further, to the point I may find it difficult to nap at an appropriate time."

Akira stood at the window with binoculars. He wore a fake mustache and headscarf. He had not moved for hours. Every so often he repeated the phrase "I am Apocalypse Now."

The Georgian family – two daughters and a father – had been pleasant to the point of irritation. It had been simple gaining entrance to their abode. After fierce negotiations led by Akira fizzled out, Wally simply offered to remove his shoes upon entry. Salaam alaykum, my brother. Wally smiled. And also with you. The entire ordeal annoyed Akira greatly, much to Wally's delight.

"May I ask you something?"

"Of course, Mr. Wally."

"What happened to your last partner?"

"Excuse me?"

"When we first met, you'd mentioned a partner. You informed me that you and he had had a disagreement."

Akira groaned. "Yes, Mr. Wally."

Wally waited, but Akira made no move to further the conversation.

"You do not wish to talk about it?"

The detective sighed. "My grandfather emigrated from Japan shortly before the Second World War," he began. "They held him in internment camps, where he suffered the sting of false accusations and prejudice. Once the war had ended, he dedicated his life to the pursuit of justice. He became a police sergeant, then a private detective, as did my father."

"But you were different," Wally guessed.

"Indeed, Mr. Wally. You have me figured out, just as you imagined."

"You wanted to be an actor."

He was quiet a moment. "I couldn't escape my fate, it seemed. I couldn't disappoint my family. I went into law and order, Mr. Wally, and I did the next best thing – I became a studio fixer. I worked in Hollywood for six years and helped many studios keep their stars in line and many stars keep their scandals buried."

Wally nodded. He began to understand. "It was not your partner who had the disagreement," he said. "It was you."

"I worked with a man named Frank Scott, a veteran Hollywood detective. We were hired onto a case that was difficult to stomach. An A-list movie star was accused of child abuse. His manager made me a deal. I was to discredit his victims, and in exchange I'd be offered a cameo spot in an upcoming blockbuster. A foot in the door, Mr. Wally."

He was quiet a long time.

"You did the right thing," Wally offered.

"Did I? I could have reported the man to the police. For all I know, the man is still out there, abusing children. Look at me. I am too cowardly even to name him. No, Mr. Wally. I was a deserter. I objected to the case and I was cast out of Hollywood, though my silence kept my reputation mostly intact. I found a demand for my services on the East Coast. I have helped locate many stray cats and dogs. I am an errand boy for hire by the rich and powerful."

"Well," Wally said, "I believe you have done good in this world. I am glad to have made your acquaintance, sir, and I apologize for my prior words."

Akira glanced through his binoculars and lowered them. His face remained stoic.

"I have two things to report," he said. "First, the sun has set and it will be difficult to maintain cover should we not snuff out the lights."

Wally shuffled in his chair. Surely they had intruded on an innocent family without purpose. Surely they should cease inflicting undue hardship on their hosts.

"Second," Akira said, "Nikole Fink is at the church."

Wally felt blood abandon his face. The bouncing of his knee stopped. He looked at Akira, then the floor, then at the nothing before him.

His heart did something strange. His momentary good will towards Akira evaporated at once. Surely the man is jesting, he thought. Why pull such a cruel trick? This has gone on far enough. I need to teach this man something. Yes. He cannot order me around. Just compare my mustache with his! I should have called the police. But for now, I must engage this man in fisticuffs. I refuse to be taken for a fool a moment longer. They will respect me for the scholar I am.

As he got to his feet he caught a glimpse through the window. It wasn't long enough for facial recognition. But it was enough. Wally felt his throat dry out.

"Engage Alpha Protocol," Akira said.

"Alpha Protocol?"

"Do you have firearm training with a rocket-propelled grenade launcher?"

"A grenade launcher?"

"Are you an expert in demolitions? Can you bring a building down? I am Apocalypse Now, Mr. Wally."

The world spun at odd angles. It was her. My God! Wally took a step, felt lightheaded, then collapsed on his back.

66

Nikole scanned the street – more a dirt and gravel path – and found all signs of life snuffed out. The world looked like an Old West film set, quiet as a stranger came to town.

Then, from an alleyway, a silhouette emerged. It was their pursuer, the one who had followed them to the lake, though she had been following Nikole for much longer.

Streetlights draped crumbling buildings in warm colors. Strips of yellow, red and white formed a pattern like a piece of steel heating up.

The figure approached and began clapping. The sound of flesh against metal thudded in the sunset.

"Bravo, Nikole," she called out, walking as slowly as she clapped.

"You burned those people," Nikole said. "Didn't you?"

"Of course I did," said Mouse. Her face entered the light one feature at a time. "One by one. I made the others watch as they waited their turn. They died in exquisite agony. I've been trained. I know how to make it good and slow."

"You wanted them to tell you about the Fountain of Youth," Nikole said. "You're obsessed."

"You aren't?" she asked. "We're talking about immortality. It's real! The elixir of life. The philosopher's stone. We could live forever. We've found the lock but we need the key."

"The cultists you lured to the cave wouldn't tell you the secret."

Sam took a single step back as Mouse came closer. She wasn't holding a weapon, though her jacket had many pockets.

"They preferred death by fire," Mouse said. "By the time I got to my eighth victim, I was getting nervous."

"So you let one escape," Nikole said. "You've been acting. Playing dumb. You wrote my name on that envelope. You doctored that photograph. You painted the goddess symbol and carved the *Kid Wizard* reference into the wall."

"There you're wrong. Helena carved those words. She had instructions from your mother. They were friends."

"So you let us track down Helena," Nikole said. "You bet that if Sam and I found her, and if it looked natural, she'd talk. You wore a mask in the cave. You bet that a determined daughter could find her mother where the Black Lotus failed. You took us to that graveyard because you knew about the messenger. You let us to do the detective work."

"I needed to get both you and the Black Lotus involved," Mouse said. "You're a celebrity. You're one of the few people on Earth the Black Lotus can't erase. If I started jet-setting about the world hunting for Sera, I'd get a bullet in the head before I could blink. But if I had *you* on my side, new BFF, it'd cause them the kind of migraine you get from a brain hemorrhage. I learned your sister had a long list of arrests for trespassing. I knew she wouldn't be able to resist the cave's riches. And you two did *exactly* what I wanted you to do."

"How did you get into the cave?"

"I'm a Black Lotus trained demolitions expert. How do you think? I blasted a hole from the storm sewer into the engineers' path. Took me five years. Then I collapsed my path and made it look like a natural cave."

"You lured random people on the Black Lotus watch list into your lair." She paused. "How do you even know all those people were cultists?"

"I don't. Collateral damage, Nikole. It's a fact of war."

"And now what? What's your end game?"

Mouse smiled. She gestured to the apartments on either side of the street with her head. "Mommy's in that church, you know. She's watching us right now."

Nikole and Sam studied the windows of the church and its surrounding homes. Some were lit. Most weren't. Behind a set of drapes, she could make out a shadow.

"Now for the fun part," Mouse said. "How much pain can a mother allow her daughter to endure? Sera will tell me about the secret of eternal life or she will watch her daughters dismembered, piece by piece."

"Alright, lady," Sam said. "You went to, like, *a lot* of trouble setting this up. Calling me Whiskers and whatnot. Running from the cops. Escaping a burning village. The shootout in Budapest. I don't get it. If you're such an elite super assassin, why not just kidnap us and whisk us around the world in your secret stealth jet?"

"Do you know how hard it is for me to walk down the street?" Mouse asked. "I'm number one on every Lotus hit list. I lived in a sewer drain for five years. I had to distract them. I had to show them something spectacular to get their heads turned. Then, well, I just got on a plane and flew back to Prague. Thanks for all that! You've been a pal, Nikole. Now you're gonna help me out one last time."

Nikole's eyes darted between stone houses and backlit shadows, from orange light trickling through slit blinds to a universe of stars blinking to life in the abyss of space.

She grabbed Sam by the wrist and took a step backwards, not quite sure what she was doing.

"Come on out!" Mouse called to the watching windows. "We'll have a nice little family reunion, just the four of us!"

Nikole eyed an alley between flaking brick buildings. Instinct took hold. She stepped aside, but not fast enough. Mouse moved like an Old West gunslinger, faster than the eye could grasp. Inside the space of a hummingbird's wings, she plunged her hand into her jacket. Nikole knew what was coming before she felt it, felt it before she heard it, heard it before she even saw the glint of gun barrel in the street lights.

She looked down. Her leg stopped working. The bullet had hit her knee head on. She collapsed to the street. Her leg from the knee down protruded at a sickening angle. Her jeans grew black with blood.

It didn't hurt. Not yet. Not like it was about to. Her body felt like it had touched electric wire. Too shocked to move, she looked at the bullet wound then at the world, wondering if any of it was real.

Mouse aimed at Sam's chest. Sam raised her arms in surrender.

"Easy, lady."

Mouse closed the distance between them, keeping the gun at heart level.

With her gun, Mouse instructed Sam to open the door. Hinges creaked under pressure, spilling shadows over the street. Mouse and Sam hauled Nikole to her one working leg and they entered the church.

Someone was waiting inside.

67

The Chemist had come decked out for chemical warfare, complete with gas mask and lab coat, lugging what looked like a beer keg. Wisps of something deadly stirred near its lid. He set down the canister with a resounding thud that echoed like a gunshot.

"This chemist," he began, addressing Mouse in a voice made mechanized by his mask, "has brought you a gift."

Genghis emerged behind them.

The church was hardly the size of a bedroom. Its walls and floor were a single shade of mossy stone. Starlight trickled in through window slits. Sagging beams held the ceiling aloft. The stink of chemicals was overwhelming.

Nikole crawled into a corner and stretched her wounded leg, trying not to look too hard at the damage.

Masked Black Lotus soldiers swarmed through the door, assault weapons raised. They leaked out of every corner of the Earth, forming human barricades across the escape route and pulling shut the ancient door.

Mouse stayed steely, almost smirking, as though she'd anticipated everything.

A man with his whole head shaved – eyebrows and all – stood at the altar. He was dressed all in black, unarmed as far as Nikole could tell, smoking a vapor cigarette. He spent a long time looking at Mouse as though she were an exotic insect pinned behind glass, a species of life he'd never known existed.

"Huh," he said.

Everyone kept one eye on The Chemist. Nobody moved.

After the gunshot, the world had its volume turned down. Nikole's mind still hadn't caught up with her body. She tried to move her leg and found the limb disobedient.

"You know," the shaved man said to Mouse, "Genghis requested that he be the one to pull the trigger. He's still sore after what you did to his partner."

Mouse kept the gun aimed at Sam.

"Think about what you'll learn," he continued. "You'll know more, at that moment, than anyone alive. You'll figure out the mystery. Everyone dead knows one thing more than the living." He puffed vapor from his electronic cigarette and dramatically stepped through the cloud. "Do you know," he asked, "about the Mende people of Sierra Leone?"

Nobody spoke.

"Sande influences every aspect of a Mende woman's life. It is present before birth and it is still present after. You're familiar with the way of the Tao, correct?"

Silence.

"Well, it's a similar concept."

Pain began rolling out of Nikole's wound in waves. Blood pooled below her knee. She felt nauseous, then sleepy. Low light painted the world the color of dreams.

"Wow," Mouse said, drawing out the word into multiple syllables. "Are things really so desperate?"

"We're going underground a couple decades," the bald man explained. "Our cover's blown all around the globe. Hope you're happy. Anyways, we thought we'd go out in..." A smile crossed his face. "Well, you'll see."

"And the quest to exterminate the Cult of the Bird Goddess?"

"Completely abandoned. You and the Lipinski sisters here are our last loose end."

"That's too bad," Mouse said, "seeing as I was about to deliver to you, gift-wrapped, the location and nature of the Fountain of Youth."

His face creased like an ampersand. He stared, half-believing, as though trying to see through a car salesman's scheme.

Blood kept seeping, slower now, through the denim tatters of Nikole's destroyed kneecap. She closed her eyes, mashed her teeth, wondered what she could say in her last moments to make things right with God. The idea of an abyss became real and horrifying. Nothing seemed abstract. It was here, the darkness, encroaching on her brain. Her knee didn't hurt as bad anymore.

"What do I say to you?" The Chemist said. "I say, boss, you do not let her speak. You let her speak and what happens? Lies. She is silver-tongued, that one. She will make you believe anything."

The boss nodded, his forehead a mountain of Klingon folds. "You mean to tell me that you got one to talk?" he asked, incredulous.

Mouse nodded.

"Impossible."

"You want it too," Mouse said. "Don't you? You'd give up everything."

The boss man looked at his men. "Stand down," he said. "Let her speak."

Mouse postured like an actor preparing for a dramatic monologue, taking her time with it, building suspense.

Sam looked at her sister. In Sam's face Nikole saw alarm, then masked calm. She moved her lips to say something then rearranged her face to project an illusion that it wasn't so bad.

Nikole couldn't believe how much blood she had inside her. As she watched her life ooze from the volcano of her knee, she kept scanning the windows, hoping beyond anything for eye contact with the woman who gave her birth before the curtains close.

Outside, a shadow moved. A dull thud and rattle echoed from opposite the wall.

Mouse shot her glance sideways. The soldiers looked confused. Even The Chemist, momentarily, shifted attention from his arsenal of chemical warfare. Sam and Nikole strained to stare through the darkness.

It's her, Nikole thought. She's come to my rescue. A mother can only watch her daughter suffer so much.

A silhouette stood framed by one of the slit windows. Slowly, a second window filled with body mass. Nikole did a triple take.

Wally?

The hulking frame of her agent was unmistakable. He and another, slimmer man stood in the church's windows. His accomplice appeared to be urging Wally to do something. Wally hesitated. There was no mistaking his mustache, even at this distance.

Shit, Nikole thought. Wally. I never called him back. God knows what went through his head after that phone call from Iceland.

"Hey assholes!" the second man bellowed. "Looking for *this*?"

Moonlight glared off curved glass. He held an object to the world.

It was the hourglass.

"Okay," Mouse said. "Now *that* I did not see coming."

The soldiers took firing position.

"The hell is this?" the Black Lotus commander asked.

Genghis shrugged.

"We demand the release of Nikole Fink," said the Asian man in the window. "In exchange, we will..."

He never finished the sentence. The soldiers didn't wait for an order. The church erupted with gunfire. The Asian man was shot and fell on his back.

The hourglass tumbled through the air.

The gunfire stopped. All eyes became fixed on the impossible object as it glinted and glared through shades of lamplight and gravity, a rendezvous with reality below. It tumbled through the church window. Mouse lunged like an outfielder, but it was too late.

The hourglass crunched against the stone and shattered. The sand within stirred, liberated from its cage. It formed a miniature tornado and swept through the enclosed space. Then the vortex flew, suspended by magic, stretched out against the stars, ascending back through the windows and into the night sky where it vanished forever.

For a moment, nobody spoke.

"Huh," said the Black Lotus commander. Then he turned to The Chemist. "Kill them all," he said.

He stepped in front of a window. A rifle cracked outside. What happened to his head was hard to describe. Later, in police interviews,

Nikole would liken it to a fishbowl meeting a jackhammer. Sam would use more colorful language, describing the sinews of gray matter with a variety of melon metaphors. One thing they agreed upon was the sound. Like two bowling balls clicking together. Incredible, really, that they independently used the same description. Nothing else on earth sounds like that.

The Black Lotus commander took more steps than he should have. He shuffled his feet in an unsettling trance, then fell flat on what was left of his face, his skull simply missing from the nose up. His throat made a gargling sound that would resonate in Nikole's nightmares for years.

Mouse wiped his brain off her jacket. She sat stunned for a moment, then dove through the door back into the village of Tabatskuri.

Nikole flinched. On instinct she glanced for an escape route. Only one. Wait for the bullet and let it be over.

A streak of fire split the night in two. Something exploded. Nikole felt heat wash over her. Then came the smell. A sandpaper of chemicals ate into her sinuses. She wretched and choked. The pain in her knee returned. She turned her head and saw The Chemist in a cult-like trance swaying through a screen of mustard-colored gas billowing into the church.

In the confusion Sam delivered an uppercut to Genghis's testicles. The big man doubled over in pain.

The window in which Wally had stood was now full of flames. The gas seemed to be catching fire, igniting the very air around them.

Mouse commandeered a gun from a stumbling soldier. She masked her nose with her jacket and took aim at Nikole.

"Get up!"

Sam hauled Nikole to her feet. Her eyes burned. Sam's skin swelled and reddened. They rushed into the street.

A bullet grazed Mouse's floppy ear, taking its upper half clean off. She hardly slowed down.

"We have to get away from the gas," she said.

Nikole's head was awash in white noise. She shuffled forward like the living dead. Every part of her wounded leg came apart with each step. The pain was gone, replaced with a numbness that worked its way up her thigh and into her torso.

The streets smelled of burning. You could feel it right away, the wall of heat. Residents filed out of their homes in chaotic fashion. The only hint of a fire beyond the heat was a single wisp of smoke.

Mouse picked a direction and followed an elderly couple.

"We're finding mommy," said Mouse. The left hemisphere of her head was coated in blood.

She started knocking down doors with her metal hand, firing bullets into the night.

"Come out!" she screamed. "I have your daughters!"

They rounded a corner as more chaos exploded in the street. Poison gas followed, trickling overhead like a volcanic flow.

Nikole felt faint. She left behind a trail of blood. Everything slowed inside her head.

Another explosion, this time closer. The world buckled and Nikole struggled to maintain her footing.

Then they were there, side by side at the end of an alleyway, in dark suits and sunglasses, like the children in *The Shining* gender swapped and all grown up. They were stoic as gunfire erupted around them. As the Mouse rounded the corner, they raised their pistols as one.

"Duck," said Agent Johansson.

Nikole hit the dirt, taking Sam with her.

Two shots rang out. On instinct, Nikole clutched her neck. She heard the body fall before she felt the weight on top of her.

Mouse was dead.

She left this world hungry and alone, friendless, never deciphering the hieroglyphics to which she'd dedicated her life. Nikole watched her crumple to the soil. Her lips fluttered. She showed momentary signs of a last-ditch struggle. She made eye contact with Nikole and in her pupils Nikole saw genuine fear. Nikole thought about what the bald man had said. Soon she'd learn the secret. Soon she'd know for sure. Okay, Nikole tried to communicate with her eyes. I'll keep up the fight. I'll see what I can figure out in this life. She felt shame at this momentary comradery with her captor. Mouse looked human then and Nikole saw in her a glimpse of the thirteen-year-old pyromaniac, pre-Black Lotus, a kid with floppy ears and a curiosity that would go unanswered. Then she stopped moving.

A burning beam fell. Nikole sat up. She felt close to death.

The agents lunged into action.

"In here!"

They led the companions through a labyrinth of alleyways until they came to a hole in a brick wall leading into an abandoned building. Inside, operatives monitored computer screens and men in camo fatigues reloaded assault rifles.

"Holy shit, you guys," Sam said. "Feel my heart. Here, secret agent dude, feel my heart. No, it's cool. Chris Hansen's not around."

Arms around shoulders, they dragged themselves out of fire as the world collapsed at their backs.

68

"It was so exciting, Nikole. The man was insane! I am not the sort of person who bestows honors upon himself. I am a simple man, a tactful man. I enjoy ballroom dancing and the taste of bell peppers. I put Just For Men in my mustache. It is important to keep up one's appearances in this business. You understand. You are looking nice and emaciated yourself."

Light rain began to fall. Police handed out ponchos and gas masks. The once-quiet village had become a circus of flashing lights, curious neighbors, firefighters and men in fatigues who Nikole would later learn were CIA paramilitary.

The church had a hole punched through its center. The roof had formed a V. Fires had stopped but smoke still billowed from the wound.

Paramedics loaded Nikole into an ambulance. Her leg stretched before her, bandaged and compressed. An IV in the back of her hand made the world numb.

They brought past Akira Murakami, the Japanese detective, sitting upright on a stretcher, clutching his chest.

A Georgian police sergeant approached.

"Akira Murakami?" he asked.

"Yes?"

"You are under arrest for destruction of property, criminal trespassing, robbery, failure to appear in court, aggravated assault, impersonation of a police officer, falsification of documents, aiding and abetting a terrorist organization, possession of illegal firearms, gnostical turpitude, public urination and the illegal downloading of music."

He raised a fist in protest as they wheeled him away and announced, quite loudly, "I am El Chapo."

Wally and Sam climbed into the ambulance with Nikole. The Agents Johansson approached, looking impeccable in crisp new suits. Remarkably, both men had now removed their sunglasses. It took Nikole a moment to recognize them without facial attire.

They climbed into the back of the ambulance. The doors shut and the vehicle pulled away, siren blaring.

Wally went rigid head to toe. He looked afraid.

"Dear sirs," he began. "Permit me to..."

Agent Johansson held up a hand to silence him.

"The blood, Mr. Algayar."

"Of course."

Wally reached into his jacket and extracted a vial of dark liquid. Nikole's heart sputtered. A transfusion, the messenger had said. It's how they initiate new members.

There it is, she thought. Eternal life.

Agent Johansson ripped the vial from Wally's hand, slid it into an opaque zippered bag and shoved it under his suit jacket.

Gone forever.

"Excellent," the agent said. "Our task is complete. The Black Lotus is no more."

"So wait," Sam said. "You guys didn't have anything to do with the cave people?"

"Oh, no. We simply saw an opportunity to draw the Black Lotus out of hiding. We never intended to solve the murders. Our task was to lead the Black Lotus into a carefully orchestrated ambush. Though you took a rather - ahem - unorthodox route, and your friend here," he said, gesturing at Wally, "nearly ruined everything, in the end it worked out nominally."

"Extremely nominal," the other said.

"But what about my mother?"

"Your mother? Oh, we're certain she's a hoax. I mean, come on. Immortality? A gravity thief?" He chuckled, holding his stomach with both hands the way rich people laugh. "Surely you don't believe in such nonsense."

Nikole said nothing.

"You acted with valiance and courage becoming of an American hero, Ms. Fink," he continued. "It is my honor to bestow upon you the highest decoration within my authority to bestow."

From the inside of his suit jacket, Agent Johansson pulled a star-shaped medal affixed to a blue-and-purple striped ribbon.

"The Order of St. Hubertus," he said, awkwardly pinning it to Nikole's poncho.

"Were you going to let them execute me?" she asked. "Were you going to let them execute my sister?"

Johansson sighed. "In any armed conflict, collateral damage is inevitable."

Nikole wrenched the medal from his hands and threw it at the ground.

The agent gasped. "The Order of St. Hubertus!"

"Fuck your medal."

The two agents regained professional composure. "I believe we're finished. You have done your country a service greater than you can know. For national security reasons, we must insist you speak of your ordeal to no one. We'll see to it that any further invasion into your personal life is minimal. Godspeed, Ms. Fink."

A medic examined Sam's face with a flashlight. She winced as he touched her nose. "Not broken," he said. He prodded her split lip. "Stitches?" he asked. She shook her head.

Nikole felt by momentum the ambulance rounding a corner. The pain had stopped but she still felt faint.

"So that's it," Sam said. "Mom's not here."

Nikole didn't know what to say.

"We came all this way. Now we'll never find her. We missed our one shot."

Wally, who had been typing furiously on his Blackberry, perked up.

"Wait," he said. "There was someone. A woman in the church. Yes. When we arrived. She seemed to be in a hurry to leave. I thought nothing of it."

"Did you see her face?" Nikole asked.

He nodded.

"What did she look like?"

He shrugged. "Pretty," he said, squinting into his phone, trying to remember a detail before insanity had washed everything from his brain. "Green eyes. Black hair. She was rattled by our appearance at her doorstep."

The sisters looked at each other.

The ambulance pulled to a stop. Paramedics pushed the doors open.

"Did she say anything? Did she give you a message?"

Wally shook his head. "She looked spooked," he said. "She seemed in a hurry to leave. Did you know her?"

A waiting cadre of nurses rushed Nikole out of the ambulance. Outside, the rain moved like ghosts. Nikole studied the sky. Clouds parted in patches, baring a cleavage of stars. She thought about ancient mariners and sea monsters, sailors from another age using night to chart the way home. She felt affixed to a piece of driftwood circling the globe, dying of thirst surrounded by salt water and sirens. She wished upon a flickering satellite that things were different.

Sam nudged her elbow. "Go get better, sis," she said. "Then we'll go home."

69

A nurse changed her IV bag. Nikole thought about the first person to get a blood transfusion, the secret of modern medicine, dangerous and forbidden knowledge. Anxiety was no match for anesthesia. She'd spent twelve hours post-surgery in comatose dreamland, waking disoriented, wondering if everything from her birth onward had been a dream.

Air conditioners hissed overhead. A wall-mounted television played the news on mute. The nurse adjusted Nikole's pillow, offered a strained smile and left.

Nikole saw her own face on the television. Text at the bottom of the screen read, in English, "RACHEL LIPINSKI HOAX DEBUNKED; ACTRESS NIKOLE FINK ALIVE AND WELL."

Sam sat cross-legged on a plastic chair in the corner of the room in the midst of an ice cream binge. She saw Nikole stir and licked the chocolate off her lips.

"How do I know that when we get back to New York you won't start abusing your pills again?"

Nikole averted her eyes.

"It'll kill you, Nikole."

"I don't want to talk about it," Nikole said.

"You need help."

"Oh," Nikole said. "Uh, no thanks."

She felt a bulging rage and tried not to let it show. Not now, she thought. Not after everything. Of course I'll get clean. But the timing's wrong. How can I make my sister understand?

Sam looked conflicted.

"Look," she said. "I get that I don't get it. Okay? I understand that I don't understand. But whatever you're going through, we'll have a better shot of beating it if we worked together. You know, as a team."

Because that worked out so well on our little vacation, she fought the urge to shout. What had they accomplished? What were the spoils of their hardships? Why had they suffered? The Cult of the Bird Goddess was still a mystery. Their mother had disappeared.

Sam paced the hospital room. A bad feeling had developed between them.

Unexpectedly, she tossed the bottle of Xanax onto Nikole's bed.

Nikole eyed the pills, unsure how to interpret the act.

"Once we get home, I'm leaving," Sam said. "You'll never see me again."

"Why?"

"You don't need me."

"What do you mean?"

Sam pouted like a child. Nikole hadn't touched the vial in her lap but felt her brain salivating. It's a test, she decided. The asshole is testing me.

Sam's silence bothered Nikole.

"You're so goddamn perfect, huh?" she snapped. "Tell me why I should care. Tell me why your opinion matters." Her voice rose. "Explain that to me."

Sam didn't speak. The nurse stuck her head through the door to observe the disturbance, then withdrew.

"What, you're too good for me?" Nikole asked. "At least I have a home. At least I've earned a roof over my head."

She waited for Sam to respond, to say, look at yourself. See what you're doing. See what you've become. But she only stood in silence, which enraged Nikole further.

Nikole swung out her leg cast from under her sheets and hobbled to her feet, holding herself up by clutching her IV stand. As she stood, blood did odd things in her body. She felt faint and saw spots.

"Hey!" she bellowed. "Look at me, asshole! I was nice to you! I treated you like a sister, like a friend. I helped you out."

Sam flinched. In the hallway Nikole saw the nurse conversing with other nurses and they took turns staring Nikole down, debating how to handle the disturbance. The machinery Nikole was hooked up to bleeped and blared like she was having a stroke.

"You think I need these?" she asked, rattling her pills. "You think I have a problem? I'll show you a problem."

Sam approached her sister.

Here it comes, Nikole thought. She waited for a fist to the face, a knee to the stomach. Something, anything. She wanted pain, if nothing else so she could feel. Sam wound up for assault. Nikole tensed her muscles.

Sam lunged into Nikole shoulder first, wrapping her arms around her sister, embracing with the sort of overbearing, suffocating love you can only get from your family. Sam sniffled. Nikole felt tears stain the shoulder of her shirt. She felt embarrassed to the point of nausea. Sam helped her settle back into her bed.

"Promise you'll never leave me."

"I promise," Nikole sniffled.

"Promise you'll get help."

She felt as though she'd stepped in a bear trap. Forced down a corridor of shame, immobile in a hospital bed for at least another few days, she'd been prodded into a dead end. Nothing mattered. The decision had been made for her, not by Sam, not by circumstance, but by something shuffling slyly behind the veil of reality.

"I promise."

"We'll work together," Sam said.

"Okay."

"I'll make sure that whatever they do to you doesn't hurt."

"Okay."

"If we team up nothing can stop us."

She heard the words, their shape, and felt their truth.

Sam smiled, wiping away tears. "So when do we call VH1?"

Nikole laughed.

"Think about it," Sam continued. "We could make a solid buck! Family drama, pill abuse, intervention and '90s nostalgia? We could at least land some inspirational Thought Catalog headlines if not a major TV deal. I could be a star. I see myself as having a career trajectory similar to that of Ron Jeremy with less splooge. Okay, more splooge. Sploogeosaurus. OMG. Best username ever."

"I'm glad you're with me," Nikole said.

"When you sign a big Hollywood deal," Sam continued, "does the Illuminati visit *you*, or are you supposed to go find *them*? In any case, I guess I should get this out of the way. Oh sweet Satan, I pledge my soul to you, Prince of Darkness. Hey, you think they've got KFC in Hell?"

"There's just one thing left that bugs me," Nikole said, recomposing herself.

"What's that?"

"The cult," she said. "Was it real? Do they really live forever? Or is it a cult like any other?"

Sam chewed her lower lip. "Maybe we'll figure it out some day," she said.

Her heart monitor deviated for a fraction of a second like a hiccup. Through her window the sun peeked over the horizon equal parts blinding and divine.

Sam held her hand and the medicine took control. She felt the world tremble as she realized what a thing it was to be alive.

70

She sat in her wheelchair at her apartment window clutching the broken hourglass, her only reminder that something was amiss about the world. A single detail. All that remains. Outside, the streets were an American portrait: the wrinkled, the dirt-caked, the unemployed, the drunk-before-noons, the brown paper bags, the hackey-sacks, the lines snaking out of shops with neon signs advertising lottery. A kid with homemade piercings darted out of a corner store looking nervous. An old blues singer sat on a folding chair on the sidewalk, looking at nothing. The street ebbed and flows as it had for decades, a river run without changing course.

The gravity thief. Infinity Point. The blood of the goddess. These were words and phrases, syllables, things you could say out loud. But none of it was real. It was a cult like any other and Melanie Fink was brainwashed. And, for a moment, I believed too. Human beings are like that.

From window to sidewalk was a five-story fall. Who'd find it? She pictured a homeless trash picker hunched like Gollum discovering his precious. She pictured the hourglass remains – nothing more than two wooden discs etched with a symbol of goddess worship – crowning a mountain of garbage bags. Drop it. Throw it. Be done with the thing.

The clinic was called Elmwood Palms. Very discreet, according to a Studio32 message board. They had a guy called Leo Bloom who goes by Dr. Magic. That's the kind of man you trust, Nikole thought. Dr. Magic had been blunt. A Xanax addition is no joke, he'd said. I've seen people come off heroin easier, he'd said. I'll be blunt, he'd said. Yes. There was no question as to Dr. Magic's bluntness.

Look at me, Mom. I'm still here. I'll wait for you. I've made a big decision, you know. I'm going to change. When you come around next, I'll still be breathing, sitting at this windowsill, waiting for you. But first I need to learn to walk again.

She dropped the hourglass remains on the floor.

Inside one of the discs, something rattled.

Nikole turned her neck. Cracks crisscrossed the wood. She scrounged at air and plucked the thing from the floor, cradling it in her palms. With delicate breath and hands, she shook it twice, three times. This was not the clatter of shards. This was the sound of buried treasure.

She wheeled herself into the kitchen and knocked it against all manner of surfaces: wooden counter, plaster wall, steel stove. More and more tiny cracks. The fall from the church window in Georgia had rattled something loose. Under repeated assault, the surface came apart and she had the feeling of unmaking the universe, a goddess with the galaxy in her hand. Her kitchen counter lacked adequate powers of destruction. Onto the tools, the next phase in evolution. Steak knife. Blunt end. Then to the toolbox in the closet. A dozen delicate taps with a hammer and the cracks began giving way.

Why hadn't we thought of it? The hourglass is not the thing. The hourglass is only its holster. Just like the goddess isn't the goddess but a conduit for our bacterial overlord. But what is the thing? A treasure map? Hieroglyphics? A virus to eradicate humanity to be released in event of failure of the species?

Nikole wound up and delivered a fatal blow.

And there it was, the big secret.

For a moment, she sat with her wheelchair against the fridge, alone in the world with this knowledge.

Neighbors spoke in the hallway. Nikole wheeled herself with fury. She hobbled to her feet and pressed herself against the apartment door and slid shut the deadbolt, then the chain. Eye to peephole, she scanned the hallway for men in black.

She moved with purpose, heart in overdrive, foyer to table to window and pulled the drapes. Carefully she fingered a slit and observed reality beyond her walls. No anomalies. The street maintained a hum of foot traffic and taxis and newspapers blowing like tumbleweed. It's in my kitchen, she thought, and the door is locked. Nobody knows I have it.

An arbiter of secret knowledge, newly initiated, Nikole rolled back to the scene and stared. It hadn't vanished. She almost wished it would.

Because making the decision is harder than the doing of the thing. Say it vanished in smoke. Self-destruct. Poof. Oh well, she'd think. At least I avoided the hard part. But things don't just disappear. Its matter was indisputable.

I could give it to Sam, she thought. A gift. I could stash it away. I could find a way to contact the Johanssons. They'd know what to do. Study it, examine it, run it through laboratory tests. She pictured stone-faced men in white, researchers behind one-way glass.

Her heart beat in her throat. This suffering. Life. Pills and pool parties, shattered dreams, al-Qaeda and bone cancer in kids. Who wants to stick around? Curious where global warming might lead? Eager for Armageddon? And what if the Bible's right? I mean, just in case. Isn't this cheating? Won't I pay a price?

She scurried to the shattered hourglass and checked its innards for a note, instructions, something to help explain the unexplainable. Nothing.

Her body trembling, she plucked the hidden treasure from its resting place and held it to the light.

A vial of her mother's blood.

She'd gifted her daughter the key to eternal life.

Is it true? Does death give meaning to life? Or is that just something they say to feel good about mortality? Because nonexistence is beyond our understanding. We can't fathom it. Electron microscopes and periodic tables are useless. So we nod our heads, softly smiling, repeating the mantra to make sense of the nonsensical. It gives meaning to life. But what is meaning? What is life?

This, Nikole thought, holding her hand to her heart. This is life. Something inside me.

She had a needle amongst her drug paraphernalia. I could do it, she thought. I could inject myself right now. Just as a test. It's probably not even real. A cult like any other.

Right?

She set the vial on the table, unable to take her eyes off it. She kept her hand on her heart, sensing its rhythm, and for a long time in her apartment she simply existed, listening and watching, not thinking much of anything at all.

Then she made a big decision.

71

The sun felt cold. Glittering women streamed out of limos, floating through the crowd wrapped and pained like Fabergé eggs, exuding exotic perfumes. A flashing camera left Nikole with momentary PTSD. Reporters scurried across bleachers. They jostled through artillery of shouts and shutters, triangulating their position, stalking their prey.

Here comes one, they sensed collectively. Here comes a big one.

The men wore bowties. Nikole couldn't believe the number of bodies squeezed in such a space. Hulking guards patrolled a waist-high barrier that was more for show than for event of stampede. Actors snapped selfies and answered inane questions. Near the golden statue, a reporter stopped Nikole, a black woman in a crimson dress whose age had been buried under cosmetics.

"I'm here with one of the nominees," she said, half-turned to the camera. "First of all, Nikole, who are you wearing?"

Natasha Kennedy chatted with Martin Scorsese under the theater awning. Fans filled out the bleachers that Nikole never knew existed, each her own paparazzo, holding iPads and smartphones to the red carpet procession below. Antonio Noon, her old nemesis, fired away with his camera. A swell of screams flared as Jennifer Lawrence materialized out of a limo. Cameras panned her up and down. Who are you wearing, who did the dress, etc. A marquee of names scrolled overhead, announcing new arrivals so the crowd knew how loudly to squeal.

The biggest names passed through a gauntlet: into a tent, before a backdrop, paraded before a horde of press, then up onto a platform where they were asked about their dresses, their dates and do they watch a lot of movies, who did the dress, what about your dress, etc. Nikole had been able to snake through the mass drawing minimal attention.

"I hear it's a pretty wild tale," the reporter was saying. "A couple years ago, you were doing shoe commercials and struggling to find work. Now you're the runaway favorite to win Best Actress for your stirring performance in Natasha Kennedy's *Orphans of the Storm.* So my question for you, Nikole, is why didn't you bring a date this evening? Unusual for a woman, you know."

She spotted Carlos amidst a sea of suits.

"Excuse me," she said to the flustered reporter.

He looked happy, grinning in a sharp blue suit. He was twitching a bit from gum withdrawal. His slick hair glistened under the lights. His date, a nose ring model named Lupita, was explaining to a reporter who designed her gem-studded dress.

Carlos smiled and waved Nikole over.

"Hey," he offered.

"Hey."

"You look good."

"Thanks. You too."

"You look clean."

"Eighteen months tomorrow," Nikole said.

"Congrats."

Lupita broke free from her interview and nearly fainted. "Oh my god," she said. "Nikole Fink. I've been waiting to meet you. It drove him crazy. When we started dating I was all like, you've gotta introduce me to your ex. Oh my god. I absolutely adored *Orphans of the Storm.* You'll win

Best Actress for sure. I mean, who are you up against? Anna Kendrick? Please."

Nikole offered a handshake but Lupita went for full embrace.

"You just had this look in your eye through the film. You know? It's like, you've seen things."

Nikole and Carlos exchanged glances.

"Lupita and I are engaged," he said.

Nikole smiled. "I'm happy for you."

Lupita continued fawning over Nikole until she spotted Jeff Daniels. "Oh my god," she said into Carlos's shoulder. "Oh my god."

She slinked off into the crowd, tugging Carlos by the wrist.

"Well," he said, "good luck tonight."

"Thanks."

"Maybe I'll see you at one of the parties."

"Maybe."

The crowd swelled, moving towards the theater – faces pumped full of Botox, wrinkled men with brides forty years their junior, incessant cameras, sobbing fans, teeth so white they'd gain citizenship by default in the kingdom of Commandant Kovac.

Nikole shivered and felt an emptiness inside. Xanax felt like a dead relative, its absence rippling through her soul.

The Oscars might be the Moon. A minefield of anxiety stretched before her. Her veins free of chemicals, mind steadied, she readied herself for the evening and followed the crowd.

Then she saw something that didn't belong.

A dozen figures stood clustered behind the press. They were a curious blend of racial features – protruding jawlines, wide noses, sloping eyebrows, tan skin and thin lips. Their hands were weathered, their eyes prehistoric. A bearded man crossed ancient arms, his hair tied in a ponytail. Nikole searched for her mother amongst them. She spied a woman hiding her face with a veil.

They looked like you and me. Hunters in painted caves, figures etched into temples, faces from hieroglyphics, names from the Dead Sea Scrolls. They shared this moment in history. Heads bowed in gratitude, they thanked Nikole with body language for saving their lives. They were safe now. They made no sudden movements, no need to rush, tucked into a niche where no one would notice unless they knew where to look. One of the men gave Nikole a curt nod and she returned the gesture. Then they walked away, one after the other, casting no shadows in their wake.

Nikole stood there a moment, then turned to the auditorium and followed the crowd, watching her shadow between spotlights grow longer then shorter then longer again, her life before her as endless as the line on the horizon.

DATE DUE

CPSIA information can be obtained
at www.ICGtesting.com
Printed in the USA
BVOW03s0830140217
476147BV00001B/20/P

9 781612 968247